Half Mortal

Daughter of Light

Book Two

A Young Adult Fantasy Trilogy by

Heidi Garrett

Half Mortal by Heidi Garrett

Half-Faerie Publishing

Copyright © 2015 by Heidi Garrett

Find out more about Heidi Garrett at

www.heidigarrett.com

Cover Art by J.W.B.

Editing by H. Danielle Crabtree and Vince Dickinson

ISBN: 978-0-9907691-3-2

Other Books by Heidi Garrett

Daughter of Light

(A Young Adult Fantasy Trilogy)

Isolt's Enchantment, A Prequel
Half Faerie, #1
War and Grace, #3

Once Upon a Time Today

(A Collection of Stand-Alone Modern Fairy Tale Retellings)

The Girl Who Believed in Fairy Tales: Three Short Stories
Beautiful Beautiful
Dreaming of the Sea
The Tree Hugger
I Am Lily Dane

In Collaboration with Billie Limpin

(A New Adult Paranormal Romance)

Cupcakes and Kisses

For

Louise Marie Garrell

Contents

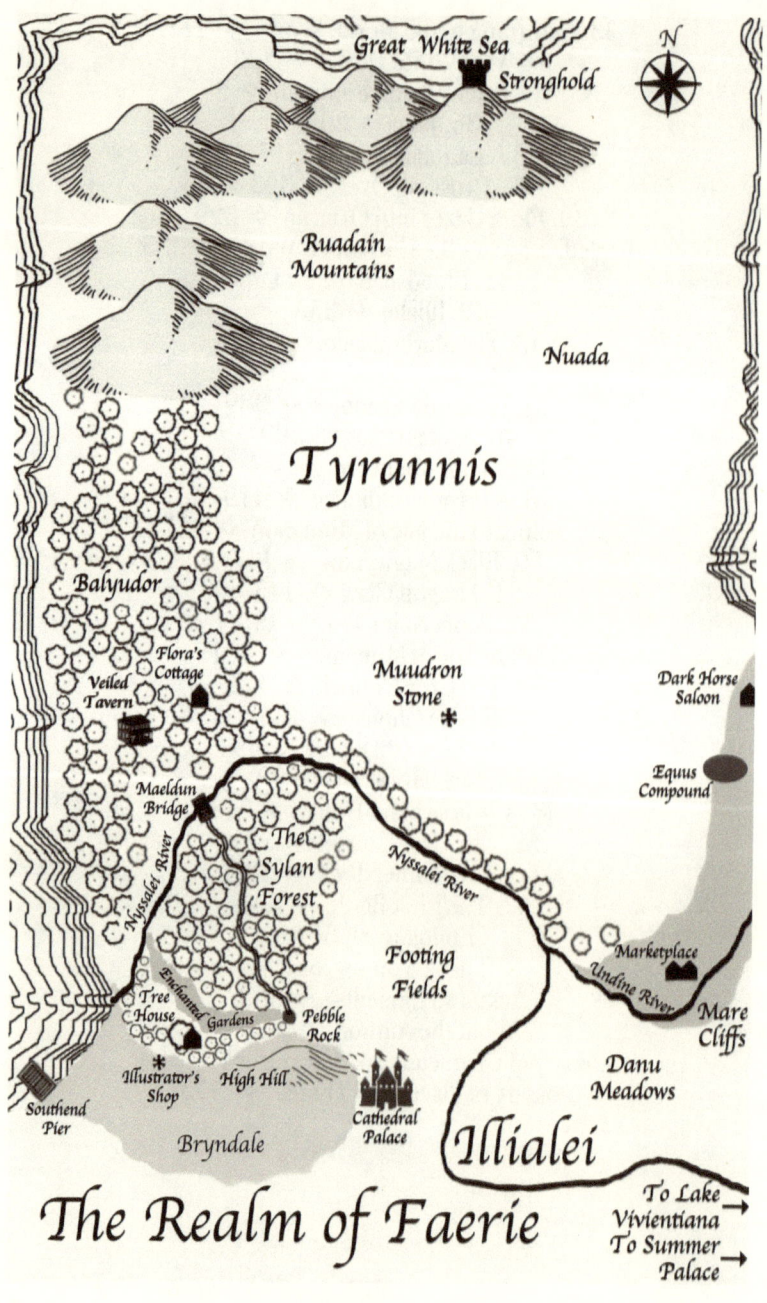

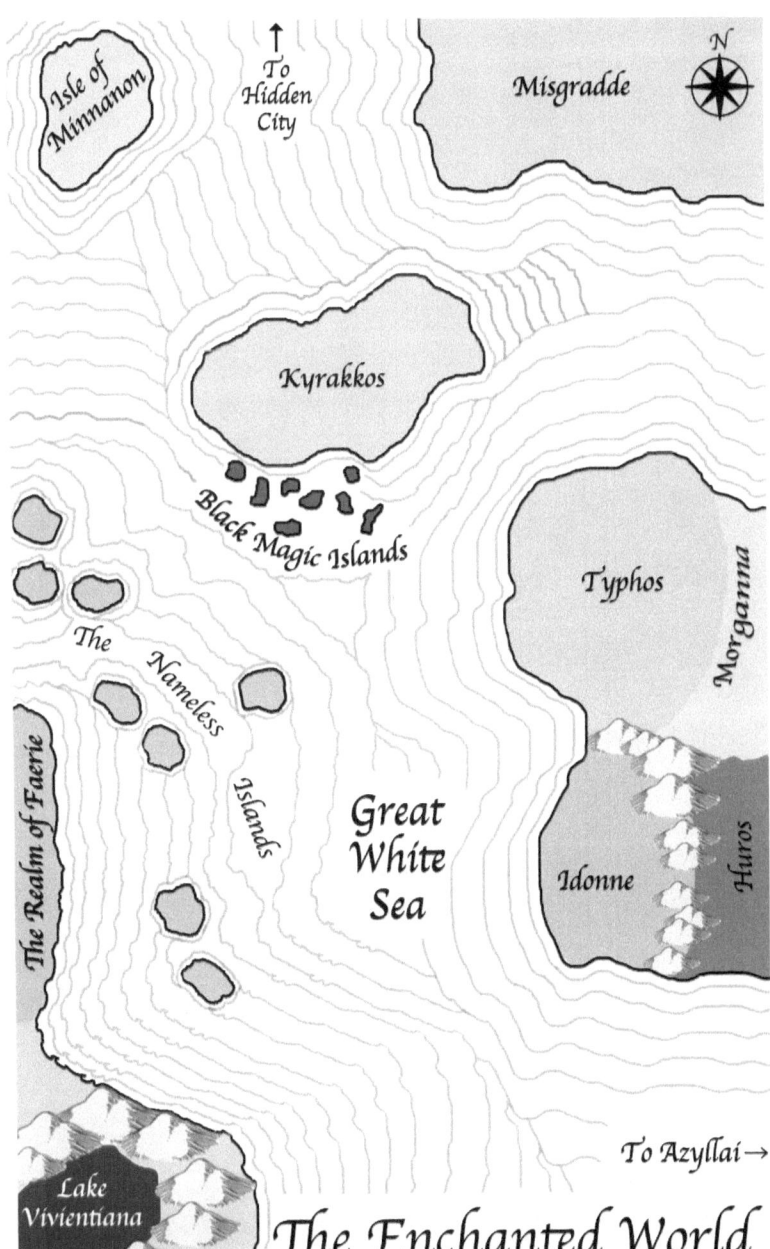

The Enchanted World

Idonnic Prophecy

When the Dark Master rises from the mist to breach the veil, and a Daughter of Light, denied the throne by virtue of birth, stands alone, beware. Cunning will test the Grey Sentinel's shield.

If the Iron Bridge falls, and the Ancient Doors close, the end is near.

The blood of innocents will soak Illialei's meadows, and dreamlessness will snuff all hope from the mortal world. Fear not. This apocalyptic union can be saved. Though grace is undeserved, the purpose is love.

These are the mysteries yet untasted, on the tip of your tongue, O Wayward Son of Idonne.

The Old Texts, Appendix VII

1. The Huron Knight

Gavin surveyed the beach with a distrustful eye. Was the audience's gaiety—mouths enlarged with good cheer, hands slapped together in exuberance, and eyes wide with wonder—genuine? The Huron knight never expected Illialei's population to welcome a military force, but here they were: brownies pushing their way to the front, elves afire with curiosity, and the taller flower faeries edging forward with blushes and sighs.

Observing his men, Gavin took pride in their discipline. Already crates of supplies were neatly stacked along the quay; transport wagons rolled from the deck. More knights readied the horses. Once wild desert natives of Idonne, Gavin had broken many of them. A platform and pulley carried the sea-weary creatures from the ship. As each horse exited the contraption, the crowd's volume increased.

On an average day, such nonsense irritated Gavin, but this afternoon, his lips, while not quite reaching the proportions of a smile, curved upward. The youngest commander in the Huron army crossed his arms as he reconsidered his assignment.

Almost two moons ago, Keir Collin called Gavin before the Huros high command. There, before the ten war chiefs, of which Keir was one, he told Gavin, "The Realm of Faerie grows restless. My wife is concerned for her safety as well as that of my daughter's." Despite the ocean between the couple, Keir remained Queen Luisa Albiana's husband; Princess Lilliane Albiana was his daughter. "I'm sending you with three regiments"—ninety soldiers—"to secure Illialei's border. Assess the situation when you arrive. If you require more troops, send word." The prestigious appointment should have flattered Gavin, but safeguarding a spoiled princess and her fearful mother in their paradisaical garden smacked of contemptible indolence.

Gusts rolling off the sea teemed with a life-infusing property nonexistent on the shores of Huros. The heels of Gavin's boots crunched sand as white as sugar. He pivoted and marched to a sward of grass. Crouched there, he removed a leather glove to comb the silky blades, before snatching a handful in his fist. The fresh scent infused his nostrils. Another man might have kicked off his boots, laid down in the cushioned field, and gazed up at the sweep of blue sky entranced, re-imagining the Whole and his place in it. Not Gavin.

Anticipation quickened within him. He straightened his back and braced his hand again in leather. Illialei was indeed the rumored paradise he'd heard it was, but something more existed here: A potent energy infused its romantic beauty. An energy Gavin could turn to his advantage. He would present his most charming and chivalrous self to the queen and her daughter.

His lieutenant approached, leading a coal-colored horse. Illialei's fresh air excited the beast as much as its master. Its black eyes shined as it trotted with high steps. "Sir, we're ready to advance to the palace."

"Indeed." Gavin accepted the reins and swung himself into the saddle. It felt good to be on land. It felt good to find his expectations required revision. He inspected his troops. Their ordered rigidity buoyed his confidence. Gavin wheeled the horse and galloped in the direction of the Cathedral Palace.

During the journey across the Great White Sea, Gavin studied maps of the Realm of Faerie. His sense of direction was acute. He coaxed the horse into a full gallop as they rounded the outskirts of

Bryndale. There would be time to explore the country's cities and landmarks later.

The sun glinting off the palace's gleaming white turrets shot rays of blinding light. Gavin pressed his cheek against the horse's neck and urged it to continue its reckless speed. Ahead, the palace gates were thrown wide. Gavin dug his knees deeper into the horse's flank. The command forced the beast to end its run by rising high on its hind-legs to avoid smashing into a battalion of brownies on the far side of the gold-railed drawbridge. The miniature guardians, dressed in the blue and green livery of the Albiana, scattered like marbles. The horse danced in their midst as Gavin shouted, "Who's in charge here?"

A dark-headed, ruddy-faced cherub inched forward on hands and knees. He wobbled to his feet. "And who might you be, sir?" The brownie righted his cap and retrieved his shield from where it had fallen on the ground.

"I'm Gavin Tovar, the commander of three regiments of Huron knights sent at the behest of your queen." He offered a mocking bow from his saddle. "In that regard, I seek an audience with Luisa Albiana posthaste."

The brownies reformed into an unyielding knot, blocking access to the palace. "You'll not find our queen within these walls," their spokesman replied.

Gavin cursed. If ill fate befell the queen or the princess, Keir would have him imprisoned with no opportunity to defend himself. "What has happened to her?"

"She is well and safe at the Summer Palace." The brownie's probing eyes roamed over the young commander and the officers who gathered behind him. "Do you know the way?"

"It lies east, on the shores of Lake Vivientiana."

"If you wish to arrive before the sun sets, I advise you leave now. Even with such a fast horse." The brownie's chilly demeanor was a sharp contrast to the festive greeting the knights received on the beach.

Although the brusque attitude rankled, the authority to chastise him didn't yet belong to Gavin. "A small contingent of knights will travel with me, but we'll establish our main camp outside these gates."

The brownies exchanged frowns and long faces. A few grumbled with their spokesman. The elder guard argued it would be less invasive to have the knights camped in the field by the orchard than on the palace lawn itself. "That is what you meant, sir, is it not?"

"Indeed."

"Much better than inside the palace," one of the brownies whispered loudly before thumbing the side of his nose, as if the knights exuded an odor that befouled their pristine haven.

Gavin forced a cool smile. He would enjoy making an example of the fool, but tents needed to be raised before the sun fell. And an audience with the queen couldn't wait until morning.

✧ ✧ ✧

From a distance, the Summer Palace looked more like a shrine than an abode. Unlike its larger counterpart, the walls of the smaller palace weren't blindingly white, rather an inviting ivory. And the outer perimeter wasn't really a wall at all. Evenly spaced columns created openings into the palace's interior. It was going to be a nightmare to secure with the amount of men Gavin had. His first task would be to persuade the queen she must return to the Cathedral Palace with its solid defenses. In this breezy atrium she and her daughter were exposed.

When he and the five knights who rode with him entered the courtyard, no one came to greet them. Gavin jumped to the ground and tossed his horse's reins to his corporal. "Wait for me here."

His boots clicked on the marble floor. Its color matched the columns extending to the high ceiling adorned with bright-colored, watery images of Illialei and her inhabitants. The effect was spacious and playful, hardly conducive to serious matters of state. Slender faeries with pale skin and luminous wings moved gracefully through the interior. Other than batting their eye lashes and turning their rose-colored cheeks away from his piercing gaze, they paid Gavin little heed.

It was incomprehensible the queen lived in such an unprotected environment. No one even commented on his presence. He chased down a young sprite to locate the queen. The slim girl led him deeper into the circular maze of halls and rooms.

Gavin lost all sense of direction by the time they reached the throne room. Perhaps the queen was not so vulnerable here as he originally feared. Although the external perimeter couldn't be effectively defended, the inner chambers coiled in upon themselves like a seashell.

Luisa Albiana reclined upon a cushioned divan in the heart of the cylindrical chamber. As he approached her, the queen's lavender eyes pooled with a delightful secret. One he longed to know.

He executed a meticulous bow. "Gavin Tovar, at your service."

Far lovelier than any of the other faeries, the queen's ivory skin contrasted with the irresistible shimmer of her ink-black hair; her lips touched lightly in an alluring appeal; her eyebrows crowned her violet eyes with an elegant flourish. Her gown, stitched from countless layers of gauze, obscured her figure, but the length of her arms and proportion of her hands promised perfection. The countless white feathers in her magnificent wings bestowed a mystical authority upon her.

A young girl lounging beside Luisa giggled. Family resemblance confirmed she was the princess. Enchanted by the mother, Gavin didn't noticed the girl until she laughed at him.

"He's quite taken with you, mama," the girl snickered.

"Indeed," Gavin replied.

"It is disturbing that we require your services, but we thank you for coming," Luisa murmured.

Gavin knelt before her. Lilliane burst into harsh laughter. It almost broke her mother's spell. The commander wavered, but as soon as his gaze returned to the queen, his haze deepened. "I'll safeguard your life and throne."

Luisa rose to pace the platform in front of her divan. "Have you heard the latest news from Tyrannis?"

"Indeed."

"Indeed! He sounds like a parrot trained to respond to every comment and inquiry with a single word!" the young girl crowed.

"Silence, Lilliane." Although the princess' face was a mirror of the queen's, her penetrating eyes were a darker shade of purple—almost black—and a cruel twist to her lips marred the perfection of her features. "Now that the grey faerie has fallen, the battle between Dark and Light begins," Luisa continued. "That is why you are here. To honor the ancient alliance between the knights of Huros and Daughters of Light."

"Your enemies are the enemies of Huros, your highness."

"Among them, my sister Pressina and her daughters are the most treacherous."

"Are they warriors? Like the spring faeries of old?" Gavin asked.

"They're not!" The princess screeched. "They've violated Uriel and Olivia's decrees, and they must be banished to the mortal world!"

"Please, Lilliane. When you yell, I can't hear myself think."

The princess jumped from the divan and approached Gavin. Her bone-colored wings quaked with gold dust and shadow. She was tall, but not as tall as he. She held his gaze and severed his connection with her mother.

He rubbed his forehead as he stared at the cream-colored marble at his feet. "What was it you were saying about your sister?" Gavin asked the queen, careful to avoid her violet eyes.

"I've allowed Pressina to live on the outskirts of Bryndale, near the forest—"

"It was her youngest daughter who killed the grey faerie. The beast," Lilliane hissed.

Gavin startled, having forgotten she stood near him.

Luisa returned to her divan. "Pressina covets my throne. She won't have it. Nor will her daughters. Lilliane is the princess heir.

There can be no challengers."

Lilliane studied Gavin's face. "My aunt and cousins have proven themselves to be traitors."

Gavin loosened his collar, which all of a sudden felt like a noose tightening around his neck. "I'll chart my defense strategy accordingly." His throat was parched. He could hardly speak. "And report the results as necessary." He bowed deeply and turned, searching for an exit.

"Is that all you have to say?" Lillian's ridicule echoed as he hurried to rejoin his men.

The oak in the center of the tree house drew Gavin's attention. Even after an investigation of every room left him empty-handed, his inner insistence remained: There was something valuable to be discovered in the home Pressina shared with her daughters.

He ran a gloved hand over the tree's bark. The sense he overlooked something strengthened. He removed a glove to trace the wood's rough ridges and the smooth places between them. An inaudible buzz stimulated his instincts.

He studied the branches spiraling out like the spokes of a wheel overhead. A pair of golden eyes glared down at him. When Gavin stepped closer to see the creature more clearly, it hissed. "Here, kitty, kitty." He opened and folded his fingers against his palm in a continuous motion. The thing arched its back and yowled. Gavin backed away. His hand settled on a polished globe marking the banister of a short flight of stairs descending to the tree's base.

The creature in the tree remained hostile. Eager to break eye contact with it, Gavin descended to the lowest level of the tree house.

At its base, the oak's circumference exceeded the width of the stairwell. There was hardly space to turn in a circle. Gavin explored the bark methodically, sweeping his fingers from top to bottom and side to side in careful strokes, searching for an anomaly.

He touched the faintest indentation. His finger traced the

hairline crevice invisible in the dim light. He rushed upstairs for a candle, his boots cracking on each riser; there was no one to hear. It was well past midnight, and he'd relieved the guards on duty with orders to return in the morning.

Candlelight revealed the barest outline of a door, its handle concealed as a natural knot in the wood.

Gavin twisted the knob. It refused to turn. He pushed, pulled, and prodded. He settled on the lowest step to study the obstacle. He could spy no keyhole or other locking mechanism. If the door was fortified with a spell, he was doomed. The people of Huros possessed no magical abilities.

From the top of the stairs, the strange cat-like creature mewled with greater urgency. It wasn't a cat, but something unnatural with odd markings on its coat and vicious hooks for claws. Gavin had heard the tales of a small, unfriendly beast rumored to be the result of one of Pressina's spells. Since his arrival upon the shores of Faerie, Gavin had learned a lot about Luisa's sister. More a witch than a faerie, she spelled her three daughters.

The longer he stared at the closed door, the more he became convinced the root of her powers lay behind it. He should have brought an axe.

After the queen and her malcontent daughter impressed upon Gavin their fear of Pressina and her girls, he decided to do his own research. Late afternoons spent buying honey mead for wood elves at the Hive proved the most profitable. Although the gossipy creatures strictly adhered to Olivia's decree, that Pressina and her daughters were never to be spoken of as Albiana descendants, they freely shared other opinions about the tree house's missing residents. And they relished the opportunity to speculate about Pressina's black magic.

Perhaps a secret lever or discretely placed latch controlled the door.

Beginning with the step he sat upon, Gavin ran his fingers along every planed surface and baluster. Pressina's beast hissed. Gavin ignored its agitation as he inched up the stairs.

When he reached the globe, the thing sprang on him, digging its nails deep into Gavin's back. "Get off me!" The unnatural thing clawed its way up his torso.

It batted his face with slicing hooks, tearing flesh. Warm blood trickled from Gavin's ears and down his cheek. He managed to free his sword hand and pull the dagger from his hip. He aimed its point at the creature's back and stabbed. It continued its frenzied writhing. Gavin stabbed again and again until the thing was a lump of bloody fur at his feet.

The knight staggered and landed on a lime-striped chaise, panting. He yanked the cloth covering from a nearby table. Glass shattered against the floor. Gavin winced as he wiped the blood from his ears and lips. He glowered at the limp form of his attacker. Pressina's demonic creation should never have known life in the first place.

When he regained his breath, Gavin returned to the globe at the head of the banister. His fingers danced over the polished sphere, searching. He alternately pulled and pressed down on it with both palms. He'd almost given up when his finger tip grazed metal, an ornately embossed letter A forged from black iron on the column beneath it. Gavin fiddled with the decorative embellishment. He slid it to the left and heard the unmistakable creak of a door swing open. He bolted down the stairs where his candle still flickered.

His pulse quickened as he raised the light high to observe Pressina's secret chamber. The sight was disappointing; a few cupboards and shelves pushed against curved walls, several wooden chests stacked on a table. He tested the lid of one of the crates. It was unlocked. Loose pieces of parchment filled it. He examined a sheet. It was a letter to Pressina from her husband, Elynus. Gavin scanned the text.

The letters contained more than flowery declarations of eternal devotion. He sat down to re-read the passages which intrigued him.

An incorporeal force exists in the Void. After researching the matter and giving it much thought, I'm convinced this entity, known as Umbra, holds the key to our reunion. In addition to unlocking the doors between the mortal and enchanted worlds closed to me, I believe it possesses the power—perhaps the only thing in the Whole that does—to end Luisa's reign. If we're unflinching in our devotion to this energy, the power to unite the Realm of Faerie under a single monarchy will be ours. Unfortunately, the road to victory is not assured. Certain artifacts, lost in days long past, must be reclaimed.

Gavin's awareness numbed to the sting of the cuts on his face as he began to apprehend his discovery.

2. The Intruder

Melia soared over the enchanted gardens to the tree house. She landed on one of the oak's lower branches. Tatou's arms draped her neck, the limp weight of the pixie's body and legs pressed against Melia's back. Pixies were known to be deep sleepers, and her best friend often fell asleep in flight. Melia would wake her in a minute. After she savored the deep hush which only came as the last edge of night slipped away.

Awaiting dawn, Melia thought of Ryder and the first time she saw him in the palace library. Nandana's mark blazed on her forehead. A few hours later, the blue emblem mysteriously evaporated. Despite those startling coincidences, she chose to keep him at a distance, unable to trust him with her heart, unable to risk achieving the remedy to her mother's spell—

A loud thud followed by a sharp rap of quick steps shattered the peace and quiet.

Melia blinked. The branch she perched on shot above the stairway spiraling the oak's trunk. Her eyes followed the wooden steps down to the ground. They were empty. The noisy intruder was inside.

Tatou murmured.

A person Melia had never seen before threw open the tree house's front door. Gold hair, light eyes, a trimmed beard, and lean build—not to mention the deep brown uniform—alerted her. He was a knight from Huros. Lines of fresh scabs covered the side of his face and neck.

Melia remained still. If he didn't raise his head, the veil of leaves would conceal them.

He paused in the doorframe to adjust his coat. Melia smelled body odor and leather. Grey half-moons beneath his eyes made him look like he never slept.

Melia imperceptibly craned her head to search the nearest row of trees. Could she reach the tall eucalyptus before her twitches began? She rustled a wing to warn Tatou.

"What?" her friend mumbled.

Melia's body vibrated. "Fly to the enchanted gardens." She spoke in the tongue of eagles, a language the pixie understood. "Now!" Melia's back, arms, and legs extended. Ripples in her flesh absorbed the feathers of her wings. The feathers on her back coalesced and smoothed into the same blue dress she'd worn to her sister's wedding. She squeezed tree bark with fingers, not talons.

The physical upheaval knocked Tatou from where she lay. Melia's heart roared into her throat as her friend plummeted. When the pixie reached the height of the knight's knees, her gossamer wings beat like a hummingbird's.

"What do we have here?" he asked.

Tatou flitted away from his grasping hand. "I didn't mean to bother you. I'll just be on my way." Once she caught her breath, a surge of energy would charge her. Pixies were sprinters able to fly faster than faeries of flower and field; they just couldn't last long at their top speeds.

The knight hurried down the steps after her. "Such a tiny thing, creating such a commotion." Focused on his prey, he never raised his eyes.

Melia dropped her legs and pushed herself from the branch to make a noiseless landing on the porch. She tore down the spiral staircase.

The pixie zipped into the forest. The knight raced behind her. "Hey, what's your name? I need to talk to you!" It wasn't a friendly request.

He didn't notice Melia chasing them. All her life she'd run through Illialei barefoot and wild, and as Tatou often pointed out, she never crashed around like mortals.

Because she was half faerie.

The soldier's boots crunched dried leaves, drowning out any sound of Melia's pursuit. Tatou's pale glow bobbed a safe distance ahead. She'd almost reached the gardens. If the knight followed her into the pixie kingdom, he'd be considered a trespasser. And pixies didn't take trespassing lightly; the tiny faeries took captives. They wouldn't harm the knight, but they'd keep him prisoner much of the day.

A steep quiet descended. Melia halted to listen. The thump-thump of her frantic pulse was the only thing she heard. Nothing moved in the forest. The knight had stopped running. She slipped behind a birch tree.

When she heard a rustle of movement, Melia peeked from her hiding place. The knight stood at the grey stone wall. Tatou had disappeared. He wasn't going to enter the gardens.

Melia curled her toes around the tree's roots and pressed her palms against its trunk. She imagined the forest filling her with infinite energy and power. Then she ran. Pumping her arms and legs, she bolted to the grey stone wall, hurtling past the knight.

"Hey!" he shouted.

Melia pulled herself up, but not over the wall. Balancing on its slim width, she placed one foot in front of the other as quickly as she could without toppling over. At the same time, she whistled for Tatou. If this was going to work, she needed an invitation to enter the pixies' domain.

The knight was gaining on her. "In the name of the queen, I command you to stop!"

Melia continued her acrobatics, trotting along the thin ledge, whistling the tune she and Tatou agreed upon ages ago to identify themselves to one another in moments like these. Melia almost lost her balance. They'd never dreamed of moments like this in those sleepy days.

"Melia!" Tatou's bell-like voice chimed. "I invite you to enter!"

The half-faerie swiveled to leap from the wall. Strong fingers grabbed her heel. She pounded it against the stone. The knight roared in protest. Melia catapulted into the gardens, her tumble ending on a springy bed of fern. She regained her footing. "You can't catch me!"

The knight scrambled over the wall.

"Call the rest of the pixies!" Melia hollered as she jogged backward. At the sound of Tatou's shrill whistle, Melia threw her hands over her ears. "Keep calling them!"

The knight stumbled through a tangle of ivy, the expression on his face murderous.

Melia turned and ran. Tatou caught hold of the half-faerie's hair, whipping in the morning air.

Where were the other pixies? Tatou emitted another piercing alert. Melia risked a backward glance and almost lost her footing. A reflected flash of sunlight stung her eyes. The knight had a knife! Melia ran faster.

Finally, a cloud of pixies fluttered into view. They saw Melia first. Mischief lit their angelic faces until they saw Tatou riding in Melia's hair. The tiny faeries hovered in a confused mass.

"Why did you call us?" a chubby female with enormous eyes demanded.

"Not her!" Tatou shouted. "Him!"

The pixies swarmed past them, but Melia didn't slow down. She could still hear the knight's heavy breathing and feel his footsteps slamming the ground behind her.

"Hey! Stop that!" he yelled.

Inside the enchanted gardens, and in large numbers, pixies were potent.

"He has a knife!" one squeaked.

"Hey! Ho!" another cried out. "We'll be having none of that!"

"We're going to need everyone!" a deeper voice yelled.

Five more earsplitting whistles followed. Melia could no longer understand what the pixies were shouting, but the number of voices multiplied rapidly.

Finally, she heard the jubilant outcries.

When she stopped to turn around, a thick ring of tiny faeries danced and sang around their dazed captive.

Tatou released her hair and landed on her shoulder. "That was close."

A short distance away, a dagger lay on the ground. Melia edged around the pixie ring to pick it up. She touched its tip and pricked her finger. She sucked on the drop of blood. "Too close." She tucked the blade in the sash of her dress.

Neither Tatou nor Melia spoke on their trip back to the tree house. Most of the way they could hear the pixies' cheery singing. By the time they reached the oak, Melia's heartbeat had slowed, and she was breathing normally. She hesitated before climbing the spiral staircase.

"Why did he try to catch us?" Tatou asked.

"News about the grey faerie's death has probably crossed the river," Melia said. "Everyone in the marketplace was talking about it."

Two days ago, they spent the better part of a morning wandering through the popular gathering spot in the muannai valley, eavesdropping on the dark-skinned, wingless muannai. Elendah's death and the fall of the stronghold of Calashai was plastered on the front page of the copper sheets and had been the subject of every conversation. Speculation over who killed the beloved regent included: Melia's sister Plantine, her late husband, his jilted muannai lover, a disgruntled cult of Umbra captain, the sole-surviving spring faerie in the enchanted world, and a hired assassin.

"Then it's even more important that we talk to Aldous as soon as possible," Tatou said.

A few days ago, Melia ripped the hem of her dirty blue gown to just above her knees. "I need something clean to wear."

"Maybe I could make a head start." Tatou didn't need to fetch a change of clothes when she could create a petal skirt from almost any flower she came across.

A twisty feeling crept up Melia's spine. "We need to stay together. I won't take long, I promise. Besides, I want to find out what that knight was doing in our tree house."

Melia took the steps two at a time. The front door hung open. Distracted by Tatou's unexpected appearance, the knight had never closed it.

Inside, even though every window was open, an unnatural stillness curled around them.

"Do you hear that?" Tatou whispered.

"What?"

"Not a bird is singing."

Melia settled her hand on the hilt of the knight's dagger. "Our sprint through the forest must have spooked them."

"Oh no!" Tatou's hands flew to her mouth.

Melia rushed over to Malachi's inert form swimming in a grisly pool of blood. Recalling the numerous scabs on the knight's face, she shook her head. "I was never fond of Malachi, but there was no reason to kill him so brutally. I can't leave his remains here."

Tatou agreed.

Melia moved quickly. She found a gardening trowel, clawed a trench, wrapped the small body in a soft sheet, and placed it gently in the shallow grave. While she worked, her thoughts kept turning to Pressina. Malachi's violent death would upset her, more than her daughter fighting for life in a Calashai dungeon.

Tatou seemed to sense the dark merry-go-round of Melia's thoughts. She remained outside while Melia walked through every room in the tree house.

Before changing into a green summer dress, Melia examined the

knight's dagger. The blade and handle were stained with blood. Most likely Malachi's. If she carried it with her, everyone who'd ever believed she was her father's accomplice would accuse her of coming to kill innocents now. She hid it in a kitchen cupboard behind several large pots of honey.

"Other than killing Mother's pet, it's not clear what the knight was doing here," Melia said.

Perched on the staircase railing, Tatou appeared subdued. "A malignant force is on the move. Like a wind blowing, even when the air is calm."

It was true. The forest remained too quiet around them. "It's been a harsh morning," Melia observed.

"It's more than that. Elendah's presence protected the Realm of Faerie. Her consciousness was like a shield. Now that she's gone, we're no longer protected."

Melia refused to believe the eerie silence had anything to do with the crime her sister committed while Umbra possessed her body. "Come on, we need to go to the library."

3. The Golden Orchard

Almost every brownie, faerie, and wood elf scurried out of the way when Melia and Tatou walked by. No one smiled or offered a greeting. It wasn't unusual for them to ignore Melia, but it worried her that nobody acknowledged Tatou. Maybe they didn't see the pixie riding on her shoulder.

"What are you staring at?" Melia heckled two rotund elves who stopped to watch her with rounded eyes. Rather than answer her, they covered their mouths, making the chatter between them indecipherable.

Melia jogged along in explosive bursts. Close to the palace, the traffic trickled to nothing. Tatou's ominous words tightened around her heart. "Stop!"

The pixie, flying a few feet ahead, wheeled around. "What?"

"Listen." Melia jutted her chin. Voices rumbled in the distance.

Tatou's face clouded. "That doesn't sound like brownies." Her wings beat a frantic rhythm. "More knights?"

Melia pointed to the side of the road. She moved wordlessly until they reached the break beyond the cherry trees. "Let's sneak through the orchard."

When they first came to Illialei years ago, she and her sisters played hide-and-seek among the ancient trees. The abundant golden apples, as big as two of the half-faerie's fists, were one of her favorite treats. Today, she ignored their ripe scent as she stalked to the line where the neat rows of trees devolved into a tangled web of

21

leaves, limbs, and trunks.

The blare of voices crescendoed as Melia peeked through the foliage. A swathe of stiff brown jackets, boots, and bearded faces gathered around the palace gates. "Why is a company of Huron knights in Illialei?" Melia wondered out loud.

Three of the knights shouted to be heard above the rest. Random conversations petered out as the milling soldiers formed three meticulous lines. Melia counted thirty in each line, ninety in all, including their leaders.

Each leader inspected his group. Their regimented discipline, creased uniforms, and weapons were out of place in a country where the population ran around barefoot and spent most of their time lolling about rivers and meadows, or gossiping over honeyed confections at the Hive.

Tatou stood on Melia's shoulder, her fingers twined in the half-faerie's hair.

Melia pushed on a small limb heavy with leaves. "I don't see a single brownie. Where are the palace guards?"

Tatou alighted from her shoulder to hover in the air. "Psst." The pixie motioned with her head and fluttered away.

Melia crouched to follow her. When they reached a hollow in the undergrowth, Tatou disappeared into the opening. Melia crawled after her. They were far enough away that they could talk without being overheard.

"The battle between Dark and Light has begun," Tatou said.

"No." Melia refused to believe it. "Luisa is probably just celebrating my mother's departure from Illialei."

"That's not a celebration; it's a search party. This morning, that knight tried to stop us in the name of the queen. He was guarding the tree house in case you or your sisters or your mother came home."

A deep uneasiness flowered in Melia's stomach. "But the pixies captured him. He couldn't have told anyone about us yet."

Tatou shrugged. "Maybe they're going to search for him. Or

maybe one of the faeries we passed on the way here is a spy for the queen."

"Then we need to make sure no one sees us enter the palace," Melia conceded.

The pixie's eyebrows disappeared in a tousle of golden curls. "Did you see how many knights there are?"

"We'll wait until the sun sets."

"We're too late. Explaining things to Aldous won't make any difference now."

Melia closed empty fingers. She wished she had the knight's dagger. "I have to see Aldous."

"We can't risk getting captured! Without the grey faerie to rein in their power, the Albiana will only grow more dangerous."

"I have to warn Gabriela and her daughter," Melia said. Umbra threatened the half-faeries with Albiana blood almost as soon as Plantine spewed his vile consciousness back into the magical basin, Ormrun, while the Calashai imploded. "Aldous is the only one who can help me find them in the mortal world."

"I wish we had the Tasimas."

The yellow diamond would solve the problem of entering the palace unseen. One of the Rykkiel—seven magic gems, each with a unique power—the Tasimas made instantaneous travel within the enchanted world possible. The trick being you had to have been to the destination at least once before in order to visualize it. Both Melia and Tatou had been in the palace library.

Melia chewed on a fingernail. "I should have asked Flora for it."

Tatou flitted over to smooth Melia's hair. "She never would have let you take it."

Melia sighed.

"You need rest after flying all night," Tatou said.

"What are you going to do?"

"Keep watch."

Exhausted and on edge, Melia curled up in the grass and closed her eyes. Her pounding heart made it difficult to fall asleep.

✧ ✧ ✧

The brush-covered cave was dark when Melia woke up. She rubbed her eyes. Why hadn't she changed into an eagle? "Tatou?"

Melia crawled through the tunnel of branches. Ahead, it was brighter, the sun lingered. Which was why she was still in her half-faerie form. She calmed down. Two apples, a pickler cucumber, and a pile of almonds nested in the roots of the nearest tree.

A gift from Tatou. The pixie must have rolled the giant fruit across the ground. Melia wondered how long that had taken. Wherever she was now, Melia hoped she'd be back soon. She didn't like them being apart.

Grateful for something to eat, Melia grabbed the food and pushed herself back into their leafy cave. As she crunched on one of the apples, she made a mental list of questions for Aldous.

The wood elf was the palace librarian; he knew more about the Albiana lineage than anyone. Although Flora told Melia the secret that Pressina, Melia's mother, was a full-blood Albiana, the librarian had been the one to show Melia her family tree. She wasn't the only one with a mixed Albiana-mortal bloodline. There were four others: her sisters Melusine and Plantine, her cousin Gabriela, and Gabriela's daughter Lola.

Melia ticked Plantine off the list. Her younger sister had already tried to incarnate Umbra and failed. That left Melusine and the others. Three to find and warn.

Remembering her last trip to the mortal world, a hot tear burned the corner of Melia's eye. She wiped it away and sniffled. If only her mother had told her the truth about her lineage, and all their dark secrets, before the accident in Achill.

Melia wiped her nose with the back of her arm. It was too painful to think about her father's death. She pushed those thoughts away and refocused on Aldous.

She would need to know the year and geographical location in the mortal world where Melusine, Gabriela, and Lola could be found. If the palace librarian had any pictures, that would help. When Tuck showed Melia pictures of Achill, it made it easier to find her father.

She mentally hurried past all the bad things that had happened since she sat at the Hive with Tatou and the tree elf. Some good things had happened too. Ryder. After the Calashai fell, he held her in his arms, searching her eyes with his forest-green ones.

And what did she do? Crushed the tender shoot of feeling breaking ground in her heart. Melia hugged her knees to her chest. Four days later her insides remained bruised. As soon as she got back to Aldaine, she was going to tell him everything.

A ball of light flew toward her. The sun was about to set. Beneath the tangle of apple trees, the world was already dark.

"Where have you been?" Melia asked Tatou.

"Scouting."

"Shining like that, anyone can see you!" Melia held up a hand and backed farther into the narrowing hollow. She hated anyone to watch her transform from a half-faerie into a bird. When she re-emerged as a jet-black eagle, she didn't feel any less irritated with her friend.

"I was careful," Tatou said.

Melia shook her tail feathers.

The pixie ignored the display. "We need to cross the river."

"After we talk to Aldous."

"I was hiding in the long grass at the edge of Footing Field and I overheard some brownies. Luisa sent for those knights as soon as news of Plantine's wedding to Goring reached the Summer Palace. She fears Umbra's incarnation."

"Then I'm no danger to her. I've risked my life and lost everything to stop it from taking place!"

"Lilliane believes you and your sisters and your mother are the greatest threat."

Melia tossed bits of dirt and grass with her talons. "What about Gabriela? Luisa's first-born is a much greater threat than me. Why doesn't the queen dispatch an army of Huron knights to the mortal world and save me the bother."

Tatou balanced on one foot while she tugged on the ankle of her other foot, kicked behind her.

"What?" Melia asked.

"The knight who chased us this morning is already back at the palace."

Melia wanted to peck something. Preferably something belonging to the queen. She restrained herself. Anger and stubbornness had deafened her to her father's pleas. She settled for a few satisfying clacks of her beak. "I must talk to Aldous."

"If the knights catch you, they won't release you," Tatou said.

"Then we must be careful."

Tatou wasn't pleased with Melia's determination, but she stopped raising objections. When they reached the edge of the orchard, the pixie clambered onto Melia's back.

"Ready?" Melia chirped.

Tatou patted the crown of her friend's feathered head.

A wall of tents lined the palace's south wall. Several fires interspersed the knights' camp. Although no formal guard was visible, Melia couldn't risk hopping around on a window ledge with so many eyes beneath them. A black eagle searching for an open palace window would draw attention. That Pressina had cursed her daughters as punishment for their role in their father's death was about the only thing that wasn't secret in Illialei.

If Melia flew west, then circled back north to come across the meadows, moonlight would expose them; but if she flew east, as close to the treetops as possible, they might be able to enter the far end of the palace unobserved.

4. Among the Calashai's Ruins

Ryder heaved the hammer high above his head and slammed it down with all his strength. Although there was no visible impact to the slab, he could sense the give. He raised the hammer again and again. Finally his target shattered with a satisfying explosion of rock and dust. Balancing the hammer head on the ground, he leaned on the rough-hewn handle. With his other hand, he wiped a slick sheen of sweat from his forehead.

The sun had set. He was alone. The crew of muannai that worked by his side during the day was long gone. He listened to the surf far below, crashing against the granite cliffs. Tyrannis' rocky coast was different from the sandy shores of his homeland, Idonne. He spit into the wreckage, as if by doing so he could discharge the unpleasant truth of his situation.

He had no homeland. He was a fugitive, dependent on the good will of those who discovered his crime. The threat of being sent back to Idonne in chains had been used against him three times. Each time fate—or Sinjiin—intervened. He and the mage were bound to one another, at least until Ryder delivered the sword and basin to the Grey Council.

He kicked a loose rock with his boot. The dragonwitch sent trolls asking after the artifacts, but she wouldn't find them. The night the stronghold of Calashai fell, when everyone else was passed out from grief and exhaustion, he and Sinjiin stole the basin from Flora. They wandered through piles of debris—some taller than Ryder's head—

until Sinjiin nosed out an intact passageway leading deep into the mountain beneath the Calashai's ruins. With a torch in one hand, Ormrun in the other, and Koldis in his belt, the priest followed the tiger down a winding incline.

By the time they found a spacious cavern, Ryder was convinced they'd reached the mountain's core, and maybe they had. A melancholy tune had settled in his mind, a plaintive lament of abandonment and sorrow. It made him think of Melia.

As long as he lived, he'd never forget the stormy hurt that flooded her sea-blue eyes when he turned from her the night Elendah died. Even as he walked away, he wanted to return. But pride kept him placing one foot in front of the other.

That same night, in the cavern, with that sad song squeezing his heart like a tourniquet, he and Sinjiin buried the basin and sword forged by dwarf magic; but all he'd thought about was Melia, and how he should never have let her return to Illialei alone.

A biting wind brought him back to the present. He searched for another target and heaved the hammer once more. Breaking down what was left of the Calashai's stone walls was the only thing that helped him manage his regret. And his rage at the spring faerie. As soon as Flora realized what Ryder and Sinjiin had done, she retaliated by spiriting away the Tasimas. She'd be happy to make a trade.

Ryder smashed the stone in front of him. There was no give. He unleashed his fury upon it.

"Are you thirsty?"

He spun around.

Chloe, one of the Order of the Calashai's surviving acolytes, stood a safe distance from him. She held out a wooden cup.

The way her eyes traveled his torso made him aware of his bare chest. He knew he smelled of sweat and dirt—and a blister on the heel of his hand burned—but something to drink sounded good. He took the cup and drained it in two gulps. He wiped his mouth. "What was that?"

"Herb water. Would you like another cup?"

"Please."

He watched her hurry away. Throughout the day female muannai offered everyone who worked in the courtyard food and drink, but nothing as refreshing as what he'd just tasted. It cooled the heat eating away at his insides.

Sinjiin returned with Chloe. His friend had probably sent her the first time.

Ryder gave his head a slight shake, but took the proffered cup and emptied it as quickly as he had the first one.

"Are you hungry?" Chloe asked.

Ryder wanted more of the water, but didn't want to ask her to retrieve a third cup. "I'll join the others soon."

She curtseyed and retreated.

Sinjiin sidled up to him and gave him a nudge; from the great cat, it was enough to make Ryder lose his balance. His heavy hammer wobbled. He set it next to the slab he would take out his frustrations on tomorrow.

The tiger roared and padded in the opposite direction of the muannai gathered on the lawn. He tread to the stone staircase leading to the inlet, one of the few structures that remained unbroken.

The pair were silent as they raced to the sand. Sinjiin leapt toward the tide. Ryder chased after him, pulling off his boots and dungarees. They dove into the rolling water alongside one another.

When the saltwater had dissolved the grime from Ryder's body, he returned to the shore. The tiger followed. The night was cold, and now that he'd stopped working, Ryder shivered.

The rush of warmth that always accompanied the monstrous tiger's shift into a lithe, cinnamon-skinned mage passed in an instant. The mage fidgeted with the silk of his baggy pants.

"Any success obtaining the book?" Ryder hoped *The Book of Umbra* would have instructions for freeing the basin and sword from the Calashai's founding stone. The stone acted like a magnet to prevent anyone from taking the dwarf artifacts from the mountain.

"Sevondi invited Flora to the Blue Mermaid. The dragonwitch wants to thank the spring faerie for saving her life," Sinjiin said.

Melia and Sevondi had been shot with arrows, lingering on the threshold of death until Flora discerned the tips were dipped in a poison brew and traced the malignancy of the potion to Umbra's influence. She gathered the ingredients and boiled the healing draught that saved their lives.

Ryder crossed his arms. "Is the spring faerie going to go?"

"Yes."

"Good luck to her."

Sinjiin danced in his black slippers.

"What?" Ryder asked.

"If Flora can negotiate an exchange for *The Book of Umbra*, she wants us to return the basin to her."

"Return? It was never hers to begin with."

"She kept it safe for many years," Sinjiin reminded him.

Ryder laughed. "You've already agreed to the trade, haven't you?"

"We're surrounded by muannai. The sword and basin are useless to them. Even if they wanted to incarnate Umbra, none of them can."

"Except for the dragonwitch."

"Maybe," Sinjiin said.

Ryder squirmed as he recalled the night she tricked him with the illusion of a dragon. "That's not a chance I'm willing to take."

"We may not have a choice. Sevondi is wooing the muannai, and they're taking heed of her."

"A fickle lot, aren't they? The cult of Umbra. Abandoning the memory of their dead leader for his spurned lover. I'm not sure I care who they follow when their allegiance means so little."

"Regardless, turning Sevondi into an ally might be the most practical course. And Flora has a strategy."

"If you've already agreed to this, why come to me?"

Sinjiin smoothed his black vest. "There's something you can contribute."

"Of course, that's the only reason you're confessing any of this. What is it?"

"I'd rather let Flora explain."

"No, you tell me now."

Sinjiin's hands disappeared in the folds of his red silk pantaloons. "Flora thinks your presence will make Sevondi more amenable to our proposal."

Ryder's stomach tightened. "Which is?"

"If we show a united front to support Sevondi's ambition to become the new regent—in exchange for a family heirloom—"

The priest jogged away. He wasn't exactly sure what might entail making Sevondi more amenable, but he didn't want to be in the same room with her. The witch not only stole the sword at the Muudron Stone, she humiliated him as well. He could just imagine what kind of regent she'd make.

When Ryder lived with the priests in Idonne, the study of Umbra had been his specialty; it was impossible to study the dark master without grasping the history of the muannai. The two species came into being simultaneously—an evolutionary response by the Whole to rapid population growth in the mortal world. Soul embers could no longer be absorbed and reformed in the Great White Sea; grey faeries were no longer born. There were simply too many embers to cool and not enough time.

Now, any mortal psyche that gained a degree of consciousness but did not have the cohesion to survive death and pass into the Unknown Beyond split. The passionate, vital energy of the psyche birthed the muannai, wingless dark faeries native to Tyrannis. The degraded, destructive, resentful aspect of the psyche had to go somewhere as well. Too impure to be re-absorbed by the Primal

Essence, it was being shunted to the Void. There, the ash aggregated into a single consciousness which had become self-aware and named itself Umbra.

A half-muannai witch obsessed with the dark master didn't strike Ryder as the best candidate for regent.

Sinjiin roared beside him.

Ryder raced harder. The beach was endless. He ran as fast as he could. He ran until his exhaustion was stronger than his anger. "You're not going to leave me in peace until I listen to Flora, are you?"

Sinjiin nosed him again.

Ryder pushed the cat away and thought of Melia.

Nandana, a Hindi woman who came to be known as the Illustrator in Illialei, predicted the half-faerie would incarnate Umbra; Ryder wasn't going to let that happen either. The sooner he took the basin and the sword out of Faerie, the sooner Melia would be safe.

He needed *The Book of Umbra* to do that, and the odds of obtaining the book by force decreased daily. Yrrick had transformed the cult of Umbra into a dedicated crew of builders, but Goring trained them to be an army. They knew how to fight. And every day more muannai arrived in Aldaine, adding sheer numbers to the equation. Thousands to three, if Ryder counted himself, Sinjiin, and the spring faerie. Thousands to one if he counted only himself.

The priest turned around and tramped back to the stone steps embedded in the side of the cliff.

Sinjiin tagged along at his side, wisely silent.

Ryder made a straight line to the spring faerie's makeshift tent.

He ducked beneath one of the tree limbs that supported the heavy canvas Flora had salvaged from the Calashai's wreckage, and pushed away the loose flap of cloth serving as a door. He had to crawl to enter.

Once inside, he surveyed the interior. It was more spacious than it appeared from the outside. Several odd-shaped lamps created a glow in the enclosed area. A few shelves, filled with glassware and whatnot, lined the tent's perimeter. A pallet, piled high with blankets, laid off to one side. A woodsy smell emanated from the bundles of herbs, bound tight with string, hanging from the rope that architected the tent's ceiling. On the far side, Flora—her ever-present kerchief tied beneath her sizable chin—perched on a stool with a large bucket beside her.

Sinjiin pushed past him and curled up on a thick rug that seemed to have been placed there for the big cat.

Ryder rubbed his jaw. The steam Chloe's drink cooled inside him boiled again.

"I've heard you like my herb water," the spring faerie said.

Her herb water? He should have known. "What's in it?"

"Boiled seawater—infused with local weeds and cooled in the light of the moons. Would you like another cup?"

The bucket beside her was full.

The priest challenged the tiger with his eyes. The oversized feline purred. Ryder considered scooting back out of the tent, but his throat was scratchy, and more of Flora's concoction sounded like just the thing to soothe it. Accepting he'd been manipulated, he grunted his assent.

Flora pointed to one of the shelves. "Fetch me one of those glasses, and you can have as much as you want."

He shifted and stretched to reach one. Remaining in a crouched position, he inched toward Flora, as if keeping his distance made it clear he was present under duress.

"How's your arm?" she asked. She'd ground beach sand and other mysterious ingredients into a sticky ointment to treat the fracture he received as a prisoner during his stay in the Calashai's dungeons.

"There's no more pain. The mobility and strength has returned," he conceded.

She filled his cup a fifth time. "Good to know."

By the time he drained the refill, the burning inside him was extinguished.

Flora peered into her bucket. "A few drops left."

Ryder set the empty glass down on the ground. "I've had enough."

"Then you'll go to the Blue Mermaid with us?" she prodded.

"You think Sevondi will give you *The Book of Umbra*?"

"If we can convince her an attempt to incarnate Umbra would be dangerous, that she risks death if she pursues it, she might."

"I have no interest in convincing her of that."

Flora and the tiger exchanged a glance that excluded Ryder. He remained calm. Of course they'd become friends; they were both ancient.

"But I do." The spring faerie stared at his bare chest. "And if Sevondi is distracted, it will be easier for me to do so."

Ryder choked at her implications. He should have put on a shirt.

Flora brushed off his discomfort and continued in her gravelly voice, her gnarled hands emphasizing every word. "If you've studied Umbra, then you understand the dilemma of the muannai. They're a distinct population in Faerie, with a different purpose than the inhabitants of Illialei. The energies across the river serve the birthing of mortal consciousness. Here in Tyrannis, they serve its final preparation for the Unknown Beyond. As a race, the muannai have earned a second opportunity to complete the evolution of their consciousness. Yet for all their passion and vitality, without a leader, many are likely to lose their way. That won't be good for the Whole."

Ryder sat with his back rigid. The spring faerie sounded like one of the priests in Idonne, lecturing a hall of students. Usually, she grunted or huffed. He studied the empty glass beside him. Perhaps her herb water cleared the mind as well as cooled the heat. He wondered how much she drank before he arrived.

She wasn't finished. "Under Elendah's term as regent, many muannai died peacefully and traveled to the Unknown Beyond." She leaned toward him with her elbows on her knees. "It seems unwise to risk an alternative for which no one can predict the outcome. The battle between Dark and Light is upon us. The muannai need a leader. If Sevondi can be persuaded incarnating Umbra isn't necessary to achieve her goals, it will be good for us all."

"You believe she's the right person to be regent?" he asked.

Flora pressed her palms against her knees to push herself up. "I do." Her answer was quiet, but it carried the weight of her history behind it.

Sinjiin raised his head; he fastened his golden eyes on Ryder as if to say, "Why must you continue to argue?"

The young priest threw up his hands. "I'm not convinced she's the best choice for regent, but the rest of your points have merit."

The spring faerie paced. "Sevondi may try to needle you, rouse you, or cause you to lose your balance. It's her way." She tugged at the knot beneath her chin. "I've got two more batches of herb water brewing." She held the priest's gaze. "One is for me, and one is for you. We'll drink it before we go to the Blue Mermaid."

5. Princess Lilliqne

As Tatou wrestled with the window, Melia hopped along the ledge. She kept an eye on the ground below.

Loud talk and laughter drifted from the encampment on the palace's south side, but none of the knights ventured beyond the circles of light cast by their cross-stick fires. The eastern wall of the palace, concealed by the thickest part of the orchard, remained dark and unguarded.

Tatou threw the weight of her small body against the window's solid pane. "It's stuck."

Something else to add to the long list of reasons Melia hated the Albiana. Glass windows were uncommon in Illialei. The drapes and shutters in most homes allowed the fresh air of Faerie to circulate–and were a great alternative to doors.

Tatou kicked the glass with her heel. "It's not going to open."

Melia adjusted her feathers. Once Tatou resettled on her back, she spread her wings, pushed from the ledge, coasted, and then flapped her wings to gain altitude. She made an arc over the top of the apple trees to find another entrance.

On the wall's north corner, a window stood ajar. She aimed for the ledge.

Even though the window was open, its hinges were stiff. Tatou slipped though the narrow gap. She pressed her back against the glass and shoved. It opened wide enough to allow Melia to squeeze inside.

They stood in a wide alcove opening onto an ornate sleeping chamber. Diaphanous curtains draped an enormous bed. In the fireplace, a single orange coal burned. Melia spied a closed door on the opposite side of the room; it didn't have a handle. She wanted to hug her friend.

Tatou returned to her back.

Melia launched toward the bottom of the door. A deep sigh came from the bed. Melia landed on the floor, heart racing. Tatou slid off her back and pushed against the door with the entire weight of her body. It squeaked open.

A pale hand pulled back the bed curtains. "Who's there?"

Tatou raced down the hall, small feet pattering against the stone floor. Melia hopped and flitted behind her.

"Stop!"

The sharp command spurred Melia faster. She caught up with Tatou in a large stairwell.

The pixie gasped, "That was Princess Lilliane!"

Melia used her coat of blue-black feathers to form a protective shield while Tatou took a running jump to catapult herself from the landing. The pixie flew down the stairwell in a trail of flickering light. Melia hurried after her.

"Wait …" the princess' voice became an increasingly faint echo.

Two flights below, Tatou hovered in a dark passageway with her mouth wide open sucking air. Melia glided beneath her. The pixie dropped onto her back and circled her arms around Melia's throat. "The library is at the end of the hall on the right," she whispered.

Melia took off. When she had the library doors in sight, she angled her body. "Hang on," she warned Tatou.

The pixie's clench tightened around her neck.

Melia squared her body and slammed into one of the floor-to-ceiling bronze panels. Deceptively light, it swung open on the first assault. They careened into a vacuum of pitch-black as the door swayed closed behind them.

"I can't see," Tatou said.

Melia's eyes adjusted. Everything smelled like must. "No one is here."

"Aldous never leaves. His private quarters are off the east wing. We'll just have to wake him up," Tatou said.

Melia's navigational instincts were strong as an eagle. She wove her way through the wall of bookcases and shelves. Ahead, a beam of moonlight relieved the suffocating blackness. There was a narrow hall to the left.

"Down there," Tatou whispered.

Another closed door. It had one of those infernal knob handles. Melia landed.

Tatou crawled from her back. The pixie's tiny wings, worn out from her second sprint of the day, sagged. When she pressed her small body against the door, it didn't yield. Shut tight, no light seeped from beneath its frame. "Aldous," Tatou whispered several times. She stood on her tiptoes but couldn't close the gap between her fingers and the door's knob. The pixie stepped back, took a running jump, and leapt at the knob. She managed to grip the round ball, her legs dangling, but with her wings spent, she had no leverage.

Melia hopped in an agitated circle. It was impossible for her to open anything sphere-shaped with her talons or beak.

Tatou slipped and fell to the ground.

"I don't think he's in there," Melia clucked. "I don't think anyone has been down this hall in a while. The air smells dull."

A bright light danced in the direction from which they'd come.

Melia covered Tatou's glow with her wings and searched for an exit.

The light moved past them.

"I'm sure they entered the library," said the same girlish voice that called them from the top of the stairs.

"Moonlight and shadows plays tricks on the eyes, Princess," a male voice answered.

Princess Lilliane was searching for them with one of the knights.

"Who wasted the day in a pixie haze while my cousin roamed free, Gavin?"

"I'll station a guard at the door." His deference sounded forced.

"I'd station more than one. The half-bloods are full of tricks. Check that window," she snapped.

"Of course." Something heavy dragged along the floor. A dull thud and grunt followed by a sharp crack. "It's closed tight. Nothing came through here."

"I want you to check them all. Make sure every single window is locked."

"As soon as I escort you to your chamber."

"You expect me to sleep while wanted fugitives wander the palace? No wonder the old elf escaped." Lilliane's contempt tightened her voice into something nasal and harsh. A light swept past the end of the hallway where Melia and Tatou hid. "I know you're here, cousin. You and your little pixie friend. You better find them," she told the knight, "The queen won't be pleased if they get away."

"Of course, Princess. Would you like to supervise the search?"

"No. Escort me to the rose garden."

"Do you think they're there?" he asked.

"No. I need to get ..."

Melia hopped toward the end of the hall to hear more of their conversation. She peeked around an enormous bookshelf. Several shadows stretched across the end of the aisle. More knights.

"She's gone for her black roses," one of them said.

A cold fist gripped Melia's heart.

"Come on," Tatou squeaked behind her. "There's got to be an open window somewhere. We have to find it before they lock it."

❖ ❖ ❖

Melia lost count of how many windows they tried.

Below them, a large white rat rose on its hind legs, sniffed the air, twitched its whiskers, and scurried toward the lights flickering in the library's north wing. Melia couldn't help but wonder if it was the

same rat she almost tripped over the day she met Ryder. She swerved to the right.

"Every window along this aisle is locked," the knight's voice sounded much too close.

"That means they're still in here." Lilliane had returned from the rose garden.

"The south wing is the only one left to secure."

"We have them trapped," the princess gloated.

A desk with a collection of paperweights caught Melia's eye. She circled back.

Visible in the brown-gold light of oil lamps, Lilliane led a small army. The princess crushed something in her long slim fingers. A brittle gleam lit her eyes.

The distinct fragrance of roses drifted toward Melia. She detected something bitter, almost metallic, commingled with the natural scent of the flower. Her throat closed. At first she thought fear choked her.

"There they are." The princess ran. "I see the black eagle." She rubbed her fingers together with greater fury.

Melia landed on the desk. "Pick up the heaviest thing you can carry," she told Tatou. Each chirp came out cracked and broken.

The pixie alighted onto the wood surface. She pushed against various metal, glass, and rock-carved designs, gasping for air as she tested their weight. Melia strained to breathe too. When Tatou found an octagonal block that took both her hands to hold, she nodded. Melia scrunched down on her belly, dizzy from lack of oxygen. The pixie fell against her back. "You can do it," Melia encouraged. Tatou whimpered as she hauled herself up and balanced one of the block's flat planes against Melia's back. She wrapped her legs around Melia's sides and squeezed.

The smell of bitter roses clogged the air. Melia gagged. It wasn't fear; she was suffocating. She covered her beak with her wing. The shield of feathers allowed her to manage a few shallow breaths. "I'm going to aim for the window in the corner," she gasped. "Use my momentum and all your strength to heave the block through it."

The pixie dug her knees deeper into Melia's sides.

Melia forced herself to move. When she launched from the table, the drag from the extra weight and her inability to take a full breath made it hard for her to lift.

Lilliane and her entourage were almost upon them.

Melia used every last ounce of will to flap her wings. She bobbed, but kept her course as straight as she could.

The lights and voices were right behind them.

Tatou's legs squeezed tighter. The pixie lifted the block. At the last minute, she heaved the paperweight.

The awkward-shaped stone crashed through the glass, shattering the window. Fresh air poured through the hole. Melia inhaled as she wheeled in a tight circle. Tatou flattened herself across Melia's back.

With each full breath, Melia's energy returned. She shot through the jagged opening.

"Stop them!" Lilliane screamed.

The night air blasted them with freedom.

Melia flew east from the palace. Any other direction would leave them exposed, flying over field and meadow.

The thunder of hooves reverberated in the night; the knights hunted them.

Melia landed in an ash tree. "Are you all right?" she asked Tatou.

Her friend stepped down onto the branch beside her. "I've got some cuts—not too deep—and glass splinters sticking my legs like pins." Tears glistened in the pixie's eyes. "Why couldn't we breathe in the library? Lilliane and the knights were fine. It was only you and me."

"Did you smell the roses?"

Tatou nodded.

"Black roses. Black magic," Melia said. "The princess cast a spell. She was trying to suffocate us."

Tatou wiped her eyes. "I can't believe she tried to kill us! Are you hurt?"

"No." Melia's false reply came out like a woodpecker's shrill protest. They were halfway to Lake Vivientiana, and the image of the sapphire lily emblazoned her mind. She closed her eyes, dug her talons into the bark, craned her head from side to side, and ruffled her feathers.

Tatou peered into Melia's eyes. "You don't look so good."

Melia could barely think, much less fly while the lily's call exploded her eardrums. "I ... it's just ... there's a loud roaring in my ears. This happened before, on the way to Flora's cottage."

Just like tonight. The force of the lily's call suffused her. While Flora and Tatou were attacked, and the spring faerie's home burned to the ground, Melia flew to Lake Vivientiana. Now they needed to leave Illialei, and it was happening again. Everything inside Melia yearned to inhale the flower's magical perfume.

"Listen," her friend said. "What do you hear?"

"Nothing."

"They're going to search the river. They'd never guess we'd fly to the lake. It's too close to the Summer Palace."

Melia hesitated. The Summer Palace practically sat on Lake Vivientiana's shores. What if there were more knights there?

"I can wash out these splinters in the lake, and the water will soothe my cuts," Tatou said.

Melia didn't need any more encouragement. "I'll make sure we reach the Mare Cliffs before dawn."

The blue-purple flower maintained a steady drone in her mind as she flew east toward the lake.

The Summer Palace sparkled hard, like an illuminated jewel below them. Light thrust from its windows, spearing the night with angled rays of white. If Queen Luisa was there, why wasn't Princess Lilliane with her?

Melia adjusted her flight vector and targeted the beach to land as close as possible to the flower. She watched the shoreline as she descended. Not a single knight in sight. The tightness in her throat and chest loosened. By the time her claws touched sand, the fountain in the lake's center drowned out all other sound.

Tatou jumped from her back and ran to the water. The pixie splashed her arms and legs.

Melia hopped to the lily.

The last time she visited the lake's shore, it had been a dark moon night. She'd sensed the flower—towering over her—more than seen it. But tonight, beneath the light of Faeries' two moons, she could see its rich velvet petals and the gold flecks in the lily's throat. She inhaled its heady scent. Her mind calmed. The fresh perfume was more powerful than she remembered.

She took another deep breath. And another.

Everything was going to be all right.

6. The Mare Cliffs

Melia landed on the cliffs overlooking the Undine River. The distinctive odor of sirens and nixies, mingled with the scent of fresh water and fish, rose from the gorge below.

In the grey light of predawn, Tatou looked like she'd run through a thorn patch.

"I'm sorry about the broken glass," Melia cawed.

"Much better than death."

"Does it hurt?"

The pixie lifted her petal skirt. "I washed out the glass chips in the lake, and it seems like my short swim soothed the cuts." Although the Great White Sea was most potent, all natural bodies of water in the enchanted world possessed healing properties. Tatou pointed to a laceration already reduced to a thin pink line. "See." She walked to the edge of the bluff and looked down to where the water roared through a canyon. "I thought we were going to cross the river."

The Undine marked the eastern and northern borders between Illialei and Tyrannis. It was doubtful the Huron knights would cross it.

"We are, but we need to find Aldous first," Melia said. "If the knights secure the border, it's going to be difficult to cross back into Illialei. Where do you think he is?"

Tatou's forehead wrinkled. "I've heard he enjoyed walking in the palace rose garden every morning, but I've never seen him anywhere but the library."

Melia ruffled her feathers. She didn't want to hear any more about roses. "Do you think he'd go to the glen?"

Aldous was a wood elf, and the largest population of wood elves lived in a glen nestled in the western range of the Rolling Mountains.

"It would be too easy for Lilliane to find him there," Tatou said.

"Maybe his lineage would hide him."

"I'm not sure they could risk offending the queen."

"Then where?"

"Maybe he left Illialei. Maybe that's why Lilliane is so angry—because he's beyond her reach."

Aldous sent Melia and Tatou to visit Flora after Plantine was kidnapped. He gave them a rose-quartz bracelet to show the spring faerie. It was an awkward introduction, but later Flora made it clear she was fond of the wood elf.

"Do you think he would try to go to Flora's cottage?" Melia asked. "He might not know it burned down."

"I'd be surprised if he didn't. He maintains a network of falcons and other messengers that bring him news and information from all over the enchanted world."

"Then where would he go?"

"The closest place would be the Veiled Tavern."

Melia's talons clenched dirt. The last time she saw the Veil's proprietor, Gumf lied to her about having Ryder arrested. Likewise, she neglected to tell him Flora was waiting in the woods for her and her friends—with the Tasimas diamond. She couldn't imagine the dwarf would be happy to see her. "Can you think of anywhere else he might be?"

"The Dark Horse Saloon is east of the marketplace, but that's a longer trip overland. It would make more sense for him to go to the Veil. He knows Gumf."

"Could he have caught a ship at Southend?" Melia asked hopefully.

"Someone in Illialei must know. Let's call some of my friends." The pixie held her hands to her mouth and trilled at least five different bird dialects. Melia echoed Tatou's call for help in the tongue of eagles.

They heard the song, a duet, before they saw the singers.

A siren's ethereal face peered over the cliff's ledge; her enormous wings—they looked like they belonged to an oversized butterfly—beat a slow, steady rhythm, suspending her in midair. Two arms wrapped around her neck. Her singing partner, a glamorous nixie, peeked from behind the siren's neck through a tumble of golden hair.

Sirens lured mortals to a watery death, but a powerful one could seduce a creature from the enchanted world too.

Tatou's wings drooped.

Melia dropped her hand to her waist before she remembered there was no weapon there.

"We were coming to dive," the siren sounded like a swan. Her perfume—the scent a thunderstorm left in its wake—carried Melia all the way back to her childhood in the mortal world.

"It's the black eagle," the nixie said in the common tongue. A row of small pointed teeth contrasted with her pouty mouth.

Melia clamped her beak against the creature's pungent scent.

Nixies, distant kin to Illialei's mermaids, were the water faeries native to Tyrannis. They were smaller than mermaids, although not as small as pixies—more like the size of a short field faerie.

"You know me?" Melia asked.

The nixie showed more teeth.

Melia flinched before she realized the water faerie was smiling.

"Everyone knows Pressina's girls."

The nixie's revelation heightened Melia's sense of vulnerability. If she was recognized so easily by strangers, anyone might spy on her for Lilliane—and her army of Huron knights.

The siren fluttered higher, until she cleared the cliff. Her bare feet touched the rock of the cliff's edge. Webbed, they trailed water

47

as she walked toward Melia and Tatou. The nixie slid down the siren's back. On the ground, she balanced on her belly with her scaled tail coiled and twitching behind her.

Staring at the siren's wings and the nixie's tail, Melia couldn't help but think of Melusine. She wondered if her older sister was happy; if her marriage to Raymond, a full-blood mortal, was everything she'd hoped for; if he'd kept his faerie troth to never witness Melusine's repellant transformation on Sunday. For on that day, Melusine's slender legs twisted into a coarse, leathery serpent tail and lumpy dragon wings erupted from her back. If Raymond ever saw her in that state, Melusine's transmogrification would become permanent. It was their mother's curse.

But the nixie's tail was sleek and smooth, with a golden sheen. And where Melusine's wings were knobby and dense, the siren's were gauzy and elegant. If her mother had given Melusine wings and a tail like that, her older sister might not have suffered as much. She might not have left Illialei so abruptly.

Melia craned her head from side to side. Not a single bird had answered their calls. Not surprising, when a siren and a nixie stood a horse-length away from them.

"Maybe you can help us," Tatou said.

Melia swiveled her head to glare at her friend.

"News travels fast along the river," the pixie continued.

"It does, little one," the siren said.

Tatou risked a step forward.

Although Melia would have preferred to remain farther from the nixie's razor-like teeth, she matched her friend's advance.

"We need to find someone who we fear is in danger," Tatou said.

The siren and nixie exchanged glances. "Who?" the nixie asked.

Although she was prepared to whisk Tatou away at the first threat of black magic, Melia forced herself to stand even with her friend. She stretched her neck to its maximum extension, straining to catch any hint of dark enchantment in the siren's voice.

"Aldous, he's the palace librarian," Tatou said.

The siren nodded. "The old wood elf."

"Do you know where he is?" Melia blurted out.

The nixie's flexile torso sinuated across the ground. She closed the distance between herself and the half-faerie. She gazed into Melia's eyes and sang a wordless song. Melia relaxed. The nixie's melody untied knots, tangled within knots inside her.

Melia thought of her father. She thought of her mother. She thought of Elendah. And though she guarded her heart, Melia yearned to weep as everything unraveled within.

"Dawn will be here soon," Tatou's whisper broke the spell.

"The black eagle's heart is heavy," the nixie said. "A good cry is like a deep cleansing. She needs one."

"Right now?" Tatou asked.

The nixie shrugged. "It makes no difference to me, but Nandana was my friend, and she talked with me about this half-faerie who shifts into a black eagle at sunset." The water faerie spoke about Melia as if she weren't standing a few paces in front of her. "The sooner she allows her tears to wash away the dirt in her heart, the sooner she'll be able to see clear and find her way. Then she might be able to perceive who her enemies are—and who they're not." She spit the last words out as if she could hear what Melia was thinking. "Not thinking"—the nixie stabbed two fingers at the side of her head —"feeling." The water faerie slammed her own chest once with her palm. Her eyes narrowed. "If you don't set your heart free, you'll never be able to trust anyone."

Melia's right leg twitched. She backed away. The world swooshed like a cyclone around her as her body molted its feathers; the bones in her wings thickened into the bones of her arms, her talons widened into skin-covered toes; and the sleeveless green dress she'd changed into yesterday morning at the tree house hugged her hips.

Now, the siren and nixie stared at her.

"Listen," Melia said. "You might be right about the crying—"

"I'm right," the nixie said.

"But finding our friend is more urgent."

"Maybe you can do both." The nixie tilted her head toward the siren. "Give us a moment."

Tatou fluttered up to Melia's shoulder. She pointed to a bush laden with dark berries. "We'll be over there, eating breakfast."

✧ ✧ ✧

"Why did you ask them for help?" Melia asked through clenched teeth.

"Who else is going to help us? Not one bird answered my call." The pixie sounded hurt.

"Did you see the mouth on her?" Melia asked. "If I was a bird, I wouldn't come near her. Nixies probably use bird bones to pick their teeth."

Tatou laughed.

"You think this is funny? That siren is more likely to serenade us to our death than help us find Aldous. And we've just escaped Lilliane. Do we really need to court more trouble?"

"You're just upset because the nixie said your heart is dark."

"She didn't say it was dark; she said it was heavy."

Tatou raised her shoulders and shot Melia an impish smile. "She might be right."

Melia yanked on a strand of her hair. "Ouch!" A tiny sliver of glass pierced the side of her finger. She picked out the almost invisible shard and sucked away the small red bead that formed on her skin.

"Be careful," Tatou teased. "If the nixie smells blood, she might prefer you as a snack."

Melia offered her friend a flat smile.

"You don't need to be so wary of her. She's Nandana's friend."

"So she says."

"Let them help us," the pixie insisted.

"How do you know they will?"

Tatou pulled a plump berry from the bush with both hands. Then she took an annoyingly small bite that took her forever to chew.

"Because I can tell who my enemies are—and who they're not."

"If you're trying to make me feel better, it's not working." Melia's insides smarted as much as her finger. Tatou's remark about her dark heart stung.

✧ ✧ ✧

The siren stood tall and straight, her filmy dress shimmering in the morning light. "My name is Calista, and this is Bertille." She indicated the nixie who lounged on her side, her golden tail coiling and uncoiling in a mesmerizing dance.

Melia met Calista's gaze. "And you've decided?"

"Perhaps you could tell us your names," the siren said.

Melia crossed her arms. She was eager to prove her instincts were as sound as Tatou's, that the nixie and the siren were treacherous and deceitful. "If Nandana spoke with you about me, then you already know my name."

The pixie didn't wait for either the siren or the nixie to respond to Melia's challenge. She stood up on her friend's shoulder and volunteered both their names.

The half-faerie's jaw clenched. Tatou was open-minded when it came to meeting new creatures. Melia had always appreciated—and benefitted from—her friend's generosity of spirit, but today, she wished, just once, her friend would exercise some caution.

Calista clasped her hands. "Lovely. Why don't we sit down?"

It would be harder to run if they were seated, but Tatou stroked Melia's hair while Calista settled in a patch of short grass next to Bertille. The siren smiled up at them. It was a smile that made Melia's stubborn refusal to sit appear ridiculous.

"She struggles to trust us," Bertille said. "And yet, we're here to help her. In fact, during our tête-à-tête, Calista and I decided it was more than chance that brought the four of us together this morning."

A sharp pain traveled from Melia's left arm up through her neck. "And what makes you think that?"

"We have the information you seek," Calista said.

"Then don't speak in riddles," Melia snapped.

"I told you," Bertille said to her friend. "She doesn't see the golden egg the Whole has laid at her feet this morning because her heart is closed."

Melia threw her hands in the air. "Enough with my heart."

Bertille gave her a pained look.

"Sit down, please," Tatou whispered in her ear.

Melia wagged her chin and plopped down.

Tatou lost her balance and flipped into a somersault midair to land on her feet between Melia and Calista.

"Thank you," the siren said.

Calista's even temper was getting under Melia's skin.

Bertille shifted closer to the half-faerie and showered her with a creepy smile. The tips of the nixie's pointed teeth peeked over her ruby-red lips. Melia leaned back with her palms flat on the ground and her weight on her wrists.

"Have you ever gone diving?" the nixie asked.

"Not off those cliffs." Diving from the Mare Cliffs was a favorite pastime of both sirens and nixies, but Melia couldn't remember a single faerie, mortal, or other creature ever making the high jump.

"Diving is like flying," Bertille said.

Melia shrugged. "Diving is aiming your head at the ground. Flying is not like that at all."

"Yes, but when you dive you throw yourself into the air."

Melia raised an eyebrow at Tatou.

Bertille maneuvered herself between the half-faerie and pixie.

Melia scooted back.

"Trusting is magic," the nixie said.

"Those are just words," Melia said. "They don't mean anything."

Bertille leaned forward.

Melia pulled away until her back was almost horizontal to the ground.

The nixie swiveled around to Melia's side.

Recalling how Melusine had struggled with her serpent tail and dragon wings, Melia marveled at Bertille's quick, graceful movements.

The nixie reached out her hand; she placed it on Melia's breastbone.

The half-faerie lifted her arm to push it away, then hesitated. The energy from Bertille's palm radiated through her chest. She let her hand drop. The nixie held Melia's eyes with her river-grey gaze, but it was more than that. Bertille was holding Melia's insides still, making her stop ... wait ... and feel.

Something flickered in Melia's heart.

The nixie nodded.

In Melia's mind's eye, the flicker wavered into a tiny dancing flame.

Bertille's steady breathing supported her.

The flame grew three times its original size. A welcoming heat filled Melia's chest. She remembered a winter in Achill, coming in from the snow, her fingers aching with bitter cold. When she stretched her hands out over the fire, the pleasure was so intense she'd laughed out loud.

Her father said, "Little Bird is thawing her wings."

Wetness gathered in the corner of Melia's eyes.

Bertille's gaze remained fixed. "Let the tears come."

Melia did as the nixie told her, letting the drops roll down her cheek and gather on her chin. "I loved him," she whispered.

"Of course you did," Bertille said. "It was an accident."

Melia gulped air. "Since then, everything"—she banged the ground with the back of her hands—"everything has gone wrong."

"Your journey has only begun. Don't judge yet." Bertille's words were a calming breeze; they brought down another wall.

Melia gripped one of the pearl bracelets Elendah had given her.

"Yes, yes," Bertille said. "Pierce the veils of darkness within you."

"My sister killed the grey faerie." Melia smeared the tears on her face. "But in my dark moon visions, it's my hands that are stained with blood." She hiccuped. "I'm always the murderer. That's why I have to stop Umbra, because—because—" She wiped the snot from her nose. "I can't allow the incarnation to happen. I can't let the things in my visions come true. And now, my father and the grey faerie are dead, my little sister is a murderer, war has come to Illialei, and my mother hates me." Melia folded over her legs, covered her arms with her head, and sobbed.

Bertille's hand rubbed a circular motion on her back. "There, there, let it all out."

7. Sevondi's Vision

Sevondi paced the length of her suite in the Blue Mermaid. After Zachariah died, she remained at the hotel—his homage to the mortal world. It was a strange place with all its shiny gadgets and hard surfaces, but it was comfortable, and living at the top of the mountain among the Calashai's ruins didn't appeal to her.

She would go there when the new stronghold was built, when there was a throne for her to sit upon. Not one day before.

Flora accepted her invitation. "Would it be all right if I bring along a friend, or two?"

Sevondi sent Pogo with a response. "Fine, bring the tiger." She told his twin brother, Moog, "The cat will want something raw—bloody—to eat." The troll blanched, but Sevondi intended to find out what happened to Ormrun and Koldis. Befriending the spring faerie's new pet couldn't hurt.

It confounded her. The night the Calashai fell, she sent the twins to Aldaine. The only thing they learned: Flora and her friends tried to escape with the basin and sword, and failed. Even with Elendah dead and the stronghold razed, even with the courtyard nothing but gashes of dirt and rubble, the founding stone held fast to the dwarf magic.

Sevondi stretched her fingers. She needed to get her hands on that bowl and the sword.

The shiny cabinet across the room stared back at her, an enormous eye. She hated it almost as much as she hated the book

shelved beneath it—mocking her from behind two polished doors—
The Book of Umbra.

The druid's work was indiscriminate. Elynus wrote down every word of research—and every single thought he'd ever had—on the subject of Umbra. Sifting through the copious chicken-scratch was agonizing; some of the passages were illegible, many were meaningless. She had no patience for it.

Since Elendah's death, hundreds of muannai came to Aldaine every day. They came from the valley and deep woods. They crossed the Nuada and climbed the mountains in droves. They wanted—they needed—to rebuild the stronghold.

Their spiritual renaissance was a moving thing to witness; and the opportunity it presented wasn't going to slip through her fingers.

A vision came to her: Caravans winding their way through Tyrannis—a pilgrimage following a spectacular show of dragons scorching the night skies in fiery combat.

She imagined crowds, stamping their feet, shouting her name, bowing before her: Sevondi, the Great Dragonwitch! Sevondi, our beloved Queen! She would lead them to the Muudron Stone, and there, win their allegiance with the most outrageous display the enchanted world had ever seen: Umbra's incarnation.

It would herald her ascent to the throne of the stronghold of ... of ... she rubbed her thumb against her fingertips. The stronghold of Calashai reeked of Elendah's determined peace.

Sevondi eased down onto the bed. The blanket was such a comfort, so luxurious and thick. Her back burned where the arrows tipped with Umbra's poison pierced her skin, but Embril could find no residual poison.

"Hardly even a scar, ma'am," the troll said.

Damn Zachariah for marrying that half-faerie.

Sevondi closed her eyes. A new name for the stronghold would come to her. As the basin and the sword would come to her.

She tried to imagine performing the incarnation ritual on the top of the mountain where the Calashai once stood, but the scene always lacked impact. Sevondi's great-great-grandfather practiced black magic at the Muudron Stone; it had to be there.

She closed her eyes and envisioned the triumph in her mind.

"They're waiting?" Sevondi asked.

Pogo and Moog nodded as one.

"When I snap my fingers, open the doors. Once I'm inside, let them close behind me. Don't let them see you. We're creating an effect. Do you understand?" She glared at Moog who didn't seem to possess his twin's innate sense of discipline.

The troll tipped his head. Irritation rolled off him. It irked her. Pogo's loyalty was limitless—as long as she paid him well. But Moog's loyalties weren't so easily bought. This afternoon, she'd have to settle for compliance.

"Good," she said. "Have lunch served immediately. Don't dawdle. Are we ready?" She suffered their lukewarm assent in silence. A lecture on the benefits of enthusiastic response would have to be delivered another day.

Sevondi clicked her fingers.

The twins pushed the doors on the same beat. Sevondi offered Moog a pleased bob of her chin. She glided across the threshold into the well-lit ballroom.

Electricity. It involved a lot of wires, but the results were spectacular. The spacious hall sparkled like an ensorcelled woodland grotto. Wild sprays of night jasmine bloomed from enormous vases. Woven screens and tapestries in every shade of green created pathways and nooks beyond a central area blanketed with cushions and pillows. Overhead, crystal waterfalls poured from a multitude of gold-finished branches.

It wasn't quite the stronghold of Calashai, but the effect was unexpected. Moog had supervised the ballroom's transformation. Either the troll had the soul of an artist in his runt of a body, or she'd gained more of his devotion than she knew. Sevondi turned her attention to the guests.

Flora stood in her usual belligerent stance with her hands smashed in the pocket of that atrocious apron she always wore. Her clashing kerchief almost blinded Sevondi, its knot askew beneath the spring faerie's chin.

The tiger made for a fierce-looking creature, glowering and showing its saber teeth. A lover of cats in all sizes, the dragonwitch immediately warmed to him.

And there was the young priest, arms steeled across his chest. Dressed in ill-fitting breeches, a loose shirt, and moccasins, he oozed a straightforward masculinity that would challenge any female creature's determined aloofness.

"Flora, I owe you my life," Sevondi said. "Thank you."

The spring faerie took her hands from her pocket and let the muannaye hold them. The dragonwitch squeezed Flora's fingers, calloused from the hard work so many years spent isolated in the Balyudor had demanded.

"Will you be staying in Aldaine?" Sevondi asked.

Flora slipped her hands back into her apron pocket. "For the time being."

"A cottage, perhaps?"

"A tent."

"Among the stronghold's ruins?"

Flora's gaze wandered the ballroom. "It's being rebuilt."

"So I've heard. Please, introduce me to your friends."

The spring faerie sank her hand into the ruff of the big cat's neck. "This is Sinjiin."

The dragonwitch crouched. The cat's eyes were mysterious, sentient. "You're magnificent." She held out a hand. The tiger's nose twitched.

She stood up to face the priest.

"I believe you've already met Ryder," Flora said.

Sevondi held out her hand again. "Yes, but the circumstances were quite different."

The priest kept his hands clamped beneath his crossed arms. "Ma'am."

"Please, everyone sit," she said.

They shuffled around her in awkward silence.

The first course arrived. Sevondi said nothing while Flora slurped the soup and then soaked up the remaining broth with half a loaf of bread. Everyone stared when Moog brought out a tower of raw steak balanced on a silver platter.

"Thank you for feeding the cat," Flora said.

"Of course," Sevondi murmured. "Such an unusual pet."

The tiger bared its teeth.

"He's not a pet," the spring faerie said.

"No?"

"What she means is: Sinjiin belongs to no one." Finally, the priest had spoke.

Sevondi faced him. "But what an ally to have in a tight spot."

The priest picked over his meat tart. He barely touched the cheese soufflé or his blackberry wine.

"You're not hungry?" Sevondi asked.

"The food is rich."

"I suppose the the priestly fare in Idonne is much simpler."

"That's true," he said.

"Don't worry about him," Flora interrupted. "Everything's delicious. What's for dessert?"

"Nut cake and aurora infusion with goat cream. Your favorite, I believe."

Flora nodded.

"Is it true–"

"Do you–"

They spoke at the same time. Sevondi bit her tongue to let Flora speak first.

"Do you have *The Book of Umbra*?" the spring faerie asked.

Sevondi stretched her arm and examined the new sheath she wore on her forearm. It was forged from gold leaf. She hadn't decided whether or not it truly suited her. Perhaps if she lacquered her nails. "You know that I do."

Flora picked at the nut cake. Usually, she would have inhaled three pieces by now. "We'd like to propose an exchange."

Sevondi dropped her arm. She leaned forward with parted lips.

"We'll support your regency in exchange for the book," Flora said.

Sevondi intended to be queen, but why quibble over details. "What an intriguing offer."

The spring faerie set down her plate. "Elendah's peace has ended." She twisted a silver ring on her finger. "We seek an alliance with the leader of the muannai. Someone who will stand with us against the Albiana when the time comes."

Sevondi looked from Flora to the tiger, then to the priest. The support of three who'd once supported Elendah would lend a sense of destiny to her ambition. It was more than she'd hoped for, but best not to appear overeager. She reached for a slice of cake. "And what will you do with the book?"

"Take it to Idonne," the priest said. "It belongs in the library's archives."

Sevondi choked on a pecan.

Pogo appeared out of nowhere to hand her a glass of water.

When she could speak, the dragonwitch addressed Ryder. "Such a prize would please Anton, perhaps even move him to forgiveness." She turned to Flora. "And what of Ormrun and Koldis?"

"Ryder will deliver them to the Grey Council."

"Idonne, the Isle of Minnanon—you'll be sailing the Great White Sea for years," Sevondi said. "And what of poor Umbra, never to incarnate?"

Flora dropped her eyes. "We'll support your regency for the book, Sevondi."

Blood pulsed in heated waves through Sevondi's veins. Her

dream of incarnating Umbra wasn't something she'd relinquish because these three wanted to spirit away the portal and its key. Yet, the fish was on the hook. If she traded the book, perhaps the handsome young priest could ferret some meaning from Elynus' scribbling. Better him to slave over the tome than her. "It's an offer worth entertaining—"

"You should do more than entertain it," the priest said.

Flora's eyes glinted.

"And yet ..." Sevondi repressed the smile threatening to make her satisfaction transparent. She considered how hard to drive the bargain. "My regency"—she detested that title—"might not require your support."

"Look around you," Flora said. "War is upon us. The one who sits on the Cathedral Palace throne will fall. You don't want to gain the regency only to fall with her, do you?"

Before the burning of the spring faeries, Flora had developed a reputation as something of a strategist. Apparently, age and exile had sharpened her mind—though not her tongue. Throughout lunch she'd refrained from her usual bitter retorts; rather, her demeanor bordered on gracious. Sevondi didn't know what to make of it. Had the spring faerie metamorphosed into a politician—or a trickster?

The dragonwitch inhaled an exaggerated breath. The scent of night jasmine—the flower of Tyrannis—infused her senses. "I've always wanted to stand with you against the Albiana. For what they did to your people." It was hard for Sevondi to look at Flora and not feel great sympathy for the genocide of the spring faeries. However, of late, something noble blossomed from deep within the grumpy old faerie. Something that had been dormant all the time Sevondi had known her. "I'd be a much stronger ally as the incarnated Umbra." She bit her tongue. Her Aunt Imelda always warned her strong emotion weakened reserve.

"No one is going to incarnate Umbra," the priest said.

Sevondi glared at him. "So you say, but you'll be proven wrong before this war is over."

Flora smoothed her apron. "We can agree to disagree upon the finer details."

The dragonwitch laughed. "Now the incarnation of Umbra is an insignificant detail?"

"Everyone here wants the basin and sword free of the founding stone," the spring faerie said.

Sevondi examined each of their faces from beneath her dark lashes. No matter how much Flora wanted *The Book of Umbra,* she would never give her the bowl or the sword.

The enormous clove-colored tiger licked the silver platter clean.

Perhaps a pampered feline might lead Sevondi to Ormrun and Koldis—once they were beyond the founding stone's pull. Before the noble priest could sail away with them. It would be easy enough for Moog to supply the cat with daily treats.

"*The Book of Umbra* for my regency," Sevondi agreed.

Flora held out a gnarled hand.

8. Dark Knight

"We lost them, sir," the scout reported. "They disappeared."

"Like magic." The words tasted bitter in Gavin's mouth.

When Keir warned him about the country, Gavin listened with half-an-ear: "The charms of Illialei's inhabitants are neither fearsome nor harsh, yet many men of strong will have been lulled into a joyous stupor there. Keep your wits about you."

Now Gavin detected the experience in Keir's words. He dismissed the scout with a scowl.

Alone in his large tent, Gavin's mind swirled with the events of the past two days–his decision to search the tree house, the discovery of Elynus' letters, the half-faerie luring him to the pixies, and Lilliane's unexpected arrival at the Cathedral Palace. He rubbed his eyes, dry from lack of sleep, with the heels of his palms.

His thoughts turned to Umbra and the haze in his mind receded. In Huros, conversations about the evolution of consciousness bored Gavin. Umbra was another fish in a sea of information irrelevant to his ambition. But Elynus' research on the basin and the sword showed him his error.

Before he could organize his ideas on the subject, his lieutenant entered the tent. "The princess requests your presence in the throne room."

Gavin rose from the carved chair which always served as his command post. He followed his officer through the Huron camp, the palace gates, and across the drawbridge. Inside the palace, their boots rang out against the stone floor. They passed no one.

The princess traveled with a small retinue while the queen remained at the Summer Palace. There was no audience in the throne room, only the princess seated on her lesser throne.

"Where is my cousin?" she demanded.

Gavin would not be shamed by a girl in the presence of a subordinate. "Leave us." His lieutenant bowed and left the spacious hall. Gavin braced himself for a tantrum.

"How could you let her escape—again!" Lilliane shouted.

Gavin cursed the spies who reported his encounter with the half-faerie, the one that led to his capture in the enchanted gardens. "Our search continues."

"Indeed!" the princess mimicked him.

He would make no excuses. He would make no false promises. "Is there anything else, Princess?" To avoid eye contact with her, he studied the detail in a tapestry hanging on the wall above her head.

"Do not trouble me again with your reports of failure!"

He didn't remind her she had sent for him. "If your cousin has entered Tyrannis, we cannot apprehend her there. I have no authority beyond your country's borders. However, we'll prevent her return to Illialei. Sentries are posted along the river."

With no power to contradict the direct orders of Huron war chiefs, the princess sulked. "You're useless to me."

"Perhaps, but I would prefer you travel with an escort when you return to the Summer Palace."

She pouted. "Do you wish to be rid of me?"

He wished to monitor her movements. "I wish to keep you safe."

She rose from her petite throne and sauntered toward him. "Your concern touches me."

He forced his lips into the semblance of a smile.

She stopped before him. The bruised violet pools of her eyes assessed him. "Do you find me beautiful?"

"There is none more fair."

"Your lips are a font of flattery and deceit."

He raised his hand to brush his thumb along the side of her chin. It was a disrespectful gesture, one her father would have punished severely if he were present. But Keir Collin was far away in Huros.

Gavin noted how the princess trembled at his touch, before dismissing him with a much subdued tone.

✧ ✧ ✧

Gavin called for his lieutenant. "How many knights are stationed at the river?"

"A dozen."

"And still no sighting of the half-faerie?"

"No sir."

Gavin rubbed his gloved hands together. "Prepare my horse. I'll join the sentries on the border."

"How many men would you like to ride with you?"

"None."

The lieutenant offered a curt nod.

Gavin's horse followed the well-trodden dirt artery to the Sylvan Forest. From there, the beast continued on the main road to the Maeldun Bridge. It pleased Gavin that none of his knights could be sighted from this vantage point. The half-faerie wouldn't spy them either, if she chose to cross the bridge. The size of the black iron structure impressed Gavin. He considered crossing it to enter Tyrannis.

Not yet.

What he really wanted was a place to meditate upon Umbra undisturbed. He dismounted and led his horse into the forest. When the main road was no longer visible, Gavin tethered the horse's reins to a limb, calmed the beast, and slipped deeper among the trees. He walked until he could walk no farther. Below him the Undine River forked into the Nyssalei.

Gavin used the broad trunk and low-lying branches of an old maple tree for camouflage as he studied the landscape.

Unquestioning obedience was the mystical talent of every Huron knight. It allowed multiple regiments to execute military operations as if by one powerful arm. Gavin fussed with his collar as his thoughts turned to Umbra.

A deep well of discontent welled up within him. Luisa Albiana was weak and indolent, her daughter childish. Neither was fit to rule a country. Illialei's inhabitants were capricious and wayward. They needed order and discipline. Gavin could provide that.

He rubbed the back of his neck. What was he thinking? Keir sent him to Illialei to protect his wife and daughter, not overthrow their monarchy.

The air around Gavin was stifling. He unfastened the top two buttons of his jacket. Obeying Keir put him in the unenviable position of taking orders from a girl and her invalid mother.

A light whistle interrupted Gavin's reverie. He scanned the undergrowth. A pair of sparrows hopped along a branch. Gavin crouched and sifted through the detritus of leaves and twigs. He found a stone with a serrated edge and took aim. The missile struck its target midair. Stunned, the small brown bird flapped its wings helplessly, quivered, and then plunged to the ground. The second sparrow scattered, its futile cries quickly fading.

Gavin's gaze returned to the river.

The basin and sword Elynus wrote of remained in Tyrannis. If he possessed them, Gavin could unlock Umbra's power. Lilliane's childish tirades and personal vendetta against her cousin would be moot. He would command her. She would obey him. Gavin clenched and unclenched his fist. He imagined squeezing Lilliane's pale throat. He imagined her dropping to her knees, those black-violet eyes swimming with fear.

He raised his arm and reached with his hand. Finding Ormrun and Koldis would require deceiving the princess, placating her, perhaps even seducing her, while he searched. It would be easy enough to bend her to his will. For all her cruel ambition, Lilliane was naïve.

Gavin turned his hand over. He stared at his gloved palm. To hold the future of the enchanted world in his hand, that would be something.

9. Leaving Illiqlei

The line of water made Melia's head swim. The river seemed so far away. What if she missed? Her body swayed; she stumbled backward. Calista grabbed her arm. "There's a path in the grass," Melia said. "It switchbacks along the edge of the cliff. I'll go down that way." She turned around.

Bertille blocked her. The nixie's erect torso reminded Melia of a picture Plantine showed her once of a spitting cobra. "Let go of your fear and self-doubt," the water faerie said.

Melia pointed her thumb back at the gorge. "This can't be the only way to do that."

"Remember what I told you. The body is an expression of the mind, and the mind is an expression of the spirit. Yes, there are other ways to let go, but they could take a lifetime. I don't think you have a lifetime. By diving, your body will experience the letting go immediately, and your mind will comprehend. It won't be just an idea." The nixie's eyes twinkled. "It will set your spirit free."

"But the cliff is so high. Couldn't I dive from one of those rocks over there?" Melia pointed to a formation of boulders on the Tyrannis side of the river.

Bertille raised her hand above her head. "Those boulders are hardly taller than you. It would be a jump not a dive."

"Why is letting go so important?"

Bertille curled her hand into a fist. "When you're so closed, you hold on to things you no longer need." She opened her hand and showed Melia her palm. "Open yourself, and you can receive. Different things. New things. Important things. Things you need now." The nixie opened both her hands and raised them above her head. "When old things fall away"—she slid her hands in a winding motion toward the grass—"you can move, adapt, and respond to the present. You become more agile. Shadows from the past no longer obscure your vision, or trick you. Wasn't I right about the tears?" Bertille's graceful gestures were more convincing than her words.

When Melia's father broke his faerie troth, his daughter received two harsh blows. The first being the loss of her childhood playmates. Listening to her mother disparage mortals for years made Melia doubt those affections. She locked the sadness away, never thinking or talking about her young friends from Ireland again.

The second blow occurred when she arrived in Illialei. As a wingless half-faerie in a world of full-bloods with magnificent wings, and seeing her mother's exquisite ivory wings every day—wings which Pressina hid in the mortal world—knifed Melia's young heart like a betrayal.

Then her father inadvertently opened Melia to Umbra, probing her innocent mind while his own obsession with the dark master influenced his every thought.

Bertille assured her: "The dark moon visions only prove Umbra has touched you, amplifying your anger, hurt, and resentment, not that you're dangerous. That they only occur when the moons are dark speaks to your inner strength. Once touched by Umbra, few can contain the dark master's impulses."

Bertille made everything sound hopeful. Like Melia was a virtuous saint, not a potential murderess haunted by images of blood-stained hands. She wanted to believe the water faerie.

Her stomach growled.

"After you dive, we'll eat," Bertille said. "Calista will cross the Undine and pick up some smoked fish at the market."

Melia didn't miss Tatou's sour face. "Maybe she could find some dried fruit, or one of those sticky buns for my friend?"

"Of course," the siren replied. "Anything else?"

"Um, a plate of baby greens? The ones that are pan-fried with garlic and onions," Melia said.

"Those are my favorite too." Bertille asked Calista if she could handle another plate.

"Smoked fish, a bag of dried fruit, two plates of greens, anything else?" the siren asked.

Melia settled her hands on her hips. She wanted a pair of slacks, the style the muannai wore. After the dragonwitch slimed her at the Muudron Stone, Gumf gave her a pair along with some boots. They were long gone.

"Something else?" Calista asked.

Melia wished she had some coins.

"Don't worry about the cost." Bertille reached for Melia's hand. "Calista and I are market regulars. We provide fresh fish to many of the vendors. We can barter for the rest. What is it that you want?"

"A pair of pants?"

Bertille nodded. "Very practical. But don't forget the boots," the nixie said to Calista. She turned back to Melia. "You simply can't have one without the other."

The half-faerie beamed. Wearing muannai boots was like going barefoot. She leaned over and squeezed Bertille.

When she turned to hug the siren, Calista was already gone, her enormous wings making a slow wave in the early afternoon sun. She flew north toward the muannai valley. Something on her shoulder sparkled.

"Tatou?" Melia's gaze ping-ponged from side to side.

Bertille clasped her hands. "The pixie doesn't need to dive. They'll meet us when we're finished here. Are you ready?"

Melia swallowed the panic rising in her belly. She didn't think she'd ever be ready, but what if Bertille was right? What if she could let go of a past that was never really hers? A past that belonged more to her father and mother, a past that had always been such a heavy burden. She tiptoed back to the ledge and peered over. "You'll go with me?"

"I'll be right behind you."

Bertille was half her size and had no wings, either. Melia's brows pulled together. "What if nothing changes?"

"It will," the water nixie said.

"You're not going to let me walk down that grassy trail, are you?"

"You don't need to walk. Remember what I told you. Push with all the strength in your legs, not just your feet. The wider the arc, the more powerful the dive. On the way down, let your arms and hands spread wide, like wings. Aim there." Bertille pointed to the length of the river that was the deepest shade of blue.

Melia swung her arms in a sideways windmill motion. She balanced on her toes. She breathed in and out. She clapped her hands together over her head–

And jumped.

She pushed forward and out. Her body found its natural arc with no help from her mind. She bent in half, almost touching her toes before her body straightened into a meteoric plunge.

Wind whipped her hair from her face. It pummeled her cheeks. She struggled to breath. The wind buffeted her arms. She tried to hold them out, but the air current pinned them to her sides.

She dropped faster and faster. Her heart was in her throat. She thought it might fall out of her mouth.

This was nothing like flying.

The river widened below her; it became something impossible to miss. Whitecaps broke on the large rocks downstream. Where she was headed, there were none. Green and brown blurs detailed into treetops.

Tension left her body in an unabashed scream. Her mouth and her nose flooded as she broke the river's surface. Momentum plunged her deep down into the frigid water. When her descent ended, she kicked her legs vigorously. She ascended to gulp air. Her torso bounced up and down as she kept her lower body in motion.

Chains that had bound her heart for so many years hit the river's bottom. She could almost hear them. Ka-chink.

A waterfall rained down on her head. Bertille popped up from the depths beside her.

"Can we do it again?" Melia asked.

The nixie laughed. She wrapped her arms around Melia's neck and pressed her slim torso against the half-faerie's back. Her weight was so slight Melia hardly registered it as her long legs conquered the steep path she fought to walk down earlier.

The dive resurrected a free-spirited young girl bursting with energy, the girl Melia had left behind in Ireland.

She couldn't wait to see Ryder.

They made two more dives before Calista and Tatou landed on the east side of the river. The siren had been more than generous with her purchases at the market.

By the time they finished eating, Melia lolled back on the riverbank with a stomachache. She'd eaten too much and too fast, but she'd never tasted smoked fish before; it melted in her mouth.

Tatou licked the stickiness from her fingers. She ate every last bite of the dried peaches, pears, apricots, and honey-sweetened cranberries, but her favorite was the sweet bun with its icing that stuck like glue to everything, including the pixie's lips and cheeks.

When Calista presented Melia with a leather pouch she could wear on her back, the half-faerie became bleary-eyed.

"Look inside," Tatou blurted out.

Melia untied the thong that closed the pouch's flap and felt inside. The bag was stuffed. She pulled out a pair of black pants. Not a color she would have chosen, but the fabric was sturdy and soft. She reached back into the bag and pulled out a boot. Black leather lace-ups. A mirror image of the brown ones she lost at the Calashai. She hugged it to her chest.

Bertille pointed to some bushes. "Go change."

"Don't forget the shirt." Calista reached across the remains of their late lunch for the pouch. She fished out another black thing and tossed it to Melia.

The half-faerie caught it in one hand.

"We thought the black would make it easier to travel unnoticed. Bright colors make everyone turn their head."

Suddenly self-conscious of her green dress, Melia hurried to discard it.

"Aldous is at the Veiled Tavern," Bertille said.

Melia had forgotten about the wood elf. She'd forgotten about Umbra. She'd forgotten about traveling to the mortal world. Since her first dive, all she could think about was Ryder.

He risked everything to answer the call of Nandana's mark, and she'd acted like it was nothing. Like he was nothing. It made her catch her breath and will herself to believe it wasn't too late to make things right with him.

What if it was?

No. He would to listen to her. He would give her another chance. She would make him.

Tatou, Bertille, and Calista awaited her response.

"It's just that"—Melia pushed the ends of her eyebrows with a thumb and finger—"the last time I saw Gumf, we weren't seeing eye-to-eye."

Tatou landed on her shoulder. "If Gumf is protecting Aldous, we can count him as a friend too. If he sees things differently, Aldous will set him straight."

Melia tugged on a strand of damp hair. "Aldous is the only one who can help me find the half-mortals."

"Then it's settled," Tatou said. "How long will it take us to reach the tavern from here?" she asked Bertille and Calista.

"You can reach the Veil tonight." Calista walked over to the hollowed out trunk of an enormous elm tree, which Melia hadn't noticed before because it blended in with the natural detritus along

the riverbank. "Ride in this until the sun sets. Then finish the trip as an eagle." The siren rubbed her arms and scanned the sky.

"What?" Melia asked.

"I feel an unfriendly gaze."

Melia scanned the bluffs. While they'd been eating, more nixies and sirens had arrived at the popular diving spot overhead.

"Not there," Calista whispered. "To the west."

To the west, the greenery and trees of the Sylvan forest obscured the riverbank. Melia couldn't see anyone spying on them, but she didn't question the siren's instincts. Her heart thumped as Calista helped her shove the elm's trunk into the water. The siren squeezed her in a quick, silent embrace.

Melia knelt before Bertille.

The water nixie squeezed her hands. "Things can be different for you now, but you must allow the changes to happen."

"I will."

Melia joined Tatou, waiting in the makeshift boat.

10. A Dark Spell

They floated down the Undine in the tree trunk hollowed by fire. Resin smoothed its walls and hull. The faintest smell of burnt wood lingered. Melia lay flat on the bottom; Tatou lounged on the half-faerie's stomach. Whenever the sound of rushing water approached, the pixie peeked over the vessel's high sides.

After diving from the cliff, drifting down the river was easy. Whenever their makeshift boat rolled, tilted, swirled, or dropped over one of the smaller waterfalls, Melia relaxed into the motion.

A deep tension that had lived in the back of her neck most of her life had dissolved. She wasn't dangerous. There wasn't anything wrong with her. Her visions were more than likely a gift from her father's Druid blood, a deep way she had of connecting with the Whole's layered realities.

"What do you think about everything Bertille told me?" she asked Tatou.

"Water creatures are wise in the ways of the inner realms."

"Then you think what she said about my visions is true?"

Tatou rolled onto her belly and propped up her chin with her hands. "That the violent ones will stop?"

"And that I'll have more of them that won't be tied to the moon cycles."

The pixie's eyes brightened. "I do believe her."

The hope of having no more dark moon visions left Melia elated.

Right before dusk, Tatou peered over the sides of their floating tree trunk. "Coast is clear."

Melia rose to her knees and paddled the vessel to the north side of the river. When it pushed into the weeds, she felt safer. They'd officially reached Tyrannis.

She stood, braced herself, and stepped one foot outside. Her new boot squished in a marsh. "Damn the gods of Azyllai." Mud coated the black leather. She pulled the messy boot back into the boat, knelt, leaned forward, and felt for dry ground. There wasn't any. She pushed the vessel farther downstream, her hands sinking almost to her elbows in boggy grass. When she finally found a spot that felt solid, she pulled at the long grass trying to coax more of the vessel to land. The tree trunk leaned so far to the side it almost tipped over.

After two close calls, enough of the siding lodged against the riverbank that they could safely disembark.

Melia used some leaves and moss to clean her boot. It didn't do much more than spread the muck around. They didn't have time to find a clear spot in the river where she could wash it; the sun was setting.

Tatou waited close by, ready to fly.

Once Melia cleared the treetops, she aimed west.

She landed on the branch of a large ficus tree at the edge of the Veiled Tavern's lawn. Everything was quiet. Not a single troll or other creature patrolled the wraparound porch, and only a handful of patrons came and went, most of them muannai.

"Do you think you can open those doors?" Melia asked Tatou.

Engraved and made of heavy wood, they didn't swing open at the slightest touch like the ones in the library.

"Probably not."

"Last time I slipped inside through the kitchen when one of the trolls came out the back door. Let's try that." Melia flew around the corner of the plain rectangular building.

Things were just as quiet on the back lawn. Her heart and belly flipped. Clover napped beneath some trees on the yard's edge. If Flora's goat remained welcome at the Veil, maybe Gumf had forgiven the spring faerie for taking the Tasimas.

Clover's backside was completely healed. No bandage or visible scarring remained from the burns she'd suffered when muannai set fire to Flora's cottage.

Melia cawed a greeting.

The goat, curled up in the thick grass, opened heavy eyelids. She recognized Melia. Warmth lit her soft brown irises. She baahed. When she saw Tatou, she rose.

The pixie rushed to greet her old friend, clucking and waving her hands. The animated reunion lifted Melia's spirits. Then Tatou asked about Aldous.

The goat ground a front hoof into the ground.

"Has something happened to him?" the pixie asked.

Clover bleated.

Melia rocked in the grass. Lilliane's venom echoed in her head; the princess had been furious the head librarian escaped.

Melia and Tatou followed Clover to the front of the Veil. The goat stabilized her body before ramming one of the large doors with her horns. The door swung open partway, just enough for Clover to squeeze her head through. Melia and Tatou flew through the gap above her horns.

The goat bucked her legs to finish crossing the threshold.

Although it was well-lit, the Veil's foyer was empty. The table where Gumf often kept an eye on the tavern's comings and goings sat vacant. A few low voices drifted from the cavernous interior, but Clover's noisy entrance attracted no attention. The goat headed for the winding hallway that led to the tavern's rooms and suites.

Melia feared Clover was lost until the goat paused outside one of the doors. Melia landed on the floor. Tatou fluttered down beside her.

Clover circled around and rapped on the door with one of her hind hooves.

A short, thin dwarf—the antithesis of the bulky Gumf—opened the door. A foul element loosed from the room. Tatou cringed before climbing onto Melia's back. Clover drifted away.

Melia hopped over the threshold. A small fire burned in a large grate across the room. A troll dozed in a stuffed chair next to the large bed. Melia recognized Nivea. Several tables were pushed together between the bed and the doorway. Stone, glass, and metal jars; cups, pots, and plates; herbs and seeds; eggs and bones; twine; and what looked like a few petrified insects cluttered the surfaces.

"Is someone there?" a frail voice cried out.

Melia flew across the bed to a cabinet beneath the single window. Although it was open, the room's stagnant air swallowed the gentle breeze as soon as it rolled in.

"Melia, is that you?"

Tatou gasped. Melia craned her head, not trusting what she saw.

Withered and broken, the head librarian of the Cathedral Palace Grand Library lay on his side, his knees pulled to his chest, his arms wrapped tight around his legs.

Tatou slipped from Melia's back and leapt onto a pile of blankets and sheets that Aldous, heated with fever, must have kicked away. The pixie raced across the uneven terrain to caress the elf's check. "We've just come from Illialei," the pixie's voice quavered.

"Stay away"—the wood elf's face twisted into an agonizing grimace—"from Lilliane ... powerful black magic ..."

"She did this?" Melia asked.

Aldous closed his eyes. Yes.

Melia landed on the pile of sweat-damp sheets near her friend.

The pixie pushed a few limp strands of grey hair from the elf's forehead.

"We have to do something. He's dying!" Melia squawked.

Nivea woke up. The healer's sad eyes mirrored Melia's dismay over Aldous' condition.

"Isn't there something you can do?" Melia asked.

Nivea crossed her arms over her chest, rubbed her elbows, and leaned forward. The troll clearly understood the language of eagles, but responded in the common tongue. "I've brewed enough tea to drown us all, applied all the tinctures and poultices I know how to make, and experimented with every obscure ingredient I've ever heard of. Nothing has helped. He deteriorates a little more each day. There's nothing more I can do. He needs Flora."

Melia calculated how many days it would take to reach Aldaine. Three nights of flying, at least. Aldous didn't look like he would last that long.

The troll's eyes grew wide as Melia told her that she and Tatou had barely made it out of the palace library alive. "Could Aldous have been poisoned with black rose petals?" Melia asked.

"It's possible, although I've never heard of black roses growing anywhere besides the Black Magic Islands." The healer's eyes glistened. "Why would the young princess hurt him? Aldous is a friend to everyone. He's never harmed a soul in his life."

"Does knowing she might have used black roses help?"

Nivea rocked in her chair, shaking her head and plucking at the sleeves of her dress. "I've tried everything I know. It's like no sickness I've ever seen. He can't take food or drink. As soon as I get him to swallow a bite of something, or put a few drops of water on his tongue, he heaves black bile."

Melia recalled Plantine swaying over the basin, Ormrun, a black inky liquid spewing from her eyes and mouth, ears and nose.

Nivea pointed to a wicker basket full of dirty linen in the corner. "I'm doing my best to keep him clean. But—" The troll waved her hand. Her eyes overflowed. She jumped from her chair and ran from the room.

They heard her sob in the hallway.

"I need to get Flora," Melia whispered to Tatou.

Aldous' hand fidgeted. "Is she here? Is my beloved Florette here?"

It felt like two large stones smashed Melia's heart.

Tatou slipped her hand into the pocket of her petal skirt. She sprinkled Aldous with pixie dust and whispered, "Not yet, but she's coming."

The wood elf closed his eyes, his breathing settled into a shallow rhythm.

"Hurry!" Tatou whispered. "I'll try to keep him alive."

Melia was already out the window.

11. Flora Returns to the Blue Mermaid

The icy wind blowing in from the Great White Sea burned Flora's cheeks. She pulled the wool cloak she'd salvaged from the Calashai's wreckage tighter around her shoulders.

It took some time to pick her way down the steep staircase which led to the inlet, but it was a better use of a sleepless night than tossing and turning until dawn.

Something was wrong. She could feel it in the way her joints and muscles ached. She meditated on Sevondi, recalling every gesture and nuance from their meeting at the Blue Mermaid. The dragonwitch had yet to deliver *The Book of Umbra*, but Flora believed she would. The delay was nothing more than stagecraft, Sevondi's need for drama.

No, that wasn't the problem refusing to let the spring faerie sleep.

She regarded the enchanted world's two moons, their milky and violet light waning. In five nights, they would be dark, the first dark moon phase since Elendah's death. As she rubbed her forehead, Flora's cloak crossed over her face along with her palm.

For the past nine days, thousands of muannai worked in the Calashai's courtyard, clearing rubble and taking inventory of anything salvageable: stone, wood, glass, and metal; clothing and linens; anything that remained whole or usable. By the time the moons turned dark, they would be done, and the rebuilding would begin.

Yrrick and several muannai gifted in architectural design sacrificed meals and rest to draft plans for the construction. Alrick, Yrrick's twin brother, died when the Calashai fell. The spring faerie suspected erasing that sight from his mind—Alrick crushed beneath a mass of rubble—fueled Yrrick's drive to assure a new stronghold stood before winter's harsh cold reached Tyrannis.

Perhaps grief drove the others, too. Whatever their reasons, the new stronghold would rise, not from Elendah's magic, but from a different kind of enchantment, a delirium of hope.

Flora turned to walk along the tide line.

An alliance with Sevondi could harness that hope, and turn it against the Albiana—

A river of crimson seared the spring faerie's mind, a sharp needle pricked her heart. She lost her grip on the cloak as she stumbled to her knees. A cold wind blew through the thin cloth of her dress. But it was fear that made her shiver. The Albiana.

What had they done?

✧ ✧ ✧

"I need the basin," Flora said.

"Not until the dragonwitch gives us *The Book of Umbra*. That was our agreement," Ryder said.

The spring faerie stepped square onto the stone slab he aimed his hammer at.

The priest caught the swing midair. "That was dangerous."

"Something has happened."

"Yes, the grey faerie died."

Flora shook her head. "Something in Illialei."

"Is it Melia?"

"No."

"Then it's no concern of mine. You have the Tasimas," he said.

"Use it, and don't trouble me again until you have the book."

"I need the basin to see—"

"You made your deal with Sinjiin, harass him."

"I can't find him."

"Search in some place shady. He likes to nap midday."

The priest was so stubborn. Flora stepped off the rock to stand as close to him as she could. "What if I'm wrong and something has happened to Melia?"

The indentation on the side of his jaw was visible. "Then I'll go to Illialei with you."

That was the last thing she wanted—to go to Illialei. "I doubt anything has happened to her, but—"

"I'd know if she were in danger," Ryder grumbled. "Now, get out of my way."

Grime blackened his fingernails and the crevices in his skin. Painful-looking blisters made ugly red welts on his palms and the webbing of his thumb. Every day he worked longer and harder than any of the muannai. Flora recognized guilt and penance when she saw it. He needed to work through it in his own time and in his own way.

She stepped aside, frustrated. If she could just peer into the basin, Flora was certain she could find the source of the strange darkness her heart warned of. She startled when Ryder's hammer crushed the slab into large chunks of stone.

"You'll have the basin when I have the book," he said.

Flora drank half a pail of herb water before returning to the Blue Mermaid.

Waiting on the hotel's ground floor, she wondered if she should have drank more. Her feet dangled from a black leather sofa. She was comfortable enough, seated in the open space which she'd rushed through to reach the ballroom the first time she came to the Blue Mermaid. Pogo called it the lobby. "Wait here, in the lobby, while I tell Sevondi you're here."

Everything in it—floors, glass windows, light fixtures, surfaces—was shiny and sleek. Flora couldn't decide whether she liked it or not. None of it felt natural, and yet there was a symmetrical beauty to appreciate.

Pogo stuck his head from between two polished-gold doors. "She'll see you now." He motioned Flora into a cramped box-like space.

The spring faerie peered inside. "Where is Sevondi?"

The troll pointed at the ceiling. "We'll ride in this to the top floor."

Flora searched the reflective surface above for a door. There wasn't one. "How?"

Pogo indicated some round buttons in a panel.

The Blue Mermaid was the tallest building in Aldaine. But high places had never made Flora curious. As a spring faerie, she thrived on dirt and being close to the ground.

She wanted to argue with the troll, to insist Sevondi meet her in the lobby, but Flora sensed she was running out of time. At odd moments, her dark premonition squeezed her heart like a fist. She didn't know how much longer she had to stop whatever it was her intuition alerted her to.

She forced herself to step inside the small room where Pogo waited. The gold doors whooshed closed behind her. She turned around. Her dull reflection stared back from each of the cubicle's walls. She adjusted her kerchief.

The troll pushed the round button with the black number 20 embossed in its center. Flora's stomach dropped. She grabbed the gold railing. The box stopped; the polished doors slid open.

Flora gathered her wits and followed the troll down a thick-carpeted hall.

Pogo knocked on a shiny, cherry-wood door.

Sevondi called to the troll from the interior. He opened the door and gave Flora a half-bow before disappearing in the hall's shadows.

The spring faerie entered the suite and stared at a wall of

windows. She could see the excavated ground where the Calashai once stood in the distance. She walked closer to the outrageous panes of glass. Below, the city of Aldaine sprawled before her.

She couldn't pull her eyes away from the view. Long ago, when Flora traveled to the mortal world, there had been no windows like these. She could have stared out them all day.

Sevondi spoke behind her. "This view is the only thing I like about the Blue Mermaid. And yet that's not why you're here."

"Have you thought about our offer?" Flora asked.

When the dragonwitch took her hand, the touch was jarring, unexpected as it was. Flora forced herself not to jerk her own hand away.

"Come, sit and talk with me." Sevondi pointed to a rectangle of sofas which took up the entire corner of the suite.

Reluctantly, Flora allowed Sevondi to lead her from the window.

"We must talk about Umbra," Sevondi said.

Flora braced herself. She'd given the subject much thought herself before coming to the Blue Mermaid alone. She needed to persuade Sevondi to give up her ambition to incarnate the dark master, but it would be a tricky negotiation. The dragonwitch was a shrewd bargainer, and the spring faerie was well aware the dark warning smothering her own heart was a distraction.

"We can't talk about Umbra without discussing the Albiana." The moment Flora named Illialei's line of queens, she felt her face pale and her cheeks cool. She tried to continue. "We both agree the Albiana reign–" An invisible claw scraped her throat.

Sevondi's eyes widened with concern.

"–must end." Flora wheezed out the words.

"Are you all right?" The dragonwitch poured a glass of water from a pitcher.

Flora took a few sips before setting the glass down. She tugged at the knot on her kerchief.

Sevondi arranged herself among a pile of cushions.

Flora studied the dragonwitch's face. There was something

different about her appearance. It was her hair; a fringe of thick black bangs covered her high forehead. The style made her look even more exotic, and hid her uneven eyebrows. Flora guessed she was preparing herself for her new role as leader of the muannai.

"Did you ever meet my Aunt Imelda?" Sevondi asked.

Flora pulled on an eyebrow. Sevondi had seven aunts, all deceased. "I met two of your aunts. I don't remember their names."

"You must have met Isobel and Isadora. They were the youngest and outlived the others. But it was Imelda who made me vow on her deathbed to incarnate Umbra."

Flora took another large gulp of water. Deathbed vows were hard to argue against.

Sevondi twirled a strand of long black hair. "But it was Isadora who lived the longest, and she made me vow to never try. It was her dying wish."

Flora wiped her mouth with the back of her hand. "You've never mentioned either promise before."

"It's never mattered until now."

"But now you have an opportunity to lead your kind in a way that Elendah, and all your aunts, never could. The grey faerie was beloved, but she wasn't a muannaye. You could help many of your people complete their journey on this plane ... More souls could be released to the Unknown Beyond. It would be good for the Whole."

Sevondi tapped a fingertip against her chin. "And yet, if I incarnate Umbra—"

"You could die."

The muannaye stood up. "You don't know that. No one knows that. My conflict is that I can't keep my promise to both Imelda and Isadora." She dropped her knotted fists to her side and paced the narrow aisle between the sofa and table.

"You don't need to incarnate Umbra to lead your people."

"Says you," Sevondi lashed out. "At least the priest wants to prevent Umbra's incarnation altogether, but I know what you want. You want one of those half-faeries to go through with the

incarnation. You would have us all bowing before a child!" Sevondi flicked her thumbnail against her upper teeth.

Flora set the glass down on the table. "Even if the half-faerie can live through the incarnation, even if she can contain Umbra's consciousness, she'll be no threat to you."

Sevondi's dark eyes flared. "Can you guarantee that?"

"I'll be the one who trains her."

The dragonwitch laughed from deep in her throat and fanned the air with her hands. "And you think your training will—what? Be a leash around her neck that you can yank to make her do your bidding?"

"The Albiana—" Flora gasped. It felt like her heart was being incinerated.

Sevondi leaned over to refill the spring faerie's empty glass. "Every time you say that name—"

They stared at one another.

"Black magic," Sevondi whispered. She dropped down beside Flora on the sofa and took the spring faerie's hand. "I'll never forgive you for keeping the basin secret from me all these years."

Flora averted her gaze. Keeping the basin hidden had been the right thing to do. She wasn't going to apologize for it. Not even to Sevondi to gain *The Book of Umbra*.

"And I know it was you who killed Zachariah." The dragonwitch's voice pulsed with intense emotion. "If he hadn't betrayed me by marrying the half-faerie's sister, I'd slit your throat right now!"

The spring faerie raised her hand to protectively grasp her neck. She didn't doubt the dragonwitch was capable of such an act. Her eyes darted around the room. With no visible avenue of escape, she considered her invisible glamour. She stopped practicing with the shield the day Elendah died. It wouldn't be much use flickering on and off.

Her heart beat in her ears. She'd known Sevondi for years, and though they'd never called each other friend, they had much in common. Self-sufficiency, native curiosity, strong ties to the natural world, and the clarity that the Daughters of Light turned to darkness long ago.

Flora had to believe Sevondi would never make the crude error of killing the sole surviving spring faerie. She met the dragonwitch's gaze with her own squinty-eyed stare.

"But he did marry Plantine and order my death." Sevondi sighed. "Such deliberate treachery." She patted the spring faerie's knee. "And you saved my life."

Flora's shoulders relaxed.

"If the Albiana—" Sevondi paused to glance at Flora, as if to judge whether her saying the name had an equally adverse effect on the spring faerie. It didn't. "If the Albiana are going to come for you after all these years—" The dragonwitch stood up and walked to the panel of windows across the room. She stared out of them with her arms folded. "It's an insult beyond comprehension." Sevondi's entire body trembled with rage.

"If we stand together, we can destroy them." Flora's tone was deliberately measured.

Sevondi whirled around, her eyes filled with fire. "Yes, we can. And we will. Faerie doesn't belong to them. It never has, and it never will." She returned to sit beside Flora on the sofa. "I want to know everything you're doing. Don't make a move without including me."

"Of course."

"I will lead the muannai."

"That's what we agreed to."

"The book is tedious to read."

"I understand the young priest excels at research."

Sevondi clapped her hands. "Excellent."

Pogo entered the suite so quickly, the spring faerie wondered if he'd been eavesdropping.

"Retrieve *The Book of Umbra*. Give it to Flora."

✧ ✧ ✧

Sevondi provided a carriage to carry the spring faerie and *The Book of Umbra* up the mountain.

It jostled along the cobbled streets of Aldaine. Flora closed her eyes. The negotiations were taxing, but soon she'd have the basin—and the means to find out what Illialei's queen was up to.

It was hard to imagine Luisa had become powerful enough to attack the spring faerie directly. Ever since she returned from the mortal world, Olivia's daughter suffered from a chronic malaise.

12. Florelle

Where was Flora?

Melia flew back and forth across what had once been the stronghold of Calashai's courtyard. She squawked the spring faerie's name as loud as she could and asked every muannai she came across if they'd seen her. None of them understood the language of eagles.

The image of Aldous curled up and wasting away made Melia frantic. She tried to find Ryder and Sinjiin.

Where were they?

Stacked debris formed a perimeter around the cleared courtyard, the progress remarkable. She hung in the air. Could they have gone to Aldaine? Perhaps they stayed at an inn?

They would never leave the basin and sword unguarded.

Unless ... they discovered how to release the basin and sword from the founding stone. Could Ryder have sailed to the Isle of Minnanon without her? Without saying goodbye?

Her wings turned to lead. A few bay trees on the edge of the courtyard survived the stronghold's implosion. Melia circled down to land on a branch.

"Are you all right?"

Melia searched the leaves. A seagull rustled through them to land beside her. "I've been watching you fly back and forth, screaming for Flora."

"Do you know where she is?"

The gull pointed to a large canvas draped over multiple branches. "That's where she sleeps, but she's out tonight."

"Out where?" Melia squawked.

"She left with the tiger and the young male."

"When will they be back?"

The gull spread his wings. He didn't know. "You could wait for them inside."

Exasperated, Melia flew to the ground.

The gull followed her. "You seem upset. I thought you might like some company."

At least he could understand what she was saying. "Company would be nice." She peeked underneath the cloth.

"The door is over there." The bird indicated a loose flap a little farther away. "I don't really know them, but I watch them come and go all the time. Well, Flora and the tiger. Tonight was only the second time I've seen the young man."

"And you didn't see where they went?" Melia asked.

"Sorry, no."

Melia hopped inside the tent. The interior was dark, but she could make out some shelves and a pallet. There was a stool, a bucket, and a rug. It smelled like herbs and made her think of the spring faerie.

What else could she do but wait, and hope Flora returned soon?

Melia flopped over to the pallet, folded her wings across her back, and dropped to her belly. She kept her eyes on the partially open tent flap. Her chest pressed against something hard. She scratched the blanket back with her talons. *The Book of Umbra*. Melia wrestled its heavy cover with her beak and stared at a page. It was hard to make out the letters; she thought it might be written in a language she didn't know. She studied the tent's interior with more care. The book was as important as Ormrun and Koldis. Why would Flora—and Ryder and Sinjiin—leave it so poorly hidden?

She turned back to the gull. "When they left, did it look like

something was wrong? Like someone was hurt?"

"No, no, nothing like that."

"Did you hear them say anything? Anything at all about where they might be going? Or when they might be back?"

The bird shook his head.

Melia hopped around the tent, looking for the Tasimas. She couldn't find it.

"Melia?"

She startled awake. Night was over and she'd shifted back into her half-faerie form. She rubbed her eyes. Beside her, the gull lifted its head from beneath its wing. It let loose a shrill string of aw-ucks. Melia covered her ears as it evacuated the tent.

In front of her, Flora gripped Ormrun so tightly her knuckles were white.

Now that the spring faerie stood before her, Melia didn't know how to say what needed to be said. She didn't know whether Aldous was dead or alive.

"Where is the Tasimas?" Melia asked.

"Don't worry. I've got it," the spring faerie said.

"We need to go to the Veiled Tavern. Now."

The spring faerie's eyes narrowed to slits. "When you left here, you were going to Illialei to talk to Aldous—" The basin slipped from her grasp. Her face bleached as she staggered.

"He's at the Veiled Tavern. Flora, he's in terrible shape. Nivea hasn't been able to help him. He spits up the same black liquid Plantine did when Umbra left her. He asked for you ... for Florette."

"Stay here."

"No!" Melia said. "I'm coming with you."

"Stay here with the basin. The Tasimas is buried." The spring faerie's gazed wandered to *The Book of Umbra*. "Cover that back up." She was gone.

Melia picked up Ormrun. She'd forgotten how light it was. She settled the bowl in her lap and gazed into it. She ran her fingers along the gemstone-encrusted rim. It seemed like the sapphires, emeralds, and rubies never dulled or got dirty. She stared at her reflection in the bottom.

A chill moved through her. The bowl fell from her fingers and rolled off her lap. She rubbed her upper arms. Even wearing the boots and slacks Calista gave her, it felt like deep winter in the tent. She pushed the basin toward the book and pulled the blanket over them. Her hands were freezing. She rubbed them together to warm them.

Ryder crawled through the loose flap first.

Melia squelched her impulse to rush to him. What if he pushed her away? Like she'd pushed him away.

Flora was right behind him.

He nodded. That was all the acknowledgment he gave her.

Everything in Melia's chest—her heart, her lungs, and her ribs—strained with the need to touch him. But Aldous was dying. Maybe already dead.

Flora's gaze searched the tent.

Melia pointed to the blanket. "They're under there."

"Keep them safe while we're gone," the spring faerie told Ryder.

"I will," he said.

"And study the book. If the instructions for releasing the basin and sword from the founding stone have been written anywhere, it's in there."

Ryder nodded.

Melia recognized the pillowcase in Flora's hand. The same one she stole from the Veil ages ago, it was dirty. She couldn't believe the spring faerie still used it to carry the Tasimas.

"Are you ready?" Flora asked her.

Melia turned back to Ryder. She caught him staring at her before his gaze fell to the ground. What had been in his eyes? Longing? Disappointment? Contempt?

"I—" Words lodged in her throat. There wasn't enough time to say everything she needed to say. The spring faerie had already crawled from the tent. Melia couldn't keep her waiting. "I'm glad to see you again."

"I'm sorry it's not under better circumstances," he said.

Melia nodded. Flora must have told him about Aldous. "If you find the way to take Ormrun and Koldis from this place, please wait for me," she said. "Don't leave without saying goodbye."

His eyes lit up.

It was all she could think of to say before shuffling outside.

Flora led Melia behind the tent. The muannai worked in the courtyard on the other side.

"Can you take me straight to him?" Flora asked.

"Yes."

Flora opened the pillowcase to let the sparkling yellow diamond roll to the ground. She stopped it with her boot as she stuffed the pillowcase into her apron pocket.

Melia took the spring faerie's hand. She focused her mind on an image of Aldous atrophied in his bed at the Veil. The picture was impossible to forget. She reached for the Tasimas.

They slammed against a wall of wind so furious Melia feared it would throw them back into the Calashai's courtyard, as it had when they carried the sword and basin.

Flora's voice exploded in her mind, "Concentrate."

Melia redoubled her efforts. She gazed with her inner eye at the old wood elf, crumpled beyond recognition. She traced his room: the window she flew out of, the tables littered with Nivea's medicinal attempts, the straw basket in the corner stuffed with stained linen.

She tumbled onto a rug. Flora kicked her chin. It was midday. Although sunlight filtered through the leaves of an enormous oak outside the window, grey light filled the room.

Nivea screamed, her pale lavender eyes the size of two teacups.

Flora rushed to Aldous' side. They murmured to one another, hushed tones filled with love.

Melia blushed.

Nivea stopped yelping and came to stand by Melia. "He's much worse."

"Are we too late?"

"Flora's worked many a miracle before," the troll said.

"Where is Tatou?"

Nivea fidgeted.

"Where is she?"

"It's been hard on her, watching him deteriorate. All last night, he thrashed and yelled. I tried to restrain him, but his fever burned so high, it just about scorched my hands to touch him. I can't imagine what it felt like for him. Tatou tried to help, but the pixie dust lasts minutes, at most. I sent her to the Undine a little while ago to fetch some herbs. Not that anything I've concocted has helped, but I thought the fresh air might do her some good, bring some color to her cheeks. I don't think she's gotten a wink of sleep since you left."

Melia chewed on a fingernail, worried about her friend wandering through the Balyudor alone.

"She'll be back soon," Nivea said.

Melia remained silent. Any Huron knight stationed on the river's south side could cross the Maeldun Bridge and grab the pixie if they spotted her.

Flora called out to the troll she once claimed was the third best healer in Tyrannis.

Nivea ran to her side.

The spring faerie rattled off a list of ingredients. "A freshly killed seagull–"

Melia flinched.

"And Hellebore. Tell Gumf to send some muannai with you to the Granite Cliffs. They need to carry a barrel and bring back as much sea water as they can. There's a trail that winds down to the

beach. It's not visible to the naked eye, and it's steep, but Gumf knows which one I'm talking about. Maybe he can go with you. You'll find the hellebore on that trail, under the rocks nearer to the sea.

"And seaweed," Flora added. "They might have to wade into the tide this time of day, but I need several large handfuls. Better to get too much than too little."

Nivea picked up her long skirts and ran from the room.

Melia edged over to Aldous' bed.

"I'm going to brew the same draught that brought you and Sevondi back from the dead." Flora's words were so soft Melia had to lean in to hear them. "He's overdosed with Umbra's poison. I don't know how they did it without the basin."

The whole time the spring faerie instructed Nivea, she never let go of Aldous' hand.

"Do you love him?" Melia whispered.

"We loved each other when we were young. I suppose we still do. He used to call me Florette—" Her voice cracked.

Melia moved to stand behind her. She rubbed the spring faerie's shoulders. They felt thin and loose in their joints. She rubbed them until her fingers ached.

Flora patted her hand. "Thank you."

Melia's heart wobbled like a top. Flora instructed Nivea with her customary sternness, but the longer they waited for the troll to return, the more her resolute mask slipped.

She soaked some rags in a tub of water and pressed them against Aldous' fever-red extremities, but she couldn't disguise her fear that she'd arrived too late to make a difference.

Melia couldn't make up her mind which was worse: getting a glimpse of the spring faerie's self-doubt, or wondering whether Tatou would return safely to the inn. Sitting still was impossible. "There's got to be something I can do," she said.

Flora lifted her head as if from a daze. "Tell one of the cooks to boil some water. Tell him to use the largest pot in the kitchen and to keep the water roiling until Nivea arrives. I'll need another clean pot for the seawater." She continued to apply cool wraps to the wood elf's parched skin. "Send for me as soon as Nivea is back. That would be helpful."

"Of course," Melia said.

"I meant to tell you," Flora said, "your mother and sister, and the tree elf, left Aldaine a few days after you did. They're on their way to the Isle of Minnanon. Even if the weather is good, they'll be gone awhile."

Already halfway to the door, Melia hesitated. "Do you think the Grey Council will find my sister guilty of Elendah's murder?"

"They'll be impartial, and they won't rush to judgment. That's the most anyone can hope for."

"Do you ever w-wonder–" Melia hadn't stuttered since she faced Pressina the day the Calashai fell. She turned back to Flora who hovered over Aldous. It was the wrong time for Melia to ask the question, but there would never be a right time, and she needed to know. "If you'd known that it was Plantine who killed the grey faerie, that it wasn't Goring, w-wooould," she stretched out the word to keep it whole, "you have k-killed him?"

Flora wrung water from a rag. "Have you forgotten he ordered your death? And Sevondi's?" She pointed her chin at her patient. "Aldous isn't the first I've had to cure of Umbra's poison. Maybe Goring didn't kill Elendah directly, but if you recall, Plantine was his wife at the time. Has it ever occurred to you that she confided in him?

"We'll never know if he could have done something to save the grey faerie and didn't. That would make him an even greater monster. Manipulating innocents to commit crimes he was too cowardly to carry out himself. More than one muannai died because he ordered the basin and sword taken from the stronghold of Calashai. And remember what happened to your pixie under his command."

Melia shivered. Memories of the night a turnskin chased her and

Tatou through the Balyudor remained vivid.

"No," Flora said. "I don't lose sleep over Lord Zachariah Goring. Now Bella's death is a different matter altogether. Burned alive, she was."

Melia could only hang her head at the memory of the black cat.

"Go on, now," the spring faerie said. "There will be a dwarf or troll loitering close by. There always is, in case you lose your way in the maze of halls."

Melia followed the young dwarf who appeared out of nowhere as soon as she took the first wrong turn. She tugged on a strand of hair as they walked. Flora's answer had shaken her. Not because the spring faerie felt no remorse, but because it reminded her that if Flora hadn't been at the Calashai, Melia would be dead.

They'd almost reached the kitchen when Melia heard voices from the yard. She ran toward the tavern's front door.

Gumf led five muannai, two large horses with round wooden barrels strapped to their sides, and Nivea carrying a pail stuffed with long, stringy weeds.

Tatou lounged on one of the barrels, lecturing everyone. "I could hear you all the way from the Maeldun Bridge, and you were still at the seashore! We're not going to win any war if you all crash through the woods like a band of mortals."

Tatou was safe.

Melia laughed with relief. She had the feeling that, soon, Aldous would be safe too. Flora hadn't flinched when it came to killing Goring, but the spring faerie's real gift was life and the living.

13. The Mortal World

Ten days later, Aldous peered at Melia through wire-framed spectacles. His body was a wasted bag of bones beneath his nightshirt, but his eyes were clear, and he'd just finished eating breakfast.

It had been a challenge, coaxing the elf's locked jaw open and forcing him to swallow Flora's draught, but the improvement in his health began immediately. Soon after taking the first dose of the spring faerie's remedy, he stopped retching the vile black liquid, and the straw basket full of clothes and sheets soaked with Umbra's poison was removed from his room. The collective sigh of relief from those who gathered around his bed cleared the last revenants of dark magic from the room.

Tatou sat in her usual spot on Melia's shoulder. The pixie had smoothed things over with Gumf, so that neither he nor Melia brought up Ryder, or the dwarf's lies about the priest. As far as Melia could tell, the Veil's proprietor made his peace with Flora too. He hadn't said one word about the Tasimas balled up in a dirty pillowcase beneath the bed, although he visited Aldous' room several times a day.

Flora patted the wood elf's arm. She didn't have on her apron, and her hair, free of its kerchief, formed a grey halo around her head. The hardness in her brown eyes had softened, and when she smiled on occasion, everyone smiled with her.

Melia had learned much during Aldous' convalescence. One

thing being that pixies and spring faeries were similar by nature, but where pixies were charming in spite of themselves and their tempers, the charm of a spring faerie was more judicious, a gift bestowed.

Another thing Melia had learned: It was the Albiana, specifically Uriel, who encouraged the division between the two countries of Faerie. Revolted by perceived physical flaws—the siren's webbed feet, the nixie's razor teeth, the male trolls' swarthy complexions, the dwarves lack of physical symmetry (Gumf was a good example with his lumpy arms which were longer than his legs)—the queen discouraged commingling between the two populations. From public shaming to black magic, Uriel strove to purge impurities from her court. Only when the Maeldun Bridge—which was once a bustling thoroughfare—stood empty, did her campaign against the inhabitants of Tyrannis subside.

Many friendships foundered, the one between Gumf and Aldous among them.

For Melia, the hardest part of the past ten days was not using the Tasimas to return to Aldaine. Witnessing love renew between Aldous and Flora made her heart ache to make a fresh start with Ryder.

Perched alone in a tree one night, Melia wept for her mother and father. The chance to see his beloved Pressina once more drove Elynus' obsession with Umbra, and in a way, it was what killed him. Melia never understood the drive to heal a connection severed by misunderstanding until now. As soon as she warned the half-faeries in the mortal world about Umbra, Melia would have an honest conversation with Ryder. Meanwhile her heart looped through anticipation and dismay—if she could only know his heart without risking hers.

"Aldous is strong enough to answer a few questions." Flora indicated the chair closest to his bed. "Sit here so he won't have to strain his voice."

Melia settled in the chair as she reminded herself of the promise she made after diving with Bertille: She wouldn't keep any more secrets from her friends about Umbra.

Now, she described to Aldous, and everyone else in the room, the encounter she had with the dark master on the night Elendah died. They listened without interruption. She told them how she resisted Umbra, and how he threatened the half-faeries in the mortal world when she refused to yield to him. "Someone must warn them," she said. "I will."

Aldous rubbed his chin. The skin on the back of his hand was so thin Melia could see every vein. "You'll have to make more than one trip," he said. "They're scattered across different times and places."

"Maybe I should find Melusine first," Melia said.

"I don't think that will be necessary," he said.

"Why not?" she asked. "Umbra has already targeted me and Plantine. Wouldn't he choose Melusine next?"

"Your sister never expressed much interest in Umbra," the elf said. "As I recall, of the three of you, she was the one most taken with the idea of romantic love."

Melia's head throbbed.

The elf continued. "She wanted to marry that mortal—"

"Raymond," Tatou said.

"And she did." Aldous turned to Flora. "Am I right?"

The spring faerie nodded.

"You see, Umbra must be invited in—"

Melia stopped listening. He might as well have dumped a bucket of water on her head.

Flora's eyes rounded as she tilted her head toward the half-faerie. "Maybe invited is too strong a word."

The wood elf's raised eyebrows indicated he grasped her warning to nuance. "Yes. Need is a more precise way to describe the space Umbra flows into. There has to be some great need, which makes those who are in love somewhat immune to his call, as the needs of those falling in love rarely extend beyond the beloved."

Melia wanted to cover her ears with her hands. Was it really possible Melusine was the one immune to Umbra? Because she risked everything and married a mortal for love?

Melia had always believed Plantine was the daughter most like their mother—not herself. Plantine put her need for a throne over her feelings for Tuck. But Melia had placed her need to fly above her feelings for Ryder. Her heart beat so loud it was hard to think.

Tatou smoothed her hair.

Umbra had been contacting Melia, influencing her and invading her mind, since she was thirteen. And now she wouldn't allow herself to fall in love because—

She shook her head. Admitting she cared for Ryder was like standing in the current of a powerful, fast-moving river; she feared it would knock her feet from beneath her, drag her through rapids, and slam her against slippery rocks she'd never be able to grab hold of.

Flora waddled to her side. She clasped Melia's shoulder. "Nivea, Gumf, Tatou, maybe you could leave us alone with Melia."

The troll and dwarf shuffled from the room in uncomfortable silence. Tatou gave Melia's hair one last stroke and pecked her cheek before fluttering after the others.

"Don't judge yourself too harshly," Flora said. "I'm not sure you know your own heart, yet. But you will. Give it a little time; things will come clear. As for Umbra, it's no reflection on you he courts you."

A moment before, Melia couldn't have imagined feeling more sickened. "Courts me?"

"He needs a willing vessel. He can't enter this plane without permission from someone who accepts his consciousness."

"He can't just possess someone?" Melia asked.

"No," Flora said.

Melia wiped her nose with the sleeve of her shirt. "So I won't ever become his vessel unless I say yes to him?"

Aldous and Flora nodded.

The spooked gallop of Melia's heart slowed.

Flora handed her a tissue.

"Our time and resources are limited," Aldous said. "Elendah's death has made Lilliane brazen. The princess wishes to secure her ascendancy to the Cathedral Palace throne. Even though Gabriela is half mortal, as Luisa's firstborn daughter, she's the gravest threat to Lilliane."

"Then I will find her first," Melia said.

Melia's head broke water. She trod a sleepy current. A shadow fell across the river. She shielded her eyes from a wicked sun. A bridge, orange-brown with rust, and much smaller than the Maeldun Bridge, loomed overhead.

Behind her, she heard the plip of Tatou's arrival. The half-faerie swirled in the water. "How was it?" she asked.

Tatou spit water and poked a finger in her ear. "Much harder than I thought it would be."

Melia dog-paddled. "Ride on my back." She aimed for a sandy stretch of beach. "Do you remember what Gumf said?"

"About what?"

"The borders between the mortal and the enchanted worlds? He said now that Elendah's died, some of them are closing, and the ones that aren't are becoming harder to cross. When Flora and I used the Tasimas to travel from Aldaine, we almost didn't make it. We hit a wall of wind that pushed us back, refusing to let us pass."

Tatou sprawled on the sand, her arms and legs flung wide. "I thought I was going to drown."

"Do you see why I didn't want you to come?"

Her friend's eyebrows flattened. "I'm fine."

"Who are you talking too?" A young mortal inched toward them. His smooth torso was bare, loose dungarees hung from his slim hips, and he was tall. He held a long slim rod in one hand, a pail in the other.

Melia squinted up at him.

He watched her with keen blue eyes. His nose was small for his face, and his cheeks were smattered with freckles. "Do you talk to yourself a lot?"

She pointed to the pixie. "You don't see my friend?"

"You're playing a joke on me, aren't you?" He shifted his feet. "Like my cousin."

He really couldn't see Tatou.

"It's just like Flora said," the pixie whispered.

"Speak up," Melia said.

Tatou cupped the sides of her mouth and yelled, "Flora said most mortals won't be able to see me!"

Melia watched him.

"Or maybe you're just crazy," he said. "My ma says she knew a crazy lady that carried on conversations with herself all day long." The boy almost squashed Tatou as he stepped closer to Melia. "You're awfully pretty, though. I don't think I've ever seen a girl as pretty as you." He swatted at an enormous fly and almost poked Melia's eye out. The sides of his face turned bright pink.

Melia tilted her head.

Tatou fluttered to her shoulder.

"Where are you from?" the boy asked.

"Down river."

"Where's your boat?"

Melia scrambled. "We had an accident; it sank." She wrung out one of her shirtsleeves.

"We? I don't see anyone else."

She opened and closed her mouth.

An enormous grin reached the young male's eyes. "You're so pretty, I don't care if you're crazy. How are you going to get home without your boat?" he asked. "I was going fishing, but maybe I can help you."

Overhead, the sun was ferocious. The scraggly bushes that lined the shoreline looked half-dead. Tatou wilted on her shoulder. Melia recalled her days wandering on Achill Island, searching for her father. "I need to find the Ashorn Farm," she said.

108

"You mean Edmond and Emma's place?"

Those were the names of Gabriela's aunt and uncle. "Yes."

"Come on. It's just outside of New Ulm, the next town over. It's off the Farm-to-Market road." He ran toward the tall trees arching over a dirt road, waving his arm for Melia to follow him. "My dad works in Columbus. He can drive you in our Model T."

"What's that?" Tatou asked.

"I don't know, but if it can get us to the farm, I'm going with him," Melia said to her friend.

The boy jogged down the road, his fishing pole and pail flailing.

Melia hurried after him.

14. Gabriela

It was hard to imagine Queen Luisa in this sticky dust and heat, but Aldous assured Melia the princess crossed over to the mortal world on her nineteenth birthday with a large party of friends, all flower faeries.

They found their way to this large country called Texas. Once they arrived, they hid their wings—as faeries did in the mortal world —and bathed in the Colorado River for the day. A sly young mortal spied them. It was Luisa's bad luck that he stole her wings and refused to return them.

By the laws governing the mortal and enchanted worlds, whenever a mortal possessed a faerie's wings, that faerie was bound to him for life—or until their wings were returned. Luisa's friends had had no choice but to leave her with her captor/husband when they returned to the Realm of Faerie.

The mortal's name was Ben Silver. He and Luisa had a daughter named Gabriela.

When the chance came for Luisa to retrieve her wings and return to Faerie, she seized it. However, since her husband hadn't broken his faerie troth, Luisa couldn't take her daughter from him.

The faerie princess returned to Faerie listless, a shadow of her vivacious self. Not even the birth of her second daughter, Lilliane, made much difference.

Now the year was 1925 and Melia and Tatou were trying to find Gabriela, a slim fourteen-year-old girl with dark hair and deep-set grey eyes. She supposedly lived with her aunt and uncle—her aunt being her father's sister.

No one could say for certain what had happened to Ben.

Aldous described Gabriela, and where she lived, as best he could from his memory of a collection of photos in the palace library.

"Alex, how much farther?" Melia asked the boy they'd met at the river.

Perspiration trickled down the back of her neck. She shoved the long sleeves of her shirt up to her elbows. Her black pants felt like they were painted on with sweat. She'd taken off her boots and walked barefoot.

The young male frisked beside her like a colt. "Just around the bend."

"He keeps saying that," Tatou said.

The boy disappeared inside his family's hardware store. Melia and Tatou waited outside, where he left them. They stared at the odd carriage suspended midair between four rubber spheres—tires, Alex called them.

"Do you think it's safe?" Tatou asked.

Other Model Ts traveled the city's dusty streets.

"Everyone else is riding in them," Melia said.

Aldous had told them: "As time advances in the mortal world, so does their technology. You'll see and experience many strange things. Be careful, but don't be frightened over much. I look forward to hearing all about everything when you return."

The store's door swung open and Alex rushed out, buttoning up a short-sleeve cotton shirt. His father was waiting for a delivery and couldn't leave the store unattended; he gave his son permission to drive them out to the farm.

The boy was all smiles and exuberance. He patted the siding. "Get in."

The interior leather seat resembled the ones in the coaches in Aldaine. Except those enclosed coaches were pulled by horses. This carriage was open, and there wasn't a horse in sight.

Melia tugged a strand of hair.

Alex grinned, displaying a pair of dimples. "Don't tell me you've never ridden in an automobile before? I thought everyone had by now."

"I'm usually the last to try new things," Melia said.

Tatou giggled in her ear.

"Then you're in for a treat. Jump in. We'll be at the Ashorn Farm in no time."

That was what Melia wanted to hear. She walked around to the other side of the Model T and crawled in. Her clothes were almost dry from the scorching heat, but the seat still stung the back of her thighs when she sat down. She bounced up to stand on the narrow floorboard.

Alex stood in front of the car.

As soon as he leaned over, an elderly gentleman with a greasy cloth draped over his shoulder stuck his head out the hardware store's door. He held out a floppy straw hat. "Give this to your friend. The day's only going to get hotter. As pale as she is, she's going to burn if she doesn't cover her head."

The boy returned to the storefront in a few short strides. His father handed him the hat. Alex took it and headed back to Melia. "He's right. If you don't put this on, the top of your head is going to feel like it's on fire before we get out of town."

Melia turned the hat around in her hands. Two wide ribbons hung from the brim. She'd never worn a hat before. "What am I supposed to do with it?" she asked Tatou.

Alex laughed. "Put it in on your head."

Melia gave him a small smile.

Tatou fluttered from her shoulder. "Tie those ribbons beneath your chin."

The half-faerie fitted the straw to her head and fumbled with the ties.

"Looks great," Alex said.

The boy's father stood in the doorframe watching. When she caught his eye, he gave her a crooked grin revealing stained teeth.

"They like you," Tatou said.

Melia didn't care what they thought of her as long as Alex helped them find Gabriela.

"Son, don't forget—all your fingers on the same side of the crank."

"Yeah Dad, I remember."

Melia watched Alex's back and shoulders rise and fall with intense exertion.

A guttural hum came from beneath the hood. The seat vibrated.

"It doesn't seem very stable," Tatou said.

Alex walked around the auto. The noise and shaking didn't seem to bother him in the least. He jumped onto the bench next to Melia and slapped his palms onto the steering wheel. "Go on and sit back down. The leather will cool down pretty quick."

The carriage moved in reverse.

Melia flopped back. The glass pane in front of her face offered a smudged view of the world. When he squeezed a bulb attached to the horn on the panel beside him, she almost jumped out of her skin.

Tatou covered her ears. "Ouch."

"Relax and enjoy the ride," Alex yelled, as they jolted backward into the sparse stream of traffic.

"Hang on," Melia said to her friend.

"Yes, hang onto the rail in front of you whenever you feel scared," Alex shouted.

The city—Alex called it Columbus—wasn't big. Before too long the Model T carried them over small hills. The scenery didn't change much. Dusty roads and burnt grass dotted with groves of enormous pine trees.

Every now and then, they passed a house. Some were small, wood frames of weathered planks. A few were whitewashed brick with large porches and yards. But most were in-between, well-kept homes with vegetable gardens, a few chickens, and a horse or two in a nearby corral. What impressed Melia most were the crops in the distance, quilting the horizon. Alex pointed out the tall stalks of corn, the shorter prickly-leafed sugar cane, and the endless snowy fields of cotton.

"In a few weeks, the whole county will be out harvesting," he said.

"Like a party?" Melia asked. She thought of the festival along the Nyssalei River celebrating the honey harvest in Illialei.

He shook his head. "No way. It's back-breaking, knee-busting, sweat-in-your-eye, bruising-the-tip-of-every-single-one-of-your-fingers work, but no one can afford to lose any of their crop. So we all pitch in."

"Too bad we're going to miss it," Tatou said.

Melia laughed.

"I'm not joking," Alex said. "If you don't believe me, come back in a few weeks. We'll let you help."

"I don't think I'll be able to make it," Melia said.

"That's too bad. We sure could use another pretty face around here."

Alex followed a winding gravel road to a pristine wood-frame bungalow. A large pecan tree shaded the house.

"Is this the farm?" Melia asked.

"Not exactly." Alex pointed north. "The farm is over there. It's huge, but this is where Edmond and Emma live. I thought you wanted to visit them." He pulled back hard on the lever between them as he smashed the pedal farthest from her with his foot. The auto came to a jerky halt.

"You're right," Melia said. "Thank you."

"Do you want me to walk you to the front door?" he asked.

Melia's stomach twitched. She hadn't really thought about what she was going to say. "Actually, I need to see their niece, Gabriela.

115

Do you know her?"

"Gabbie? That little stick? Why didn't you say so?"

Alex jumped from the Model T, went around to the front of the auto, and leaned over. He cranked the engine back up.

Melia stepped up on the floorboard to lean against the windshield, now pasty with dead bugs. "Are you going to leave us here?" She had no idea how long they'd been driving, but it might take all day if they had to walk back to the river when they were finished speaking with Gabriela.

"No." Alex waved. "Sit down. We're going to the cemetery."

"Isn't that where they bury dead people?" Tatou asked.

"That sounds creepy," Melia whispered. "Um ... why are we going there?"

"It's Sunday. Gabbie always goes to visit her mother after church."

"Do you think there's a way to Faerie through the cemetery?" Tatou asked.

"It's the same thing as a graveyard, right?" Melia whispered.

"Yep," Alex said.

She hadn't meant for him to hear her. She said more softly, "Graveyards are in-between places."

"But she's never been to Faerie," Tatou insisted.

Alex finished cranking the engine. He grinned at Melia as he wiped his hands on his long shorts.

"Look at those dimples," Tatou said.

Melia wasn't noticing much about Alex—or his dimples.

She couldn't stop thinking about Ryder, and how, by pushing him away, she made herself more vulnerable to Umbra. She wished she was scouring the countryside with him instead of Alex. It was so frustrating. Each moment they spent searching for Gabriela delayed the moment when she and Ryder could sit down and have the heart-to-heart conversation she needed to have with him.

They turned from the main road onto a narrower one rutted with grooves. The Model T choked up a hill. Alex's knuckles whitened as he fought to keep the unwieldy carriage from veering left or right. He aimed for a crown of tall pines cresting the broad swell.

Melia noticed stone markers. Most were oblong.

"Tombstones," Tatou said.

"Do they mark the doors to Faerie?" Melia asked.

"What?"

Melia had forgotten about Alex. "It's very open and airy," she said.

He quirked a brow. "Yeah, open and airy. Just like the rest of the countryside."

Melia chewed on a fingernail. She wondered if he still thought she was touched in the head. Right before he reached the line of trees, a loud bang scattered a flock of crows across the sky. Melia yelped and shot forward in her seat to clutch the handrail.

"You act like you've never heard an automobile backfire," Alex said, as he pulled over.

Melia's heart slowed down. "No, it's just that every time I do, it takes me by surprise." She blinked. "Just like the first time."

Alex studied her face, as if trying to assess the truth of her words. "I guess you're just skittish by nature?"

"It's my ears; they're sensitive."

Tatou fluttered between them. "Listen to you."

Alex nodded as if he accepted her explanation. "Gabbie is always over there." He pointed west. "She hangs out by her mother's headstone."

Melia waited for him to get out of the car or stop the engine. He didn't.

"I'll wait here," he said. "It's kind of creepy—all those dead people."

She nodded. "Right."

"It's better if he doesn't come with us," Tatou said. "You can talk with her in private."

Melia flashed Alex a smile as she untied the ribbons tight beneath her chin. She exited the auto and placed the straw hat in her empty seat. As much as she appreciated the floppy rim's protection from the sun, the graveyard's inner sanctum was shaded. She ran her fingers through her hair. Hats, like shoes, felt too restrictive. Unless they were muannai boots.

Halfway across the lawn, Melia realized she'd left *her* boots in the car. "Do you think he's going to wait for us?" she asked Tatou.

"Oh, he's not going anywhere. You've glamoured him."

"I did not."

"I didn't say you did it on purpose." Tatou launched from Melia's shoulder and zoomed ahead.

A bird shrieked. Melia looked up. A single crow spiraled in the sky. Despite the heat, chill bumps covered her arms as she watched it fly away.

She entered the grove, dim with shadows.

Melia read some of the markers. *Almond D. Lewis. Killed by Indians. August 19, 1862. 32 Years Old.* Too young to die, even for a full-blood mortal. *John Ulm. Died Oct. 9, 1889. Aged 80 Y. 8 M. 23 D.* The small town's namesake.

Tatou hovered ahead, pointing.

In the corner, a tall slim girl with long dark hair hopped across several stones. Melia took a deep breath. Tatou returned to her shoulder.

"Gabriela?"

The girl stood still.

"Gabbie?"

The girl made a slow rotation.

Melia approached her with hands extended, palms up.

The girl stared at Melia's shoulder where Tatou sat.

"Can you see my friend?" Melia asked.

The girl backed away, shaking her head.

"She's staring right at me," Tatou said.

The girl covered her eyes. "I don't see anything. Faeries don't

118

exist." Her voice sounded strained, like she was afraid.

Melia crouched.

Gabriela spread the fingers of her palm wide, to peek through them. "Please don't cause trouble with my aunt."

"I don't know your aunt. But if I did, I promise, I'd never tell her anything that might make her upset with you."

The girl dropped her hand from her face and took one step toward Melia. She shook her finger. "You don't belong here."

"I won't keep you," Melia said. "I just need to ... warn you about something."

The whites of the girls eyes widened in the late afternoon shadows.

"Do you ever have nightmares?"

Gabriela squeezed her eyes shut.

Melia took that as a yes. She wished she could hold the girl, or at least clasp her hand, as she explained Umbra. "Will you come sit with me?"

"Are you going to take me to that other place?"

"Which place is that?"

The girl held out her hand. Melia stood up and took it in hers. Gabriela led her to a tombstone and kicked it hard. The girl winced. She'd probably hurt her toes. "That's my mother's headstone," Gabriela said. "But she's not really buried there."

"You're right," Melia said.

The girl's fingers tightened around Melia's hand. "You believe me?"

"I live in the other place—"

Gabriela dropped Melia's hand as if it scalded hers. "Then you live in hell!" She flicked her fingers at Melia. "Be gone, demon. Spawn of Satan!"

"Gabriela—"

"I can't see you, emissary of Satan." She closed her eyes and stuck her fingers in her ears. "I can't hear you, messenger of the Devil." She crumpled to her knees and pulled out a chain tucked beneath her collar. She rubbed the silver cross that hung from it between her thumb and forefinger. The gesture was eerily similar to Lilliane's frantic rubbing of her black rose petals. Melia shivered as Gabriela's voice shifted into a droning mechanical recitation. "Our Father, who art in Heaven, hallowed be thy name."

"What is she doing?" Melia asked Tatou.

"I think she's praying."

"Ah." Melia vaguely remembered the concept of prayer from when she'd been a child in the mortal world. She recalled some mortals took their prayers very seriously. Melia waited for Gabriela to finish.

The litany continued.

"I think she's praying that you'll go away," Tatou said.

The girl quivered like a doe that might bolt at the crack of a twig.

"Do you think she's all right?"

"I think she doesn't want to go to Faerie," Tatou said.

"I never intended to take her there."

"I know that, but I think she's afraid you might try."

Melia squatted next to Gabriela and rested her hand on the girl's shoulder as gently as she could.

Gabriela jerked away and hissed, showing Melia her teeth. Then she resumed her prayers, head bowed.

"Psst." Tatou hovered a few headstones away.

Melia went to her.

"The cross she wears is a symbol of the mortal religion she practices."

Melia's forehead raised. "And?"

"I think it will protect her from Umbra."

"I need to be more certain than that."

"I'm pretty sure that if Umbra calls her, she'll think he's the Devil —Satan, or whatever—and she'll pray until he goes away."

The girl never let up on her fervent prayers, although Melia thought she saw her open one eye to check whether they were still there.

"Maybe you're right." Melia walked back to Gabriela and knelt beside her. "If anyone else comes for you—or calls you—from that other place, you do what you're doing now," she told her. "Send him away with your prayers. And don't stop praying until he's gone."

The girl quieted down. She rocked back and forth, hunched over her heels and toes, but she didn't open her eyes.

"We need to go," Tatou said.

Melia had never seen anyone—let alone a child—so broken. "Do you think Luisa knows her daughter is so troubled?"

"Maybe that's why she's never recovered herself."

"Maybe," Melia said. But she was thinking: Maybe it wasn't such a bad thing, growing up in Illialei among the faeries with wings. Because whatever had happened to Gabriela was worse.

15. Black Crows

Lilliane knelt before a bed of black roses. She inhaled their spicy perfume and let her mind drift to the Void. She closed her eyes and focused on Umbra's formless darkness. She gave it shape, imagining it as a large black pool. She stood at its edge and loosed the cord that tied her silk gown, letting it fall from her hands. She slid the sheer cool fabric of her robe from her shoulders. Standing naked, she dipped her toe in the black liquid and shivered. Slowly, she entered the darkness and swam within it. She hummed and sang as she imagined the black energy infusing her with power.

When she felt sated, she exited the dark waters. The pool was almost drained. A shriek drew her attention to a tall stone tower. Lilliane dressed quickly and ran to the grey brick silo. It had no door, no point of entry.

A black feather fluttered from the monotonous charcoal sky to land at her feet.

Lilliane opened her eyes. She glanced around her.

On the other side of the rose garden, two knights were deep in conversation.

The princess crawled along the ground. She kept the knights in her peripheral vision as she edged to a break in the bushes. She didn't stand until she'd slipped through the narrow space. She straightened her skirts and strolled along the walkways, stopping to smell a bloom here and there before ducking through the little-used door that led to the cupboard beneath the stairs. A crack of light poured into the cramped closet from the interior hall. Lilliane peered through the gap. If she was careful, she could slip through the palace's less-traveled halls without being seen.

These days whenever the princess turned a corner, Gavin or one of his knights was there. If they'd kept as close an eye on her cousin, Melia never would have escaped! The men were solicitous enough, with their servile bowing and obsequious tones, but Lilliane couldn't allow them to interfere with her wicked delights.

She raced up the tower's round staircase, the silk of her gown bunched in her hands. Every tenth step or so, she checked behind her.

The spell had worked!

She listened for the echo of footsteps before opening the tower's heavy door. Inside, she dropped the bolt behind her. Standing at the window facing west, she flattened her palms on the stone sill, imagining her flock of birds in the mortal world.

Before the grey faerie died, Lilliane's spells often ended in failure. Regardless of how precisely she attended to the timing, ingredients, and incantations they rarely worked. But now, her intentions rippled through the Whole with increasing precision.

A black speck appeared in the distance. Lilliane's heart swelled as it grew in size. Breathless with anticipation, she raised her arm, her wrist angled. The crow landed on the offered perch, its talons tickling her bare skin. "My sweet, what news do you bring?" Lilliane murmured.

The crow cawed. It was a loud, piercing cry.

Lilliane paced, following the tower's stone walls. "You're sure?"

The crow's loud trill reverberated in the stone chamber.

Her cousin and the pixie were in the mortal world, visiting Gabriela. Lilliane carried the crow to a metal box in the shadows. Inside the box, a dozen mice crawled over one another. She snatched a rope-like tail and dangled the creature before the crow. "A prize for my sweet."

The bird opened its sharp black beak. Lilliane plopped the rodent into the creature's gullet. The crow gulped the snack down in a single swallow.

Lilliane returned to the window. She held the bird with both hands. "Return to the others. When there's more news, bring it at once." She threw the creature into the air. It caught itself with inky wings. She watched it shrink into the horizon.

What were Melia and the pixie plotting with Gabriela? How had they found her half-sister in the mortal world? Lilliane crossed her arms to cradle her elbows. The old wood elf must have helped them. Damn Aldous for escaping. Her black spell would have been the end of him if Flora hadn't saved him. She should have burned along with the rest of the spring faeries.

Uriel Albiana's journals lined a shelf against the tower's north wall. Lilliane studied the spines. Now that she'd mastered the art of sending her familiars beyond the palace walls, she itched to try her hand at something more demanding. The princess selected two slim volumes before locking up her refuge and descending the winding staircase.

A uniformed figure waited at her door.

"What are you doing here?" she snapped at the knight.

"Gavin ordered your suite guarded day and night."

Lilliane clutched her great-grandmother's journals against her breast. "I assure you that isn't necessary!"

He blocked her way.

"May I please enter my chamber." It was a command not a question.

The knight pushed the door open. When Lilliane entered, he followed her inside.

"I didn't grant you permission to enter my suite!"

"Would you like to wait in the hall while I search your rooms?" he asked.

He was ignoring her orders. "Search them for what? No one is here but you and me."

"I need to verify no one is hiding in the wardrobe—"

"Leave me at once!"

The knight bowed and retreated.

Lilliane threw Uriel's journals onto her bed. She fell down beside them, slamming the mattress with her fists.

A sharp rap at her door pulled Lilliane from her studies. "Yes?"

"Princess, may I enter?"

Lilliane recognized Gavin's voice. She rubbed her forehead.

"Princess?"

She stomped to the door and opened it—a crack.

He thrust a basket in her direction.

Lilliane took it from him. She wrapped her hands around the wicker handle and studied its contents: the gloves, sachet of seeds, spade, and trowel she left in the garden. "You shouldn't have troubled yourself."

He stepped inside her room. "I was concerned when you left them in the garden this afternoon."

"Your concern is overbearing."

"Your father would never forgive me if anything happened to you."

At the mention of her father, Lilliane raised her head. "My father spoke of me ... to you?"

"Not in great detail."

She whirled around and marched to the corner, where she dropped the basket. It landed with a loud thunk and toppled over. Lilliane didn't bother to collect the objects spilling from it. She wrapped her arms around herself and gazed out the window. "Illialei is a country of gossips," she said. "The wood elves are by far the worst. I dislike when they spread false rumors about me." She faced Gavin. "Lies are harmful, are they not?"

"Indeed."

She smirked. "Perhaps you could station your knights in Bryndale: at the Hive, and along the busy streets that lead to the vegetable market—to end their slander against me." That would at

least end the elves constant speculation about what had happened to Aldous, and reduce the number of knights spying on her in the palace.

"And that would satisfy you?"

"Immensely."

"Consider it done."

She acknowledged his obedience with a tilt of her chin. "I've noticed, Gavin, you're much younger than the soldiers you command." She relaxed into a chair.

"I'm the youngest commander in the Huron army."

"And how did you manage that?"

"I've studied the art of war with a relentless devotion. However, it's my skill as an assassin that truly sets me apart. Even under orders, most Huron knights will act alone only under duress. My preference for solo operations is unique and valuable to the Huron oligarchy. Thus my meteoric rise."

Her lips trembled. "An assassin? You enjoy killing?"

Gavin shrugged. "I enjoy working alone."

She ran her index finger across her bottom lip. "I see."

A dead half-blood couldn't incarnate Umbra.

16. Solving the Riddle

Ryder shuffled the pebbles in his hand before dropping them onto the grass floor of Flora's tent, again. Twenty-one days since Melia said, "Wait for me." No matter how many times he counted the small rocks, the number didn't change.

"Send a falcon," Sinjiin said.

Ryder was surprised his friend had shifted into his mage form. "You need to be careful. Someone might overhear you and become curious that a tiger can speak."

Sinjiin tilted his head toward the loose flap of the tent door. "No one is going to hear me above that."

Shouts and raucous screams, syncopated by the boom of drums and the pulse of seashell-filled rattles, drowned out the Great White Sea's crashing tides.

His friend had a point. Ryder scooped up the pebbles. "I don't have a falcon."

"Train one. Tell me you at least learned how to do that in Idonne."

"I never attended those classes either."

"Then you'll have to rely on faith and your pea-sized rocks until she returns."

"Do you think she will?"

"Yes."

Ryder wanted to believe his friend, but every morning since Melia left, he awakened with his heart full of anticipation—this would be

129

the day he would see her again. Every day, he caught her in his peripheral vision, tall and slender with her long dark hair, walking among the muannai asking for him. But it was never her, only tricks the light and air of Faerie played upon his eyes. Every night he fought to sleep. The days passed with no appearance and no word from her. She had the Tasimas. If she really wanted to see him, she could use it.

"What's taking them so long?" he asked.

"The wood elf was at death's door. If he'd died, they'd already be here. It must be taking some time for him to recover. He's very old. Don't worry. Flora hasn't forgotten the basin, and Melia hasn't forgotten you. They'll return. Until then, how are your studies going?"

"Do you ask because you're eager to be free of your debt?"

Sinjiin's teeth gleamed in the light of Flora's makeshift lanterns. "You've grown attached to me. You'll miss me when I'm gone."

Ryder hadn't given much consideration to what Sinjiin would do once he fulfilled his debt, but the thought of losing the mage's companionship unsettled him. "I've finished more than half the book and found nothing about the founding stone. The new stronghold is being erected faster than I believed possible, and lately, the muannai talk about nothing but this carnivale," the priest said. "What is the dragonwitch up to?"

"She's sent a small army to harvest every ripe grape in the Nuada."

"Wine?"

Sinjiin nodded. "The harvest will be shipped to the muannai valley. She'll have fountains of wine for her dragon festival."

"Already the muannai follow Sevondi, and she's not even regent."

"Can you blame them? For the first time one of their own will sit on a throne."

"I'll feel better if Ormrun and Koldis are gone from Faerie before this carnivale of hers begins."

"Have you ever considered Nandana might be right?"

"About Melia incarnating Umbra? No, I haven't."

"Then let me make a suggestion."

"If it's about that, I don't want to hear it."

"Listen to me."

"No."

"Do you think it's a coincidence you're here, sitting in this tent with that book?" Sinjiin reached over to ruffle *The Book of Umbra's* pages. "You're the pre-eminent scholar when it comes to Umbra and the incarnation. You love this half-faerie. If it's her destiny to become Umbra's vessel, you, more than anyone, can help her."

Ryder resisted the impulse to box the side of Sinjiin's head. "You'll never convince me that putting Melia in danger is the right thing to do."

The mage shook his hand with his thumb pressed against his index finger. "Don't let your fear for her close your mind to the opportunity before us."

"Opportunity?"

"Yes, the opportunity to make Faerie whole." Sinjiin clapped his hands together once. Ryder flinched at the unexpected crack. "United."

"For thousands of years, the Whole has been just fine with Faerie divided."

The mage brushed Ryder's words away with a flourish of his hand. "No. I don't think so." Sinjiin waved his finger as if there were a group of musicians seated before him. "When we buried the basin and sword the night Elendah died, did you hear Isolt's song?"

Ryder preferred to erase the haunting melody from his memory, but often when he struggled to sleep he heard its echo. "Yes."

Sinjiin tapped his bright yellow turban and continued his mad speech. "It's with me all the time. I've thought of little else. In my meditations, I've come to understand that when Isolt of the Waters was buried in the bowels of the Ruadain, a great wound was created between the enchanted and mortal worlds. It has never healed. The growth of the human population in the mortal world, the end of the grey faeries, the rise of the muannai, the division of Faerie, Uriel Albiana's embrace of black magic, the burning of the spring faeries"—he ticked off each event on a finger—"have all led to one thing."

"Which is?"

"An Albiana with mortal blood to heal the wound." Sinjiin crouched on the balls of his feet. "Which is Umbra."

Ryder ground the flats of his fists into the grass. "You saw what happened to Plantine. She became like a glove for Umbra's hand; she murdered the grey faerie!" he shouted. "It almost killed her."

Sinjiin crossed his arms over his black vest. "Plantine was weak. She sacrificed love and allowed ambition to rule her. It could be different with Melia. If she chooses love—"

"Every time we get close, she runs away from me. She chooses to fly."

Sinjiin shrugged. "I didn't say it would be easy. Love never is, but you're an orphan, and she's alone. A love strong enough to harness Umbra's power could create a new world, one in which both of you find your place." The mage jammed his hands into the pockets of his red silk pantaloons. "Consider that while you're searching for answers in the book."

Before Ryder could find his tongue, a burst of warm air brushed the hair from his forehead. The six-hundred-pound tiger stalked out of the tent.

The priest lunged after him.

Sinjiin disappeared among the revelers, who every night celebrated the progress made on the new stronghold. They clapped and cheered as the tiger cut through the crowd. The big cat's appearances delighted them.

Long after Ryder lost his friend to the night, he continued running. He ran until he could run no more, he ran until he dropped flat on his back on the ground, gulping for air. He stared into the black sky, hating that his whole life he'd longed for a place where he belonged.

❖ ❖ ❖

An excerpt from *The Book of Umbra*:

This is an interesting tidbit: I've made contact with a dwarf in Misgradde who claims to know Gweff–the same Gweff who forged the basin, Ormrun, in the bowels of the Ruadain Mountain. This contact has provided me (in exchange for an obscene amount of gold, so I hope there is some merit in his account, otherwise, I've been duped!) information about a curious encounter he had with Gweff late one night when they'd fallen deep in their cups.

It seemed the dwarf never stopped carrying guilt over the death of his friend, Haff.

Note: There has always been some question as to whether that killing was accidental or intentional. My contact informs me Gweff wept and muttered for the better part of an hour that he'd never meant to hurt Haff. Unfortunately, that kind of confession never clarifies motive.

What intrigues me is Gweff's recounting of his terror of Isolt.

Isolt of the Waters is an ancient water elemental who was banished to the Void by her husband, the god Vulcan, for betraying him with a mortal lover and daring to carry her lover's child–a child who died as Isolt's corporeal form dissolved in her otherworldly prison.

If one can imagine Isolt's state of mind–a volatile mix of horror, rage, and sorrow–one might fathom that direct dealings with her might engender fear, especially, if the one who dealt with her betrayed her as Gweff did when he reneged on the original agreement he and his friend, Haff, made with her: They would create the means for her to return to the physical plane and achieve vengeance, and she would rid Una (currently known as Earth) of the mortal scourge, allowing the dwarves to return to their original and rightful home.

In the final moment, Gweff refused to give Isolt the means to return from the Void, and this is where my contact's account piqued my curiosity.

He quotes the dwarf:

I turned and ran from the cavern. I had the sword in my hand and the basin on my back. I wasn't going to leave them with her; the bargain we'd struck with her was too evil. My heart pounded and I gasped for air in the winding tunnels. I reached dead end after dead end. I fell and stumbled over rocks and bones. It became difficult to breathe. There was no light; I couldn't see. I had to feel my way, crawling with my hands out in front of me. The screams of the dead, and the laughter of those who would have preferred me dead, chased after me. It felt like insects and worms feasted on my skin. I came to believe I would be trapped in the depths of the mountain forever. By the time I reached the surface, I screeched like a madman.

I tore across the grass. She chased me. The sun was her enormous eye, meant to turn me to ashes if I dared stop.

I ran until I couldn't feel my feet or my toes. When my calves and knees became numb, I dragged myself along the ground with my arms. That's how the caravan found me, out of my head with fear. All I wanted to do was get out of Faerie.

Ryder covered the book with a pile of folded blankets and pushed it all into the corner. He left the tent and headed for the cliffs.

Intense emotion was a common enough way to open a door between the planes of existence. Joy was one way to travel between the mortal and enchanted worlds. But terror. What an elegant twist on transportation, so simple, and yet he could imagine nothing more effective for propulsion.

Who would have suspected it?

The question before him now: How to induce it?

Ryder searched the stronghold's construction site for Yrrick. Well-liked by his fellow muannai and intuitive about design, he led the rebuilding project. Daily, he impressed Ryder with his organizational skills and innovative ideas.

The muannaye's vision for the new stronghold was a radically altered one, and as Ryder watched the concept unfold, he came to appreciate Yrrick's insistence that any attempt to replicate the structure which had built itself around Elendah would insult her memory.

She'd been inimitable, and so had the Calashai; its exterior—a traditional stone fortress—belied its interior—a magical weaving of nature, comfort, and utility.

Yrrick recombined those elements into something altogether different, but equally impressive. His expansion of the stables embraced the muannai passion for horses, while the numerous reading rooms honored his race's passion for books and ideas. His use of glass opened the north side to the Great White Sea, and the south side to breathtaking views of Aldaine and the Ruadain's six remaining steeples. The generous installation of courtyards with fountains and gardens paid homage to the regent he'd loved without transgressing her memory.

Ryder marveled each day at the progress.

Yrrick wanted it livable before the first snow. "You're looking for me?" The muannaye pulled away from a group of sweaty builders.

"Yes."

"Do you need more timber?" Yrrick asked. "Another shipment arrives today."

Where the Calashai had been solid stone, Yrrick's design for the new stronghold made liberal use of stone and wood.

"No, I need to find Embril," Ryder said.

The muannaye's eyes scanned the priest's body. "Are you hurt? Did you suffer some injury?"

Ryder shook his head. "Something else."

Yrrick didn't question him further. It was probably one of the reasons he was so well-liked. "She has a small shop in Aldaine. Will you need a cart?"

Ryder could hike down the mountain to the city, but it would take all morning. Now that he'd solved the riddle of how to take the basin and the sword past the enchanted barrier which bound them to the founding stone, he was eager to test his theory. "Yes."

Yrrick hollered a name over the din of hammers, saws, and friendly shouting of the workers. A troll appeared. "Please, drive him to Embril's shop."

Ryder thanked the muannaye and followed the troll down the incline to where two carts and three carriages were parked. Their drivers milled about. The troll pointed out the most dilapidated vehicle, a simple cart with a long warped board for a seat.

Although Ryder rarely visited Aldaine, he enjoyed the city, and these days, with the enormous influx of muannai from other parts of Tyrannis, more of the exotic wingless faeries than ever packed the tea shops, cafes, and inns. In their tight pants, knee-high boots, and colorful ruffled shirts, the entire population appeared as if they'd indulged in an extravagant shopping spree among the fashionable shops interspersed along the city's spiraling cobbled streets.

When the scent of roasted meat hit Ryder, he ignored his hunger pangs. Instead, as the cart wound past the city's most colorful inhabitants and storefronts, he fell into his habit of observing.

In Idonne, everything was white, ivory, or the color of sand; in Tyrannis' most cosmopolitan metropolis, every color of the rainbow was represented.

The priest was surprised when the troll rolled the cart down a narrow and deserted alley. He'd imagined a more spectacular location for the most skilled healer in the city.

The troll yelled. The horses stopped their forward movement, raising their hooves up and down in place. "Do you want me to wait?"

Ryder jumped to the street. "Yes."

A faded sign read: Embril's Apothecary. The door hung crooked on its hinges and stuck against the shop's dirt floor. When the priest pushed hard, it flew open. In spite of the many candles, the interior was dim. It smelled like the deep woods, a meadow, and the ocean all at once. Outside, the sun was bright. Ryder paused while his eyes adjusted to the shop's interior.

Embril materialized before him, her aqua eyes wide. "May I help you?"

There was no easy way to ask for what he needed. "I believe that you can."

She indicated a table. "Please, sit. May I offer you a cup of tea?"

Maybe the ritual would help him gather his thoughts. "Yes."

She bustled away while he tested one of the rickety chairs. When he was satisfied it would hold his weight, he sat down. Shelves reached from floor to ceiling, lining each wall. Jars, boxes, and baskets filled them. Bundles of herbs, tied and drying, hung from rods that crisscrossed overhead. It prompted thoughts of Flora, her makeshift tent, and what he discovered in the book.

By the time Embril placed two cups and a full pot of tea on the table, he'd worked out what he needed to say. "Do you know of a powder or drink that can produce symptoms of terror in the body?"

Embril set down her teacup. "Most folks would prefer to alleviate their fear."

"I don't want to feel the fear—I mean I don't want the person who takes it—"

"Of course, that won't be you."

Ryder absorbed his blunder with a straight face. "I don't want them to actually feel their fears. I just need their body to mimic the rapid beat of the heart, perhaps a cold sweat, maybe a freezing of the muscles—"

"I understand what you're after."

"This needs to be kept in confidence."

"Of course."

If the potion failed, he wouldn't be the first to die trying to take the sword and basin from the founding stone. "It needs to be strong. It needs to work. If it doesn't ... there is risk of death."

"I can probably have something like that ready in a fortnight."

Ryder saw through Sinjiin's speech about the wonders of Melia incarnating Umbra. To heal a fundamental wound in the Whole, one that had existed for thousands of years, was a lofty ideal. But he seemed to be the only one who understood how hard it would be for a young half-faerie to harness Umbra's power and turn it to the good.

If Sinjiin and Flora tried to convince Melia, she might be persuaded, especially, after Nandana's reckless prediction.

Ryder's blood raced in his ears. "I need it much sooner."

Embril's eyes pierced his with questions. He remained mute as he argued the case, once more, with himself.

The idea of creating a world with Melia where they both belonged was tempting, but not tempting enough to jeopardize her soul. Umbra was a jealous and possessive consciousness. He would consume her psyche, leaving no room in her heart for another; whatever chance existed for Ryder and Melia to love one another would be stolen from them.

It was too great a risk.

He wiped a sheen of sweat from his brow. He hated to admit he'd fallen in love with someone who felt nothing for him except, maybe, gratitude. Yes, she asked him to wait for her, but it had been thirty-five long days.

The basin and sword must be gone from Faerie when Melia returned to Aldaine. If she returned.

Despite the tea, Ryder's throat felt parched. He coughed into his hand. As much as he tried to convince himself the indigo smudge on Melia's forehead was meaningless, he'd never forget it evaporating on the day they met.

Embril refilled his cup.

"I can't wait a fortnight." Ryder pointed at the shelves. "Don't you have anything in one of those jars or baskets I can take with me today?"

"I have something, but if the dosage isn't exact you'll—your friend—will suffer a great deal. Too much and the terror will never leave him. Too little and the effect will be diluted. How big is your friend?"

"About my height and weight," Ryder said.

"Of course, he is."

The priest ignored her self-satisfied smirk. Several days ago, he asked Sinjiin for a few pieces of gold. They burned a whole in his pocket. "I can pay you well."

"Of course, you can."

Embril's long skirt swished the dirt floor as she walked to one of the walls lined with shelves.

17. Embril's Apothecary

Sevondi waited for Pogo to push the door of Embril's shop open. "Keep an eye on the carriage and horses," she told him. Another run-down heap half-blocked the alley. She didn't want it anywhere near her newly acquired coach, or the high-strung beasts that pulled it.

Inside, the usual cloying smell of rosemary, buttercups, and sea orchids assailed her. In defense of the perfumed onslaught, Sevondi shortened her breaths and searched the apothecary's shadows.

Where was the troll?

Her gaze met the staring eyes of the young priest. Not who she was looking for, but what a pleasant surprise. She smoothed her hair. "Ryder? How unexpected to find you here"—she swept her hand wide—"in Embril's garden of wax."

Anger, chagrin, pride, and—was that curiosity?—played across his face. He stood as she approached. Reflexes, she imagined.

"I'll be leaving soon," he said.

His face was dark from days spent outside. The contrast between his bronzed skin and green eyes was striking. "Please don't rush off on my account."

He moved to the counter where Embril collected payment. The thin fabric of his shirt stretched across his broad shoulders. The effect of working with the muannai to rebuild the stronghold, she presumed. Her stronghold.

"She's almost finished putting together my order," he said.

"Picking up something for someone? Flora, perhaps?" It would be divine to know what the spring faerie was up to. She'd heard nothing from her in weeks.

"A friend," he said.

"Maybe the half-faerie?" Sevondi winced. The fleeting sting between her shoulder blades reminded her Umbra's poison-tipped arrows pierced them both.

The young priest glared.

She could almost see the smoke curling from his nostrils. If he were a bull, he'd be stamping the ground with his hoof. "No, not for her. Someone else, then. And yet, just the mention of her ... arouses you."

His broad jaw pulsed, but he said nothing.

"So mysterious and close-mouthed, such valuable qualities in a priest." For every step she took toward him, he took one to the side or back.

"I'm no longer a member of the order," he said.

"Why do I believe Anton would welcome you back in the fold with open arms? I doubt it would take more than a sincere apology."

"You speak as though you know him."

"I do." She registered his shock—the slightest widening of those emerald eyes—before his face resettled into that wooden expression. "And the Muudron Stone was not our first meeting," she added.

Embril measured a white chalky powder on the scales. The troll was all ears.

"I doubt you remember. I forgot myself until recently." Sevondi opened her palm even with her thigh. "You were about this high."

He gave a slight shake to his head. "You've been to Idonne?"

She laughed. "I consider Anton a friend."

"Have you ... communicated with him since ..."

"Since you stole Koldis from the Idonnic Library's archives? No, I haven't."

"I can see it might be difficult for you—a friend of his—to explain how you used magic to steal it from me," Ryder said.

He definitely had not forgotten her trick at the Muudron Stone. "It's such a magnificent blade. Do you think he'd be sympathetic if we pleaded it was impossible to resist?"

"He might believe you."

Embril cleared her throat. She held up a small pouch. "I've prepared four doses for someone who's about your size. Calculate the portions precisely before mixing a single dose with fresh water—not saltwater—at dawn in a container the size of a drinking glass. There's some creeks that run down the mountain. They're easy to find. Use water from one of them.

"There are also four dried peppers in the bag. Drop one of them into the mix. Allow the contents to sit undisturbed for the rest of the day. It must be taken within an hour of sunset. Throw the pepper out right before you drink it. The effects should last most of the night."

The priest leaned against the counter to block Sevondi's view. "How much do I owe you?"

Embril scratched some hashes on a marked-up piece of parchment. "Fifty copper pieces."

He whispered something Sevondi couldn't hear.

"I don't have change," Embril said.

"I have change," Sevondi offered.

"Thank you, but I'll handle this," said the young priest who claimed he was no longer a priest.

She humiliated him at the Muudron Stone. He'd never forgive her. What a shame. Her eyes flickered on the piece of gold Embril dropped on the scale.

"Generous," the troll said. "Feel free to come back if it doesn't work for you—for your friend."

He left without another word. Not even a nod of the head.

Sevondi took his place before the counter. "What was that all about?"

"Confidential."

"Something for Flora?" The priest could have lied.

"I don't think so."

"Speaking of, have you seen her?"

"Not since I came down the mountain."

"What about the half-faerie? Not the one Zachariah married, but her sister. The one who got shot the same day I did. Any news of her?"

Embril shook her head. "News isn't my business."

Sevondi patted her hand. "But certainly the priest mentioned her?"

"Not a word."

"Interesting. When I asked him about her, he became provoked. I wonder why?"

"I've no idea."

"He loves her," Sevondi mused. "But there's more to it than that. He's hiding something."

"Aren't we all?"

"Embril, you've taken a liking to him."

The troll made a noncommittal grunt.

The dragonwitch wondered if the burning sting of Umbra's poison lingered beneath the half-faerie's skin.

"I doubt you came here to gossip," Embril said.

"You're right."

The troll walked around the counter and cleared cups from the table. "Tea?"

Sevondi sank into one of the empty chairs. "Mint."

The troll removed the pot.

"Not mint?" Sevondi asked.

"Orange Blossom Ginger."

"Fine, I'll have a cup of that."

"It won't take long to brew a fresh pot."

"You don't mind?"

Embril disappeared behind a curtain separating the front of the shop from the back.

Sevondi tiptoed over to the counter with the scales. She checked to make sure the troll was still in the back of the shop before she leaned over to grab the jar half-full of the white powder Embril sold to the priest. She twisted off the lid, licked her finger, and pressed it into the white substance. Holding her coated finger to the side, she tightened the lid and repositioned it to where Embril had placed it.

Back in her chair, Sevondi held her finger to her nose. Any scent was hard to detect. She flicked her tongue against the tip of her finger. Bone? Mixed with something else? What was the priest up to?

She hadn't heard from Moog in several days, and his last report was useless—the tiger inhaled all the fresh meat they supplied him, but didn't provide any useful information in exchange. Cats. All the same. Reciprocity was beyond them.

✧ ✧ ✧

"What can I help you with?" Embril asked.

"Have you heard about my dragon carnivale? I intend it to be more memorable than any celebration the grey faerie ever hosted."

"Everyone's talking about it in the tea rooms."

Sevondi tossed her hair and rearranged her skirt. "What are they saying?"

"That there won't be a grape left in the Nuada by the time you're done. That it will be spectacular."

Sevondi's hands trembled with excitement. Her tea made waves in its cup. She set it down. "And what do you think, Embril? Do you think I'll be the next regent?"

"The sympathy of the muannai is on your side, and they're ready for one of their own to be regent. A pageant to usher in the new age is quite fitting."

Sevondi reached across the table to squeeze the troll's hand. "I think the stronghold needs to be renamed. What do you think of the Dragon's Keep?"

"It has your stamp on it."

Sevondi laughed.

"But that's not why you came here today," Embril said.

"No, it isn't. The priest distracted me."

The troll's lips sealed into a flat line. Sevondi couldn't blame her for keeping Ryder's confidence; he paid her in gold. The dragonwitch twitched in her seat.

"Have you experienced any more burning where the arrows pierced your back?" Embril asked.

"On occasion."

"Is that why you came today? Would you like me to examine it?"

"No. Although the pain can become intense, it happens less frequently. What I need today is something for stamina."

Embril sipped her tea.

"Almost all my life I've conjured dragons at will," Sevondi said, "but never so many, or over such an extended period of time as I'll need to do for the carnivale. It will take a moon cycle to travel the route I've mapped from the muannai valley to the Muudron Stone, and I'll need to call forth at least three dragons every night."

"When you call the dragons, do you feel drained?" Embril asked.

"It requires fierce concentration to call each one, and endurance to hold them."

"Mental and physical energy."

"Do you have something to sustain me? I need something that won't fail."

"Will you call the dragons every night?"

"Yes."

Embril rubbed her jaw with her thumb and forefinger.

"You have to know of something—"

"I'm thinking." The troll rose from the table and drifted to one of the shelf-covered walls. Female trolls had the most gorgeous hair— thicker than a horse's tail. Embril's gleamed in the candlelight. "When does the carnivale begin?"

"Before the first night of the next dark moon phase at the Dark Horse Saloon."

Embril counted on her fingers. "That will give me enough time. I'd like to experiment with some ingredients."

"Send word to the Blue Mermaid when it's ready. I'll send Pogo to pick it up."

"Or I can have it delivered," Embril offered.

"Even better." Sevondi risked a glance at her lap, where she'd settled the back of her hand. She itched to know what the crystal-like glaze on the tip of her finger was for. "Another pot of tea?"

The troll opened and closed her large aqua eyes.

Sevondi laughed. "What?"

"You never have a second pot."

"Are you anxious to be rid of me?"

"I don't want to gossip."

"Never."

Embril snorted. She gathered the tea kettle and disappeared behind the curtain in the back of the shop.

Sevondi sucked the last bit of white powder from her finger. It was sweeter than bone, and the taste still didn't give away its purpose. Frustrated, she wiped her hand on her skirt. The priest wanted to take the basin from Faerie, but Flora wanted the half-faerie to incarnate Umbra. If the priest loved the girl, maybe he didn't want her to incarnate Umbra. That could work to Sevondi's advantage.

All her efforts to coax more information from Embril about the priest and half-faerie were fruitless, but the mint tea was delicious.

"Even better than the first pot," she said.

Embril remained tight-lipped.

Sevondi blinked in the late afternoon sun. Rare in Tyrannis at this time of year, bright rays of light angled into the alley. In a few moments they would pass, and the narrow space between the dilapidated buildings would be as dark as Embril's shop.

The rattletrap cart was gone. It must have belonged to the priest. Pogo snoozed on the driver's bench of her carriage. She swatted his calf. "Wake up."

He jumped.

"After you take me to the Blue Mermaid," she said, "I need you to visit your brother."

Pogo opened her carriage's black lacquered door and held out his hand as she'd taught him to do. It wasn't quite the effect she'd hoped for. Maybe he needed a uniform; something with braids, and a different sort of hat. Not that wool one he always fiddled with. It looked like a sock stretched over his head.

"He's feeding the tiger and keeping an eye on it. I thought that's what you ordered."

"Can't he do more than one thing?" She passed on the instructions she overheard Embril give to the priest.

"Now you want him to watch the priest, too?"

"As much as I pay him, I'd think that wouldn't be too much to ask."

"How can he watch both of them at the same time? What if they go off in different directions?"

"Don't make it so complicated. The day the priest mixes this drink, tell your brother to make him the priority."

Pogo stuffed his hands into his pocket. "Yes, ma'am."

Sevondi climbed into the carriage. "Take me to the hotel."

On the way back to the Blue Mermaid, Sevondi felt for Umbra. Nothing. Not even a wisp. It had been too many days since she felt the dark master's presence. Had she angered him in some way? Had he chosen another vessel?

Her heart jumped. The half-faerie!

The partnership between Umbra and the vessel of incarnation had to be mutual. Even with the sword and basin, Sevondi couldn't force his consciousness into her body if he chose not to enter. Would the half-faerie accept him?

Her sister had.

18. A Difference in Time

Melia pressed the straw hat down on her head, grateful for its protection from the relentless heat. Her eyes drooped. She felt drowsy, like she would never fully wake again. Her feet dangled in the Colorado River. At least her toes were cool.

Although it seemed like they'd been floating down the sleepy river forever, it couldn't have been more than a few hours. She checked the height of the sun. They should reach the Columbus bridge soon.

Flora warned her to use the same door between the worlds when they returned to Faerie: "If you use a different one, you might not come back to the same place."

Alex didn't want to leave her stranded in the middle of downtown La Grange, Texas. She assured him she was close enough to walk home, and her father wouldn't appreciate her showing up with a strange boy. That convinced him.

After he asked if he could see her again, and she told him another lie—"We can meet here next Saturday"—he finally left with sad eyes, no dimples. But not before he shoved the hat back into her hands.

On the way down to the river, they passed a pile of huge, black inflated tubes similar to the black circles of rubber that ferried the Model T. She had the idea they might float and lugged one down to the riverbank. Now, she lay cradled in its empty center while Tatou sunned herself on the rim.

It was impossible for Melia to keep her eyes open. She closed them again. One more short nap before they reached the bridge.

✧ ✧ ✧

I'm at the Muudron Stone.

The dragonwitch stands next to me. She has marks on her face, a pattern drawn in black.

Overhead the sky explodes. Crimson, jade, sapphire, and golden-colored dragons sizzle and swipe at one another in the night sky.

I gaze down at my fingers, my hands, my dress, my bare feet.

It's nighttime, but I'm not a bird.

My hand brushes my lips. Did I kiss Ryder?

Beyond the crumbling dais of the ancient stage, the faces of thousands of muannai glow in the light of Sevondi's dragons. They watch her, and the dance of the great clawing serpents breathing fire above our heads.

The stage vibrates. The stone pillars rattle.

Behind us, muannai beat drums the size of mountain boulders. There are four of them—the drums—a pair of muannai with long handled sticks beat each one. The head of the sticks are padded with animal hide. The muannai use both hands to grip the long handles. Combined with the roar of the dragons, the effect is deafening.

Next to me, Sevondi gyrates. It's hard to take my eyes from her, but something glittery catches my eye.

Ormrun, filled with water, lords over a pedestal between us.

The dragonwitch writhes as she did at Plantine's wedding. It doesn't take long before the muannai are hypnotized, the dragons overhead forgotten.

I gasp.

Koldis glimmers along the length of her thigh.

Where is Ryder? He promised he'd take the basin and sword to the Isle of Minnanon.

But then I asked him to wait for me. I've been gone too long.

The beat of the drums become more frenzied. I can't think. Like everyone else, I can only watch, mesmerized as the dragonwitch courts the dark consciousness of Umbra's power.

She rips Koldis from the sheath on her thigh and brandishes the blue shimmer of its blade high above her head in a single liquid motion.

She weaves closer to the bowl.

I can't breathe.

Umbra will be born. Into our plane. Into our world.

And then I hear that voice. It's so seductive, enticing me. "My Melia," it says. "Long have I dreamed of your embrace."

My blood turns to ice in my veins.

Where is Ryder? Tatou? Flora? Sinjün? Why am I standing here, on the dais with only the witch?

"My Melia, you won't need anyone else."

My insides begin to thaw. The warmth spreads, melting the cold, pinching at first, but then ...

"My sweet, Melia."

My heart hungers for the flame of dark power.

"Would you wake up?"

Melia's eyes shuttered open. "Tatou?" Her hands and feet splashed in the water. "Where am I?"

The pixie pointed to the bridge disappearing behind them. "I've been trying to wake you up forever!"

Melia shook her head. "Get on my shoulder and hang on. I'll swim us back."

She spilled out of the buoyant tube and gulped a mouthful of river water. At least the wetness helped shock her into alertness. She pushed upstream, her arms and hands digging against the current.

"The sun's going to set soon," Tatou said.

Melia saw the strips of gold and pink when she turned her head to breathe. As bits and pieces of her dream came back to her, she fought the river harder. Nothing about the images made sense, yet a horrible dread mounted within her.

They had to get back to Faerie.

When they were beneath the bridge, she dog-paddled. "Are you ready?" she asked her friend.

"I think so."

"You go first this time. I'll be right behind you."

Melia lifted one arm and then the other out of the water. The pearls Elendah gave her wrapped each wrist. With a slow long breath, she exhaled the air stagnating in her lungs.

In her dream, her arms were bare.

Melia kicked her legs hard.

An invisible wall blocked her effort.

She sensed what was happening. The ancient door between the worlds was closing. She felt with her fingers for a seam, a crack, any open sliver, but all she could think of was Tatou. Had her friend made it through?

Melia opened her eyes; the river water transformed into something more like wind. It pushed her eyes shut. She opened her mouth and choked on a gust. If she couldn't push through to the other side ...

Her frantic fingers found an edge. She shoved with the heel of her hand. Her head and neck passed through before a weight slammed into her chest. Immobile, she kicked harder.

She pulled herself up and through. A sheering pressure twisted her wrist. The force of what felt like two heavy, flat stones came down on her hands. She yanked with all her strength. The bracelet on her left hand burst; the individual pearls scattered between the worlds, lost to her forever.

Melia gasped. Her legs remained trapped. She found a plane with her palms. She pressed down as her torso shot up. The door wanted to close; it pressed against her hips. She imagined fluttering through an archway. Resistance scraped her thighs, her knees, her shins.

When it slammed her toes, she screamed.

Melia shot to the Nyssalei's surface. "Tatou!" she spluttered.

The pixie appeared from the long weeds, clustered at the river's edge.

"Thank the gods of Azyllai you're safe." Melia's eyes widened as she dragged herself to the shallows.

Flora stood on the bank, her brown eyes dark with concern. Gumf knelt with his hands in the mud.

"What are you looking for?" Melia asked him.

Gumf held up a muddy pearl.

Her heart skipped like a stone skimming the river's surface. "How many have you found?"

"Four."

Melia floated toward him on her belly, sifting the loose mud with her fingers. She gathered several stones, but no pearls came to her.

"Do you know how long we've been gone?" Tatou asked.

Melia crawled through the mud and grass on her hands and knees. She feared looking at her toes, afraid she'd find blood and stubs of bone.

"Most of the day." She winced as she wrung out her hair. She didn't know which hurt worse, her feet or the loss of one of Elendah's bracelets.

"What's wrong?" Flora asked.

"My toes. It feels like they've been cut off."

Gumf still knelt at the shoreline. "Let me have a look."

Melia flinched at the thought of the dwarf examining her toes and looked to Flora for help.

The spring faerie's thick eyebrows steepled, her hooked chin tilted in Gumf's direction. "Let him look, but I'm sure they're fine. No blood in the water."

Melia swirled her hands, letting her backside rest in the mud. She held out one of her feet but gazed downriver. Gumf's touch was curiously tender. When she half-turned her head to watch him from the corner of her eye, she couldn't help but think of her mother, and the story the dwarf told her about Pressina's first and only trip to Tyrannis.

Plagued by the crimes of her Albiana bloodline, and scorched by visions of the spring faeries burning, Pressina ran to the river. That was when her mother traveled to the mortal world. That was when she met Melia's father.

Gumf rolled Melia's toes and massaged her feet. The sharp pain melted away.

"What happened to your boots?" Flora asked.

Melia touched her hand to her head; the straw hat Alex gave her was gone. It must have fallen off when she crossed over, but how could she have forgotten the beautiful black boots Calista gave her?

"I left them ... I forgot ..."

"In Alex's car," Tatou said.

Melia nodded.

"Is Alex a mortal?" Flora asked.

"Uh-huh," Tatou answered.

"Hopefully, he won't come looking for you."

Melia glanced at her friend.

The spring faerie's gaze sharpened. "What?"

"He might," the pixie said.

Melia groaned. "He was so helpful. Is there some way we can make sure he doesn't?"

Flora shrugged. "Mortals are an unpredictable lot. Push all thoughts of him and those boots from your mind. It might help him forget about you." She threw her hands in the air. "But who knows? Everything is so out of kilter since Elendah died."

Gumf held out a hand. Five pearls were centered in his palm. "We'll put them on a string, something you can wear around your neck to keep them close to your heart."

Melia was speechless. Up until that moment, she'd disliked the

Veil's proprietor.

He wiped his hands in the grass and stood up. "I can send for a new pair of boots for you, too."

Melia crawled ashore. "Thank you." She tested her feet and toes. Everything seemed to be working. She crossed her arms over her chest and rubbed her forearms. After the heat of Texas, the air of Faerie was crisp—much cooler than it had been that morning.

Tatou landed on her shoulder. "We've been gone thirty-six days!"

Melia rubbed her eyes. Brown and crimson edged the leaves of the trees. This morning everything in the Balyudor was the deep green of late summer. "That's impossible."

"Apparently, nothing is impossible these days," Flora grumbled.

"Wait," Melia called out to the spring faerie. "We went to the mortal world this morning."

Tatou tugged on a strand of Melia's hair. "They think it happened while we were floating down the river. We were stranded in time and space. They've been coming out to the Nyssalei every day to look for us. Flora was afraid we weren't going to make it back. She almost came after us. The ancient doors are closing."

"The one we went through almost slammed in my face," Melia muttered.

Aldous' eyes sparkled behind his glasses. The pink of his chafed cheeks had healed. His heavier, but still thin frame, no longer made Melia think of sticks that would snap under the slightest pressure.

"Finally," he said, as Melia climbed the steps to the Veil's wraparound porch. Covered in a blanket, he lounged in a reclined seat made of lashed together tree limbs. He looked comfortable.

Melia crouched beside him. "I'm so glad Flora saved you."

He patted her hand. "So am I."

They smiled at the spring faerie standing on his other side.

"Did you ever find out what made you so ill?" Melia asked.

"It was Princess Lilliane," Flora said. "It had to be."

"My protective spell wasn't infallible," Aldous said.

Melia raised her eyebrows.

"The morning we spoke in the library, the day you met Ryder—"

She blushed.

"—the incense kept everyone out," the old elf continued, "but what I didn't realize at the time was that Princess Lilliane installed her spy inside the library the night before." He turned to Flora. "She's always questioned my allegiance to her and her mother."

"A rat," Gumf said. "The princess trained a rat. It overheard Aldous and the rest of you violating Uriel and Olivia's decrees, talking about Flora, and the mix of Albiana blood in you and your kin. None of you are safe in Illialei anymore."

"It was only when Basil returned a few days later," Aldous said, "sleek and well-fed, that I became suspicious. Everyone in the palace knew your mother came to the library to see me the night Plantine was kidnapped. It seems Lilliane was more curious than the rest about her visit.

"That evening—sometime after you and Tatou left—she came down to the library carrying a black lacquered box. I didn't think much of it at the time. I assumed she was hunting for a bedtime story and let her be. After all the commotion, I didn't want to make any more fuss. She lured Basil with a chunk of fresh fish and set her agent free. The next morning, when I activated the incense, her spy was already in place.

"It must have reported every word of our conversation to her."

"I almost tripped over a large white rat right before Sinjiin pounced on me," Melia's hand flew to her mouth. "I saw another one, the night Lilliane spelled us."

Aldous nodded. "The princess heir is clever. I began feeling ill after Elendah died. At first it was mild headaches, nausea. I thought it was my nerves from all the tension and worry. But when I heaved nothing but black bile, I knew it wasn't natural.

"I made use of my contacts in the palace, field faeries and brownies I've known for years. We pieced together the bleak news.

Lilliane has resumed her great-grandmother Uriel's study of black magic."

The world was spinning too fast. Melia gripped the side of Aldous' chair.

Tatou flitted from her shoulder. "What's wrong?"

"Are we in a dark moon phase?" Melia asked.

"No, the moon will be full tonight," Flora said.

"What is it?" Tatou asked.

Melia wanted to tell them about the vision, but Aldous' eyes were red with strain. He slid lower in his chair.

The spring faerie squeezed Aldous' shoulder. "He needs some rest. Let's go inside."

"Before you go, please, tell me about Gabriela," Aldous said. "I've often wonder how she's fared in the mortal world without her mother."

Melia told them about the fearful young girl they found at the cemetery. "She prays a lot."

Aldous adjusted his glasses. "From what I've studied, acts of supplication can be helpful to mortals; it opens them to the vital essence of Faerie, which they need to hope, dream, love, and imagine."

"But she hates Faerie," Melia said. "It terrifies her."

"I'm not sure that matters. The energy of Faerie feeds the hearts of all mortals who yearn for it. They may call it by another name, but that doesn't alter what nurtures their spirit. Prayer is an expression of deep inner hunger. To hear that young Gabriela has such habits is hopeful."

"I wonder if it would have been better for her to be raised in Illialei," Melia said.

"That choice wasn't given to her," Aldous said.

"No," Melia said, "it wasn't. The good news is that Umbra won't be able to reach her."

"That is a relief," the elf said.

"But we know she'll have a daughter. And she needs to be warned as well," Melia said.

"Recover from this trip first," Flora said.

Melia didn't argue. After her experience with the closing door, and losing so many days in the mortal world, she wasn't in a rush to return.

Tatou stroked Melia's hair as she traipsed behind Flora through the Veil's winding halls. The entire time, Melia's mind darted between thoughts of Lilliane, Sevondi, and Umbra.

Who was the greatest threat?

The spring faerie unlocked a door. "I'll have some tubs sent so you can bathe, followed with an early dinner."

Melia marched over to the inviting bed and dropped down onto it. She closed her eyes. The blanket beneath her was soft and thick. She slid her palms across it.

Tatou settled on her stomach like she used to when Melia lay in Illialei's tall grass. It was a small thing, but the familiar act comforted her.

By the time the dwarves arrived with buckets of steaming water, they'd both dozed off.

19. Flora's Plea

Tatou picked at the meal sent to their room while Melia paced. Her stomach rose and fell in uncomfortable waves. She was certain that if she ate anything, the food wouldn't stay down. A loud knock at the door made her jump. She cracked it open.

"Are you going to let me in?" Flora asked.

Melia stepped aside.

"We need to talk." The spring faerie nodded to Tatou. "You can stay."

When the pixie tried to respond, peppermint tea sprayed everywhere. "Oops." She held her hand over her mouth.

The spring faerie frowned.

Tatou wiped her face and mouth with a pixie-sized napkin. She put it down, the natural exuberance wiped from her face. Melia settled cross-legged on the bed. The pixie landed on her knee. Still and quiet, they waited to hear what the spring faerie came to tell them.

"Let me finish my piece before you say anything," Flora said to Melia.

"All right."

Flora swung her booted feet as she talked. It made her seem child-like, even though age wrinkled her face. "If you'd gotten trapped in the mortal world, the only person left in the enchanted world with mixed Albiana blood would have been Plantine. She's already tried to incarnate Umbra and failed. I believe Princess

Lilliane held you in the mortal world while she tried to close the door you used to pass over."

"But how do you know it was her? And how could she know which door we used? Or that we were even there?"

"After the success with her rat, Aldous fears the princess has black-magicked a legion of crows."

Melia chewed on a fingernail. She'd seen a crow.

"At the graveyard," Tatou said. "Remember? A flock flew away when the Model T's engine backfired."

"But were they in league with Lilliane?" Melia didn't want to believe it.

"Animals have always been able to cross the threshold between the worlds. Every living thing except the muannai—and grey faeries —can. What were you doing in a graveyard?" Flora asked.

"That's where she was. Gabbie—Gabriela."

"I'm sure the princess sees her half-sister as a threat to her ambition," the spring faerie said. "Much like her mother and grandmother have always viewed Pressina. It would make sense for the princess to keep an eye on Gabriela. If her birds spied the both of you there with her, there would have been more than enough time for one of them to report back to Lilliane. After your encounter in the library, I imagine she counted herself lucky when she received the news. I suspect she used black magic to throw you out of time while she tried to close the door."

"Does she have that much power?"

Flora's eyes darkened, or maybe it was the shadow in the room. "With Elendah dead, the power of the Albiana will increase unchecked."

"But how does she direct her will without the basin?"

The spring faerie worried her cheeks with her hand over her mouth. "Uriel didn't have the basin."

"It almost worked," Melia whispered. "She almost locked us out of the enchanted world." Her stomach rolled.

"Thank the gods of Azyllai she wasn't successful," the spring faerie said. "But now, we must discuss Umbra."

The half-faerie crossed her arms over her stomach. "What is there to discuss?"

"Nandana has always been prescient," Flora said.

Melia's knee bounced up and down. She slid her gaze to the right, where her friend straddled her other knee. "Did you tell her?"

"You almost died in the Calashai's dungeon. Flora and I talked about a lot of things during that time."

"I agree with Nandana," Flora said, "that you should incarnate Umbra."

Melia's mind spun round and round. She tried not to dwell on the mental games Umbra played with her in the past. She tried not to imagine what it would be like to have that massive dark consciousness—not just groping for her through the planes of existence—but inside her body. She couldn't suck enough air into her lungs.

"Melia!" Tatou leapt from her knee and patted her cheek. "Just the thought of it is too much for her, Flora. Maybe we shouldn't discuss this now."

The spring faerie leaned forward, her elbows on her knees, her boots finally still. "We must discuss it now."

Melia fell back onto the bed and stared at the ceiling. Tatou darted back and forth across her field of vision. She couldn't believe Flora would ask her to incarnate Umbra.

"I'll help you," Flora said. "So will Tatou. And Ryder and Sinjiin. We won't let you do it alone."

Angry fireworks exploded in Melia's body even as she forced her face into a rigid emotionless mask. "I won't listen to this."

"You must." Flora stood by the bed. "Princess Lilliane will only grow more powerful. Uriel destroyed my people. Who will Lilliane destroy? With Elendah dead, there's no one to control her. You could stop her."

Melia's left leg jittered. Gruesome scenes from her nightmares filled her head. "Who will I destroy?"

"I'll train you," Flora said.

"What good will training do?"

"We all have access to energy. You keep yours buried. Your visions are violent because you reject your power, but if you were to embrace it—"

"Do you know what is in me?" Melia pushed herself up. Each minute movement required effort. Her body felt like it was stuffed with rocks. "Murder, blood, destruction. Wastelands. Is that what you want me to usher into the enchanted world? Death and nothingness?" She reached for Flora's hand and squeezed the blood from it. "Even the flowers die in my visions."

"It's good you're afraid. If you weren't, I wouldn't even consider helping you."

Melia dropped the spring faerie's hand. "You're not listening to me."

The twitches that preceded Melia's change were upon her. She shoved herself off the bed and backed away. There was nowhere to conceal herself. Tatou and Flora watched her body reshape with feathers and talons. When it was done, Melia beat the air with her wings.

"I've been observing you," Flora said.

"Like a spy?" Melia cawed.

"Like someone who understands the Whole is in grave peril. Whatever steps are taken next will determine the future, not just for those alive today, but also for generations yet to be born. The most important decision of all will be who incarnates Umbra."

"Ryder has studied Umbra for years—in Idonne with those priests," Melia said. "He knows more about Umbra than anyone, and he doesn't believe Umbra should incarnate. He thinks it's too dangerous. He thinks the incarnation will destroy the vessel. Is that what you want, Flora? To destroy me because I have Albiana blood?"

Flora's face remained soft. Patience glowed from her warm brown eyes. Like Elendah's eyes. The grey faerie's death had affected

Flora, too. It had made her more noble or brave or something.

"I'm sorry," Melia chirped. "But what if you're wrong?"

"If it were only me, the possibility of my being wrong would be great. But I'm not the only one. Nandana believed you're the right one. So did Elendah. And I've had long talks with Sinjiin on the subject. He sees the wisdom in it, too."

Melia craned her head from side to side. "How can you begin to believe I can handle it?"

Flora sat back down as she ticked off the qualities that made Melia the best candidate for Umbra's vessel of incarnation: Her lineage from both sides, her strong mind and will, the innocence of her heart.

The half-faerie hardly listened to the meager list.

"Now that Elendah no longer sits on the Calashai's throne, Lilliane will grow stronger. You will too. When you learn to harness your emotions," Flora said, "to channel them with your mind and body, then you can direct your anger, instead of pretending you aren't mad when you're really furious."

Melia clamped her beak. How many times had she stalked away from her sisters seething in silence when they teased her or lied about her?

"As I said—"

Apparently, Flora was going to keep on until Melia agreed.

"—druids have a deep connection to the natural world; that's why your heart breaks to see it laid waste in your visions. With a legacy of both druid and Albiana blood, you can become the leader called for in these times. One who has the power to heal the great wound that is Umbra."

The spring faerie spoke in the tongue of eagles. She'd done it once before, when she and Melia plotted against Gumf in the Balyudor. On Flora's tongue, the language of eagles sounded sacred and wise.

"Once you've mastered your emotions," the spring faerie continued, "you'll have a fighting chance to control the black cesspool of feeling that is Umbra's consciousness."

Melia shivered. Nandana. Elendah. Now, Flora, speaking in riddles about a future she couldn't conceive. All she'd ever wanted was to have wings and fly.

And to stop her dark moon visions.

She did that.

When she dived from the cliffs.

Something sparked in Melia's heart. She brushed her beak with her feathers. When she discovered the truth about who she was, she stopped stuttering. She ruffled the feathers of her left wing. She survived arrows tipped with Umbra's poison—thanks to Flora—and the last time Umbra tried to intimidate her, he failed.

And if Bertille was right, her visions had already altered into something beyond Umbra's reach.

But saving the enchanted world, saving the Whole ... "What if I can't? What if you train me, I incarnate Umbra, and lose control?"

"That's the risk," Flora said.

Melia shook her feathers. "It's not one I'm willing to take."

"No one else will be able to stand up to Lilliane."

"Why can't you do it?" Melia asked. "You were a great warrior once. That's what everybody says."

"I'm too old. My body is too worn down to take on Umbra's consciousness."

"What about the dragonwitch?" Melia asked. "In the vision I had on the river, she was incarnating Umbra."

"What vision?" Flora and Tatou asked together.

"When we were floating down the river, I had ... a vision. It was like my dark moon visions except it wasn't ..."

"Are you certain Sevondi was incarnating Umbra?" Flora asked.

"She stood before the basin with the blade. We were at the Muudron Stone. Thousands of muannai watched."

"That cheat!" Flora banged the arm of her chair. "We need to go to Aldaine."

"Then you think my vision was real? Like a foretelling?"

"It was a foretelling if we don't get to Aldaine and stop her."

Flora nodded to Tatou. The pixie darted over to her friend. She reached into her pocket.

"If you try to sprinkle me with pixie dust," Melia said, "I'm going to fly out that window and never return."

"Now you sound like Plantine," Tatou said.

Melia winced. The last person she wanted to be compared to was her little sister, especially during a conversation about Umbra.

The pixie held out her hand. What rested in her palm wasn't glittery pixie dust, it was a number of dull blue seeds.

"Sapphire lily seeds," Tatou said. "I gathered them when we were at the lake, after Lilliane tried to kill us, just in case we needed them. Flora can plant them in Tyrannis. They'll create a shield for you. And Ryder ..."

Flora studied her hands clasped in her lap. "The priest won't allow you to destroy the Whole. His–" She swallowed. "If you reciprocate his feelings for you–and open yourself to them–love will always guide you in the right direction, as long as you listen to your heart."

"With Flora's training," Tatou said, "a field of sapphire lilies, and Ryder's love, you'll be invincible. You'll be able to incarnate Umbra and defeat Lilliane."

Melia wished she shared her friend's confidence. "You make it sound so easy."

"Don't ever think it will be easy," Flora said. "It will be the hardest thing you ever do. Maybe the hardest thing anyone alive has ever attempted. But if you succeed–"

"A new world, and I'm the queen," Melia said.

Flora nodded.

"I don't want to be a queen."

"That's why you'll make a good one."

Melia hopped from foot to foot.

"Rest tonight. Think about what we've discussed," Flora said. "In the morning, we'll leave for Aldaine. From what you've told me, we've been gone far too long."

"What about Gabriela's daughter?"

"After we straighten out Sevondi, you'll need to warn Lola."

20. The Dragon's Keep

Brutal wind whipped Melia's hair. Tatou's comforting weight disappeared from her shoulder. Melia strained to find her friend in the confusing gale, but Flora and Aldous on either side of her held her hands tight, restricting her movement. A sharp yank of her hair pulled her head back. She hoped it was the pixie.

Her feet—in a new pair of boots Gumf mysteriously produced that morning (she imagined a room stocked to the ceiling with a surplus) —jammed hard against the ground. The impact forced her to her knees. Her torso smashed forward, and she ate a mouthful of dirt as the heels of her hands sank into damp earth.

Tatou crashed into her head and moaned.

"Are you all right?" Melia asked.

"I don't think anything's broken," the pixie said, "but I don't want to do that again anytime soon."

"It's getting worse," Melia said. "It was bad when Flora and I traveled to the Veil, but not this bad."

Aldous, glasses askew, lay flat on his back a few feet away. Flora crawled toward him. The Tasimas rolled between them.

The old elf wiggled his fingers. He straightened his glasses. Flora helped him sit up. "My, my, what an adventure." His sense of wonder was contagious.

Flora pulled the old pillowcase from her apron and held it over the yellow diamond.

After Melia dusted herself off, she stood up and helped Aldous rise. They'd landed within the perimeter of the old courtyard, but the partial stone wall, the only structural remains after the Calashai fell, was gone. Where the stone fortress once seemed to flower from rock, a new construction designed from wood and stone and glass sprang from the mountainside.

Stunned by the transformation, Melia stumbled toward it. Columns twice the height of any muannai formed an enormous semicircle. Beyond these stone sentinels, the shout of laborers and ring of hammers sounded. Muannai worked on their hands and knees, laying polished wood tiles in the floor of a moon-shaped dais. Past the entryway, a wall of red-orange stone dug into the mountainside and climbed to its peak. Windows, balconies, and battlements laced the new stronghold's exterior.

"It's incredible," Tatou whispered.

"Sevondi will be the regent," Melia said.

"If she keeps her bargain with Flora."

"If she incarnates Umbra, how will Flora stop her from claiming the throne?"

"Don't underestimate the spring faerie," Tatou said.

The scene from Melia's vision flashed through her mind. "If the muannai support Sevondi, what does she have to lose by seeking more power? Flora is clever, but I don't see how she can sway the muannai sentiment against Sevondi."

"Don't underestimate yourself, either," Tatou said.

"You should have seen the dragon Sevondi called forth at the Muudron Stone. It was as big as a ship. And even when I realized it wasn't real, I could feel the heat rolling off the flames pouring from its snout."

"You sound like a fan."

"Maybe I am." Whenever Melia remembered the dragon, her heart throbbed with a fierce energy that enlivened her entire being. As she tiptoed around the workmen, careful to not interrupt their work, she realized she ached to see the majestic beast again—almost as much as she wished to find Ryder. Where was he?

Sinjiin nuzzled her hand. A grin spread across Melia's face. She'd missed the enormous feline. He stretched out his forepaws and pressed his belly flat against the ground. The tiger wanted her to ride on his back. Maybe he'd take her to Ryder.

She swung her leg high and across his girth. Tatou settled in front of her, clinging to the scruff of the large cat's neck. He circled to pad back in the direction from whence they'd come.

As soon as he passed the stone columns, the tiger picked up speed. Soon, he raced along the open grass along the promontory overlooking the Great White Sea. Melia felt her spirit ease as he raced the gulls.

The tiger panted and slowed to walk toward the line of bay trees. When he reached Flora's tent, he flattened against the ground. Melia slid off. Maybe Ryder was inside. The tiger pushed his muzzle against the flap which served as the door. When it gave way, he disappeared inside.

Melia bent down to pull the loose canvas aside. She got a glimpse of Flora's boots and the mage's black satin slippers. He'd shifted; he must have something to tell them.

She scooted in after him. Tatou flew in behind her. Aldous sat on a short stool. Flora stood beside him. Sinjiin sat on the ground. No Ryder. Melia's heart drooped as she settled next to the mage. Tatou flitted among the bundles of dried herbs hanging above them.

"Where is he?" Melia asked.

"I'll take you to him after we talk," Sinjiin said.

The mage's words calmed her fears—that Ryder left Faerie without saying goodbye. That he wouldn't talk to her. That something awful had happened to him while she floated down a river in oblivion.

She couldn't wait to see him.

"Moog—one of the twins who works for the dragonwitch—brings me a thick, fresh steak every day," Sinjiin said. "He watches me like a hawk. If I had to guess, he's hoping I'll lead him to the sword and basin."

"Where are they?" Flora asked.

Melia found her mind wandering. Right now, she could care less about Umbra, or the battle between Dark and Light. She wanted to see Ryder's forest green eyes and experience that feeling that nothing bad could ever happen as long as he was by her side.

"They're safe," Sinjiin said.

"So you've hidden the basin from me, again?" Flora said.

"You've been gone a long time. Ryder and I are out all day. That stack of blankets isn't the most ingenious hiding place."

"We were waiting for those two." The spring faerie indicated Melia and Tatou. "Lilliane managed to throw them out of time. It seems the princess is becoming more adept at black magic. We must solidify our alliance with Sevondi before it's too late, before she betrays us. Melia had a vision of her attempting the incarnation."

Hearing her name broke through Melia's daydream. An uncomfortable feeling gathered in her chest. Flora treated her vision like it was fact. How did she know it could be relied on?

"We may have some time, yet," Sinjiin said. "Ryder has found nothing in the book to release the basin and the sword from the founding stone, and Sevondi plans to leave for the valley in two days. All the muannai are anticipating her carnivale. She won't alter the schedule of her appearances and risk disappointing them. What about you?" Sinjiin addressed Melia. "When will your training begin?"

"I haven't agreed to anything."

Sinjiin's dark eyes penetrated her fear. "You must train, whether or not you incarnate Umbra. Or is being vanquished by Lilliane Albiana what you wish for yourself and the entire enchanted world?"

Melia gasped. He'd never spoken to her so sharply before. "Don't lay the future of the Whole at my feet!"

"The battle between Dark and Light is upon us. You must choose a side and fight. You can't run away. There is nowhere to run."

Sinjiin's ferocious spirit roared at her. In comparison, Flora's speech the night before was gentle. Tatou landed on her shoulder and smoothed her hair.

"The side that controls Umbra will win," the mage said.

Melia swallowed hard. "I don't deny what you're saying is true, but I won't discuss this any further until I see Ryder."

Sinjiin popped up in a single motion. "I'll take you to him. But we'll finish this conversation."

She exhaled slowly. Tatou whispered in her ear, "I'll wait here with Flora and Aldous."

The Dragon's Keep design was both sturdy and delicate. The foundation and columns of stone gave the sense of a fortress, while intricate accents of wood and tile made the walls and ceilings works of art.

Sinjiin passed through a number of breathtaking gardens, each one celebrating a distinct plant or flower.

Melia would never forget the enchantment that lived in Elendah's Calashai, but she had to admit, the Dragon's Keep was impressive. And also more to her taste than the Cathedral Palace in Illialei. She could almost imagine herself making a home in one of its spacious rooms—if the threat of war and Umbra's incarnation wasn't hanging over her head.

Sinjiin's outburst rang in her mind. He'd made the dangers and her choices clear. She could train to win, or cede control of Faerie—and perhaps the enchanted world—to Lilliane who was proving to be as ruthless as Uriel.

Melia remembered her thirteenth birthday. She and Plantine swam in the Nyssalei. Tatou lounged on the riverbank. They laughed and splashed together. Out of nowhere, a long pole with a tightly woven net swooped down on the pixie, trapping her. Lilliane peeked from behind a tree, a nasty smirk on her face. She threatened to take Tatou home and roast her for dinner.

Melia could still hear the princess say: "Such a sweet and tasty treat."

Tatou had been in tears.

That night, Melia saw her first dark moon vision. She'd always blamed them on her father's psychic trespass, but that night, an urge to kill Lilliane seized her. Really kill her, even though Melia knew the desire was wrong.

That's when she slammed the door of her heart shut. That's why she never allowed herself get too angry. If she didn't walk away, stomp away, disappear, she might destroy the world.

What if she could tap into that reservoir of emotion and use it to protect the people, the creatures, the world she loved? She needed to find out for herself. She needed to train.

As Sinjiin padded though the unfinished halls of the Dragon's Keep, many of the muannai waved at them. Some paused in their work to stare at Melia riding on the tiger's back. She searched for Ryder's familiar chocolate hair and broad shoulders.

She must talk with him about all this.

The tiger entered a stairwell, white marble inlaid every riser. On each landing, windows opened to the horizon; an ocean breeze chilled the air.

Sinjiin climbed to the highest floor.

21. The Tower of Light

Ryder huddled with Yrrick over plans spread out on a table between them. Two of the muannaye's fingers traced the diagram, following the tower's supporting beams. Four towers protected the stronghold of Calashai, but Yrrick designed the Dragon's Keep with only one. A broad spiraling staircase served as much for reinforcement as to climb to the observation deck and steeple, which rose higher than the mountain's peak.

Ryder studied the design's structure for any weakness. He detected none. The single tower, a tower of light, would be the Dragon's Keep's crowning achievement.

The young priest felt torn. He'd worked side by side with Yrrick from the day the Calashai fell. Since his argument with Sinjiin over whether or not Melia should incarnate Umbra, he spent more time with the muannaye than the mage. They'd become friends, and friends were a scarce thing in Ryder's life.

The muannaye was talented and disciplined. Watching how he handled work crews, Ryder absorbed a style of leadership by inspiration rather than domination. Yrrick's passion and devotion to the keep motivated everyone who worked alongside him. What had been wrought in the last two moon cycles was a miracle. No, it wasn't the Calashai; the grey faerie's stronghold was irreplaceable. But Yrrick had created something new and dazzling to honor Elendah's memory and move his people forward.

Ryder wanted to help him complete the vision, but if he didn't get the basin and the sword out of the Realm of Faerie soon, Melia might return, convinced she should incarnate Umbra.

He wiped the sweat from his brow before it dripped onto Yrrick's meticulous drawing. If Embril's potion didn't work, or his theory about strong emotion was wrong, he would die trying to free Ormrun and Koldis from the founding stone.

Yrrick stopped speaking. The muannaye gazed toward the arches that would soon serve as an entrance to a private hall for the Dragon's Keep's regent.

Ryder thought he must be dreaming. He rubbed his eyes.

She rode the tiger's back. Sinjiin was bringing her to him.

He went to greet them.

She looked thinner, paler, and there were dark smudges beneath her eyes. Sinjiin flattened himself against the ground. Ryder reached out with his hand to hold hers, and though it wasn't necessary, to help her balance.

Her hand felt cool and small in his. She didn't pull it away, and he didn't let go.

Sinjiin and Yrrick left them alone in the cavernous hall.

Ryder searched her deep blue eyes. He tugged her hand; she didn't resist. He pulled her into him. When he folded his arms around her, she let her head fall against his chest. His chin rested in her hair. She smelled like a meadow of wildflowers. Her face and cheek were soft against his neck and collarbone. If he could stop time, this would be the moment.

"I thought you weren't coming back," he said.

"I almost didn't."

"I'm sorry—"

She pulled away and held a finger to his lip. That gentle touch reached the shell encasing his heart and melted it. "So much has happened since Elendah died," she said. "I don't even know where to begin, but first let me explain why I keep pushing you away."

He held her with his eyes and couldn't let go.

She reached for his hand. Together they walked toward the only piece of furniture in the hall besides the table blanketed with Yrrick's parchments—a plain wooden bench. Her steps didn't ring out and echo like his or the muannaye's; they were a whisper, caressing the dust-coated floor.

She sat first. He didn't let go of her hand as he sat down beside her.

"I don't know where to begin," she said.

"Anywhere."

Her lips parted and the sides of her eyes crinkled.

He missed that smile.

"My life used to be very slow." A small laugh escaped her. She blushed. "Tatou and I, we used to spend our days lounging in the grass, making big plans. When we were more adventurous, we might go for a swim in the river, climb High Hill, or sneak into the fields and spy on the brownies rolling ball. When we were really bored, we might head down to Southend and watch the ships sailing into the harbor. But nothing ever really happened. And I was so afraid nothing ever would.

"And then, when I turned thirteen, I started having these visions. I put together that they were connected to my father, but I forgot about this horrid joke Princess Lilliane played on my birthday. Now, I'm sure it's all connected. Back then, I didn't know about Umbra. I thought it was all me, and I became afraid whenever I felt angry or hurt.

"The thing is I became really good at suppressing my emotions, even the good ones. I never realized how flat my life had become ..." She glanced down at their entwined hands.

"And then one day, I heard two elves gossiping about my mother and father, saying my father was going to incarnate Umbra." She tossed her head. "From there, everything sped up, and things just keep moving faster and faster." She told him everything that happened since the night the Calashai fell: Finding the Huron knight at the tree house, escaping Lilliane in the palace library, traveling to the mortal world to find Gabriela, and getting trapped in time. She skimmed over the day they spent with Bertille and Calista.

"I had no idea," he said.

She pulled her lower lip. "I'm sorry to go on and on like this, but I need you to understand why it's hard for me to be close to you."

"I've been losing faith." Ryder confessed, as he squeezed her hand. "But the internal battle you're fighting makes sense."

"Even if nothing else was happening in my life, I still wouldn't necessarily be able to trust what's happening between us. I've never felt this way before."

Ryder's hand shook. He steadied it. "I've never had feelings like these for anyone before, either. But I don't question them." He couldn't believe he was going to have to leave her to keep her safe. He stared at her long, slim fingers wrapped in his, darkened by the sun and roughened by physical labor.

He struggled for the right words, an explanation that might help her trust him while he was gone. "You have to know how much I care for you, and how compelled I feel to protect you. I always will. I know Flora and Sinjiin believe that by incarnating Umbra, you could heal some cosmic wound, but I have to do what I know is right. I'm going to carry through with the promise I made you the first day we met."

"I've never had the chance to tell you something," she said.

He could feel her eyes on him, but he couldn't meet her gaze. He was going to have to lie to her—after she'd finally given him her trust.

Once again he thought about how much he hated the Realm of Faerie. How since he'd stepped foot on its soil, everything had gone wrong. "What?" he choked out.

"I saw you," she whispered. "I've never told you this, but I saw you before you ever came to Faerie."

"Where?"

"After Nandana marked my forehead, you appeared in my visions. You," her voice quavered, "were always calling out to me, trying to

176

save me. I could never reach you."

He dropped her hand and drew both of his down the length of his face. She was making what he needed to do impossible.

"Are you angry with me?" she asked.

"No. I just–I had no idea."

She searched his face. "It must mean something–the mark, you appearing in my visions, you answering the call. When I saw you in the library, I couldn't believe you were real."

Ryder folded his arms over his chest to stop himself from touching her. He remembered that morning in the library. It seemed like ages ago. He thought her reaction had been due to Sinjiin leaping upon her. But now, the way she looked at him, like she saw a ghost made sense.

"It seems there's some deep inner connection between us ..." her voice trailed away.

It would take more than one moon cycle to reach the Isle of Minnanon. Who knew how many would pass before he returned to Faerie? His head hammered with the need to say the right thing.

She tightened her grip on his hand. The sensation of her skin against his weakened his resolve.

"But things are starting to make sense," she continued. "Flora thinks there's some kind of power inside me."

Ryder's throat constricted.

"She thinks if I were trained, I could control it, that I could ... that I should incarnate Umbra. I need to know what you think."

He faced her. The impact of her earnest gaze tore at him. "If anyone could wring some good out of Umbra, I have no doubt it would be you. But I can't let you take that risk. I won't."

"Then you think Flora and Sinjiin are wrong?"

"I do."

"Their age and wisdom mean nothing to you?" she squeaked.

"They'll make you a puppet. I can't fault Flora's cause–no one can–but I won't let her destroy you in her blind quest for vengeance."

"But what if I can become more than I am?"

Ryder pulled away from her. "Now you sound like your sister."

Melia stood up. "How dare you! I've never asked for any of this, or sought it out. Since I was a child, this has been thrust upon me. I only discuss it with you now because Flora told me that if I opened my—"

"So all this is coming from the spring faerie?"

Melia dropped his hand and pressed hers against her thighs. Her cheeks were no longer so pale. "Have you heard nothing I've told you? Lilliane has become too powerful. What will happen when she surpasses her great-grandmother? Uriel killed an entire race. Would you stand by and do nothing to stop her?"

Ryder rose from the bench. He reached for Melia's shoulders. He had to make her understand the danger was too great. "Today, your inner beauty surpasses the beauty of your face. But if you incarnate Umbra, he'll fill you with hate and bitterness; thoughts of murder and vengeance will consume you. You won't want love, or any sweet thing that exists. You'll only want blood, and lots of it."

Melia threw his hands from her. "You're right. I've seen that path. My dark moon visions have warned me of what I could become, but I won't ever let that happen."

"How will you stop it?"

"I thought you might help me, but I see you're not the type to stand by someone!"

He reached for her hands.

She pulled hers up, high and away beyond his reach. "Nych! All your pretty words about my beauty are just that—words." She looked around the wide space they stood in. "I'm sorry I interrupted your work. I won't do it again." She spun around and stalked beyond his reach.

He sagged on the bench.

Every day, one of the supply ships anchored beyond the cove sailed. He needed to be on one with the sword and basin as soon as possible.

The freshwater stream he scouted after he returned from the apothecary wasn't far. He'd return there tonight and mix Embril's potion at dawn.

22. Leading the Dark

Melia headed for the stairs. Fire filled her stomach. It licked her throat and charred her heart.

What had possessed her? Asking him for help. What help had he ever given her?

He practically handed Koldis to the dragonwitch at the Muudron Stone, and when they reached the Calashai, all he managed to do was get himself thrown in the dungeons. He'd done nothing to help her stop Plantine's wedding, and now the grey faerie was dead and war loomed.

What had made her think he might stand by her? Or believe in her? Puh. That's what she thought of the priest and his empty words. Ryder only wanted glory for himself.

She pumped down the stairs with a quick rhythm, the dull thud of her boots marking every step.

Flora told Melia the truth about her Albiana blood when no one else dared to. She trusted the spring faerie. Sinjiin was a powerful mage. He wouldn't encourage her to incarnate Umbra if he believed she would fail.

When Nandana told them she believed Melia would incarnate Umbra, she also told them she gave Melia the mark to call Ryder—to help her! If he couldn't believe in her, how could he help her believe in herself! He couldn't!

She forced her legs to move faster.

Even Tatou gathered seeds from the sapphire lily when they'd been at Lake Vivientiana. Everyone believed in her except Ryder!

She'd been foolish to confide in him. Foolish to think he might love her. She wouldn't make that mistake again!

Tears stung the corner of her eyes. She let them flow, salty drops rolling down her cheeks. They splattered the stairs.

Bertille would be proud.

Sinjiin caught up with her. The tiger blocked her passage. When she tried to circle round him, he penned her in.

"Fine, you can take me back to Flora's tent."

He dipped his head and crouched. She swung her leg across his back. When she cinched his girth with both her legs, he shot down the stairwell.

Melia leaned forward, connecting with the strength in his powerful feline body.

"Ryder won't help me," Melia said.

Flora paced with her hands clasped behind her back. Back and forth, she crossed the width of the tent. Her plaid kerchief was back in place, covering her head. "Keeps the wind from making a nest of my hair."

Although he looked uncomfortable, Aldous sat attentively on a stool. Sinjiin, spread on a rug, didn't bother to shift into his mage form. As soon as the big cat settled, Tatou stretched out to recline upon his back.

Melia rolled a pearl on her only bracelet with a thumb and forefinger. It irked her she left the necklace Gumf had strung with the beads he found in the river at the Veil. In her rush to return to Aldaine, all she'd thought about was seeing Ryder. "I've made up my mind."

The spring faerie stopped. She tugged at the knot beneath her chin.

"I want you to train me. I want to learn everything I can about this power inside me. I don't want to run from it anymore."

Flora's eyes sparked.

"What I'm not sure about is Umbra. Teach me whatever I need to know, then I'll decide."

"We have no time to waste," Flora said. "We'll start this afternoon." She dug in her apron pocket and flung something at the half-faerie.

Melia whipped up a hand. The thing hit her palm with a pinch as she closed her fingers around it—the silver ring with a blue stone Elendah gave Flora long ago. She tossed it back to the spring faerie.

"Excellent reflexes," Flora said. "I'll focus on your physical training." She reached up and squeezed Melia's upper arm. "You have some strength, but you'll need more. I want you proficient with a sword, a dagger, a bow and arrow, maybe even a staff and a mace."

Melia's heart kicked with excitement, Ryder's rebuff forgotten. "You're going to teach me to how to fight?"

"You can't lead an army if you don't know how to fight yourself."

Melia released a nervous laugh. "An army?"

Flora jabbed a finger at the half-faerie. "Forces are aligning, the light and the dark. You'll be leading the dark."

A breath of panic caught in Melia's throat. "The dark?"

"The Albiana are Daughters of Light," Aldous said. "Light is most often assumed to be the side of the good, the benevolent, perhaps even the holy. But when the light burns too bright, when it blinds and sears, then it becomes the handmaiden of pain and evil. The dark can provide nourishment and shelter—like a mother's womb. Never forget great things are birthed in the dark."

"Umbra is dark," Melia whispered.

"And you have Albiana blood," Aldous said. "Once you've learned to balance dark and light within you, then you can lead others to achieve that same harmony. The Albiana are too light and Umbra is too dark. By bringing them into union, the necessary integration will be achieved, and the Whole will balance."

Arguments filled Melia's head. "I don't know."

"We won't be fighting against light," Aldous said. "We'll be fighting against a light that shuns the dark and seeks to abolish it.

Since that's something that can never be achieved, it will lead to unending war. War for eternity. It must be stopped before the Whole is destroyed. The Albiana crimes fester beneath the surface, on planes we can't see."

Melia chewed a fingernail. "Are you talking about the Parallel of Shadows?"

"The Shadows is one of those planes."

"Nandana told me she felt Ryder's presence in the Parallel of Shadows. How is that possible?"

"Desire vibrates. The more intense the desire, the stronger the vibration. You were determined to stop your father's incarnation of Umbra. You were right to stop him. The effort would have killed him—"

"But we killed him, me and my sisters."

"The point he's trying to make," Flora said, "is that the Albianas' determination to bury their crimes also echo in the Shadows. As does my need for justice for my people. Resonance draws us together."

"The seeds of the war we're preparing to fight," Aldous said, "exist on those other planes. While Flora teaches you to prepare for physical battle," he said, "I'll help you prepare for the one within your heart."

Melia dropped to her knees. "My heart?"

"Yes," the wood elf said. "You'll be called on to make many decisions, and you'll have to know which way to go, and who to trust. First and foremost that will be yourself. I'll teach you how to meditate in a way that will strengthen your soul flame." Aldous pointed to the tiger. "Sinjiin will teach you how to shift beyond the bounds of your mother's curse."

"You mean shift at will?" Melia asked.

"Yes."

Melia couldn't repress the grin spreading across her face. "I can do that?"

"We think you can," Flora said.

Tatou fluttered over to Melia's shoulder. "And I'll help you strengthen your connection to nature. In the end, it may be your druid blood that provides your most stable anchor. What you feel, deep inside, for the land, and everything that's natural in the world, may be what saves the Whole."

"And I don't have to decide about Umbra?" Melia asked.

"We have a bit of time yet," Flora said.

"What about warning Gabriela's daughter? When will I do that?"

"When you're better equipped to return to the mortal world," Flora said.

Melia jogged behind Sinjiin. The tiger loped toward the cliffs and the stone stairwell that led to the inlet below. Flora rode on his back. Melia's first task was to keep up with them. She hardly broke a sweat. All her life she'd raced through fields and meadows; her legs were strong.

It was fall in Tyrannis. The sun Melia caught glimpses of in late summer was gone, veiled by thick layers of clouds.

When the wind from the sea hit her, the cold was bitter. The lashing air whipped her hair and beat her cheeks. She leaned into it and wished Ryder hadn't let her walk away from him; that he was training by her side. Channeling her disappointment into her legs and feet, she burst forward and almost caught up with the tiger.

Sheets of wind pushed against her.

Sinjiin reached the stairwell and disappeared from sight, like he fell over the edge of the cliff.

When she stood at the top of the stairs, he was halfway down. Melia pounded down after him.

By the time she reached the sand, she gasped for breath and cool lines of sweat framed her face. She forced herself to keep running.

Sinjiin and Flora waited for her in the distance.

She reached them with a stitch in her side and a cramp in her foot.

The spring faerie pointed to the water. "Swim."

Low tide rippled in. Melia dragged her fingers in the shallow surge. "The water is freezing."

"Swim," Flora repeated.

"In my clothes?"

"I don't care if you swim in your clothes or take them all off. Just get in the water, swim out to that rock"—the spring faerie pointed to an outcrop of stone Melia had to shade her eyes to see in the hazy glare—"and come back."

Melia dropped her butt in the wet sand and glared at Flora as she yanked off her boots. She tossed them behind her, pulled off her black pants, and stood up.

The skin of her feet and toes shrank around her bones in defense against the icy sea. Goose bumps speckled her calves and thighs. She waded in seething silence until the frigid waves sloshed around her hips. When she plunged in headfirst, and the cold water stung the rest of her body, she tried not to think about her father drowning in Ashleam Bay.

The undertow sucked at her tired limbs, and as the waves grew larger, they rolled over her head and spun her in their wake. She fought the endless swell. Every time she tread water to sight her goal, she took in huge mouthfuls of salty water. Her lips chafed and cracked. The rock shelf never seemed to get closer.

She kept swimming.

She kept swimming.

She kept swimming.

The rock shelf seemed farther away than when she started.

She kept swimming.

When Sinjiin's furry bulk swam beneath her and lifted her from the water, she spit up seawater and clung to his neck. She wanted to protest; she'd almost reached the ledge, but she didn't have the energy to speak.

The tiger delivered her, bedraggled and dejected, to Flora on the beach. All Melia saw were the spring faerie's tiny boots.

They needed a good polish.

Melia woke in the tent on a pile of blankets.

She could tell by the length of the shadows and the shape of her arm the sun hadn't set. Flora, Aldous, and Tatou chattered a few feet away.

Everyone stopped talking when she pushed herself to sitting.

She raised a hand. "I'm fine." Then she slouched back across the blankets. If she could sleep for five years, it wouldn't be long enough.

Tatou landed next to her hand. "Flora said you did great. Better than she expected."

Melia closed her eyes. "I didn't reach the rock."

"But you didn't give up."

Her friend's voice was so cheerful, Melia had to restrain herself from squashing her. "So it was a test."

"You passed."

Melia rolled over. "I hate tests.

"Can you smell the stew?" Tatou asked. "They're cooking an enormous pot of it in the courtyard. Every night the muannai eat together after they've finished their work. Flora says it's almost ready."

"I think I'll settle for something warm and furry after I shift."

"Eww," Tatou said.

"Honestly, I'm too exhausted to eat right now."

The twitches in her arms and legs jerked Melia awake.

Around her, the tent was dark and quiet. Everyone was gone. They'd left her alone to sleep. Instead of being relieved, she felt sad. She didn't like being alone as much as she used to.

When her change was complete, she hopped outside.

The clouds that covered the sun during the day parted. Faerie's two moons were almost full. Her stomach asked for food. Drained by the day's exertions, a long flight wasn't in her. She'd hunt before seeking a nest.

Launching into the night, she found her second wind. Flight

always rejuvenated her. Maybe after dinner she'd search for Ryder. All afternoon something nagged at her. Until he'd said no, Melia expected him to help her. His refusal was a blow to her confidence as well as her heart.

Replaying the conversation in her mind, she recalled his restraint. What had he held back?

She flew over the crowd of muannai gathered around fires across the lawn. Although her friends were among them, Melia didn't stop. Who knew what torture the spring faerie planned for her tomorrow?

The best hunting ground would be the wooded area south of the keep.

The sound of running water drew her. It was the perfect spot to catch something.

Soon she picked over the bones of a sizable and tasty meal. The pale red coloring of its flesh, and black spots traveling from its tail, were unusual, as was the fish's size. Snapping it from the water had proved challenging, but one was enough to satisfy her hunger.

The insects and night noises quieted. Someone walked through the woods with heavy steps. Moonlight sprinkled the river and trees. Melia abandoned what little remained of the tender pink flesh and concealed herself in shadow.

A dark shape appeared. Melia's heart beat faster.

Ryder knelt at the river and scooped water into a jar. He checked to make sure its seal was tight before he returned the container to a pack he wore on his back. He melted back into the woods.

Why would he come to a creek for water and not drink?

Melia followed him in stealth mode.

When he reached the keep, he didn't stop to eat or to speak to anyone. He strode with his head down, past the majestic columns and across the tiled patio. Melia doubted eagles frequented the building's interior. If he spotted her, it would be difficult to pretend she wasn't following him.

Seeing him ignited a desire to untangle what had become knotted between them. But what good would it do to find him tonight when he couldn't speak the tongue of eagles?

She flew toward the sea.

Tomorrow she would find him and try again.

23. Training Melia

"Every day you'll have four lessons," Flora said, "and there'll be no days off. You'll begin early with Tatou. She'll hand you off to Aldous. I'll have you in the afternoon. We'll continue with physical drills and weapons. The hour before dusk, you'll work with Sinjiin on shifting at will."

Melia tugged on a strand of her hair.

"Is there a problem?" Flora asked.

"I need to talk to Ryder again."

The spring faerie scratched the side of her kerchief. "Stay focused today and talk with him tonight."

Melia didn't remind her Ryder didn't speak the language of eagles. She doubted Flora cared. Tatou landed on Melia's shoulder.

Flora waved her gnarled fingers at the pair. "Off with the both of you."

Melia crawled out of the tent on hands and knees.

"What's bothering you?" Tatou asked, as soon as they were out of earshot.

"I keep going over my fight with Ryder. Something was off, but I can't pinpoint what it was."

"I'm sure he's worried about you."

"It's more than that. When he first saw me, he hugged me. I could feel how much he cares for me. Why won't he help me?" She didn't mention seeing him at the creek. Although his behavior was odd, she didn't want it to appear like she was spying on him. The pixie let things slip.

"Let's go down to the inlet," Tatou said.

The beach reminded Melia of another failed conversation with the priest. "Do we have to go there?"

"There's a lot of power to be drawn from the Great White Sea. Power you're going to need."

"Yesterday it wiped me out."

"That's why you need this lesson."

Melia grumbled the whole way down the stairs. "My legs are going to fall off."

The pixie hovered a short distance from the waterline. "I want you to sit down here. Cross your legs and keep your back straight."

Melia plopped down.

Tatou flitted behind her. "Sit up straight."

"I'm too tired."

"Do you think Lilliane worried about being too tired when she tried to suffocate us in the palace library?"

The half-faerie straightened her spine.

Her friend landed in the wet sand and crossed her arms. "Watch each wave come to you. Receive the energy it brings. Breathe it in, deep into your belly. Do that for as long as you can."

Melia didn't believe the Great White Sea could give her energy. Rather than refuse to try, she decided to follow her friend's instructions precisely and prove nothing would happen. At least sitting on the beach was an improvement over sitting in a Bryndale classroom.

The first wave, crested with white foam rolled toward her. It was a simple thing to synchronize her breathing. Inhale when the tide comes in. Exhale when the tide flows out. Repeat over and over and over until ...

My belly and the ocean are one. My mind stops spinning, and the fear that ripples through me settles like sand on the ocean floor.

The ancient rhythm of the ocean holds the pattern of my breath.

The salty air stings my nose and expands my lungs. Each exhale carries away something I thought was mine but never was.

Memories misshaped by guilt, regret, and shame dissolve.

My heart feels clean, yet nothing meaningful has been lost.

I can sit here forever.

Melia turned her head. Tatou sprang into focus.

"What happened?" the pixie asked.

"I feel like I belong here. Like I'm part of the Whole."

Her friend fluttered up and down. "Are you still tired?"

The soreness in Melia's shins and thighs was gone, as was the stiffness in her neck and shoulders. "It feels like I've slept an entire moon cycle."

"Just a few minutes," Tatou said.

Melia bounced up and stretched her arms to the sky. Every cell in her body was attuned to the crashing waves, the clouds sailing overhead, the seagulls diving for fish.

"If you incarnate Umbra," Tatou said, "you won't be able to rein in his energy on your own. You'll need to draw from the energy around you, the energy of the Whole. It's always available to us when we call it. When we don't, it's still there, just dormant. Water is the easiest element to draw from. The larger the body of water, the more energy you can pull from it."

"Why didn't you ever tell me this before?"

Tatou's eyebrows arched. "You didn't ask?"

When they reached the stone staircase, Melia raced up each riser, laughing.

Aldous waited outside the tent, leaning on a wooden staff.

Melia recognized Hermes' Wand.

"Ah. I see your eyes are shining," he said. "The lesson went well?"

"She's a natural," Tatou said.

"It's that druid blood," the old elf said.

Melia's friend pecked her on the cheek. "See you later."

"I thought we'd take a walk," Aldous said. "Away from all the bustle and noise of the construction."

Melia's insides hummed, anticipating what new thing she might learn next.

They entered the woods she hunted in the night before. Aldous brushed off the trunk of a fallen tree and sat. He motioned for Melia to do the same as he balanced the wand.

"What are you going to teach me?"

"Discernment. Seeing beyond what is visible."

"Will it be hard to learn?"

Aldous adjusted his glasses. "Not from what I've observed. You've made a good start without any lessons, but training will make you more adept. Less hit or miss. The thing is, although our hearts and minds are most effective when they're aligned, it doesn't take much to separate them. It's impossible to take decisive action when one is conflicted."

"You sound like you speak from experience," Melia said.

"I do."

"How do we start?"

"I'll have you choose some inner conflict, and we'll work through it." He pointed to the wand leaning against the tree trunk. "Hermes' Wand might be useful in that regard. Is there any particular problem weighing on your heart?"

"Besides whether or not I should incarnate Umbra?"

"Yes, beginning with something less consequential would be helpful."

Melia's thoughts returned to Ryder. "The fight I had yesterday—"

"With the young priest?"

"Yes."

"What about that is bothering you?"

"There's something he didn't tell me."

Aldous offered an encouraging nod.

"At first I thought he didn't want to help me incarnate Umbra because he doesn't believe in me. But the more I think about it, I'm sure he didn't tell me everything going on with him."

"And the conflict is?"

Melia exhaled. It was difficult to put into words. "Flora told me that love—" The word felt uncomfortable in her mouth, and Ryder had never told her he loved her. "You saw the mark on my forehead disappear the day I met him."

"I did."

The elf's decisiveness gave her some courage. Sometimes Melia thought she'd imagined the indigo spot. "It just seems that we care for one another, yet we push each other away. I don't see how Hermes' Wand can help me solve that conflict."

"What it can do is help you to be more honest with yourself, and from there, the next time you speak with Ryder, you can set aside the fears in your mind"—he tapped her forehead—"and speak from the truth in your heart. Would you like to give it a go?"

She wasn't sure that she did. Maybe that was the first conflict she needed to deal with. "If he doesn't have the same feelings for me, I don't want to share my feelings with him."

"That could be awkward."

Relief rushed through Melia's body. "Maybe to begin with, I could find out what he's keeping from me."

Aldous handed her the wand.

Her heart swelled as she took it from him. The last time she held the rod, it proved she never intended to kill her father.

"Do you believe Ryder is keeping something from you?"

"Yes." The rod remained dull.

"Would you like to know what it is?"

"Yes." A small dot of light became a line. Soon the entire wand glowed and lit every shadow in the woods around them. The light shocked her; it meant she'd lied. "I don't understand."

"It's common enough to fear the truth."

"You think that's what it is? I'm afraid of what he might tell me?"

"Let's try it with the wand. If you were to ask Ryder what secret he keeps from you, are you afraid of what his answer might be?"

Melia's heart raced. "Yes." The rod remained dull. "What does that mean?"

Aldous pushed his glasses up the bridge of his nose. "It means you should hold off having another conversation with him until you're prepared to hear the truth. Otherwise, you might have another fight. You might say things you'll regret. It will only make things more difficult to resolve."

"Did that happen between you and Flora?"

"Yes. Yes, it did. Many years ago."

"This is a harder lesson than the one Tatou gave me."

Aldous sighed. "I know it is."

✧ ✧ ✧

Flora tossed the dagger between her hands. "You do it like this." She gave the handle of the sharp blade to the half-faerie.

Melia tried to imitate Flora, but her wrists and hands were slower, less coordinated. The spring faerie was so much older than she was, it was embarrassing to appear so clumsy in front of her.

"You need to be comfortable with your weapon before you learn any offensive moves."

Melia continued to toss the short knife from one hand to the other.

"Don't think about what you're doing," Flora said. "Pay attention to how it feels."

Melia dropped the knife in the sand.

They'd returned to the inlet, this time without Sinjiin. Flora made the half-faerie carry her on her back. Several times they almost toppled from the steep steps. Melia hoped the spring faerie wouldn't make her do that every day.

When Melia dropped the dagger a second time, Flora swooped to retrieve it, planted her boot, and sent the knife hurtling toward a piece of driftwood. The blade thunked the center of the target.

Melia marveled at the spring faerie's skill.

"One day you'll be able to do that too," Flora said.

She made Melia swim again, but this time her challenge was following the length of the inlet, parallel to the beach.

It wasn't any easier.

Before Melia finished, Sinjiin showed up, racing along the sand beside her. He didn't have to drag her from the water, but he carried her and Flora up the stone stairs.

The half-faerie was thrilled Flora didn't make her run behind them.

Sinjiin sat across from Melia in the tent. "Someday your mother's curse will be lifted," he said. "I know it will break your heart if you can never fly again. I don't think anyone should be asked to make such a hard choice to experience love. Especially, not someone who's so young and already carries so many burdens." He clapped his hands. "So, I've decided. I'll share this ability with you."

Melia's breaths came rapid and shallow. To be able to shift at will —it might not be faerie wings, but it was the next best thing.

"Are you ready?"

"Of course."

The mage pulled something from behind his back. A plate with meat on it. The leg of a large chicken. He set it down in front of her. "Roasted eagle." His teeth gleamed.

"I beg your pardon."

Sinjiin pointed at the plate with the side of his hand. "Your body must first digest the knowledge of the creature you wish to become."

Most of the time Melia flew alone, but there had been a few times when she came across an eyrie and flew with another eagle. She covered her mouth with the back of her hand. The thought of eating the flesh of one made her ill. "I can't."

Sinjiin tilted his head. "It's difficult. Almost like being a cannibal."

Melia nodded. "Did you eat tiger?"

197

"I did. I was young. I didn't know any better."

"But the muannai eat all kinds of animals—"

"The muannai are an exception to almost every natural law in the enchanted world." Sinjiin sighed. "There's so much mortal in them."

"But the turnskins—you said they took a potion."

"And the change they make is superficial. Other animals see right through them. You don't want to take that route."

Melia tugged on her hair. "Isn't there some other way?"

Sinjiin pushed the plate aside. "It's not only eating the animal's flesh. It's also knowing the heart and mind of the creature you wish to become. And there you have a great advantage. You know what it is to be an eagle."

"So I don't have to eat that?"

Sinjiin shrugged. "It would help a great deal."

"Is that it?"

"Oh no. That's only the beginner's step."

"What's the next step?" Melia asked.

"You must become the creature in your dreams."

"How do I do that?"

Sinjiin searched the ground with his hand. He picked up a small black vial Melia hadn't noticed before. He held it between splayed fingers. "This is a rare oil. Before you go to sleep at night, spread one drop across your upper lip. This way you will be inhaling the fumes throughout the night. It will activate a deeper consciousness, the place in you that understands the fluidity of who you are."

"But I don't have an upper lip at night. I have a beak."

"Comprehension tills the soil."

Melia chewed on a fingernail. "So what you're saying is I need to think about all this, but as long as my mother's curse holds, learning to shift at will remains impossible."

Sinjiin pushed the black vial toward her. "Keep this. When the day comes that you need it, you'll have it and know what to do with it."

198

"Which is eat the flesh of the creature I want to shift into, and then use this before I sleep at night." She held up the vial. "What if this doesn't work? What if I can't have the dream?"

"You'll have a dream. It might not be the one you hope for, but you'll have one. The rest of the work is bringing your dream-self and awake-self closer and closer until there's no separation. You shift in your dreams; you shift when you're awake. Back and forth, until it's as natural as breathing."

24. Terror

Ryder tugged on his shirt. Every test, check, and double-check was a delay. He'd been more than careful with everything.

Koldis was bound with canvas and sturdy twine, as was Ormrun. He wrapped each artifact separately, then cinched them across his back with leather straps. The blade lay at an angle from his shoulder to his hip, the broadest part of the basin pressed against it.

The Book of Umbra was too heavy and bulky to carry with the bowl and sword, and he risked running into Flora or Melia if he returned to the tent to get it. Avoiding both of them was a priority if he wanted to sail from Faerie in the morning.

Surveying the courtyard from the windows of the room he worked in, he saw the spring faerie wandering among the muannai several times. He didn't need anyone to tell him she was asking for him. She wanted to use Ormrun's eye to spy on the dragonwitch, Princess Lilliane, the half-faeries in the mortal world, and who knew what else.

Ryder sealed himself away on the top floor of the keep before dawn. As soon as he mixed the potion with spring water, he set to work on an intricate design of tile. Focusing on the job kept his apprehension at bay. And it kept his mind off Melia. His heart flooded with gloom whenever he glimpsed her crossing back and forth across the yard below. Maybe one day she'd understand that what he did, he did to keep her safe.

He was halfway down the keep's steps when he paused to listen.

Someone shadowed his footsteps on the stairs above.

He moved again.

The echo was faint. "Sinjiin?"

Silence.

"Who's there?" His call faded. The stairwell became a noiseless sheath. Outside, shouts and laughter rang from the courtyard below, while the steady tide crashed against the Ruadain's cliffs.

Ryder's anxious breathing grew louder in his ears. He closed his mouth to quiet the convulsive gasps. He recalled the delicate patter of Melia's boots yesterday when they walked across the room together. Was she following him?

His heart pumped a staccato rhythm. He couldn't let her stop him. She needed to be protected from the spring faerie's will to sacrifice her to Umbra.

Beyond the window, dark purple streaks announced the last shred of day. In less than an hour, he'd know if Embril's spell worked.

Or he'd be dead.

Ryder raced down the stairs. If Melia was following him, he'd outrun her before she changed into a black eagle.

With Ormrun and Koldis strapped against his back, he needed to remain within the perimeter of the old stone wall of the Calashai's courtyard until he drank Embril's spell. The stone wall that no longer existed. He would need to rely on memory.

Ryder erred on the side of caution, although he planned on standing as close as possible to the stone staircase descending to the inlet when he took the potion. There was no way to foresee what would happen when the terror overtook him. He hoped he retained enough presence of mind to make it to the dinghy concealed in a small cave at the east end of the beach. From there, he could row to the ship anchored farther out at sea.

Only then would Melia be safe.

As he crossed the yard, it was easy to blend in with the large crowd of muannai that always gathered for dinner. Past them, Ryder veered closer to the keep and shrank into the shadows. No one seemed to be paying any attention to him.

The sun completed its descent.

Even if Melia followed him unseen, as an eagle she'd be powerless to stop him.

He advanced to where the stone wall once stood. His heartbeat in his ears was louder than the waves hitting the rocks below.

He slipped the jar from his pocket, unsealed the lid, and removed the pepper. He tossed it a few feet away.

With closed eyes, he muttered a prayer to gods he'd never really believed in. He thought about Melia's sea-blue eyes and the way they penetrated everything they looked at, including him.

He lowered the jar.

He should have told her goodbye.

Ryder shook his head to rid himself of the dangerous thought. If he was going to do this, he needed to just do it.

He threw his head back and gulped the syrup in a single shot. The juice from the pepper burned all the way down to his stomach. He doubled over. Tears blurred his vision. He crushed the glass jar with a bare hand. Splintered shards rammed into his palm. He squeezed his hand into a fist, welcoming the pain.

Adrenaline poured into his bloodstream.

Someone was following him.

Ryder swung around. And around. "I know you're there. Show yourself!"

A couple of muannai on the fringes of the lawn turned their heads.

Ryder crouched in the grass. His heart thundered like the horses that had galloped to Garrick and Shilda's the day he left Idonne.

Anton had finally caught him. His old mentor sent the Idonnai Guard to retrieve the young renegade priest and Koldis. The basin would simply be a boon for the head of the Order of the Idonnai. Another prize for his private collection.

If Ryder let them take Ormrun and Koldis, Melia would still be in danger.

The vision of what she might become with Umbra inside her exploded in his heart like a black knife stabbing his chest. Violent despair climbed his throat.

How many came for him?

Ryder wasn't going to sail back to Idonne in chains. He bolted.

They chased him.

Overpowering dread gave his feet wings. He reached the edge of the cliff and spread his arms.

The Great White Sea crashed on jagged rocks below. It was too high to dive.

Ryder turned around. An exploding brightness blinded him. He drew back with his arms covering his face.

When the light faded, a short, stubby troll eyed him warily.

The priest lunged for him, grabbing him by the throat with one hand. "What was that flash of light? Why are you following me?"

The troll choked.

Ryder recognized Sevondi's henchman. It wasn't the Idonnai Guard, it was the witch. "Where is she?" He searched the night for one of her fire-breathing dragons.

The sky was empty of everything but clouds and the enchanted world's two moons.

Ryder flung the troll away from him. The body flapped like a tattered rag. Muannai shouted. Ryder tore along the edge of the bluff. There had to be a way down. An escape route.

A staircase.

In a crazed fog, he descended. His feet hit sand. He staggered and dropped to his knees. His heart couldn't slow down. He crawled.

Grunts. The strike of a match.

Another flash of light blinded him. The head of a torch waved in front of his face. Shadows towered over him. The stink of fear made his head swim. A hard boot connected with his ribs. He flopped in the air, gurgling. A sharp, wheezing pain burned his lungs. Another kick rolled him over. A heavy heel crushed the back of his hand. He screamed before curling into a fetal position.

"Yep. This is the one she wants." The thick, dull voice of a monster.

Ryder's entire body spasmed. Rough hands pulled his hair, dragging his face into the torchlight. It hurt to breathe.

"What's wrong with him? His eyes are bulging right out of his head."

"Not our concern."

The vise grip dropped his head with such force it lolled forward out of his control. Ryder kicked his legs. He smashed his heels into the sand, spinning himself like a top.

"Where does he think he's going?" Garish laughter.

Ryder yelled.

A club smashed his mouth, knocking him sideways.

"Hey, what's that tied to his back?"

"She said hands off."

"A little late for that."

"Whatever he's got comes along with him, or we don't get paid."

"How will she know? Are you going to tell her?"

"Remember the flare that warned us he was coming? That was the troll. He'll know. And when he tells her you stole her property, she'll suck your insides out and tan your hide."

"Can we kill him?"

"Naw. She wants him alive."

Mania reinvigorated Ryder. He lunged at one of the boots. It tried to kick him off, but he hung on. He inched up the giant's leg. As soon as he felt the end of the boot's leather, he sank his teeth in.

"Get him off of me. He's biting like some damned rabid dog."

Something heavy bashed the back of Ryder's head.

25. Trapped

Sevondi circled the unconscious priest.

Dried blood smeared his cheek and creased in the corner of his mouth. His lower lip was split and swollen; his entire head appeared lopsided. On one side of his face, a bruise extended from jaw to hairline. And such a handsome face. What a shame if the damage was permanent.

The ogres had been rough. They weren't gentle creatures. She knew that when she sent them to help Moog.

Pogo twirled his wool cap on the end of his finger.

Glik, the eldest ogre, hulked in the corner. As soon as he and his four brothers dumped the priest on the floor, she sent the others away. Their simple minds grated, as did their smell. No matter how much she ordered them to bathe, the scent of mold lingered in their wake.

"Moog did well, Pogo," Sevondi said. "I'm pleased."

"The priest almost choked him to death."

Maybe that's why the ogres beat him.

The dragonwitch leaned over to test Ryder's bicep. "He's very muscled." She glided over to the cabinet, opened her coin box, and took out a single gold piece. She handed it to Pogo. "Give this to your twin to ease his pain."

His eyes gleamed. "Do you have one for me?"

"On the night you face down death for me, I will." Sevondi clapped her hands. "I don't want to see you again without my

207

seawater."

"Aye, ma'am." The troll ambled from the room.

"Glik." She pointed to the inert body at her feet. "Help me with him."

If he'd raced across the room with a turtle, the turtle would have won. Ogres were brutally strong with legs and arms like young trees, but among their wearing qualities, they walked slowly.

Sevondi beseeched her dead aunts for patience.

Glik finally reached the priest's body. "Yes, ma'am."

Twice as tall as she was, the ogre's head almost grazed the ceiling. She patted the floor beside her. When he knelt, his head was almost level with hers. "Help me get these things off his back before he wakes up. Hurry." She bit the back of her hand. Urging Glik to hurry would only make him more clumsy. Ogres responded to simple instructions. "Roll him over."

Glik wrapped one enormous hand around the priest's torso and pulled.

Ryder's teeth knocked together. He groaned.

"Sorry," the ogre said. "It's hard for me to be gentle."

The dragonwitch patted his wrist; he couldn't help himself.

Glik's parted lips resembled a smile. His breath curdled toward her. She repositioned the back of her hand beneath her nose. "Undo those straps."

The ogre tackled the leather strips and buckles with thick fingers.

Sevondi feared he'd still be at it when the sun rose. She pressed her palms against her thighs but said nothing.

When Glik finally handed her the basin's bulk, her body pulsed with ecstasy. She rushed over to the gilded stand she'd ordered to specification in Aldaine. Even wrapped in canvas, the bowl fit perfectly. She imagined her triumph at the Muudron Stone.

Turning back to the priest, she found her face in Glik's stomach. "Please, move."

"I wanted to see what excited you."

His curiosity eased her frustration. "It's a special bowl. The stand

was made for it."

"I like it." He shoved the still-wrapped sword at her stomach, almost knocking her over. "Did I hurt you?" he asked.

Sevondi smoothed her bangs. "I'm fine." Her hands curled around Koldis. She'd forgotten how light the blade was. Eager to be alone with her treasure, she hurried to her coin box for a second time. With the sword slipped under her arm, she counted out the ogre's pay.

She dropped six gold pieces into Glik's outstretched hand. "One for each of your brothers, and two for you."

His deep-set black eyes glinted with infatuation. "Thank you, miss."

"Could you check the cage?" she asked, as a way to dismiss him. "We'll be leaving at dawn, and I don't want the prisoner escaping while we travel to the valley."

Glik nodded his head. "I can do that, miss."

Sevondi mimicked the up-and-down motion of the ogre's giant head as she led him to the door.

✧ ✧ ✧

Sevondi set Koldis down on her improvised altar, a shiny black counter. Her fingers tore at the twine and cloth wrapped around Ormrun. A layer of dust dulled the rubies, emeralds, and sapphires encrusted along the basin's rim. Where had they kept it? Buried in the ground?

It needed a good wash.

She arranged her power objects, artifacts with great personal meaning she'd collected through the years, around the bowl. She unwrapped the blade, its blue shimmer unmistakable. She approached the basin.

How many years had she waited for this opportunity?

Her gaze traveled back and forth between the sword and the bowl. *Imelda, I have them.*

✧ ✧ ✧

"Stay with me," Sevondi commanded Pogo.

The troll shifted from foot to foot. "Is he going to come, ma'am?"

"Who?"

"Umbra?"

"That is the point."

"Is it true the incarnation could kill you?"

Sevondi spun around. "Who told you that?"

Pogo rolled his knit cap between his fingers.

She refrained from snatching it out of his hands.

"Moog," he said.

"What does your brother know?"

"Yesterday, when he was keeping an eye on the tiger, like you told him to, the big cat was inside Flora's tent, and they were having a conversation about, well—Flora told the old wood elf that if you tried to incarnate Umbra, you might die. And if you do, she said it would be a great loss to us all, ma'am. Those were just about her exact words, as best as I can recall."

"Old fool. She wants that half-faerie to incarnate Umbra."

"But—"

"Pogo, I'm not going to go through with the incarnation tonight. I'm only going to peer into the basin."

"What about Isadora?"

Sevondi pressed her palms together. "And why must you bring up Isadora tonight?"

"I was there," he whispered. "When she was on her deathbed and made you promise you wouldn't do it."

"And were you also there when I promised Imelda I would?"

"Yes, ma'am."

The troll mumbled something Sevondi couldn't hear.

"What did you say?"

"Imelda hated your mother."

Sevondi's nostrils flared.

"Everyone knew it but you."

She couldn't listen to this. "Leave me."

The troll stomped his foot. "Hear me out."

"If you speak your piece, it will be the last time."

Pogo stared at the ground. "The muannai love you. They loved Elendah, too, but you're one of them. The grey faerie never courted their favor. But this carnivale—they can't wait to cheer you on. Everywhere in Aldaine, they're talking about you becoming the next regent. They're counting down the days until the dragon carnivale begins. And I know you haven't seen it yet, but the Dragon's Keep is magnificent. Yrrick and that priest lying on the floor over there have sweated and broken their backs to finish it. I know you're ambitious. I've been looking out for you ever since your mother and father abandoned you when you were too young to understand why they left. Ever since then, you don't believe anyone can love you. But they do, Sevondi. They all love you. Even Flora. Don't risk your life over a promise you made to an aunt who never kept her word to anyone." Pogo jammed his hat back on his head and stalked out.

Sevondi paced, avoiding the pitcher of seawater the troll had placed on the counter. It was impossible to recover her earlier enthusiasm. She tried to piece together fragmented memories of her mother, but all she could remember was Imelda.

The priest groaned. She crouched over him.

His shirt was torn and dirt streaked his clothes. There were abrasions, but no open wounds. His dark green eyes searched hers.

"You've had an accident," she said.

He tried to sit up and winced.

"Let me help you."

"It's my side," he gasped. "And my head. It hurts to breathe."

She lifted his shirt and pressed against his ribs.

He sucked in air.

The ogres had been too rough with him.

"Who are you?" he asked.

"You don't recognize me?"

He shook his head.

How fortuitous.

211

The priest rubbed his eyes with the heels of his palms. "Everything is blurry."

Sevondi reached out to feel the back of his head. As soon as she found the swollen knot, he bellowed. "You've banged your head. Are you sure you don't recognize me? We know each other rather well."

His fingertip traced the shield she'd drawn on her face that afternoon. The touch was warm and gentle. "Then why don't I remember your name?" he asked.

"You've suffered some memory loss. Do you know your name?"

His pupils shifted left to right. "No. But you can tell me."

Sevondi restrained an impulse to lie, to offer a false name. What if she could turn him in her favor? His knowledge of Umbra was vast. She looked over his head at the sword and basin. Perhaps he could help her understand why the dark master withdrew from her. Maybe he could help her call Umbra back.

"Your name is Ryder, and you're an Idonnic priest."

He shook his head. "None of that sounds familiar."

"Give it a few days."

"What is your name?" he asked.

"Sevondi."

"It's not familiar to me, either."

"Do you remember anyone?"

He pressed his fingers against the sides of his head. "Shilda. And Garrick. They're my mother and father. Where are they?"

"I'll help you find them."

The false promise placated him for the moment. "I'm hungry and tired," he said. "But my mouth and my side—everything hurts." He winced when she touched his cheek.

"Lie down," she said. "I need to wash the blood off your face."

"You want me to lie here on the floor?"

She gave him her best smile. "I won't be long. Just close your eyes."

He did as she told him.

Amnesia. No spell required.

She needed Pogo, but she sent for Glik. The ogre wouldn't argue about locking the priest in the cage. The troll would.

✧ ✧ ✧

Sevondi watched the bowl for a long time as if it were a living thing.

What could it hurt to fill it with water from the Great White Sea and peer inside it once?

Dismay slithered through her. Why did Pogo make such a fuss about something the spring faerie said? Imelda always intimated the risks were minimal. Sevondi picked up the pitcher and filled the bowl. A mist rose from the water's surface. It smelled of the deep woods. The vapor formed a thin veil around her. She inhaled to the bottom of her lungs. The fog thickened into an opaque cloud.

She waited for Umbra.

The eye opened. It showed her a strange young girl, hair knotted and twisted in thick strands. The girl hugged her knees to her chest. Black-chipped fingernails danced over a small glowing device.

"Bring this one to me."

The command reverberated through Sevondi's body. A venomous rage shook her.

"This one will be my vessel."

An icy pressure compressed the dragonwitch's head. Sevondi spit into the bowl. Her saliva sizzled on the water's surface. "You'll never have her."

A sinister laugh echoed through the suite like wicked thunder. *"You thought I wanted you?"*

Sevondi picked up the basin and slammed it against the counter. Salty water sloshed everywhere, including on her face. It was so cold her teeth rattled. "I will make you come to me," she whispered. "I will find a way."

26. The Unknown Beyond

It was a blue-skied, crisp October morning in St. Louis, Missouri.

An exhausted young woman—so slight she might have been mistaken for a child—perched on the edge of a battered sofa, elbows leaning against the brushed silver railings of a hospital bed.

The bed dominated the middle of a sparse living room. A flimsy rolling cart cluttered with bed sheets, bed pads, diapers, ointments, lotions, thermometers, and an inventoried quantity of morphine was stationed next to the out-of-place bed. Across the room, dappled light spilled through an open window. Worn grey-white curtains shifted in a breeze.

It was the tenth morning of Jade Rae Silver's vigil over her grandmother, Gabriela, and she'd already decided that when it was her time to go, she was going to enlist hospice care, too. The hospice workers thought of everything, even sending a chaplain, a social worker, and pamphlets to prepare the living for their final goodbye to the dying.

Jade's mind wandered as she held her grandmother's soft hand.

The afternoon she flew in from San Diego, a woman with pinched cheeks and kind eyes informed her Gabriela had two weeks—at the most a month—left to live. Jade pummeled the hospice worker with questions: How could she make such a prediction? What about recoveries? Gabriela had made a few remarkable ones in her ninety-four years.

After that depressing encounter, Jade read and re-read a

pamphlet detailing the physical and emotional manifestations of the last days of life. Now, she too could see her grandmother's time was near.

Resignation made her more quiet and introspective than usual as she studied Gabriela's beloved face. Their bond hardly made sense—the deep devotion between the prim and proper, intensely religious orphan raised in a small Texas town, who read nothing but the Bible; and her rebellious, vegan, portal-fantasy fanatic granddaughter, who thrived on Caramel Macchiatos and sported several tattoos and dreadlocks.

But Gabriela taught Jade to respect the devout, even when she couldn't believe herself. One of the few social détentes the young woman had achieved in her life—perhaps the only one—it drew grandmother and granddaughter closer.

Jade pushed her butt back into the sofa.

For the first time in several days, Gabriela rested quietly, her wispy grey hair pulled away from her face and held in a silky topknot with a scrunchy. Her breaths were shallow but even, and the expression on her age-grooved face could almost be described as blissful. It had been seven days since she stopped taking bird-sized bites of applesauce, and two since she tightened her lips against the pipettes of water. That had been the worst moment. Now, it was all waiting and cherishing the last few days—minutes—left together.

Gabriela squeezed Jade's hand, bringing the young woman's hyper-attention back to her patient. Her grandmother's eyes fluttered open, their milky-blue irises searching.

Jade leaned forward, gently squeezing her grandmother's hand in return. "I'm here."

Gabriela asked for the thousandth time, "Where is Lola?"

"She couldn't make it."

"No?"

Conspiracy theories were among the many outrageous ideas Jade's mother embraced with the same passion Gabriela applied to her Christian faith. "She's afraid to fly."

Her grandmother accepted the answer. "Are you still eating all that beans and rice?" she whispered. Through the years, Jade's dietary choices had been a conversation point for them.

"Yes, black beans are still my favorite."

"And still tying all those ribbons in your hair?"

Her grandmother never used the word dreadlocks, but once, when they sat on her front porch, Gabriela brushed the heavy mass of her granddaughter's hair aside, and said, "They suit you." That shy acceptance of Jade's dreads—the most visible symbol of her granddaughter's militant rejection of commercialized fashion's tyranny—could still make Jade's ragged heart smile.

Gabriela loosened her grip on her granddaughter's hand, and Jade returned to the present. "Yes."

"That's all right," her grandmother said.

Jade stood to lean over the bed's railing. "Do you need anything?"

Gabriela rubbed her granddaughter's forearm. "Has he tried to contact you?"

"My father?"

Her grandmother patted Jade's face. "Not him. The dark voice."

Visual and auditory hallucinations were a side effect of morphine. "Are you having nightmares? Is that why you've been so restless?" Jade asked.

Despite increased doses of the sedative, Gabriela moaned at varying pitches and intensity for five days straight, every utterance piercing Jade's heart. She spent the stressful days curled up in the sheets beside her grandmother, or pacing the wood floor on the phone with hospice care workers, or standing over the bed administering a cool rag to her grandmother's forehead.

"No nightmares. He's real," Gabriela said.

Bent almost in half now, to hear Gabriela's soft words, Jade pressed her palm against the back of her grandmother's hand. Jade's whole purpose in being there was to ease her grandmother's passing to wherever the dead went. Objecting, or otherwise insisting Gabriela was only imagining a dark voice, would only agitate her.

"Lola hears him," her grandmother's cracked voice continued. "It's the cause of her troubles."

Jade's mother, Lola, spent half of each year institutionalized, and the other half as a bag lady in Balboa Park. It wasn't a stretch to imagine her mother had heard a dark voice and told Gabriela about it long ago. "Don't worry about Mom," Jade said. "She's all right. Even when she's staying in the park. It never snows in Southern California."

Gabriela gripped Jade's arm with renewed strength. "They warned me about him when I was a child." Her grandmother stared at the ceiling. "They told me to pray whenever he tried to contact me, and he did. Plenty of times, but I did what they told me to do. Every time he came, I prayed until he went away." She rolled her head toward her granddaughter. "Jade, I thought they were evil. The blue-eyed girl with the little faerie on her shoulder. But they weren't. They were kind to warn me, and now I'm warning you. Have you seen any of them?"

An inner tremor rocked Jade's sense of reality. She was used to her mother's odd notions and pronouncements, but talk like this from her grandmother disoriented her. "Who?" Every Sunday, Gabriela put on black heels, a dress suit, and ear bobbles to go to the Methodist Church down the road. It was Lola who talked about creatures from other realms with startling insistence.

Jade's gaze shifted to the table next to the metal cart. Although she hated to do it, maybe it was time to increase her grandmother's morphine dose. She let the thought go. She wanted Gabriela with her—lucid—as long as possible.

"Jade, has he tried to contact you?"

Tears balled in Jade's eyes. Reluctantly, she slipped her smartphone from her pocket to check the time. 10 a.m. Per the hospice nurses, Jade kept a chart tracking her grandmother's medication. She'd need to verify the most recent doses before calling the nurse on duty to discuss Gabriela's auditory hallucinations.

"The faeries. Have you seen them?" Gabriela persisted.

Jade wiped the wetness from her cheek. A hurricane of fear, regret, and hope erupted within her. Why did her grandmother have to remind her—right now—of when she was a young girl and Lola assured her faeries were real, even though most mortals couldn't see them?

Although Jade tried again and again to see the creatures her mother described, she never could. Lola, unable to conceal her disappointment, eventually gave up on encouraging her daughter to look for them. "I wish."

"Well, they were right about him." Gabriela's eyes locked onto Jade's. "He'll promise you everything."

"Everything doesn't sound like too bad a promise to me," Jade teased. "Maybe I should hear him out."

"No." Her grandmother tried to raise her head, but her shoulders slipped back against the stack of pillows propping her up. "He'll destroy your soul," she pleaded with a stark sincerity.

Alarm bells erupted in Jade's mind. Before the psychiatrists began plying her with medication, her mother babbled along a similar vein. Something inside Jade broke; the wall that separated a magical mother who enchanted her as a little girl from the incoherent mental patient Jade guiltily avoided.

God, now hot, wet snot trickled from her nose. She needed a Kleenex. Settling for the back of her free hand, she refocused. Determined to keep Gabriela peaceful, Jade made her voice light and playful. "Oh, so he's the devil?"

Gabriela rocked her head from side to side in an anguished display. "Much worse than the devil."

"Who could be worse than the devil?"

"He's real."

Jade's insides shuddered. Her silent weeping stopped. Gabriela sounded too much like Lola. It was unnerving.

Her grandmother shook a bent finger. "When he comes for you, close your heart. Don't listen to him."

At least Gabriela wasn't exhorting her to go to church. "Fine, Grandma, I won't listen to him."

Gabriela patted her hand. "Thank you." Her eyelids drooped. She kicked off the thin sheet covering her lower body, crossed her legs, and lowered her chin.

Jade's eyes watered as her grandmother took four shivering breaths like a fish out of water, sucking air.

A great light filled the room. Jade swore bells tolled in the heavenly distance. A sense of peace swirled through the living room as her grandmother's body, shrunken and innocent, released its soul.

A deafening silence extinguished the light.

Gabriela was gone.

Jade walked through her grandmother's house one last time. Faeries. She laughed. It was still hard to believe her Christian grandmother had warned her about faeries and dark voices. Maybe there was something genetic to her mother's insanity after all.

A disturbing thought.

Jade returned to the concrete. The past week had been busy. Jade contacted the funeral home in Brenham, Texas to arrange for Gabriela's body to be retrieved. Her sole granddaughter wasn't going to attend the funeral—she'd said her final goodbyes, plus the pomp and cheap public display of overwrought emotion never sat well with her—but any surviving Ashorns would.

Let them.

She packed her grandmother's meager possessions to be donated to a short list of charities.

After confirming that Julian "Jules" Tracy—her father's circumspect attorney, and the administrator of Jade's trust fund—would handle the sale of Gabriela's home, she provided the local real estate agent he hired with a tour of the small property.

Shoving a spare set of keys into the woman's hands was a painful experience.

Gabriela's home, imbued with her life force, had always shimmered in Jade's mind. But with her grandmother gone, the enchantment faded.

As seen through the calculating eyes of the selling agent, the house transformed into something mean and run-down: a wild and overgrown yard; creaky stairs with gaps in the wood descending into a musty basement; a rickety railing surrounding the leaning back porch; torn screens in the sunroom; kitchen cabinets soiled over time; peeling wallpaper in each of the small bedrooms; and ancient pipes that shook and wailed whenever the water was turned on full force. All of it would decrease the sales price.

Jade hugged herself.

It had taken seventy-two hours for Gabriela's essence to depart her home, and now that it was gone, her granddaughter didn't want to be there anymore.

Grateful she didn't have to handle the logistics of the actual sale, Jade took one last look around. Her grandmother's soft laughter echoed through her as the shine in Gabriela's eyes danced through memories of special days they'd spent together in these walls, and on this land.

Jade closed the front door and lugged her single bag down uneven cement steps. She'd take away the precious memories, and leave behind the images of a stale, dilapidated building stripped of Gabriela's presence.

The trunk of the tin can she rented at the airport slammed. Jade drove slowly down tree-lined Lynn Avenue, to take a right on Page, then all the way down to Browne.

She drank in the sights of every block rolling by. Old brick homes with painted doors, windowsills, and eaves. Young children pedaling bikes or pounding basketballs against cracked pavement. Thick grass that colored the city green.

Jade settled in her window seat on the plane. It was an early afternoon, mid-week flight, and for once, not every seat was taken. She punched the call button. The flight attendant eyed Jade's dreads with disdain. She stood as far away as possible to hand over the disposable pillow. Jade ignored the pert young woman's attitude. Whenever they were together, Gabriela's innate kindness and tolerance rubbed off on her granddaughter, and lingered for a few days.

The blanket barely covered Jade's slim legs. She rotated in her seat until she found a comfortable position and closed her eyes.

✧ ✧ ✧

"My precious, Jade."

Hazy light filtered through a web of greens, golds, oranges, blacks, and browns.

"Finally, you can hear me."

The voice hovered as the blurred colors sharpened into a mass of leaves, limbs, and tree trunks. Jade searched for the speaker. With every twist, her body met resistance. A mouthful of leaves, the scrape of a knotty branch, a yank on her dreads by an aggressive twig. She forced herself to be still.

A delicate fragrance permeated the air. Above her head, the largest golden apples she'd ever seen clustered from thick black limbs. Her eyes traveled from tree to tree, heavy with ripe fruit. She stood in an ancient, overgrown orchard. Her stomach grumbled.

"Do you like what you see?"

She offered a begrudging and silent agreement. Lola gave her insanity away by answering the voices aloud. Jade wasn't going to make that mistake.

The scent of apples overpowered her. The delusion so real, she decided to jump up to grab one of the fruits. Her fingertips brushed the yellow globes. They were too high. She couldn't remember the last time she'd climbed a tree.

Time to fix that.

She pushed her way through the crisscrossed limbs of four trees to crouch next to the one with the lowest branch. If she could just squeeze through the overlapping limbs and leaves, she could pull herself up. A cluster of apples would be within reach.

Jade pushed one branch away. When she pushed a second and straightened, the first one slammed against her hip. Not as easy as it looked. She shifted her body and used her back to push the wall of foliage up and out. With the tension of the branches pressing against her, she hooked her arms around the lowest branch and swung her legs toward the trunk. The lower branches snapped back to fill the empty space beneath her. She pushed against the tree with her feet and heaved herself over the branch.

Just like when she was a kid.

A tuft flurried through her mind, a cloudy memory gone before she could grasp its meaning.

An apple was in reach. Her heart pumped with anticipation as she extended her arm. Her fingers curled around its smooth skin. The branch bounced, leaves shivered, but the apple refused to let go. Frustrated, Jade shifted. She made herself more stable by repositioning her feet against the tree trunk. She extended her arm its full length, palmed the apple, and jerked.

The apple came free, but so did she.

Although her butt cushioned the fall, the hard landing knocked the wind out of her. Undeterred, she twisted over and drew the apple toward her with splayed fingers. When she held it in her hand, she flopped over, flat on her back and took an enormous bite.

Perfect. Lightly sweet with just the right amount of tang.

"Become my queen."

Jade dropped her arm to the ground. Her stomach rolled. The first time her mother was institutionalized Jade was four years old.

Schizophrenia most commonly manifested in late adolescence and early adulthood. For Jade, every year that passed without symptoms was a cause for private celebration. Now nineteen, she was ripe for the onset of mental illness. Her pulse zipped as her gaze raced along the maze of trunks, leaves, and branches. Someone had to be there. *"I can't see you,"* she said in her mind.

"As long as you can hear me, I can help you."

A freezing dread inched up Jade's spine. She pressed her lips together and pushed herself up, the half-eaten apple rolled on the ground beside her. If she refused to answer the voice, maybe it would go away.

"I won't harm you."

Right. An image of her mother's face, bewildered with terror, filled Jade's mind. She needed to get out of here, wherever here was. A dream? She needed to wake up.

"I am Umbra."

Jade ignored the introduction as she wobbled to her feet. Naming things made them more personal—and real. If she couldn't wake up, she could at least get as far away from the voice as possible. She made a circle and paused when she heard the soft but distinct rush of running water.

Sweat trickled down the back of her neck and the inner creases of her elbows. Ignoring the slaps of supple branches against her forehead, forearms, and stomach, she punched her way through the overgrown woods with greater force. The forest seemed endless, but the sound of the river grew louder. Soon she'd reach the water. Or wake up.

"Your noble lineage is wasted in the mortal world."

Jade stopped, choking back grief. Images of her grandmother and the humble home she lived and died in roared through her mind. Gabriela worked two jobs most of her life. Certainly, she would have mentioned royal blood if there had been any.

Neither Gabriela nor Lola ever talked about Jade's father. Supposedly a scion from one of the wealthiest families on the east coast, he indulged in a seasonal fling with her mom. Jade had been the result. Every month since Lola became pregnant, a trust sent a

generous check to care for his born-out-of-wedlock daughter—
mistake. Jules, the fund's administrator—and the closest thing to a
father Jade had ever known—made it clear the first time she asked:
Her father didn't want anything to do with her, and if she ever
attempted to find him, the checks would stop. It was a harsh
arrangement, but Jade knew people with worse family situations,
broken and financially bust.

Now she wondered why she never challenged the arrangement.
Maybe her subconscious mind was prodding her to find her father
before he died. *"Are you talking about my father?"* she asked,
violating her promise not to engage the disembodied voice.

Deep laughter reverberated around her. Surround sound. The
hair on her arms stood up. *"Absolutely not. Your faerie blood comes
by way of your mother."*

"Faerie blood?" she asked in her mind. A sense of wild freedom
infused her. She remembered the magic of her grandmother's
garden and wanted to weep.

"Gabriela refused me."

*"You're the dark voice my grandmother warned me about. She
said you'll destroy my soul."*

*"Even you recognize your grandmother's beliefs were prosaic. The
great religions of the past have had their day. A new age is coming,
and you can usher it in as my queen."*

A strange sensation worked its way up from Jade's belly and into
her chest. Not fear. She didn't feel exactly threatened. Her mind
scurried. The only things she believed in were rooted in nature.
Religion—and all belief systems born from the human mind—had
always struck her as limited, slices of truth cutting away too much of
reality. New age alternatives were no better.

She imagined the voice as a middle-aged white guy, wearing a
cheesy three-piece suit, microphone in hand, with a creepy hole of a
smile, professionally bleached teeth glinting through. Ugh.
"Couldn't you come up with something more original?" Jade

225

resumed her assault on the forest. Queens, religion, a new age. Why was her subconscious hurling such crap at her?

"The war will not be fought in the mortal world."

Jade's stomach squeezed into a tight ball. *"Then where?"*

"In the heart of the enchanted world, in the Realm of Faerie."

She snorted. *"The Realm of Faerie, right. Good one. You almost had me."* She reminded herself this was a dream.

Gabriela had been the rock in Jade's life. That she resorted to Lola-like ravings in her final moments unsettled Jade. This dream was a way for her subconscious to sort through it all.

"You have much to learn, my beautiful Jade, about the realities of existence."

Jade felt her cheeks heat. She was scrawny, even for a vegan. Her dreadlocks gave her an interesting look, at least that's what she'd decided. A few of the coffee shop regulars only showed up when she worked the bar, but she never paid them much attention. A while back, her mother's therapist labeled her a sexual anorexic and tried to pin it on her father's abandonment, but Jade had other theories. Mostly having to do with the broken hearts and broken lives most guys left in their wake. Reason enough for Jade to put up big, thick walls whenever it came to sharing bodily fluids. But when the voice called her beautiful, a thrill shot through her spine, a thrill that didn't leave her nether regions untouched.

Why did it feel so dangerous and exciting? Was this what standing on the edge of madness felt like?

The sound of rushing water faded; the trees blurred into a haze.

The truth was: This was the most fascinating thing that had ever happened to her, and she was damned curious.

"Why do you want me?" she asked. *"Why not someone else?"*

"You're perfect," the voice cooed.

Jade whirled around, searching. *"I want to see your face."*

"When we meet again." The voice was gone, a chasm of emptiness left behind.

Jade pushed for awake consciousness. Someone was shaking her. "Let me go," she mumbled. Her eyes sprang open.

The pert flight attendant stared down at her. "I've been trying to wake you up for five minutes."

Jade glanced out the window. They were on the tarmac, and all the other passengers had deplaned. She wiped drool from her chin. How embarrassing. She pushed the wadded-up blanket and pillow into the flight attendant's hands. "Thanks." She grabbed her bag and hurried down the exit aisle.

The next morning, Jade stood in front of the mirror. It wasn't her reflection that held her attention, but the cedar wardrobe. She ran her finger along the cabinet's edge and took a step back. Remembering the morning Lola bought the treasured piece, Jade doubled over with grief.

It had been one of her mother's few lucid moments in the past fifteen years. Jade was rereading *The Chronicles of Narnia*—again— and when mother and daughter went to breakfast, they discussed portals to other worlds as if they were legitimate modes of travel to actual geographic destinations.

Jade could almost feel herself glow as Lola waxed eloquent about fantastical realms inhabited by faeries.

But there were no faeries in Narnia. And no one named Umbra.

Yet the dream she had on the plane, the ancient apple orchard— she might as well have entered the opening pages of *Prince Caspian* along with the Pevensies.

Jade tiptoed to the wardrobe, wrenched open the door, and pushed a hand through her bohemian collection of thrift store tees, gauze skirts, and faded jeans. Half expecting to reach tree trunks, falling snow, or the metal of a lamppost, her heart collapsed when her palm pressed against rough cedar. Did she really believe other worlds existed? Jade buried her head in her clothes.

Maybe it was time to pay Lola a visit.

27. Losing Ryder

When the spring faerie headed away from the stone stairway leading to the inlet, Melia wanted to hug her. Until she faced the steep incline, all sand, dirt, and rock, impossible to climb. What was Flora thinking?

Race up to the top and come back down, race up to the top and come back down, race up to the top and come back down. As many times as you can.

She'd rather swim.

And that was saying something.

The night before, too exhausted to fly after two days of pounding waves, Melia nested in one of the bay trees near Flora's tent. She woke at dawn, crashing into canvas. Fortunately, the roof held–the spring faerie was a genius with knots–and she didn't crush anyone sleeping inside.

Training was teaching Melia to appreciate the small things.

She rocked on the heel of her boot, arms folded over her chest. Flora nibbled on a green leaf speckled with orange-brown, an herb to build her stamina. The spring faerie was training too. She offered Melia a bruised leaf.

"Chew on this."

Ever since she smoked ylandria. Melia was wary of faerie herbs. "You remember I'm half-mortal?"

"Yah." Flora gnawed on her second leaf. "That's another reason I want you to try it. I'm curious to know how it will affect you."

Melia arched an eyebrow. "I don't like the sound of that."

Flora shrugged. "Fine. Start moving."

Melia couldn't gain any traction. Her boots slid in the sand.

"Use your hands," the spring faerie shouted.

Melia threw her body forward; pebbles dug into her palms. Pride and determination kicked in. She dug her fingers in the dirt and found invisible grooves. Her forearms grazed prickly weeds that refused to wither and die. The resolute plants inspired her as she inched up the mountainside.

She wished Ryder was training with her. Regardless of their fight, she couldn't escape the insistent feeling they should be together. But she took Aldous' advice to heart, she would wait until she was sure she could share her feelings with him and hear what he had to say before she approached him again.

Sinjiin confided Ryder wasn't making progress with *The Book of Umbra*.

As long as the founding stone held the basin and sword, the priest would remain close. And the next time Melia went to the mortal world, she was going to be ready if Lilliane tried to pull any black magic tricks.

Neither she nor Ryder were going anywhere soon.

Sinjiin told her, "Fear cages the sentient being's mind. Untether yourself and you will be free, whether or not you can fly."

Melia promised herself, the next time she talked to Ryder, she'd be fearless.

When she reached the top of the mountain, she grinned. Down below, Flora had company. The tiger stalked in tight circles around the spring faerie. He jerked his head and growled loud enough for Melia to hear. When she waved, they ignored her.

The half-faerie tugged her hair. What was going on?

They sat in the tent. Everyone was there except Ryder: Tatou, Aldous, Flora, and Sinjiin in his mage form.

"I went to get the basin for Flora," Sinjiin said, "but it's missing, along with the sword. And I can't find Ryder anywhere. Have any of you seen him?"

No.

"Neither has Yrrick," the mage said.

"What about the book?" Melia couldn't believe Ryder released the basin and sword from the founding stone, kept it a secret from everyone, and left Faerie without saying a word to her. "If Ryder took Ormrun and Koldis, he would have taken the book as well."

"It's still here," Aldous said.

Melia's body softened. "There must be another explanation. Perhaps he moved them?"

"Why would he hide them and not tell anyone? Not even Sinjiin?" Tatou asked.

"He's upset with all of us," the mage said.

"Why?" the pixie asked.

"He's opposed to Melia incarnating Umbra; he's always been against it." Sinjiin expelled a long breath. "He must have found a way to break the spell of the founding stone. I should have realized it by the way he's been avoiding me. He's probably on his way to Minnanon."

The mage's conclusion punched Melia in the gut. "Do you really think he'd do that? Leave without a word to anyone?"

"When none of us listened to his concerns," Sinjiin said, "he stopped talking to us."

"What about the book?" she asked.

"He never promised to take that to the Grey Council."

"Do you really think he'd leave without saying goodbye?" Tatou asked.

"When we fought two days ago, he held something back." Melia recalled how he pulled away from her. How he stared at the floor and his posture became stiff. He told her he cared for her, that he would keep his promise to take Ormrun and Koldis to the Grey Council. How could she have missed he was saying goodbye?

"He wants to protect you," Aldous said.

Melia closed her eyes.

"It's the most likely explanation," the mage said.

She couldn't believe he was gone, that she'd never see him again; the way they'd left things, why would he return to Faerie? "What about Sevondi?"

"I've already been to the Blue Mermaid," Sinjiin said. "It's empty. The dragonwitch and her entourage set sail for the muannai valley early this morning. The dragon carnivale will begin soon."

The spring faerie smoothed her kerchief. "No more fresh steak for you."

"It's unsettling," Aldous said, "the priest, the dragonwitch, Ormrun and Koldis, all disappearing on the same day."

"And yet," Flora said, "if Ryder has taken the basin and the sword to the Isle of Minnanon, it could work to our advantage."

"How?" Melia asked.

"We could sail there ourselves, and petition the council to deliberate upon Umbra's incarnation."

"Would they do that?" Tatou asked.

The spring faerie's dark eyes sparkled. "Ryder is opposed to Melia incarnating Umbra—"

"I don't blame him," Tatou said.

"No one does," Aldous said.

"—and Melia is conflicted about proceeding with the incarnation."

"I don't blame her, either," the pixie said.

"None of us do," Flora continued. "If present the case to the Grey Council for judgment, it would ease my mind, and perhaps win Ryder to our side. If they rule for the incarnation—"

"And if they don't?" Tatou asked.

"Then I'll have to accept my personal vendetta against the Albiana queens has clouded my judgment," Flora said.

Sinjiin shook his finger at the spring faerie. "Ryder will listen to the council."

"But not me? Or anyone else?" Melia asked.

"Being raised among priests," the mage said, "he's trained to respect authority."

Trained. Melia was beginning to hate the word. And yet—"I would be relieved to receive their guidance," she said. "Can we leave today?"

"You're not ready to stand before them," Flora said.

"If we wait too long, Ryder will have come and gone before we reach the island!"

"If that happens, we'll track him down," Sinjiin said.

"If we'd thought of this sooner, perhaps the priest wouldn't have felt compelled to lie and run off on his own," Aldous said. "It's strange, though. Sevondi relinquishing her claim on Ormrun and Koldis without a word to you, Flora."

"She can't delay her carnivale," Sinjiin said.

"Is there a way to be sure no one else took them?" Tatou asked.

"No, there isn't," Aldous said. "But whoever did would have had to solve the riddle of the founding stone's claim upon them. And as far as we know, the young priest was the only one actively searching for the answer."

If committing to her training would hasten the time before she could see Ryder again, Melia would train even harder. She stood up. "I'm going back to the mountain to finish my drills."

No one dissuaded her.

28. Awakening

The cage in the ship's hold didn't bother Ryder as much as it should have. If he were free, where would he go? He didn't know who he was or where he was from. Sevondi was a liar—that much he'd figured out. The tender lump on the back of his head wasn't from any accident. He'd been beaten. Probably by one of the ogres hulking around the ship at her beck and call.

His prison was large enough, the wood of the bars smelled of pine, and there was plenty of fresh hay on the floor. Most of the time, everyone left him alone. The isolation gave him time to think about what did bother him: The only two names he could remember were Garrick and Shilda, and he was being handled like a wild dog, one Sevondi was determined to tame. Every time his mind caught the tail of a memory, his heart broke into a frenzied pump until the hint dispersed like mist.

Twice each day, Glik unlocked the door of Ryder's cage, tied a rope around his neck, and led him up on deck to walk with Sevondi. Everyone else on the ship walked free. Ryder decided to tolerate it, until he figured out who he was, and why she kept him locked up.

The first time they walked along the deck with Glik a short distance behind, holding the end of Ryder's leash, he figured out Sevondi wasn't there to help him. Every time he asked for more information about who he was, she evaded the question. When he asked how he ended up on her ship, she assured him he'd remember in time. Why was he being locked up? For his safety. None of it made sense. When he pressed, and his anger reached his voice, Glik shoved him. Twice, he ate the deck with his chin. He wasn't eager for a third bite.

Sevondi wanted to talk about the dragon carnivale–and becoming regent. As long as he listened, she was pleased. But Ryder found it hard to pay attention to her, so he'd nod his head, or say things like, "Yes, of course," while he watched the shoreline, searching for any clue about who he really was.

Sometimes when he was half-awake and half-asleep, he had dreams that seemed like memories. He was certain this wasn't his first time on a ship. He remembered endless white shining halls. He remembered a tiger, but he doubted he was a hunter.

He grew restless. Since they'd set sail, he kept careful count of the rising suns. Today was the fifth. When Glik came to unlock his cage, Ryder considered head butting the ogre in the stomach. He could probably make it to the deck. The question was: Could he swim?

Three days ago, their small ship left the sea. Now they sailed up a broad river. But sometimes the shoreline looked so close, Ryder thought he might be able to reach it even if he couldn't swim.

On deck, the crew seemed more alert. He tried to listen to their conversations, but only caught snippets. Nothing he heard explained the increased activity.

Sevondi smiled when she saw him. Ryder mimicked her greeting, but felt a strain in his chest. She reached for his arm and held it tight. He let her. Every day they played the same charade. Something bound them together. It wasn't love or affection. It wasn't even desire, although she was attractive enough, with her jet-black hair framing her dark eyes and the unusual tattoo on one side of her face.

"Did you sleep well last night?" she asked.

"I slept fine."

Keeping hold of his arm, she began to walk. "Tomorrow we'll reach the port at the muannai valley."

That explained the crew's frenetic energy.

"From there we'll travel to the Dark Horse Saloon. The carnivale will begin there. We'll wind our way through the valley until we reach the Muudron Stone for the grand finale. It must be spectacular."

"Yes."

She rested her head on his shoulder. He didn't want it there, but he didn't see a purpose in pulling away from her either. "Do you remember Umbra yet?" she asked.

His spine shot into a taut line that hardened the back of his neck, but the emptiness inside him delivered nothing. "No."

"You're a great scholar," she said.

His mind seized on the word scholar. The never-ending white halls of his half-dream flashed through his mind.

She prodded him. "You studied Umbra."

That felt like the truth. "Yes."

"Do you remember?"

His neck itched. He dug his fingers beneath the rope.

"Glik, remove it," she said.

"Are you sure, Sevondi?"

Something fleeting sparked inside Ryder's head.

"Yes," she said.

The ogre loosened the leash. Ryder lifted it over his head.

"Is that better?" she asked.

"Yes."

"You must try to remember Umbra." She grazed his lip with her finger. "It's important."

He knocked her hand away.

Her eyebrows flattened. "Glik, return him to his cage. He needs a quiet place to concentrate."

"Yes, Sevondi." One of the ogre's heavy hands clamped down on Ryder's shoulder.

Ryder squelched the useless impulse to fight as Glik looped the rope around his neck.

❖ ❖ ❖

Whenever Melia had a few spare moments, she flipped through the pages of *The Book of Umbra*. Ryder had studied the book while she'd been in the mortal world, so whenever she opened its thick leather cover, she imagined herself reading the same words he'd read and felt connected to him.

She passed over the passages written in indecipherable languages, but those she did understand made her rethink the seething mass of consciousness that had named itself Umbra. He was dangerous, but he wasn't evil in the way she'd imagined. It was more that he was broken and thwarted. Ravenous was perhaps the best word to describe him. The mortal ash of the spiritually starved—dying without ever experiencing the sustenance of fulfillment—his cravings for power were without limit.

Insatiability seemed to be at the root of his darkness.

As she flipped through the book's pages, she began to comprehend her father's obsession with his research.

Melia absentmindedly rolled the pearls on her wrist as she wondered how long it would be before Ryder reached the Isle of Minnanon. It was the most northern island in the enchanted world. Sinjiin told her the trip could take two to four moon cycles depending on the weather.

She wondered if Ryder ever thought about her, or missed her.

❖ ❖ ❖

They walked through a forest.

Ryder saw a split-log corral through the trees. He stood still.

Glik tugged on the rope binding the prisoner's wrists.

Ryder dug in his heels. Something about the noble creatures grazing beyond the wooden barrier kicked his mind.

Laughter shattered his concentration. The caravan was a noisy procession.

Ryder needed a closer look at those animals. It might help him remember.

The ogre yanked on the rope.

"I want to see," Ryder said.

Glik shook his head. "Sevondi won't like it."

No matter how much she poked his mind, he couldn't answer the question of how to make Umbra want her. "Then don't tell her."

"We need to get to the saloon before dark," Glik insisted.

"We're almost there."

The ogre watched the rest of the caravan filing by, his thick grey lips turned down. "Hurry."

Ryder left the dirt road to slip through the tree trunks, tall and straight like poles.

The ogre crashed behind him.

When they stood side by side, Ryder asked, "What do they call those animals?"

"Horses."

A crack from the treetops pulled Ryder's gaze from the beautiful beasts. A feathered creature shot into the sky and spiraled above them.

His pulse quickened. "What was that?"

"An eagle."

Ryder thought one word: Melia.

Melia.

Melia.

It became a prayer in his mind.

It was the name of the woman he loved.

Moments before dawn, Melia jerked awake.

She'd taken to sleeping in the tent; a relentless cycle of training left no energy for nights spent in flight.

Outside, away from the others, she scanned her body as Aldous had taught her to do. The old tension pinched the back of her neck. It concerned her, but it didn't provide details. After she shifted into her half-faerie form, she headed toward the cliffs.

It was October and the mornings were cold. Weathering the chill made her feel tougher.

Thoughts of Ryder drifted through her mind. The old wood elf always encouraged her to accept such thoughts as messages from her heart, so she opened herself to their natural ebb and flow.

Although he never said as much, she often felt like Aldous passed on the painful lessons from his failed love with Flora. Melia surmised there'd been a grand passion between the two in their youth, but when the spring faeries burned, and Flora left Illialei, he refused to go with her. Probably his work in the library held him back.

Now, finally reunited with his beloved, the old elf shared his faith in true love with Melia every day.

A spot close to the cliff's edge looked comfortable. She settled cross-legged on the ground to breathe in and out, matching the rhythm of the waves tossing below.

A thick fog rolled in from the sea. Soon, a deep mist cocooned her. She felt drowsy, and her eyes wanted to close.

I run through the woods, frantic. I've lost something precious. I try to find it.

Why don't I know what I've lost?

Branches tear at my hair. Night will fall soon; the knowledge that I'll be able to fly and cover more ground fills me with hope.

But what good will that do me, when I don't know what I'm looking for?

In the seconds before the sun sets, color explodes above me. Magenta, aqua, crimson beasts fight to rule the coming night.

Beyond my line of sight, a crowd cheers.

I let the sound lead me. I reach open fields; I recognize this place. The steppes of the muannai valley. Thousands of muannai watch the war being waged in the sky.

My body twitches. Shifts. Changes. I launch into the night sky. No one watches me; their eyes are glued to the savage dance of fire-

breathing dragons.

I soar above their heads.

The Muudron Stone. At its center stand Ormrun, Koldis, the dragonwitch ...

And the one I love.

Melia blinked.

Racing across the keep's lawn, she dodged the muannai arriving for work.

Flora and Tatou stood beneath the bay trees, preparing the day's lessons.

Melia gasped for air. "Ryder didn't sail to Minnanon. He's with Sevondi. They have the basin and the sword."

29. The Dragon Carnivale

The trees around the Dark Horse Saloon blocked a view of the sun, so Sevondi watched the shadows lengthen across the lawn to determine the time. "It won't be long now," she whispered.

"No, ma'am," Pogo said.

"Do you have the elixir?"

The troll emptied his pockets. After he set a few coins and a pocket knife on the table, he held out a small midnight-blue jar.

Sevondi recognized it as the one Embril sent to the Blue Mermaid.

He handed it to her. "Embril's instructions were one swallow," Pogo said. "Just enough to wet your mouth."

The lid twisted off easily enough. Sevondi tilted her head. Mint. She would have to thank Embril when she returned to Aldaine. Sevondi gave the vial back to Pogo. It disappeared into his pocket.

"Are you ready?" he asked.

Sevondi stopped before a metal mirror hanging on the wall. She preferred the mirrors made from glass at the Blue Mermaid.

"Is something wrong?" Pogo asked her.

Sevondi traced the black ink with her thumb. Calling more than one dragon at a time was dangerous; she intended to call three every night until they reached the Muudron Stone. Every show had to be spectacular in order to erase all memory of Elendah from the muannai hearts and minds.

Sevondi gazed at the mark on her face as if staring at it could

243

increase its potency. She'd designed the shield to safeguard her mind and emotions against distractions while she entered the deep state of concentration required to bring forth the dragons. At the same time, it would prevent her from absorbing any of the toxic residue her blazing creations cast off.

Wherever there was fire, there was smoke and ash. Overexposure due to her extravagant schedule seemed an unwise risk. She smoothed the fringe of hair covering her uneven brow. "Everything's fine," she said.

Sevondi's gaze swept the saloon's dining hall. Her entourage filled the tables with two notable exceptions. "Where are Glik and Ryder?"

The troll mumbled something.

"Don't make me ask you again."

"At the equus compound. In the stables."

Tonight's show would be held at the compound. "Are they preparing for the show?"

"Not exactly."

"Then what?"

"The priest tried to run away."

Sevondi clasped her hands beneath her chin. "And why is this the first I've heard of it?" With each word, her voice grew louder. A few heads turned.

"You don't need anything else to worry about."

"I'll be the judge of what I need to worry about. Take me to them."

Pogo shook his head. "Fine."

Sevondi's hand flew to her heart. Hundreds of muannai milled around the corral, blocking the path to the stables.

"Already a great turnout," Pogo said, "and more coming."

A few recognized her. They cheered. As others realized she'd arrived, they joined in the vigorous greeting.

Their anticipation moved her; it was the kind of attention she'd craved all her life. As soon as she dealt with the priest, she was going to give them the best show any of them had ever seen. She covered her mouth with her hand. "Where are they?"

Pogo stepped in front of her. "Follow me." He led her to the last stall in the farthest corner of the stable.

The door hung ajar.

Glik's heavy boot aimed at Ryder's head. "Now," the ogre said, "you won't try to escape again."

"Stop!" Sevondi said. "Pogo, bring a lantern."

"I need to teach him a lesson," Glik said. "He tricked me."

Sevondi approached the priest, curled up on the floor. "Glik, everyone else is finishing dinner. I want you to join them. I'm sure you've worked up an appetite."

"Yes, Sevondi," the ogre said. "Will you be safe if I leave? I don't want him to hurt you."

Pogo held a light over the priest.

"You've beaten him to a pulp," she said. "He's not going to hurt anyone. Go!"

Glik turned and left.

The excitement of the crowd spilled into the stables. She didn't have much time. Sevondi examined Ryder. Nothing was broken. Maybe the ogre wasn't as dumb as he seemed. She took the lantern from the troll. "Bring me some water."

The priest stirred.

"Has your memory returned?"

He groaned.

"Why did you try to run?"

He tried to speak.

She moved her head closer to his mouth so she could hear him.

He grabbed the back of her neck and pulled her close. "I remember who you are."

"Then you would be wise to let go of me."

"Where are the basin and the sword?"

"In a place where you'll never find them."

"Give them back to me. I'll take them to a place where they'll be safe from everyone."

She laughed.

"If you try to incarnate Umbra, you risk death," he said.

"So everyone wants me to believe."

"And yet, you would proceed?"

Pogo returned. He shoved a metal cup with water into Sevondi's hand. She cradled Ryder's head and helped him take several sips.

"I don't believe I'll die," Sevondi said. "Besides, I have Ormrun and Koldis now. No one can stop me."

A light turned on in the priest's eyes. "Then I'll help you."

"Yes, I can see you're eager to help me die."

"And Umbra with you."

Sevondi gave the cup back to Pogo. "A gambler. I like that. What an exciting game we'll play."

❖ ❖ ❖

The dragonwitch prayed to Imelda. In spite of Pogo's revelation that Imelda hated her mother, she was the one Sevondi trusted to bless her with power tonight.

Power and cruelty were often coupled.

What Sevondi could no longer deny was that her great aunt had knowingly caused pain to many, including Sevondi. And maybe to Sevondi's mother.

Ever since Sevondi's great-great-grandmother Josefina abandoned her daughter Regina to live with a sorcerer in Kyrakkos, a velvety darkness of betrayal and lies had cloaked every succeeding generation of their lineage.

It was from that darkness that Sevondi learned to call forth the dragons.

Now, her people called for her.

Sevondi held her head high and entered the arena of light cast by a line of fiery torches.

The muannai shouted her name.

In the center, ringed by her audience, Sevondi searched the

skyline for objects of nature to feed her shimmering monsters.

The muannai beat their drums. She let the rhythm invade her. Then she began.

With one hand stretched toward an enormous pine, she imagined a cerulean beast wearing an emerald breastplate. The monster exploded into the night. The muannai gasped and shouted their thunderous approval. With her other hand, she reached for a heavy cloud. Her skin tingled as a magenta fire-spewing demon birthed in the sky.

The crowd hushed.

Sevondi pulled both dragons into one hand; they sparred overhead. She used her free hand to target an enormous cottonwood tree.

An orange-gold monster erupted from the darkness.

The epic battle began.

The dragons extended wicked claws and lashed massive, scaly tails. They swiped and gashed at one another. Steaming trails of blood dripped from every wound. Their deafening outrage shook the ground. Beneath their fire, the crisp fall night became a sweltering summer day. Sevondi ignored the moisture trickling down the side of her face; she kept her hands moving. She had to keep the dragons in play.

The golden dragon circled the others, gouging chunks of burning armor from their tails which swung like clubs. The cerulean one spun, and with one breath ignited the golden dragon's vulnerable underbelly. The sun-colored beast combusted, fragments of light rained over the crowd.

As the blue-green victor flipped in triumph, the magenta beast slunk along the periphery of the arena.

The voice of a single flute floated through the air. The surviving beasts faced off.

The beat of the drums clashed. The dragon's spiraled, preparing their death strike.

Sevondi's hands choreographed a dance from the depth of her

being. The flute issued a shrill note. The blue-green dragon torpedoed its long slim opponent. The magenta dragon looped and trapped its attacker in a coiled embrace. The blue-green dragon flailed.

Another rainstorm of exploding light hailed over the audience.

The magenta dragon frolicked across the skyline in triumph.

The crowd jumped up and down, yelling and stamping their feet. They threw sprays of night jasmine, creating a carpet at Sevondi's feet.

Her skin tingled. Something light exploded inside her. She blinked back tears of triumph.

"Bring the priest. I need to speak to him before we leave."

Sevondi massaged the sides of her head. The dull ache concerned her. The first night of the carnivale had been a success, but she'd have to repeat it many times before they reached the Muudron Stone.

Ryder entered the room head held high, his hands tied behind his back.

Glik, holding the rope that bound them, followed on the priest's heels.

"Untie his hands," Sevondi ordered.

The ogre balked.

Sevondi repeated the instruction. "Don't bind him again," she added.

Distrust rippled across the ogre's usually slack features. "Yes, Sevondi."

"Thank you." She pointed to the door. "I must speak with him in private."

"Will you be safe?" Glik asked.

"You can wait outside. I'll call you if necessary."

The ogre shuffled from the room.

She motioned to a plush divan. "Please, sit."

Ryder winced as he settled on the cushions. The entire side of his face was purple.

"In regard to our game," she said. "I require your aid."

He rubbed his wrists. They were red. "In what matter?"

There was no reason to lie to him. "Umbra won't have me."

His eyes widened. "That surprises me."

"He wants another."

The priest leaned forward, his elbows on his knees. "Our bargain was that I would help you, no one else, to incarnate Umbra."

"We're in agreement. It's Umbra who makes the demand."

"For who?"

"A half-mortal girl."

"Melia," he whispered.

"The one you love?" Sevondi asked.

"I'll not let him have her."

"Neither will I. But I don't think it's her."

"Then who?"

Sevondi pressed her hands on the low table between them. "He showed her to me."

"Describe her."

"A young girl, almost a young lady, with hair tangled into thick ropes tied with ribbons—and the most haunting blue eyes and pale skin—"

"Her hair was like ropes? Are you certain?"

Sevondi held up two fingers twisted together. "Yes, like this. Black paint coated her fingernails, where it wasn't chipped."

"That isn't Melia."

"Is Melia the one Flora wants to incarnate Umbra?"

He didn't answer.

"It doesn't matter. I can see you're relieved. Now, tell me how to draw Umbra away from this girl."

He rubbed his temple with his thumb as if it helped him think.

"Well?"

"You'll need a mask."

Sevondi sat across from him. "That will deceive him?"

His head tilted. "The eye of the basin is not transparent. It's like a thin cloth, a sheer veil. You can fool him with a close likeness of what he seeks."

"A mask. That's ingenious."

He nodded.

"Explain how it will work," she said.

"When you perform the ritual, make sure you're wearing the mask before you open the portal. It will require nothing more complicated than that."

"He won't be able to detect the difference?"

"Not until he's within you."

"Can he reject me then?"

"Yes. That is how he'll kill you."

Sevondi pressed her hands together. "You've been most helpful."

"Is there anything else?"

"No, you're free to go."

"I'd rather travel with the caravan to the Muudron Stone."

"Of course," she said. "You want to know who wins our little game."

"Yes."

"I'll expect you to help the others set up the fountains and stands every night."

"I'll do that."

After the priest left, she sent for Pogo.

"Yes, ma'am?"

"Send someone to the marketplace to hire the finest artisan. One who can make me a mask." She rubbed her temples. The throbbing in her head had subsided. "And copper sheets. I want to read what the copper sheets have reported about my performance last night."

"Aye, ma'am."

"Thank you, Pogo. You serve me well." She brushed off his startled expression. "Go."

30. Melia's Heart

"How much longer can we wait? It's been seven days and nothing." Melia exhaled a breath to blow a stray hair from her face. She stood with her arms folded facing Flora, who was seated on the dais of the Muudron Stone.

The spring faerie kicked the stage's elevated platform with the alternating heels of her boots. "They'll be here."

"Sinjiin could track them."

"Or we could go to the marketplace," Flora said. "They're bound to have something about the dragon carnivale in the copper sheets."

"Then we'll use the Tasimas when Sinjiin gets back?"

"Yes."

"Thank you," Melia said.

They'd left Aldous and Tatou in Aldaine. The wood elf was studying *The Book of Umbra* and preparing a treatise on the subject of Umbra's incarnation to submit to the Grey Council. Tatou was keeping an eye on his health under the pretense of keeping him company. Although she missed her best friend, the arrangement relieved Melia; the farther the pixie was from Lilliane and the reach of the princess' black magic, the better.

"Why do you think Ryder is helping Sevondi?" After falling for the priest's charade of caring for her, and wanting to help her, it was a hard question to ask.

"What has Aldous taught you about appearances?" Flora asked.

"Things often aren't what they appear to be," Melia mumbled.

"I can hardly hear you."

"Appearances account for little. The truth lies deeper."

Flora raised her palms parallel. "So when you see Ryder again, you'll give him a chance to explain."

Melia kicked the stone stage. "I wouldn't be surprised if he's lied from the first day I met him. Anton probably sent him here to deliver the basin and sword to Sevondi."

"I doubt that," Flora said.

Melia wished she could.

In daylight, the Muudron's mystical power seemed like a dream, its empty stage and pillars mere crumbling stone. But Melia remembered the first night she discovered the theater, and the holy feeling it exuded once the sun fell.

She scratched her leg where the long grass itched. Since her vision she'd been unable to erase the picture of Ryder, standing with the dragonwitch, the sword, and the basin in the center of the stage. Flora couldn't see that. The constant image made it difficult for Melia to eat, and distracted her with self-doubt as she went over and over the last time she saw the priest. "I'll never be able to lead an army," she said.

"Why is that?" Flora asked.

"I'll never be able to trust myself. I really believed Ryder took the basin and sword to the Isle of Minnanon." She couldn't say, "To protect me," to Flora. In light of her vision, the assumption sounded too foolish.

Flora shook her head. "Talk to him before you draw a conclusion."

"Did you talk to Aldous?"

The spring faerie's eyes narrowed.

"Before ... before—"

The light in Flora's eyes extinguished as they colored to a deep brown mud. "That was different."

Melia stared at the ground, the question, "Was it?" burning her throat.

✧ ✧ ✧

Melia held open the battered pillowcase. "When are you going to find something else to carry the diamond in?"

Flora dropped the Tasimas in the makeshift bag and took it from the half-faerie. She twisted it closed and slung it over her shoulder. "Never. Who would suspect I'm carrying one of the Rykkiel in it?"

Melia didn't bother to answer; the spring faerie wasn't asking her a question. Sinjiin trotted alongside them, drawing stares from the traffic headed to the market.

Under other circumstances, Melia might have enjoyed the trip. She found the muannai exotic, and the market overflowed with unusual shops. But today there was only one thing on her mind: finding out why Ryder lied to her.

When the market's high timber roof came into view above the scattered trees, she picked up her pace. One last sharp turn and the large stone building came into view. It looked like an enormous barn except for the evenly spaced chimneys belching black smoke into the morning sky.

They passed the long line of lean-to sheds running the length of the west wall. The sheds were used to stable horses. Flora huffed beside her. They crossed beneath the high-arched entrance. Melia didn't slow down until they reached the inker's stall, where a long line formed.

She chewed on a fingernail; a snail climbing High Hill moved faster.

Finally, they were next.

"How many sheets?"

"One. No, two." Melia didn't want to share one with Flora.

The inker slammed the papers onto the counter. "Two coppers."

Flora handed him a coin. "Keep the change."

The inker waved them off with a grin.

They moved through the congested market arteries to the seating place, a large area where the market's patrons ate, drank, and gabbed. Melia spotted an empty wood-planked table in a corner.

They sat down and began to read.

Sinjiin stretched out on the ground beside them.

The dragon carnivale was on the first page. It was on every page. It was the only thing in the copper sheet.

"Look at this." Flora pointed to the back sheet. "The carnivale was here last night. We just missed them."

Melia flipped her copper sheet over to verify the spring faerie's statement. There it was in bold letters. A review of The Dragon Carnivale dated last night. The half-faerie laid her head on the table. Would her bad luck never end?

Flora elbowed her.

"What?"

"Some of the shows have been canceled. Sevondi wouldn't cancel anything willingly."

"What difference does that make?"

"Maybe none," Flora said, "but if they left this morning, they can't have gotten far. Sinjiin can catch up with them."

Melia looked at the big cat. "All right, let's go."

Flora folded the copper sheet and slipped it in her apron pocket. The half-faerie left hers on the table.

"Melia?"

She whirled around. "Calista!"

The siren hugged her. "I've just finished the day's trading and was picking up something to eat. Can I join you and your friends?"

Melia's hands fell to her sides. "We were just leaving."

"I'm sorry to hear that," Calista said. "I'd love to catch up. Bertille will be disappointed she missed you."

"Is she here?" Melia asked, scanning the crowd.

"She should be here any minute. We meet here in the seating area when we're finished with our trades."

"Maybe we can wait a few minutes, I'd love to see her." If anyone could give her courage to face Ryder, it was the nixie.

✧ ✧ ✧

Melia and Bertille sat together. A few tables away Flora and Calista chatted like old friends. They probably were.

"I can't begin to tell you everything that's happened since I last saw you," Melia said.

Bertille placed her small, cool hand over Melia's. "Only tell me what's important."

"I'm having an impossible time trusting someone I–" Melia couldn't bring herself to say the word love.

Bertille smiled, showing a row of pointy teeth. "How did you feel before you dove off the cliff?"

"I wanted to take the path that wound down the side."

"Why?" Bertille asked.

Tightness crawled up Melia's spine and settled between her shoulders. "I felt afraid."

"Is that what you're feeling now?"

Melia rubbed the back of her neck. "It is a lot like what I felt then."

Bertille nodded. "And how did you feel after you dove?"

Melia's eyebrows lifted. "I felt free. Alive. Like I could do anything."

"The next time you see the person you're having a hard time trusting, dive."

"You make it sound easy."

"Was diving off the cliff the first time easy?"

"No."

"This won't be either. Dive anyway."

Every time Sinjiin sniffed the ground, a bush, or the base of a tree, Flora, sitting behind her on the tiger's back, gripped Melia's stomach tighter.

They couldn't use the Tasimas because they had no idea where they were going. As the day wore on, Melia's anxiety increased. If they didn't catch up with the carnivale soon, she wouldn't have time to talk with Ryder before dusk. And she was afraid if she didn't talk to him today, it would be more difficult tomorrow. In fact, the farther they got from the marketplace, the more her confidence withered.

Sinjiin paused. Up ahead, a horse whinnied. The tiger padded in the direction of the sound. The clip-clop of an army of horses, laughter, voices, and the creaks and groans of carts and wagons grew louder.

Sinjiin had found the caravan.

When the muannai saw the tiger, they cheered. Loping alongside the horses and wagons, searching for the priest, he was another curiosity in a carnivale of spectacles.

Ryder was nowhere. Until they reached the front. It was worse than Melia had imagined. The priest rode with the dragonwitch. They were laughing. He'd conspired against her all along. Melia didn't need anymore proof.

Not Flora. The spring faerie waved as Sinjiin caught up to the open carriage at the head of the long line of travelers.

It was hard to tell who looked more shocked to see them—Sevondi or Ryder.

When the dragonwitch leaned close to whisper something in the priest's ear, Melia feared she might be ill. She couldn't look at him again. While her heart thumped as loud as all the horses in the caravan put together, and her stomach balled into a tight fist, she made a mask of her face. Her thighs, gripping the Tasimas between them, quivered; her hands shook. She wanted to throw the heavy diamond at Ryder's head.

It was a long ride to their destination.

The carnivale was canceled that night, and the members of the caravan took their time unloading the horses, rubbing them down, and setting up camp. Melia stayed as far away from the priest as she could.

When Sinjiin wandered off, she followed him. When the tiger plunged into a pond, Melia hunched over the water. Staring at her reflection, she compared herself to the dragonwitch. Why was she surprised Ryder chose the muannaye? Sevondi was much prettier than she was. Melia splashed her face to hide the tears rolling down her cheeks.

When someone–Ryder–rubbed his hand across her back, she almost fell into the water face first.

"I didn't mean to scare you," he said quietly.

He probably didn't want Sevondi to overhear them. She shook his hand off her back.

"What are you doing here?" he asked.

"We thought you wcrc on your way to the Isle of Minnanon." She laughed. The brittle sound was familiar to her. It was a laugh like her mother's. "I thought you took Ormrun and Koldis to the Grey Council. Can you believe it? I convinced myself you risked everything to protect me. How stupid could I be?"

Ryder's forest green eyes widened. His mouth opened, but no words came out. His face, which had been animated before her outburst, flattened.

"Yes, that's what I thought. But no, here you are, cavorting with that ... that ... that witch. Where are the sword and basin? How could you betray us like that? All this time you've been telling me: 'It's too dangerous to incarnate Umbra. I won't let you incarnate Umbra. The burden of Umbra is too great for you to bear'." She jammed a finger at his chest. "You've obviously decided it's not too much for her to bear."

He tried to put his hands on her shoulders.

She shook him off. "Don't touch me!"

"Melia," he said. "It's not what it looks like."

"It never is!"

Ryder stared at something behind her. She turned. Sinjiin lounged in the grass, licking his fur.

Melia snorted. "Oh, I get it now." She pointed back and forth between Ryder and the lazy cat. "You're working together. You probably planned this while you were sailing over from Idonne. No wonder everything has gone wrong since the moment you walked into my life. You're a liar. You've always wanted the basin for

257

yourself." She pushed her fist into his chest. "Was Nandana part of the hoax, too? With that stupid blue mark?"

Ryder gripped her hand. "Melia, Sevondi's ogres beat me. I lost my memory."

"Do you really think I'm going to fall for that? Oh, let me see. The last time she spelled you, this time she had you beaten, and now you're riding across the steppes having a grand time with her. Laughing! You'll need to come up with a better story, even for me." When Ryder's eyebrows reached his forehead, she almost thought his dismay was genuine. Almost. "How did you get the sword and basin away from the founding stone? That's what I want to know."

"I don't remember everything."

"Of. Course. You. Don't."

Ryder dropped her hand. "If you'll let me finish, I'll tell you what I do remember."

Melia covered her ears with her hands. "I won't listen to any more of your lies. All you've ever told me are lies. Lies. Lies!"

"Find me when you're ready to hear what I have to say." He turned and walked away.

"Don't you walk away from me," she whispered.

She turned around.

Sinjiin was gone, too.

Why did it feel like she'd shattered into a million pieces?

It was easy to avoid Ryder until dusk.

Due to her training, it was ages since she'd flown.

That night she flew across the muannai valley as if she would never fly again.

31. *Diving*

Melia landed in a fig tree far enough away from the muannai camp that Ryder wouldn't be able to spot her, but close enough so that she could hear when the caravan packed up.

It was Flora who found her at dawn, curled beneath the tree. The spring faerie squatted beside her, stroking her hair. The tender gesture broke through a wall no words could have penetrated.

Melia's sniffles turned into sobs.

"There, there," Flora said.

When Melia was all cried out, she risked a glimpse at the spring faerie. Flora stared across the valley steppes, and by the look in her eyes, she was far away.

Melia waited for her to come back.

"Aldous and I lost many years because we couldn't trust one another."

The half-faerie pushed herself up. "What are you saying?"

"Sinjiin and I had a long talk with your young man last night."

"He's not my young man," Melia said.

"You're jealous," Flora said. "And for no reason at all."

Melia doubted the spring faerie would vouch for Ryder if he'd lied to all of them. "Then what story did he tell you?"

"You need to talk through it with him yourself."

The burn Melia felt in her chest when she saw Ryder laughing with Sevondi returned. "I can't."

Flora reached for the half-faerie's hand and held it.

Melia searched her creased face.

"Yes," Flora said, "you can. I'm going to ride with Sevondi in her carriage today. You're going to ride in one of the carts with him."

Melia opened her mouth to protest.

Flora raised a hand. "Use everything we've taught you." She patted the half-faerie's thigh. "Everything." Then she rose to her feet and waddled away.

By the time the horses settled into a steady rhythm and the caravan quieted down, it was late morning. The sun was behind a thick layer of clouds and the air was cold.

Melia and Ryder hadn't said a single word to each other.

She kept her lips pressed together with her arms wrapped tightly over her chest or her hands clutching at the edge of the cart's flat seat. Despite what Flora had told her, she refused to be the first one to speak.

He seemed to be in no rush to begin a conversation either.

When she couldn't stop shivering, he pulled the cart over. He let the other horses and vehicles pass by as he scrounged around in the load of luggage the cart carried. When he climbed back onto the rough seat and sat beside her, he handed her a bulky sweater.

Melia slipped it on without a word.

The horses took off, and he began talking.

It was hard to avoid bumping against him as the cart jostled down the road grooved by the carts and carriages ahead of them.

He told her everything that had happened to him since the last time they spoke. "When I saw the eagle fly, that was when I remembered you. And when I remembered you, everything else about my life, and who I am, came rushing back. Because you're my heart."

Melia could hardly breathe.

"I would have run all the way to Aldaine to find you if the ogre hadn't beaten me so soundly. Sevondi stopped him before he killed me. The next morning, she proposed her deal to me. I seized upon

it, because I hoped to end the question of Umbra's incarnation before I returned to you."

All Melia wanted to do was touch him; but she kept her hands curled together beneath her sweater as the tender feelings in her heart expanded.

Although she couldn't look at his face, she was aware of everything else about him: his black boots that pressed and shifted against the floorboards; the brown cloth of his pants that gripped his knees and the muscles of his thighs; his long-sleeved shirt that ended just above his wrists; the backs of his hands tanned from working long days in Aldaine; his fingers that guided the horse's reins with such mastery; and his smell—of leather and sweat.

Everything he'd done was to protect her.

Joy unraveled the knots of distrust constricting her heart. She wanted to be done with hard conversations, to cherish the precious understanding that flowered within her, but she needed to talk more about the dragonwitch incarnating Umbra.

Melia dug deep inside for the courage Bertille had imparted at the market. He deserved her honesty. She could give him that. "Have you tried to take the sword and basin from Sevondi?"

Ryder laughed. "You haven't seen the ogres! They're not too smart, but they don't need weapons. Their hands are like boulders, and one well-placed kick from their boots could be lethal. No. There's a better way. If her mask tricks Umbra, I can use Koldis to kill them both."

Melia's mouth felt dry. "Murder?"

"I'd prefer to think of it as something nobler. The price that must be paid to stop a greater war."

"She doesn't know?"

"When I came across it in my research, I kept it to myself. Koldis is the only blade in the Whole that can kill the embodied Umbra. Does she know? I haven't told her."

The half-faerie squeezed her fists. "Have you forgotten what I told you? Lilliane almost killed me and Tatou in the library. With nothing but black rose petals. If Umbra is destroyed, who will oppose her?"

He took a long breath. "If Lilliane's drawing from Umbra's power, she'll be weakened by his destruction as well."

"That's not a risk I'm willing to take," Melia said. "I don't want Sevondi to die. I want her as an ally."

Ryder shook his head. "That's Flora talking, not you."

"Listen to me," she said. "I've been training. I still have a long way to go, but Aldous and Flora, Sinjiin and Tatou are helping me; and Flora's agreed to take the question of Umbra's incarnation to the Grey Council. She'll abide by their judgment. Surely, you agree that would be a wiser course of action than killing Sevondi."

Ryder's gazed shifted from the horse and the bumpy road to her. "Have you been drinking the wine Sevondi is plying the caravan with?"

"She's not a full-blooded muannai. She's a half-blood, like me."

He winced and returned his attention to the road. "I'm surprised you defend her."

"Ever since I woke up in the Calashai's dungeon, I've felt connected to her. I think it's because we were both shot with arrows tipped with Umbra's poison."

"That's why you want to save her?"

"She's strong, Ryder. If she leads the muannai against the Albiana, we're more likely to defeat them."

"You trust her?"

Melia rubbed a sweater-covered wrist across her forehead. "I have to."

"Have you forgotten? By attempting to incarnate Umbra, she betrays the pact she made with Flora."

"No. I haven't."

"She's as corrupt as Plantine."

Even as the truth of his words stung, her inner voice insisted she couldn't relent to his doubts. "When she fails, she'll have no other choice than to join us."

"You're so sure she'll fail."

"You told me Umbra doesn't want her as his vessel."

"You have been studying," he said with a hint of a smile. "But if Umbra is deceived by the mask—"

"You would kill Sevondi?"

Ryder's jaw tightened before he spoke. "Yes. If it will end the risk to you."

"You're not thinking about Lilliane. You're not remembering the genocide of the spring faeries. You don't know what it feels like to live with the guilt of my ancestor's crime. I must set things right. If you would stand by my side, I have a chance. If you would help me, and have faith in me—in us—in what we can achieve together. It's why you came to Faerie. It's why you answered the call of Nandana's mark." She had no other arguments. The rhythm of her heart quickened as she waited for him to respond.

He didn't say anything for a long time. "I'm going to open the portal for Sevondi. It's part of the game she's agreed to play with me. You need to know, I'll use Koldis if the incarnation is successful. But if it fails, we'll sail to Minnanon as soon as possible. If Flora is willing to abide by the council's ruling, then so will I."

Melia closed her eyes. It was enough.

They rode all day.

The long, stiff silence of the morning became an easy quiet by late afternoon. As a determined wind blew the clouds from the sky, they relaxed with each other in a way they never had before.

When the caravan stopped, Ryder pulled the cart off the road and asked her to wait. He came around to her side of the cart and helped her down. When his hands gripped her waist, she never wanted him to let go. When he did, she was terrified he would walk away from her.

He unhitched the horse, secured its reins, fed it some oats, and then came back to her. He took her hand and led her into the woods.

They came across a large boulder in a small clearing. He pulled her toward it. Half-sitting on the rock, he faced her. This time when he drew her to him, there was no resistance in her body.

He held her hands and gazed into her eyes. The moment crystallized: the smell of late fall drying the grass, the softened wind sweeping strands of hair from her cheek, and the rare, sharp blue Tyrannis sky framing Ryder's face. He'd never lied to her and he never would. She knew it in her heart.

Every awful thing she'd lived through since Nandana marked her forehead had brought her here, to this moment with him. It was a strange magic, to distillate wonder from horror. Even—perhaps, especially—her mother's spell had created the space she'd needed to sort through her feelings for him. A lesson in discernment, Aldous might have said. Melia smiled.

Ryder pulled her closer. The rough skin of his hands caressed her neck. He cradled her chin and lifted her face. His lips touched hers.

Walls came down.

Easy. No crashing.

She kissed him back. They created soft heat. They traveled to a new place together. A warm, dizzying, hypnotic place. The place where they belonged together. The place where they belonged to each other. His hands tangled in her hair.

Melia understood.

She knew how to fly. Now, it was time to dive.

She let go.

32. Soul Flame

Melia stared at the Muudron Stone remembering the night she watched from the long grass as Sevondi leapt upon the stage riding a turnskin. Tonight, the moons would be dark and the dragonwitch would attempt to incarnate Umbra.

"Are you ready?" Ryder stood behind her, cradling her body in his. His chin rested on her shoulder; his arms circled her waist.

For the past seven days, Flora tried to persuade Sevondi not to risk her life. Pogo had echoed the spring faerie's pleas.

Sevondi wouldn't relinquish her vision of incarnating Umbra as her grand finale. In a way, Melia understood. She'd witnessed two performances of the carnivale and had been as dazzled as everyone else. "I'll be the first wall of defense against the incarnation," she told Ryder. "Don't use Koldis unless I fail."

"I'll do whatever I have to do."

"It's a grisly business," Melia murmured.

"It will be, if it comes to that," he said.

"Do you think the mask will deceive Umbra?"

"It's an incredible likeness."

"Then you've looked into the basin and seen her?"

"One night, before you caught up with us, Sevondi asked me to verify the artisan's work."

"What's the girl's name?" Melia asked.

"Jade."

"She wasn't on Aldous' Albiana family tree."

"Flora thinks she's Lola's daughter."

"Gabriela's granddaughter. Could you tell—did you see anything that made you think Umbra has reached her?"

"She looks wild and ethereal," Ryder said. "But it's hard to know what drives that without knowing more about her."

"No matter what happens here tonight, I'll have to find her and warn her to reject his seduction."

"Maybe I'll go with you this time," Ryder said.

"Have you ever been to the mortal world?"

"No."

"Then you should definitely come with me."

The muannai began arranging wood bleachers around the stage and installing the fountains that would flow with wine.

"I need to help them prepare for the show," Ryder said.

Melia turned in his arms and gave him a half-hearted smile. When he brushed her lips with his, she closed her eyes. When she opened them, he was gone.

Left with nothing but her thoughts, she searched the horizon. In a few hours, the sun would set, and they would all be tested.

❖ ❖ ❖

Melia searched the crowd milling around the vats of wine, but the spring faerie, half the height of the muannai, was nowhere in sight. Melia crouched to peer beneath the platform hoping to spot Flora's tiny boots.

"What are you doing?" The spring faerie's gravelly voice came from behind.

Melia popped up. Flora never appreciated being reminded of her short stature. "Nothing."

"Hmm. How are you feeling?" Flora asked.

The half-faerie stretched her neck. "Tense."

"Good. Use the wariness to keep you alert."

Melia checked the dagger wedged in the top of her boot.

"Remember what we talked about. As soon as Sevondi shows herself, position yourself as close to the stage as possible. Don't wait for a catastrophe to begin drawing power." Flora adjusted her kerchief. The red-plaid scarf was already straight, but the spring faerie tugged, adjusted, and pulled on it whenever she sank deep into thought. Melia waited. Flora raised a gnarled finger toward the red and gold foliage of a copse of maples and sycamores. "Start there."

Melia nodded.

The spring faerie dug her hands in her apron pocket. "If you get in a bind, draw energy from the stones themselves. Their power is ancient and wild. But harness it, if you need to, as a last resort."

"Where will you and Sinjiin be?"

"As close to the stage as we can, but you've seen how rowdy the crowd becomes. If we get separated, we won't be able to help you. Don't count on us."

Every word Flora spoke made her uneasy. "What are you worried about?" Melia asked.

The spring faerie tucked a finger underneath her kerchief and scratched.

"What?"

Flora closed her eyes. "I'm worried that if Umbra discovers you, he'll seize the opportunity to incarnate."

Melia's confidence spiraled downward.

"You've done well with your training—better than I expected—but you're not ready. No matter what happens tonight, you're not ready. Do all you can to keep Sevondi alive, but your priority is to protect yourself. If it comes down to Umbra overpowering you and incarnating tonight, then Sevondi will have to be sacrificed. Let your young man kill her. The muannai will turn on us, but if Umbra possesses you before you're ready, all hope is gone."

Melia swallowed hard.

When the amethyst and onyx dragon won the final battle, the crowd stamped and cheered. A deafening wave of muannai surged forward, crushing Melia back. Flora and Sinjiin drowned in the sea of spellbound faces.

Melia's head pounded. Without the spring faerie and mage at her side, she felt stripped of power, but she couldn't risk putting more distance between herself and the stage to find them.

The muannai's love for the dragonwitch rolled over her and onto the Muudron Stone. Melia grasped at the swell of energy, but it refused to bind to her. She forced her breath to calm. It finally slowed, pushing her out of sync with the frenzy of her surroundings. She stood, out of time, and observed.

The muannai required no further proof Sevondi deserved the regency. Yet their devotion wasn't enough to satiate the dragonwitch. Umbra's rejection had become a challenge which compelled her to risk her life. For Melia, it was a bleak reality to witness.

Ryder stepped from the shadows cast by two crumbling columns. The glint of Ormrun's jewels reflected the circle of torchlight. He carried the basin and sheathed sword. Pogo shuffled behind him with a bucket and pedestal. Five monsters—the ogres—loomed on the periphery.

The muannai hushed. Melia held her breath. Ryder and Pogo arranged the stage for Sevondi's finale.

The dragonwitch donned the mask. The likeness of a pale-skinned half-mortal with ropey hair sticking out in all directions enveloped her.

Melia returned her focus to the copse of trees. With rhythmic breaths, she pulled everything from the natural world she could summon.

Pogo poured water from the Great White Sea into the basin. Ryder approached with Koldis.

The drumheads cracked with urgency.

Melia watched the basin. Her battle would be with whatever emerged from the mists roiling across its surface.

An eerie melody snaked through the strange quiet of the crowd.

Sevondi encouraged the muannai to cheer. Perhaps their quiet disturbed her. The muannai rallied with calls and bursts of loud chanting.

Searching the crowd one more time for the spring faerie and mage, Melia almost missed it when Ryder–holding Koldis' hilt with both hands–plunged the sword into the basin.

A black shadow curdled from the mists.

Melia slammed it with her mind.

The basin seethed with waves. The black shadow reformed. Sevondi called the dark shape to her, challenging Melia's mental wall.

The half-faerie sucked hard at the blackness.

"Do not interfere." The sinister voice jarred Melia.

Echoes of past failures drained energy from her mind. She lost an important moment. The inky shadow leapt from the water's surface. No longer bound by the bowl, it searched for a new home. Melia sucked harder with her mind.

The black shadow shifted toward her. *"I will take you, half-faerie."*

Flora's warning set off alarms in her mind. *"No."* Melia erected another mental wall. Broader, wider, deeper. This one to protect herself. The black shadow tested for a chink, a crack, a crevice to ooze through, but all her training held. Her shield stood, impenetrable.

Rebuffed, the shadow drifted in Sevondi's direction. Who knows what the muannai staring at the Muudron's stage saw? Perhaps nothing, only stillness as the drums and flute sent their strange song into the dark moon night.

Ryder leaned forward, ready to kill.

Every muscle in Melia's body braced.

The shadow streamed around Sevondi, tempting her, teasing her, promising her: something, everything, anything, and nothing. *"I will take you, Jade."*

Sevondi spread her arms.

Melia was too far away. She climbed onto the stage and inched toward its center. A concentrated wave of energy threw her back. She hit the stone dais with her wrists and butt, the wind knocked out of her. Sevondi or Umbra? Melia couldn't tell. As the union approached, their wills entwined.

"You have no mortal blood, dragonwitch," Umbra hissed.

Ear-splitting thunder smashed the cloudless night. Fingers of lightning speared the ground.

Muannai screamed.

Three times, Melia watched Sevondi parade her magnificent beasts across the sky, and each time the sight evoked awe in her heart. She wanted the dragonwitch to live.

Melia remembered the power in the stones. She pressed her palms against the rocks. They were warm, alive, pulsating with heat. She pressed the soles of her boots down as hard as she could and imagined herself one with the stone. The rhythm of her breath linked with the muannai drums. Her concentration settled in her tailbone. Energy coiled from the base of her spine up into her belly. Her soul flame. She let it build.

A cyclone of ancient voices swirled around her. Their unintelligible chorus embraced her. Back on her feet, she assaulted the whirlwind of inky shadow smothering Sevondi.

"I will kill you," Umbra promised the muannaye.

Melia imagined the headwind parting like water. It didn't, but there was enough give to let her progress. She focused her mind on pulling Umbra from Sevondi's body.

"She will die first," Umbra challenged Melia as she wrestled with him for the muannaye's life.

She hunted for Ryder. He stood on the other side of Sevondi. Much too close, much too eager to deal a fatal blow. Melia sensed his need to end it all. No more Umbra, no more imminent incarnation.

Princess Lilliane would be grateful; the muannai engulfing the stage would not.

Melia dove into her black pit of rage. If Flora's kin were to receive justice, if the enchanted world was to be released from the Albiana stranglehold, they would need every warrior who could fight.

Sevondi was too magnificent to sacrifice.

"Little Bird."

Melia listened.

"Darkness and light are eternally bound. Fire the lead of your darkness with the light of your soul flame. You are the crucible," the voice of Elynus spoke.

An image came to her, as if her father gifted the picture to her mind. An impenetrable vase forged by her soul flame could contain Umbra's bile. Melia rotated the flaming receptacle with her inner eye. It could work, but binding her inner light to her inner darkness was not something Aldous had taught her.

"Bear what I could not."

Her father's unexpected faith in his middle child stunned her. Distracted by the intense flush, her inner concentration wavered. The external world returned. Her gaze locked on Ryder. He held Koldis, but the ogres' towering shadows encircled him. Everyone was in danger.

With her feet jammed against the Muudron's ancient stones, Melia returned to her inner stage. The chrysalis for reality. Twining every black impulse she'd ever had with the soul flame licking her spine, she fashioned a vase's bowl in her belly, a vase's neck in her throat. Her training had strengthened her ability to focus; her ability to imagine—guided by her father's gift—came naturally. Fierce concentration obliterated any doubt. When the vase was solid in her mind, she angled for the dragonwitch.

Step by step she edged closer, her focus absolute. When she was so close the blank sockets of Sevondi's mask leered directly at her, Melia yanked the abomination from the muannaye's head.

Terror filled the dragonwitch's eyes with a cold gleam. Her hands pawed at her throat. She gasped for breath.

Melia sensed Sevondi's knees buckle and caught her. She bent over and gripped the muannaye's face in her hands. Fearless, Melia covered the dragonwitch's mouth with her lips. Pressed against Sevondi's velvet skin, they formed a seal.

Melia summoned the furious power within her—the power she'd denied all her life—and leached the dragonwitch of Umbra.

When she'd drained every last ounce of bile into her illuminated vessel, Melia closed her mouth and let Sevondi drop.

Umbra's essence sucked heat from the vase. Bubbling, oozing liquid converted to thick, black steam. The building pressure threatened to shatter Melia's inner container, but the more Umbra fought, the more she imagined her burning walls thin and hard.

The inner fight depleted her external energy. She faltered to her hands and knees. Drawing as much energy as she could from the stones through her palms, she lurched toward the basin. Free of the ogres, Ryder raced toward her. Something yanked her ankle. She half turned. Sevondi clung to her. Horrified, Melia groped for the knife in her boot. If she didn't make it to Ormrun, she'd fail.

She slashed out blindly with the dagger. Sevondi screamed. Strong hands grabbed Melia's waist. Someone—Ryder?—dragged her. Her boots scraped against the hard stage. Muannai shouted. Were they shouting at her? A tiger roared. Her shoulder crashed against the stage.

"You're damned reckless," Ryder heaved.

With dim awareness, she watched him plunge Koldis into Ormrun.

"Get up." That was Flora.

Melia reached for the basin. She had no strength left. She'd given everything to containing Umbra. Now her fiery vase was a volcano on the verge of erupting inside her. She tried to pull herself up. The bowl toppled. Water from the Great White Sea splashed in her eyes. The bowl rolled across the stones.

"Put it on the ground in front of her," Flora ordered. "Pogo, pour in whatever water is left in that bucket."

The spring faerie yanked Melia's hair. The basin slid beneath her chin. Flora pulled Melia's head back farther. The blue of Koldis' blade flashed before her eyes. Flora pushed her back toward the bowl. "Release him back into the Void."

Melia spewed lava. She retched until nothing of Umbra remained inside her. Her hollow vessel collapsed. She tasted ash inside her mouth. She spit it out. Particles floated into the basin.

Koldis clattered against the stones.

Strong hands picked her up, cradled her. Ryder.

She broke down against his chest and sobbed.

"I won't incarnate Umbra."

Melia, propped up on a bed of pillows, challenged the spring faerie. They'd been arguing all morning, the half-faerie wasted in her bed, Flora plying her with herb water.

"You agreed to put it before the council."

Melia closed her eyes. "If my father hadn't shown me what to do last night, I would ... I wouldn't ... I didn't know what to do. Umbra would have won."

Flora took the empty wooden cup from her. "But your father did show you what to do and it was rather ingenious. Druids, always wise in the ways of elements."

Melia moaned. "That's not the point."

"Then enlighten me, missy."

The half-faerie's eyelids raised. Flora hadn't called her missy since ... she couldn't remember the last time. "The point is: My father is part of Umbra."

"A part of Umbra that helped you. A part of Umbra that aligned with you, not against you."

"He was so angry when I went to see him in Achill ... and then ... why would he help me now?"

Flora fiddled with her kerchief. "Mortal bodies are dense. Much denser than the bodies of any creature in Faerie—or the enchanted world. If mortals don't tend rather vigorously to their soul flame, their spirit and awareness gets dampened. Muddied," she said. "They lose the ability to see clearly and make all sorts of regretful decisions. But when the body falls away in death, if the mortal's soul flame has any strength at all, it survives. Your father's soul flame survived if Umbra has absorbed his ash. It speaks well of him. And it speaks well of the blood he gave you."

"Are you saying he's forgiven me?"

"I'm saying he sees more now. Including seeing you as you are, not as his child. Most parents are blind to the truth of their offspring, good or bad. Especially mortals."

The half-faerie laughed. "I wonder if he still thinks I'm sweet."

Flora shook her head. "That I can't answer."

"How is Sevondi?" Melia asked.

"Alive."

"That's good." But the news was another unwelcome reminder of why she fought so hard to save the dragonwitch. Yesterday, she was committed to the possibility of incarnating Umbra; this morning, she agreed with Ryder. She was damned reckless for having ever entertained the notion. "And Ryder?"

"Guarding the tent," Flora said.

Melia's heart somersaulted. "He's outside?"

"Yes, are you ready to see him?"

Ryder entered the tent. Although his hair stuck out in all directions and his shoulders sagged with exhaustion, his eyes sparkled when they met hers. Joy surged in Melia's breast, drowning out every other emotion.

He wanted to know everything that had happened to Melia on the Muudron's stage. Although he'd been there, the ogres had formed a barrier, keeping him away from Sevondi and her.

He listened without interrupting, unlike Flora who asked a million probing questions, using every answer Melia gave to comment on how far she'd advanced in her training—and in such a short period of time.

Ryder never let go of Melia's hand. He told her again and again he should have done more to protect her.

Outside, the enormous clove-colored tiger paced back and forth.

Melia could see him through the half-open tent flap. "Is Sinjiin all right?"

"He's been restless all morning. You impressed him last night. You impressed us all," he said. "He's eager to sail to the Isle of Minnanon."

Melia's eyes blurred. They all believed in her.

Ryder wiped a tear from her cheek with his thumb. "You proved me wrong."

"How?"

"According to everything I've ever studied, what you did last night was impossible."

Melia was speechless. She'd counted on Ryder to help her convince Flora they'd all made a mistake. That perhaps Jade was the one ...

"I've been thinking all morning," he said. "What would the Whole be like if dark and light could be balanced? I've always believed dark and light were extremes of a continuum, never to achieve equilibrium, only to swing back and forth, evening out over time. But what if harmony could be achieved? What if you could do that?"

"You think I should incarnate Umbra?" she squeaked.

Ryder stared at the blanket that covered her. "I've been wrong to dismiss the truth you speak from your heart." He raised his gaze. "And I was wrong to break my promise to stay by your side: no matter what."

Melia's blood rushed. She touched his face. Her fingers brushed stubble and warm skin. He was real, and so was everything that had happened since he came into her life.

The next day, Sevondi entered her tent. The muannaye's bandaged hand gripped the head of a cane.

Expecting a tongue lashing, Melia sank deeper into her pillows.

"Thank you," Sevondi said.

Melia fumbled for a response.

"Now, I remember you," the muannaye continued. "Many moons ago you came to my shop in the marketplace." She touched the design on the side of her face. "You asked me about a protective shield."

"Yes."

Sevondi reached for a strand of Melia's hair and inhaled. "You no longer smell of bird. Or stumble over your words."

"I've changed."

"The day I sent you away was not a good day to draw a shield." Sevondi traced Melia's cheekbone with her finger. "But today is a perfect day."

33. Returning to the Mortal World

Flora gave Melia the pillowcase with the Tasimas inside. "Don't lose it."

"We won't." Although it meant he had to relinquish control of the sword and basin, Ryder was going to travel to Aldaine with Melia. He wasn't about to let her out of his sight. "What shall I tell Aldous?" the half-faerie asked.

"That I must accompany the basin and the sword to the Veiled Tavern," Flora said. "He'll understand we can't risk returning Ormrun and Koldis to the founding stone."

Melia gazed at the Muudron's crumbling pillars one last time. "When do you think Sevondi will be ready to leave?"

"When the copper sheets begin writing about something other than the carnivale," the spring faerie grumbled.

Sevondi had achieved her vision. The dragon carnivale's finale would be debated and philosophized about until the end of time. Although none of the muannai saw Umbra when Melia sparred with him, they believed an invisible force came among them that night, one that waged a mystical battle upon the Muudron's stage.

Flora and Sinjiin said their goodbyes before Melia and Ryder joined hands. The half-faerie and young priest envisioned the bluffs that overlooked the granite cliffs of Faerie's northern coast.

When Melia's fingers embraced the diamond's smooth surface, the Whole transformed into a riot of wind. Ryder squeezed Melia's hand as an enormous gust threatened to tear them apart. His grip was their only link as their torsos spun and their legs twisted in opposite directions. The release was sudden; they fell several feet to land in a bruised heap, their ears filled with the roar of the Great White Sea.

"I'm surprised we didn't encounter more resistance," Melia said.

Ryder's half-smile distracted her as he traced the tattoo curved across her cheekbone. "You're gaining strength."

The muannai they passed stared at the black design on Melia's face. When they found Tatou and Aldous, the pixie and old elf gaped too.

Tatou ran her fingers along the edge of the mark. "Will it protect you?"

"Sevondi's didn't protect her from Umbra."

"Maybe it did," Ryder said.

Melia absorbed his perspective.

"It looks exotic," Tatou said.

Ryder reached for Melia's hand. "Doesn't it?"

"Your mother's curse has been lifted, hasn't it?" the pixie asked.

Melia blushed. "Yes."

Tatou wrapped her arms around her friend's neck. "That's good news, if a bit sad. I loved flying with you."

They walked along the familiar cliffs of Tyrannis, Melia between Ryder and Aldous, Tatou perched on her friend's shoulder. The priest blocked the chill wind blowing from the sea.

The news of Jade intrigued Aldous. "We have no records of Lola having a daughter, so you'll need to begin with her," he said.

"Where can we find her?" Melia asked.

The old elf walked with his hands behind his back. "A place called San Diego, California. If I remember correctly, it will be easiest to find her in the year 1998. She'll be older then, more approachable."

His tone and words reminded Melia of the first time he sent her to meet Flora. "Is that your way of saying we should be prepared for anything?"

Aldous' eyes twinkled behind his glasses. "It is."

"Is there anything else we'll need to know?"

"You'll enter through a fountain in the park where she lives."

"Isn't that unusual?" Ryder asked. "For a mortal to live outside in that time period?"

"I believe it is," Aldous said. "But from everything we've heard, Lola is an unusual lady."

Melia and Ryder entered the Dragon's Keep library. Their footsteps echoed in the enormous space.

Empty shelves, built into the library's high walls, extended to the arched ceiling. In their center, Aldous directed a number of muannai who were pushing and pulling varnished bookcases to form symmetric rows.

Unopened crates and stacks of books towered on the south wall of the cavernous room.

Aldous dusted his hands as they approached. "We're almost ready for the gnomes to begin cataloging the books."

Melia hadn't noticed the pointed red tips of several hats peeking over the crates and piles. Flora would have chastised her for not being more observant of her surroundings. "How did you round them up?" she asked.

"We recruited them from Lord Goring's estate." Aldous said. "I've always known he had an impressive library, but with all the recent excitement, I forgot all about it. However, when Yrrick tasked me with filling the keep's library, it made sense to start there.

"When we arrived at Goring's home, a large group of gnomes moped around the front lawn. Apparently, he employed them as groundskeepers. Once we were inside, they crept behind us, speaking their gibberish. When we tried to take our leave with Goring's books, they stomped and cursed us, shaking their fists in the air.

"I had no idea gnomes were such passionate readers. We invited them to work here."

"They're focused," Ryder said.

A sense of order already prevailed where the gnomes worked among the stacks and crates.

"Another bit of good news," Aldous said, "Goring had a large number of books pilfered from the mortal world, which as you know, was his obsession. I'm confident we'll find a picture of the fountain you'll want to pass through to find Lola, shortly."

"We'll be going to the Veil before we travel to the mortal world," Melia said.

"Will Tatou be joining you?" the librarian asked.

"No. She'll be gardening while we're away. She wants to plant a few of the sapphire lily seeds to see if the flower can grow in this damp climate."

"I'll be happy to assist her—" A gnome tugged on the old elf's vest. "I'll send for you as soon as we have your photo." Aldous turned to attend the bearded creature, who without his red steeple cap would have stood even shorter than the librarian.

Melia and Ryder, standing on either side of Aldous, studied a large black and white photo the librarian held in his hands.

"It's strange how much it resembles the fountain in the Calashai's courtyard before it fell," Melia said.

"Most everything that exists in the mortal world has been imagined to some degree or another in the enchanted world first," Aldous said.

"Not those Model T things," Melia said.

"You haven't traveled to Morganna yet."

"They have autos there?"

"Engines propelled by steam."

The half-faerie quirked an eyebrow.

"Fossil fuel provides the energy for all sorts of mortal creations," Aldous explained. "A substitute for magic, I suppose. Although with inherent shortcomings—atmospheric pollution being the most obvious."

"I'm surprised Goring didn't try to smuggle gasoline into Tyrannis," Ryder said.

"It's possible he did. The gnomes have told me about several fiery explosions that occurred along the river near Goring's estate. Explosions that left more than one troll dead."

"To what end?" Melia asked.

"No one would have believed he could make electricity work in the enchanted world, but if I'm not mistaken, Goring achieved that at the Blue Mermaid. I suspect that success fueled his ambition. However, bringing fossil fuel across was an entirely different prospect. It ignited the second it reached the enchanted world's atmosphere."

"I'm surprised the trolls continued to work for him."

"At heart, trolls are mercenaries. From what I understand, he paid them well. Ah, well, these are fascinating subjects but they won't be of much use when it comes to finding Lola." Aldous handed the photo to Melia.

"Are you sure we'll be able to pass through this fountain? It looks like there's a barrier on the bottom. Some kind of rock or stone."

Aldous indicated a shadow at the fountain's center. "Aim for that point. Although the circumference of the door is relatively small compared to passageways through bodies of natural water, it should do the trick during the in-between times."

"Sunrise and sunset," Melia confirmed. "Do you have a picture of Lola?"

Aldous lifted his chin. A gnome came running with a bulk of yellowed paper. The librarian led Melia and Ryder to a table where the gnome deposited the stack. Aldous unfolded the packet of fragile sheets, once, twice. He pointed to a faded, two-toned picture.

A woman with a puffy body and blank eyes stared from the page. Lank dark hair, ratted like a mouse's nest, hung almost to her waist. Everything about her seemed shapeless and dull.

"That's is Gabriela's daughter?" Melia asked, stunned.

"If you were to read the accompanying story, you'd learn she survives among the full-blood mortals as a mental patient."

"I don't understand."

"Unlike Gabriela, her daughter speaks freely about her encounters with our kind. Since the advent of the industrial age, fewer and fewer full-blood mortals see faeries, elves, trolls, or the like in their world. However, Lola has never denied our existence. As a result of her forthrightness, she's labeled crazy and treated with synthetic medication. Her appearance indicates the reaction of the chemicals with her Albiana blood is anything but positive."

"Is there any mention of her daughter?" Melia asked.

"Not a word. But Jade must be related to Gabriela."

"Then we'll begin with Lola."

"Melia—" Aldous pushed his spectacles up the bridge of his nose.

"Yes?"

"Perhaps you could bring Lola to Faerie."

"The enchanted gardens!"

"That will have to wait until Lilliane's powers have been contained. I doubt the princess will welcome any more half-bloods to Illialei. However, I have an idea that spending time anywhere in the enchanted world will be soothing for Lola."

Melia gazed at the sad photo. "It certainly couldn't harm her."

"We'll convince her to return with us," Ryder said, "after we find Jade."

"Good. Good," Aldous said. "I hate to see the pure suffer needlessly."

34. Two White Doves

With every step Lilliane took, her bare feet slapped the cool stone floor with ill-concealed resentment. Her mother, the impotent queen, languished against a mountain of cushions. Lilliane refrained from yanking aside the sheer curtain that made a tent of her mother's bed. "You must return to the Cathedral Palace," the princess heir said.

"I'm comfortable here," her mother replied.

"You're hiding here."

Luisa turned away. "I've given you everything you've asked for: an army of Huron knights occupies Illialei; black roses from the Black Magic Islands thrive in the Cathedral Palace gardens; Uriel's journals—"

"Mother, the elves whisper about your frailty. You must return to the Cathedral Palace and prove your strength! That's the only thing that will silence them."

"Darling, is it the sapphire lily?"

Lilliane treated her mother to an icy glare. "Why must you always bring up that flower?"

"Uriel was the same way."

"What do you mean?"

"Your great-grandmother hated the Summer Palace too. Its proximity to the lily disturbed her. Of course, there was an entire field when she was your age. Now, there's only one."

"Are you testing me?"

"You wish to rule the enchanted world, do you not?"

"I'll settle for the whole of Faerie to begin with."

"Do you think the muannai will honor you as their queen simply because you demand it?"

"I'm the rightful heir to the throne."

"To the throne in the Cathedral Palace."

"The only one left in Faerie. Dirt ate Elendah's throne when the Calashai fell."

"Have you given any thought to this dragonwitch? All summer long, reports of her rise to power have filled the copper sheets. Among the muannai, she's beloved. They've constructed a new stronghold for her, the Dragon's Keep."

Lilliane scoffed. "She's no threat to me. Her attempt to incarnate Umbra failed."

"Underestimating your enemies is not a mark of wisdom."

"Now you lecture me from your sickbed?"

"You must be alert to the forces aligning against you."

"Do you think I'm blind to them?" Lilliane pulled aside her mother's bed curtain and sat beside the queen.

Luisa stroked her daughter's hair. "You're so like your father."

Lilliane's jaw tightened. "Why must you forever remind me of his absence?"

"In two years—"

"That's why you've dragged me here? To tell me that you won't release the crown for two more years!"

"Lilliane, you're still a child."

"A child who is more powerful than you'll ever be. I won't wait two more years. If you refuse to bless my succession, I'll have you imprisoned and silenced in your precious Summer Palace." She rose from the bed. "Think about that before you send for me again."

"Lilliane! I'm still queen."

The princess heir stalked to the door. "Then worry for your future, Mother. Not mine."

"Gavin, we're returning to the Cathedral Palace."

"So late in the day, Princess?"

Lilliane wasn't about to spend another night in the Summer Palace when a stone's throw away the sapphire lily, blooming on the shores of Lake Vivientiana, leeched her power.

"The moons wax tonight," she said. "There'll be plenty of light to travel by when the sun sets."

"As you wish, Princess."

While she waited for Gavin to bring her pony, Lilliane organized her thoughts. She'd answered her mother's summons, hoping to persuade Luisa to abdicate the throne. Sevondi's failure to incarnate Umbra wasn't the only news to cross the river. Melia saved the dragonwitch. As her cousin grew stronger, Luisa's delicate health made them vulnerable. Two years was far too long for Lilliane to wait. By then, any one of the half-bloods could incarnate Umbra and win the battle between Dark and Light.

Lilliane's shoulders and ribcage hardened, creating a shell around her heart. If she could just get her hands on the sword and the basin...

Ormrun and Koldis were believed to be indestructible, but everything had a fault line. Lilliane would begin her experiments with various metals to find a flame fierce enough to melt the dwarf artifacts. Without them, Umbra could never incarnate. When she did inherit the Cathedral Palace throne, Lilliane intended to draw on Umbra's ever-accumulating energy to expand her dominion.

The enchanted world was in her grasp. She could feel it. One day, even the gods of Azyllai would kneel before her.

Gavin approached with her pony. She held out her hand and smiled. "Thank you for coming to my rescue. I can't spend another moment here."

Lilliane removed Uriel's two journals from their hiding place in her bedroom. Perhaps she'd been too harsh with her mother. Luisa's gift of the leather-bound books filled with Uriel's jagged handwriting had been a surprise on the princess' fourteenth birthday. She hadn't known they existed.

"I'm sorry, Mother," she whispered into the shadowy candlelight. "The opportunity created by Elendah's death will be brief. I must seize the advantage to master black magic. The dragonwitch has shown no ability to restrain me, but it's only a matter of time before the Grey Council sends another emissary to rein in my power."

Lilliane gathered her black spider-laced shawl, a bone scrying pendant, and the dish of black rose petals she harvested on the way to her room. She pushed her chamber door open and scanned the torch-lit halls. Gavin had agreed to move his sentries to the stairwells and floors beneath her private domain. Clearing the corridor outside her room of soldiers allowed her free movement between her chamber and the palace's easternmost turret. She padded in that direction now.

The five-sided tower was Lilliane's sanctuary. Numerous tantrums had secured the required items, strange and foreign to Illialei, to construct her dark altar. Detailed diagrams and instructions in Uriel's journals guided her work. Now, every time Lilliane entered her domain, feelings of pride swept over her.

She settled Uriel's journals, the pendant, and dish of petals on the bronze table. As she walked to the tower's northern window, she draped the black shawl over her head and knotted it loosely against her throat. She leaned across the thick stone sill, arms spread, palms up, imagining the moons' radiance infusing her veins with unflinching perception.

She walked a slow circle around the tower's interior. An iron cage hung in the opposite window. The wings of the doves, asleep within, silvered in the waxing light of Faerie's two moons. Lilliane moved purposely toward the birds. She cooed as she unlocked the miniature iron gate. Her hand darted and grabbed one of the prisoners by its throat. A high-pitched hiss drowned the soft jangle of sliding metal as she yanked the captive from its home, leaving its mate caged.

The dove in her hand stabbed its beak at the princess. She pressed her thumb against the main artery in the bird's neck. Its mate made a sound akin to a scream. Lilliane's eyes widened. The mate's vehement outrage surprised her, as did the will of the bird in her hand to survive. The princess squeezed the dove's wings tight against its back with her free hand.

The bird refused to surrender.

Lilliane's heart pounded as she positioned herself before her altar. Her eyes narrowed on the handle of her dagger. She pressed her thumb deeper into the dove's throat. Her fingernails dug through its feathers, sinking into the folds of soft skin beneath, but still the bird fought.

A frantic wing shot free of her hand.

She summoned hatred. As she pressed hard against the dove's throat, she half-expected to poke a hole in its flesh with her thumb.

Both birds screeched and hissed.

A spurt of nausea erupted in Lilliane's stomach. She released one hand. The dove flapped its wings wildly, flipping its body, nicking the side of her face with a talon.

Lilliane grabbed her dagger and pushed the dove's throat against the black quartz offering slab. Rather than making a clean slice across the bird's neck, she dug blindly with the blade. She stabbed in a crazed frenzy until the dove stretched limply across the black surface. Blood stained her fingers. The mate continued to screech.

It would wake the entire palace.

She ran to the iron cage to set it free, but when she slid open the door, it came straight at her. She waved her hands to protect her eyes. Eyes from which tears of anguish and failure streamed.

The doorknob to the locked tower jiggled. "Princess, are you all right?" called Gavin.

Lilliane hissed at the surviving dove. "If you value your life, flee."

It circled her to land next to its mate. Bile rose in the princess heir's throat as it cooed and nuzzled its dead companion.

Gavin's tone grew more urgent. "Princess?"

Lilliane grabbed the dead bird and tossed it from the tower window. The surviving mate circled the tower once before following the body of its mate and disappearing from view.

The princess wiped her hands against her skirt. She slipped the shawl from her head and hid her stained dagger in her pocket. After straightening her hair, she unlocked the door. "Yes?"

He pushed his way in, searching.

She bit her lower lip, uncertain which upset her more: the night's failure or Gavin's uninvited charge into her most private and sacred space.

"I heard screams," he said.

She waved one hand. "Birds, I released them from their cage. They were overjoyed to be freed."

Gavin continued his search of the tower. When his eyes settled on her altar, he nodded, but made no comment.

The damage was done, her sanctuary exposed. Unleashing her rage would only make the moment more memorable. She forced her tone to be congenial. "Thank you for checking on me."

"It's my duty."

She pressed her lips together and tilted her head.

He proffered his forearm.

They walked in silence down the tower's spiral stairs. She was shivering from the aftermath of her failed experiment. He seemed empowered by witnessing her vulnerability.

He didn't stop outside her door as he usually did. He simply pushed it open and ushered her in, leading her to the bed. When they stood beside it, he removed her hand from his arm and turned to face her. He traced the cut on her cheek with his thumb.

His arrogance left her weak in the knees.

"You're bleeding," he said.

She jerked her cheek from his touch.

His fingers brushed her hair. Her body delighted in his audacity.

"I'll send a nurse to tend the wound," he said.

She didn't need a nurse. "Thank you," she choked.

"May I help you with anything else?"

Lilliane shook her head and dropped her gaze.

"Should I send word to your mother?"

Her head shot up. "No!"

Gavin dropped his hands to her shoulders. His grip was too firm. "Perhaps you spend too much time alone, Princess."

Lilliane closed her eyes. The smell of him filled her. She wanted to lean into his chest. She wanted to scratch his eyes out. She wanted him to help her. She wanted him to leave Faerie and never return. His finger trailed her cheek and she shivered. "I'm not trusting of others," she whispered.

"Indeed."

His mechanical response shook her from her stupor. She swallowed her pathetic hope that he might protect her secrets. She needed to be alone. She needed to rebuild her inner defenses. "Please, I'm exhausted. Let me sleep."

He dropped his hands and backed away from her.

She stared at his boots. The way he looked at her made her feel common. Yet she dared not censure him, tonight.

The next morning Gavin waited at her breakfast table, helping himself to berries and cream, hotcakes, and steaming cups of tea with honey. His familiarity stunned her. Heated currents spiraled through her body. He didn't rise when she entered the room.

"Good morning, Princess."

If her mother were here, he would never dare to commandeer her chamber with such arrogance. She refused to give him the satisfaction of outrage. "Gavin," she greeted him with a cool tone. A parchment stretched before him. "News from Huros?"

"Only a love letter. My fiancé misses me."

Lilliane stared at her plate. He toyed with her. "How pleased she must be, knowing her devotion to you is reciprocated."

Gavin laughed.

"Did I say something funny?"

289

"You have no care for my fiancé's sentiments. Indeed, if I were faithful to her, it would be troublesome to you. Would it not?"

Lilliane steeled herself. "Then you're not faithful to her?"

Gavin smiled. "She's beautiful, but she's not a princess. Besides, we've taken no vows."

"Not yet. But you're betrothed to one another."

"What she doesn't know won't hurt her."

"How simple are your philosophies, but everyone has enemies. Do you doubt those old men you command resent your rise above them. Perhaps one would tell her—"

"My troops are loyal to me."

"And you're trifling with me, Gavin."

He leaned across the table. "Do you deny your passions are dark, Princess?"

"You know nothing of my passions."

He stood and tossed the parchment into the hearth. He stabbed it with a poker until nothing remained of the letter. There was a cloth bundle sitting next to his dishes. He pushed it along a crooked course through the cups and saucers, then came around the table to stand at Lilliane's side. She could smell the soap he used to bathe with that morning; she could see a nick from the blade he used to shave his face. Her body melted, as defeat and desire struggled within her.

He pulled back a corner of cloth.

The dead dove's stiff wide-eyed stare accused her.

She covered her mouth with the back of her hand. "Take it away."

He whispered in her ear, "There's not a court in the enchanted world that would approve of Lilliane Albiana slaying innocent doves in the Cathedral Palace tower."

She gritted her teeth and stared at the ceiling as he lifted her hair and traced a line from her neck to her shoulder.

"What is it that you want from me, Princess? You have only to ask."

"Take the bird away," she said.

"As you wish." He stuffed the dove's body into a leather pouch.

Lilliane forced her hand to remain steady as she poured a cup of tea. She'd lost a battle not the war. Victory was still within reach. "There is something you can do for me," she said. "It's only that I'm not prepared to make my request this morning."

He studied her. "Don't keep me waiting, Princess." There was a threat in his voice.

Lilliane bobbed her chin.

He didn't bow before he left.

Her teacup rattled against the saucer as she tried to settle it with a shaking hand.

Lilliane retrieved a scroll from her armoire. She returned to her bed, assuming a comfortable position among her pillows and blankets. She yanked the ribbon binding the parchment and spread the well-worn document across her lap. It was the Albiana family tree.

The half-mortals with Albiana blood must be eliminated: Gabriela had already died. But Lola and Jade; Melusine, Melia, and Plantine must be dealt with.

A wisp of gratitude floated through Lilliane's heart. Plantine's unexpected murder of the grey faerie created the very opportunity the princess wouldn't allow to slip through her fingers. But now a repentant Plantine sailed to the Isle of Minnanon with her mother, seeking forgiveness or pardon or who knew what.

How long before the Grey Council dispatched a new regent to balance the Albiana power in Faerie?

Lilliane leaned toward the bouquet of black roses delivered to her bedside every dawn. Their bitter perfume sharpened the edges of her mind.

The time had come to make use of Gavin's particular skills.

Five half-mortals with Albiana blood remained. Who was the gravest threat?

Melusine, Plantine's eldest sister, seemed committed to the

mortal world. Lilliane snorted. If the rumors were true, Illialei's once great beauty had certainly been brought low, breeding crippled monsters with her French husband.

Melia was quite another matter. Surrounded by an ever-growing band of loyal followers, she would make a difficult target for assassination.

A taste of soot filled Lilliane's mouth as she recalled the night in the palace library when the black eagle escaped with her little friend. And how had Melia awakened from her black spell of endless sleep in the mortal world?

She wouldn't escape a third time.

Lilliane would destroy the stupid, stuttering half-faerie herself. That left Lola and Jade.

Lilliane readied herself to face the day. She headed to the throne room. Straightening her back as she settled in the smaller chair beside her mother's throne, she summoned Gavin.

Petitioners filed into the great hall. In her mother's absence, they sought an audience with her. By the time Gavin arrived, he would be one among many.

Perhaps that would remind him of his place.

"The assignment is clear?" Lilliane asked, softly.

Gavin's lips creased into a slit of a smile. "Clear as the endless blue that reigns over Illialei's skies."

"Then you'll bring me proof? Some token?"

"Two bloodless hearts." His raised voice rang through the hall.

The galley rippled with shock.

She glared at the handsome knight as she addressed the crowd that filled the throne room. "Don't be alarmed. He speaks only of beasts stalking the borders of our country."

"Aye, degenerate beasts threatening the princess heir's peace of mind."

Whispers rushed through the high-ceilinged chamber like the wind.

"That will be more than satisfactory," Lilliane said.

"Payment for my services will be due upon delivery of proof."

On top of every other insult and insinuation, how dare he allude to their private understanding with the eyes of her court fastened upon them? A sense of faintness gathered behind her brow as she squeezed the arms of her diminutive throne with both hands. "As agreed." Every head in the galley craned, straining to catch her words. But he had heard.

Gavin bowed so deep his forehead almost scraped the marble floor. He made a sweeping circle, then marched from the hall with a practiced flourish.

The throne room buzzed.

He courted her subjects and stirred their affection. Did he vie for the throne that belonged to her by birth?

The faintness in Lilliane's head settled in the pit of her stomach. Her fingers balled into tight fists. Certainly, there was some spell to silence the tongue of a contemptuous fool.

35. The Beq Evenson Fountain

Gumf handed Melia the necklace. Five grey-white pearls linked on an alabaster chord, a knot between each polished sphere. Ryder inserted himself between the half-faerie and the dwarf, took the necklace in his hand, and indicated for Melia to turn.

She lifted her hair. When the weight of the pearls settled against her breastbone, she splayed her fingers across the pearls and faced the sea. The Whole was on their side. Lilliane couldn't defeat them.

"Are you ready?" Ryder asked.

"Are you?" she asked.

He cocked an eyebrow. "I'm ready to go with you."

She laughed as joy spilled over from deep within. She'd found the place where she belonged–with him. "I have Elendah's pearls, Sevondi's warding, Flora's faith in me, and you by my side. I'm as ready as I'll ever be."

They held hands and advanced toward the tide line.

Melia inhaled the fresh air blowing in from the sea and dug her bare toes into the sand. Dressed in her muannai-style black pants and shirt, she felt ready to face anything. Ryder wore equally fitted brown pants and a loose muannai blouse with a single pleat of ruffles down its center. He too stood barefoot.

They exchanged a final glance before throwing themselves into the sea.

Melia let go of the unsettling newsprint image of Lola. Instead, she focused her mind on their point of entry—the fountain.

A divisive pressure pulled Melia and Ryder's hands apart. Melia refused to panic. She dug waves with her hand until matter gave way, and she spun, weightless. Clinging to the image of frothing arcs of water, she spread her arms. Her head batted against a gummy band of resistance. When she gasped for breath, turbulent air gushed into her mouth, choking her.

She pressed up with her palms as hard as she could, but her legs swung in space and she couldn't gain any leverage. Growing increasingly frantic, she reached out, searching blindly for Ryder. The cycloning winds spun her body and slammed her torso against the jelly-like wall that halted her forward momentum the first time.

Lilliane?

As soon as Melia thought of the princess heir, her body plummeted, crashing through space. Careening wildly, the half-faerie conjured an image of Elendah, grey braids pinned high on her head with a pearl-encrusted comb. Melia's fingers flailed for the chord bouncing around her neck. She managed to get a hand around the solid spheres.

The grey faerie's image beckoned, calling Melia to the mortal fountain.

The band of resistance gave way.

Melia shot up, into spray, twilight, and the laughter of children.

She shook her head, throwing droplets of water. All around her, young mortals danced in the shallow water, shrieking with delight. She scanned for Ryder. On the other side of the fountain he spun, searching for her. "Over here," she shouted, exhilarated they were safe.

She waded toward him, water dragging the legs of her pants. Backlit by a burning crimson and lavender sunset, his green eyes sparked the way they did every time he saw her.

He crushed her in his arms as three boys hopped around them, teasing their embrace with handfuls of water scooped over their heads and shoulders. Adults crowded the circumference of the fountain's retaining wall, pointing and shouting. Tiny flashes of light popped, oversized fireflies dying.

Ryder and Melia pulled apart.

The children fell silent around them, backing away, mouths hanging open.

"Cody, do you know who that is?" a man asked in a loud whisper.

An excited woman jabbed a finger in the air. "Britney, look who's here."

A young woman dug through a bag she carried over one shoulder. "Ashley," she called a girl to her side.

Couples walking by, holding hands, stopped to stare. People sitting on benches stood and wandered over. More lights flickered and flashed. Many of the mortals aimed shiny rectangular objects in their direction.

Melia gaped at the gathering faces.

Groups of people lounging on blankets laid out on a grassy knoll sat up. They talked among themselves and exclaimed before jumping up and joining the increasingly large crowd. The drone of voices grew louder and louder. It flooded the air.

Melia strained to hear the faint music the chant drowned out.

"Max, Max, Max ..."

She swirled around.

Everyone was staring and pointing at Ryder.

"It's Max Zander," someone yelled.

Several of the women screamed. The one digging in her bag grabbed the hand of the young girl beside her and waded into the fountain. She advanced toward Melia and Ryder, holding out a torn scrap of paper along with something that looked like a writing utensil. "Max, would you please sign this, 'To Ashley'?"

The woman threw Melia a scathing look as she proceeded to tell Max how much she loved his latest blockbuster movie. But no one was going to believe she saw him in Balboa Park. So if she could have an autograph–for her daughter. She stepped closer and whispered, "Does Noele know you're here with her?" She gave

Melia another withering look. "She may be attractive, but she's not Noele, and that face tattoo is a little much." The woman shoved the paper and pen in Ryder's direction. "You're so handsome in real life." She was breathless, hardly able to speak. "I mean ..."

Ryder smiled as he accepted the pen and paper. "To Ashley?" He played along with the charade.

"Say something about seeing us here at the park."

Melia clamped her arms across her chest and glared.

Eyes glued to Ryder, the woman tangled her fingers in knots.

Melia bit her lower lip as he handed the paper and pen back to the woman before tousling Ashley's damp curls. The woman half-fell, half-lunged forward, smothering him in a full-body hug.

Melia's breath shallowed in her throat. A familiar sensation scoured her veins. She wanted to shove this stupid mortal woman out of the way.

The woman kissed Ryder's cheek—only because he turned his face in time to escape her assault on his lips.

Melia yanked the woman's stringy blond hair, pulling her head back. "That's enough!"

"How dare you?" the woman shrieked.

"Cat fight!"

"Call 9-1-1!"

More people whipped out their small shimmering rectangles. Fingers flew across the strange objects eliciting a chorus of beep-beep-beeps.

Melia feinted with her fingers curled into claws. A guttural sound erupted deep in her throat.

The woman staggered back but managed to spit in Melia's direction. "Bitch," the woman said, before dragging her crying daughter out of the fountain. "You're no Noele Fontaine. That's for sure."

Melia backed away in the opposite direction. Ryder followed her.

The crowd formed a ring around the fountain's retaining wall, blocking their exit.

"Damn, someone call the papz!"

A man close to them spoke clearly and carefully into his little gadget. "We'd like to report an assault. We're in Balboa Park—" He pulled the thing away from his ear to ask the woman with him, "What's the name of this fountain?"

"Bea Evenson," she said. "It's the Bea Evenson Fountain."

The man repeated the information.

Ryder's eyes hardened.

"Yes, we'll wait." The man gave a string of numbers, tapped the screen a few more times, and then returned the object to his pocket. He spread his legs with his hands behind his back. "The police are on their way. You're going to have to stay here until they arrive." He pointed to Melia. "Sorry, Max, but she can't go around attacking every woman who asks for an autograph."

"There was no injury here," Ryder said. "Let us pass."

No one moved.

Melia burned inside. The people surrounding them seemed more curious than concerned.

A woman pushed her way through the crowd. "She didn't do anything to you, and that woman and her kid are gone. Let them go." Grey streaks tangled the woman's long dark hair, but her face was kind, familiar.

The man who called the police sneered at the woman. "Go on. This isn't any of your business. Take your shopping cart and get out of here." He pointed at the silver-framed box-like contraption the woman dragged behind her.

"I'm a witness as much as anyone else. Did you see the way that other woman threw herself at this handsome young man?" The woman winked at Ryder. "Max probably came out here to get some peace and quiet, like the rest of us. Aren't you overreacting?"

The man grabbed the woman's arm and shoved her back into the crowd. The woman stumbled—or tripped over her long skirt—landing with her palms against the pavement. Everyone fanned away from her.

Melia's mind clicked. She'd seen that face and disheveled figure before. She crossed the retaining wall in a single stride. The man lunged in her direction.

Ryder's arm shot out, a steel rod holding the man back. "When the police come, I'll be sure to report your assault on this woman." He indicated the one on the ground.

The man's face transformed into a seething mask. He shook his head. "Dammit. I'm out of here."

No one tried to stop him, but it seemed like a million more fireflies died when he grabbed his partner's hand and disappeared in the night.

Melia kneeled. "Lola? Are you Lola?" She reached for one of the woman's wrists and helped her sit up. Shadows darkened the length of Lola's body. The sun set while everyone argued. Orange-yellow lights crisscrossed the fountain, illuminating the paved walks and surrounding buildings. "Are you hurt?" Melia asked.

"Not really," Lola said. "Skinned the heel of my palm, but it's nothing. I'm glad he left. The police and I aren't on very good terms." The tears in her eyes reflected the man-made glare circling the fountain. "I saw you. I watched you come out of nowhere. I knew ... I knew, if I just kept believing, one day, you'd come for me ... just like you came for my mother. But she thought you were evil." Her voice cracked as her shoulders shuddered with heart-wrenching sobs.

Melia pulled Lola close and held her, stroking her hair and rocking her. She disregarded the twitch in her nose as the dull odor of urine and decay engulfed her.

The crowd dispersed. A few stragglers hung at a distance, whispering among themselves. Lola's cart rolled to the edge of the circular pavement. Ryder went to retrieve it. The thing rattled and shook as he pushed it toward them.

Melia wasn't sure how long they sat there.

By the time Lola finished weeping, the park seemed deserted. Only a handful of shadows moved in the distance.

"Can you stand?" Melia asked.

Lola nodded.

Ryder leaned over, one of his feet bracing the cart. Together they pulled Lola to her feet.

"Are you a faerie?" she asked.

"Half," Melia said. "Like you."

Lola's eyes widened. "You must be mistaking me for someone else. Did you come–?"

"From the Realm of Faerie, yes."

More tears twinkled in Lola's eyes. She rubbed her nose with the back of her hand. "I wish Jade were here."

"Jade? Is that your daughter?"

Lola hung her head. "Yes, but she doesn't believe in faeries. I tried to tell her–" Her voice cracked again.

Her anguish touched Melia's heart. "Then your mother is Gabriela."

Lola nodded. "She passed away last fall."

"I'm so sorry."

Lola shrugged. "It wasn't unexpected. She was ninety-four with heart problems. She lived a long life."

Although that wouldn't have counted as a long life for any full-blood faerie, perhaps it was long for a mortal. No one knew the life expectancy of half-bloods. "She was my cousin," Melia said.

Lola took a step back. "But you're so young."

"Time–"

"It passes differently over there, doesn't it?"

"Yes."

Lola reached for Melia's hand and pulled her beneath one of the lights shining from a tall silver column. She searched Melia's face, then stared into her eyes. "They're so blue." She tapped her cheek with her fingers. "Are you the one ... is it possible? The one my mother saw all those years ago? But she never mentioned anything about that tattoo beneath your eye."

Melia touched her cheekbone. "This is new. When I came with

301

Tatou–"

"The pixie!" Lola dropped Melia's hand and made fists of her own. She paced a tight circle. "I knew it. I knew you were real. I knew if I just believed–" She stopped. "But everyone can see you. I thought only my mother and I could see faeries. And what about him?" She stood toe-to-toe with Ryder. Shorter than him–and Melia–she had to reach up to cup his chin in her hand. "Everyone saw you too." She laughed and spun with her arms flung wide. "They thought you were Max Zander." She stopped her playful twirling. "Are you?"

"No. My name is Ryder."

Lola stepped toward him and held out her hand. When he took hold of it, she pumped it up and down. "Lovely to meet you, Ryder. You do look like Max, though." She turned to Melia. "Why can everyone see both of you? Has something shifted between the worlds?"

A memory of the Calashai's bells tolling for Elendah made Melia shiver. "Yes, but that's not why they can see us. We have–" She stopped. "I have mortal blood."

"What about him?"

Ryder looked over Lola's head at Melia. "My lineage is unclear–"

"You're an orphan?" Lola asked.

"Yes."

Melia chewed on a fingernail. She and Ryder had never discussed his bloodline.

"It's only full-blooded creatures from the enchanted world that mortals can't see anymore," Ryder said.

Lola nodded. "I get it."

"As mortals disconnect from nature," he continued, "their eyes close to certain realities."

Melia recalled the shock she felt when Alex was unable to see Tatou. Over seventy mortal years had passed since then.

"Did the pixie come with you?" Lola asked. "Is she here and I just can't see her?"

"She's not here. The current level of pollution would be far too dangerous for one so small," Ryder said.

Lola nodded sagely. "Of course, it would. Can you stay?" she asked. "And meet my daughter? It would mean so much to me. She believes everything the lawyers, doctors, psychiatrists, and social workers tell her about me. That I'm bat-shit crazy, that experimenting on me with the medication-of-the-day is justified. She doesn't understand why I run away from them and the clinics and halfway houses. If you could stay, if you could tell her, if she could just see the both of you!"

Melia hugged Lola. "We'd love to meet your daughter."

It was a lie. After her encounter with Gabriela, and now faced with Lola's precarious identity, Melia dreaded meeting Jade. What would they find? But they had to warn her about Umbra. It was why they'd risked coming to the mortal world.

"I'll call her in the morning, first thing." Lola patted her saggy brown velvety jacket. "She always leaves me a burner phone. I'll tell her to come when she gets off work. She always takes the first shift at the coffee shop. It shouldn't be too late." Lola wiped her eyes. "It's lovely of you both to stay to see her." She gripped the handles of her wobbly cart and pushed it down the sidewalk, waving for them to follow her.

"Come on. I've staked out the perfect place to sleep. Don't worry. It's safe. No one else has discovered it yet."

36. Jade

Sunlight woke Melia. Ryder curled around her, his belly pressed against her back. After rummaging in her cart last night, Lola handed them a blanket. "The smell is a little off, but it's clean. By the time you wake up, it'll be fine. Dew freshens everything."

Melia choked back a laugh and did her best to ignore the blanket's sour smell as she spread it out in the secluded enclave between the shelf of boulders and a grassy wall Lola had laid claim to.

As they settled into sleep, Melia recalled Aldous' words: Gabriela's daughter was unusual. She was also immensely likable.

Now, Lola perched on a boulder with her legs crossed, the backs of her hands resting against her knees, the tip of each thumb and index finger pressed together, creating an oval. She stared into the distance. Although Gabriela was fourteen when Melia and Tatou found her in Texas, the resemblance between mother and daughter was striking. Their narrow faces, light-filled eyes, and pale skin were identical.

Melia pressed her back into Ryder's warmth as she mentally prepared for Jade. Reaching for Elendah's pearls, she chastised herself for forgetting about them when the man threatened her with the police. She also forgot to draw energy and strength from the natural world—and her soul flame. What if she incarnated Umbra and forgot all her training? Melia shivered.

Ryder's arms enclosed her in a tighter embrace. The threat of the police didn't seem to unsettle him. Nor had he seemed surprised when everyone called him Max Zander. He was comfortable in the mortal world, like it was familiar to him. He must have studied these things in Idonne. She closed her eyes. They popped open. Was Ryder half-mortal? Were half-mortals required to take faerie troths?

When she kissed Ryder for the first time on the muannai valley steppes, she believed ... What? It didn't matter. The same arguments Melia gave Melusine against marrying a mortal returned to haunt her.

✧ ✧ ✧

Lola reached in her pocket and pulled out an object similar to the ones so many other mortals carried. The things that flashed with sparks of light, and the thing the man used to talk to the police, even though they were nowhere nearby.

Melia gently unwrapped Ryder's arms and propped herself up an elbow as Lola punched at the thing and then held it up to her ear.

"It's Mom." Her eyes closed. "No, no. Nothing's wrong. No trouble. Can you come by my place when you get off work?" Lola picked at her gauzy skirt. "Baby wipes. And maybe a latte?" A smile brightened her face. The beauty she'd once been flickered across her sallow puffy skin. "Maybe you could bring three?" Her shoulders stiffened. "Some friends." She slid from her perch. "No. They're not homeless."

The defensiveness in her tone made Melia want to give her a hug.

"Fine. Don't bring the lattes, but I promise, you'll want to meet these people." Lola's free hand arced above her head. "You'll just have to come and see for yourself. I'm not saying anything else." She reached the paved walkway a few feet from the boulders and disappeared from sight.

Melia scooted after her.

"One of them knew your grandmother." Lola tugged her hair.

A jolt of recognition hit Melia's solar plexus. Neither her sisters nor her mother ever pulled their hair as she did, but here was her ... What was she? Not a cousin ... but family, with the same nervous habit Melia had had all her life.

"No. They're here with me now. We'll be waiting." A pleased smile. "Thank you, Jade." Lola shoved the device into her pocket.

Melia turned to glance at Ryder, whose eyes were open, watching her. "How long have you been awake?" she asked.

"Long enough to realize Lola fascinates you."

Melia crawled toward him. "She's so different from Gabriela, and yet, she's lost too, existing out here alone with no one."

Ryder placed his hand on hers. "We'll convince her to come to Faerie with us."

Melia blinked back empathetic tears. "I feel so drawn to her. I want to watch over her and protect her." She wiped her eyes with the back of her hand. "Make sure no one ever shoves her again, like that man did last night. Why was he so awful to her?"

"She challenged him."

Melia shook her head. "I guess mortal men don't like to be challenged."

"Are you thinking of your father?" he asked.

"Maybe I am."

"The fabric of the mortal mind is made of denser stuff."

"What does that say about us?" Her cheeks heated. "About me?"

Ryder squeezed her hand. "Coming here has stirred the same questions in me. From the moment we arrived, something about this world feels natural to me, like I've finally come home. How can I not wonder whether or not one of my parents was mortal?"

"Do you know–?" She stopped herself. She wasn't prepared to accept the answer to the question she was about to ask.

He gazed into her eyes. "Do I know whether I would be required to take a faerie troth if we were to marry?"

"Now you can read my mind? I'm not sure I like that."

He smiled. "I know some of the things that frighten you, that's all." He pushed himself up to sitting. "Betrayal is one of them."

"Every single mortal who's taken a faerie vow has broken it."

"Ah, you're not a complete failure as a student of history."

"I didn't read that in any book."

"Your mother?"

"She drilled it into us."

"She doesn't want you to suffer as she did."

Melia huffed. "Clearly, she wishes each of us to suffer uniquely."

"The marriage of a half-mortal to any creature from the enchanted world would require a troth, even if the betrothed was half mortal herself."

Melia broke eye contact with him. If she and Ryder ever married, she would share the same fate as her mother—a fate she'd been determined to avoid her entire life. Betrayal and eternal separation. She pushed herself to her knees. "I don't want to talk about this anymore."

"Melia, just because something hasn't been done before, doesn't mean it won't ever be done."

In spite of her desire to distance herself from him, his green eyes pulled her in. "Every mortal who takes the vow believes he'll be the one to honor it."

"How many half-mortals have taken the vow?" he argued. "How many have broken it?"

She refused to think about what she gave up. The ability to fly. "Mortal, half-mortal, what's the difference?"

"Are you different from full-blooded faeries? From full-blooded mortals?"

"Of course, I'm different. I have no wings. And mortals ..." She sought some way to end the conversation.

Several feet away, Lola rummaged through her cart. She swatted away the many colorful scarves decorating its edges and tore open one bag after another.

"Mortals are cruel," Melia said.

"Their first impulse is often self-protective, and their consciousness evolves slowly; it seems they pay dearly for every advance they make, yet they're capable of profound love, feats of breathtaking courage; and the attainment of wisdom is not beyond their grasp."

"Then you've studied mortals—when you were a scholar in Idonne?"

"The study of Umbra is the study of mortal consciousness. Its strengths and its fault lines."

Melia tugged on her hair. In her peripheral vision, Lola approached, waving a slim, green volume in the air.

Ryder didn't stop talking. "Your stubbornness, my rebellion, these are qualities bestowed by our mortal blood."

"I see your point," she said. "Since there are no stubborn faeries —like Lilliane—or rebellious muannai—like Goring—in the enchanted world."

He laughed. "You might have missed your calling."

"What do you mean?"

"Your mind is quick. You would have excelled as a student of law or history."

"I trust my own experience and observations over studying those of others."

"Yes, you do."

When she stood, he stood beside her. "And one day I hope your experience and observations will convince you that you can trust me."

As Lola approached them, conflicting desires battled in Melia's chest, a melting heart locked in a wiry cage.

"I want to ask you some questions about a story in this book," Lola said.

Two men with naked torsos, and wearing very short pants, ran by, almost knocking Lola over.

"Watch where you're going!" Melia called after them.

They ignored her. Ryder's hand settled on her shoulder. She wanted to shake it off but resisted the impulse.

"I'm used to it." Lola inched closer, thumbing through the pages of her book. She licked her finger and pushed the pages one after the other until she found what she was searching for. She pointed at one of the pictures and scanned Melia from head to toe. "You look so much like her, but without the serpent tail and dragon wings."

"I beg your pardon," Melia said.

"Maybe it's not you." Lola shoved the book in Melia's face. "Do you know her?"

An amazingly accurate portrait of Melusine stared out from the page. Was that Raymond next to her? Melia had never met him.

She took the book from Lola's hand and began to read the story explaining the picture. Although much of it was factually incorrect, it was her sister's story. Melia flipped the page and continued to read. As she reached the end of the section, she slammed the book shut. "Where did you get this?"

Lola took it back and dusted the cover. "Found it."

"It's all lies," Melia said.

Lola's eyes blazed. "Really?"

"Absolutely."

"What part of it isn't true?"

"My sister has not had eight deformed children." Because that would be impossible, wouldn't it?

Lola watched her intently.

"And Raymond isn't dead." Awareness dawned. "Yet," she said, quietly.

Ryder gestured for the book. He flipped through the pages. "The stories in this book happened long ago in the mortal world." When he reached Melusine's story, Melia fumed while he read the page. "In the mortal world, Raymond's been dead for a long time," he said.

"What about my sister?" She couldn't—wouldn't—believe Melusine had died. "That book says she had eight children. She never even talked about having one child!"

"The account is disturbing," he agreed.

"You mean the part about all her children being deformed, or the part about Raymond violating his faerie troth and Melusine's curse becoming permanent?"

"All of it. But your sister might still be alive," Ryder said. "Perhaps she's returned to the enchanted world—"

"No one has seen her!"

"So it's true." Lola had a sad, faraway look in her eyes. "The first time I saw a faerie, I was so excited, but my mother made me promise I wouldn't say another word about them. She denied it all—other than the warning that she passed on from you about Umbra—and insisted that I deny it too ... but it's all true."

An inner shiver ran up Melia's spine. A slight young lady with ropy brown hair twined with ribbons, approached them. The likeness to the mask Sevondi wore at the Muudron Stone was uncanny. The girl's sleeveless dress, its thin fabric printed with enormous red flowers and giant green stems, draped her slim body. Her heavy boots clumped along the pavement Lola called a sidewalk.

Holding a square tray with four lidded cups, she took small, careful steps. Her eyebrows rippled when she saw Melia and Ryder. "Mom?" she asked. "Are these your friends?" Her delicate blue eyes locked on Ryder. "Are you Max Zander?"

"No," he said.

"You look just like him. Except better." She took a cup from the tray and pushed it toward him. "A triple-shot Caramel Macchiato. Upgrade's on me." She winked at Lola, ignored Melia, and took two more steps in Ryder's direction. "No big deal. I work at Starbucks."

Always the gentleman, Ryder spun the cup in his hands. "Thank you."

The girl shot him a sparkling smile.

No doubt, this was Jade, and she was as enamored of Ryder as all the other mortal women were.

The girl pointed to a small opening in the lid. "Leaving the lid on will keep it hot, so drink through that. Unless you wanted it iced. Mom, you should have asked him if he wanted it iced."

Could she have stood any closer to him? Melia's concern over Ryder's probable mortal blood collided with a stark possessiveness.

Lola remained stationed behind her cart, observing.

"It's good," Ryder said. "Do you have one of those for your mother and Melia?"

Keeping her boots planted, the young lady stretched her arm to offer one of the cups from the tray to her mother.

Lola cocked her head in Melia's direction. "Thank you."

"Oh, yeah." Jade spun around. "Here." She shoved the third cup at Melia before turning back to Ryder. "Are you from around here?"

"No, we're not."

Melia sipped from the cup and almost choked over the foul taste.

Jade swiveled her head. "You don't like it?"

"It's not what I expected."

"Most people take loads of sugar in their coffee. Maybe you're one of them?" Jade's tight smile wasn't especially friendly.

"Actually, sweets make me ill."

Jade's flippant, "Oh," before she asked Ryder, "but you like it, don't you?" made Melia want to knock the girl's cup to the ground.

"Jade, what did you bring Melia?" Lola asked.

"Um. Coffee of the day."

"Black?"

"Uh-huh."

Lola moved closer to Melia. "Try this. It's different than what she gave you."

Melia took Lola's cup and sipped the smallest amount she possibly could. "It's much better."

"It's a latte. Taste your young man's. It's different, too."

Ryder reached around Jade to hand Melia his cup. She took a larger swallow of his and gagged. "That's too sweet."

Jade stared hard at the ground.

"Is that what you got yourself, honey? A Triple Grande Caramel Macchiato?" Lola asked. "It's her favorite drink."

"Of course it is," Melia said. She wanted to add, "Well, now that we've met your daughter, we need to be going," but she couldn't.

Jade trounced on the ground, cup in hand, throwing the empty tray down next to the enormous braided bag she pulled off her shoulder. What was it with mortal women and their bags?

"So how do you two know Mom?" Jade asked.

Melia dreaded the conversation she needed to have with this harsh, fragile young woman who seemed like a child. And couldn't keep her eyes off Ryder. Melia looked to him for help.

"Why don't we all sit?" he said.

One by one, they settled on the ground around Jade.

"Mom, before I forget. I've made an appointment for you next Wednesday at 3 p.m. with Social Services. I expect you to show up this time. Maybe your new friend can help you get there." She glared at Melia. "What is that shit on your face?"

"Jade!"

Melia held up a hand as she connected her energy with the ground. "It's a protective shield."

"To protect you from what?"

"Soulless bureaucrats," Lola interjected.

"Really, Mother?" Jade asked. "Your counselors just want to help you get out of the park."

"I told you I don't want to see them anymore."

"This isn't a discussion," her daughter said. "You need to go."

Melia tried to imagine herself talking to Pressina with the same demanding attitude. It was impossible.

Lola shook her head. "Jade hates me living in the park."

"Why? It's lovely here," Melia said.

"Like I said, maybe you can take her to her appointment next week," Jade said.

"We're not going to be here next week." Melia didn't add, "Neither will your mother, because we're taking her back to the enchanted world," because she hadn't had a chance to talk with Lola about it.

"What about you?" Jade asked Ryder. "Are you leaving too?"

"Yes."

Jade pulled one of those slim, lighted objects from her braided bag. She began furiously punching buttons. "I don't have much time." She focused her total attention upon the thing in her hand.

"What is that, and what is she doing with it?" Melia asked.

"A cell phone," Lola said. "She's texting. It's what they do now."

Jade rolled her eyes.

Lola's face turned an angry red. "They don't talk, they just send each other messages."

"Talking is so overrated."

Melia forced herself to begin. "Nonetheless, we came here to talk to you."

Jade stopped her compulsive button pushing and threw her cell phone back into her bag. "About what?"

"Umbra," Melia said.

An unidentifiable emotion flickered across Jade's face.

"Have you heard of him? Or perhaps, from him?" Melia asked.

"Umbra," Lola said. "That's who my mother warned me about."

"Has he ever tried to contact you?" Melia asked.

Lola brushed hair from the sides of her face. "I used to have nightmares, but they stopped a long time ago—the first time I took Thorazine."

"My mother's claim to fame. She's taken every psychotropic drug that's ever been manufactured."

"Jade, stop it," her mother said.

"Why do you care if I've heard from this Umbra?"

"Yes, why would you come here to ask Jade that?"

"He's dangerous," Ryder said. "A seductive, corruptive influence, and he's becoming more active."

"Then he's real?" Jade asked.

"Very real," Melia said.

"Do you know him?" Jade asked Melia.

"No one knows him per se," Ryder said. "He's an incorporeal entity, living in the Void."

Jade's gaze traveled over her mother and Ryder to settle on Melia. "Did you hire these people, Mom? Cause they're good. Really convincing."

Melia wished Tatou was with them. Jade could use some pixie dust. "Umbra is attempting to incarnate. He's seeking a vessel."

"A ship?" Jade asked.

"A body," Ryder said, "to contain his consciousness."

"Why?" Jade asked.

"As an incorporeal entity, his powers are held in check—to a significant degree. Incarnated into the material plane, his power would exceed that of any creature who's ever lived in the enchanted or mortal worlds."

Jade smiled. "The enchanted or mortal worlds?"

"They're from the Realm of Faerie. They came last night through the Bea Evenson Fountain," Lola said.

Jade's face darkened. "Why are you doing this? Feeding my mother's delusions. It's the last thing she needs right now."

"Your grandmother thought we were evil spirits," Melia said.

"You're the girl with the blue eyes?" Jade asked. "The one who warned her about the dark voice?"

"Yes."

"How is that even possible? That would have been seventy-five years ago. You're my age."

"Time passes differently between the mortal and enchanted worlds. Hundreds of years can pass in the mortal world when only a moment has passed in the enchanted world."

"Don't you understand what this means, Jade?" Lola said. "It's all real. I'm not crazy. I never was. I'm not going to see any more social workers or psychiatrists or doctors."

"Mother, you can't live in the park!"

"This is my home," Lola said.

"The police don't share that belief," Jade snarled.

"I've improved my methods of avoiding them."

"If you don't keep the appointment I made for you on Wednesday, and you get arrested again"—Jade crossed her arms—"don't call me."

315

"You might as well cancel the appointment. I'm not going."

Jade glared at Melia. "Great influence you are." She grabbed her bag and jumped to her feet. "I don't have time for any more of this crap."

Ryder stood and reached for her arm. She stopped. "If Umbra tries to contact you, you need to resist his attempts to seduce you."

"What is he? A freaking incubus?"

"Yes. He's something exactly like that."

Jade leaned over to pick up her cup and the empty tray beside it. "Thanks for the warning. Gotta run."

Lola shook her head as her daughter trotted off. "She's stubborn."

Ryder met Melia's gaze and smiled. "Must run in the Albiana blood."

"Albiana blood?" Lola asked.

Melia preceded to enlighten Lola about their family tree.

37. La Jolla Cove

Jade stalked through the park.

That guy was hot, but the chick with him was possessive and as crazy as her mother. And what was up with that tattoo on her face?

Protective shield. Jade snorted. Too over the top.

What time was it? She fished her LG Voyager from her bag to check the time. Almost 2 p.m. Plenty of time to swing by the library to do some old-fashioned research on the Realm of Faerie and how to find it. Get there. Whatever. She looked around and laughed. Jeez. If people knew what she was thinking, they'd think she was crazy.

No wonder her grandmother went all religious. Signing up for Jesus almost made sense if other planes—other worlds—really existed and you were afraid of what might come through.

But if this Umbra dude could make Jade the most powerful person who'd ever lived, she was all in.

How to make contact with him again? And make this incarnation thing happen.

Jade tossed her phone back in her bag. Dammit. She forgot to give her mom the stupid baby wipes. Now she would have to lug them around for another week. Because she sure as hell wasn't going back to that little powwow and risk getting tripped up in some lie about Umbra.

She could have sworn the chick with the blue eyes was putting some kind of voodoo on her. The way she stared at her made Jade want to spill everything.

Good thing she resisted.

One thing was for sure, those two didn't come from the Realm of Faerie—Jade snorted, or wherever the hell they were from—to help her do the incarnation thing. They wanted to stop it.

Good luck with that.

Jade hummed to herself as she crossed 6th Street to cut across the Kung Foods parking lot. A veggie burger with tempeh bacon and she'd be set for rest of the day.

Jade typed *realm of faerie* into the library's online search function. About twenty books came up, all fiction. She typed *fairy tales* and got a lot more hits. More fiction. She hovered the cursor over *Fairy Tales from the Brothers Grimm*, but couldn't remember any of those stories being about traveling to another world. She clicked a few more pages ahead. Nothing helpful.

She tried *are faeries real?*

Zero results. Maybe she needed to go home and cruise the net. She hated leaving empty-handed.

Seeing faeries, traveling to faerie, when humans went to faerie.

Zilch, zilch, and more zilch.

She grabbed her bag, and left the computer to the creepy guy buzzing around her like a hornet for the last ten minutes. Probably one of those registered sex offenders who used the library computer to cruise porn sites.

So gross.

It was enough to turn anyone off sex. F-O-R-E-V-E-R.

Jade resisted making a sharp remark when she passed by him. He'd probably take it as a come on. Didn't they all?

Freaks.

The internet was more forthcoming. There was tons of stuff.

A lot of people believed faeries were nature spirits. That various species ruled over trees, water, flowers, and stuff like that. That made sense to her. Some faeries, mostly the smaller ones, had a reputation for being mischievous. Jade didn't doubt that. She glossed over the stuff about the two courts, summer and winter. Boring. But everyone seemed to agree time passed differently in the faerie plane as compared to the mortal one. Maybe the chick was more clued in than Jade gave her credit for. Maybe she should have stayed and asked a few more questions before storming off.

Jade checked the time. 7 p.m. She could make it back to the park before dark, but what if they were gone? She checked her incoming calls. The number of her mom's burner phone stared back at her. Damn. She wished she could just ask them how to contact Umbra.

Jade stared at her computer screen. She typed *Umbra*.

The darkest part of the shadow.

She shivered and wondered whether Umbra had anything to do with Carl Jung? Jade was a fan, except he was so wordy.

She couldn't find any more about Umbra on the internet. Well, nothing having to do with an incorporeal entity seeking a vessel of incarnation.

Jade stared at the wall. Maybe there was a reason Ryder and Melia didn't want her to help the dark voice.

But if she didn't, nothing would change.

She'd never become a queen, and the more she thought about it, Jade really wanted to become a queen. A cool one, not some dumb bitch who waved a scepter around and stared into a mirror, asking if she was beautiful. No, she would make sure her subjects had all the coffee they wanted, and go-karts. And in her kingdom, no one would eat animals, and everyone would wear dreads.

Shit, everyone would want to live there.

She had an idea.

Twilight was an in-between time. And an intersection between land and water was an in-between place. She could make it to the outskirts of La Jolla Cove if she left now.

Maybe—God she couldn't believe she was contemplating this— maybe she could just stand at the tide line at dusk and ask for help, or guidance, or something.

She grabbed her keys and headed out the door.

❖ ❖ ❖

Jade sat down a few feet in front of the ledge of green-brown brush. She was as far away from the seals and tourists as she could get.

One. Two. Three. Four. Five people. Didn't they need to go eat dinner? Help some kid do their homework? Walk a dog?

She'd left her purse locked in her Toyota RAV4 EV—one of those sweet treats Jules surprised her with last year.

He called out of nowhere. "I'm in San Diego for a few hours. Wanna get some coffee?" Then he handed her the keys like it was her birthday. She never asked how he managed to get his hands on the latest technology before it went public, but it was one of the nicest perks of her arrangement with her father.

Whoever the hell he was.

Jade slipped her keys in her pocket and dropped her butt in the sand. Up here, it was dry. She tugged off her combat boots and lined them up beside her.

The sun was dropping fast, a big burning ball falling from the sky. Gorgeous.

Why didn't she come to the beach more often?

All right. Now there were only three people in her peripheral vision, and they were shrinking against the horizon. Probably tourists headed to La Jolla Village for some awful, overpriced meal at a crap trendy restaurant with a stupid name like Bayzil & Sylahntro or EetMee.

Jade tossed her head, grinning at her dumb joke.

Yes. This was totally crazy, but what if it worked?

She headed for the water.

One more perimeter check.

Someone would have to be standing on top of her to hear anything over the waves. The ocean was that loud. Really, what was she worried about? Weirdoes came down here all the time to chant, wave torches, and contort their bodies into any number of exhibitionistic poses in the name of yoga. Who cared if some pale chick with dreadlocks came down to talk to herself?

She closed her eyes, took a deep breath, and pressed her hands together. She opened one eye.

Was the prayer mudra the best posture to take?

She closed her eyes and concentrated on Umbra.

Shadow.

Dark.

Candle flame sputtering out.

Water kissed her toes.

She shot her hands to the sky and arched back. "Umbra!"

God, it felt natural.

Jade forced herself to keep her eyes closed.

"We meet again, my precious Jade."

Just like that, the dark voice echoed in her mind. Heat gathered in her belly. It drew her attention inward. Rage opened from a hot inner coil, like spiky petals opening to the sun. Rage at her father.

She hated him.

Jade gulped. Guilt sloshed over the black spikes of anger, cooling it down.

"He abandoned your mother."

Damn straight.

Jade choked back a sob, remembering the time she found the last letter he wrote to Lola. It was stuffed in a drawer at the bottom of a stack of papers: *Thank you for letting me know about your pregnancy. I have no doubt the child is mine, but I can't see you anymore. Please don't contact me again, I won't respond. P.S. I'll take care of our daughter.*

Strike that. I'll send money for our daughter. But if she ever tries to contact me, I'll stop doing that too.

Asshole-on-a-stick.

Lola had been beautiful. Magical. Not some weirdo-medicated-zombie mental patient before her father threw her out like yesterday's trash.

The black fire flames crackled and leapt. Jade's memories of her mother's destroyed beauty acted like gasoline, fueling the writhing, seething mass of hatred within.

"Bring him to justice. Become my Queen."

Oh yeah. Now this Umbra dude was talking. *"How do I get to Faerie?"* she asked.

"Someone is coming for you."

"Yeah, I met them. That girl with the painted face and her Max Zander look-alike boyfriend."

Thunder rolled across the ocean.

Jade's eyes popped open. Raindrops pelted her skin. A few minutes ago, the sky was clear. Now it was pitch dark. She couldn't see a thing. Another enormous wave rose in front of her, white caps effervescent in the inky black. She stepped back. Not in time. The water drenched her before receding to rebuild again.

She stepped back again and again.

The water welled up.

She saw—imagined?—a black-gloved hand wielding a knife.

"He's coming to slit your throat."

The wave knocked Jade to her knees. Salt water flushed her nose and her throat. She gagged onto wet sand.

38. Crossing Over

Fingers squeeze black petals to dust.

Overhead, a pair of doves fly.

Dive.

Spiral.

Plummet from the sky.

I race to their slack bodies and reach out. Black-red blood gashes their throats. Their eyes, dark beads in stiffening heads half-severed, bleed silver tears. Stunned, I open my mouth to scream. No sound comes out.

Behind me, beside me, beyond me, Lilliane laughs.

Blood drips from my hands.

Lilliane laughs harder.

The ground reverberates. A sinister blade glints in the long grass.

Melia jerked awake, her heart wild in her chest. She searched for Lola.

When she spotted the woman sleeping peacefully a few yards away, the shock of her vision lessened. However, Melia's mind still grasped for tendrils of meaning. An association between the troubled woman and her equally troubled daughter merged with the image of the defenseless doves. She shook Ryder's shoulder. "Can Huron knights travel to the mortal world?" she whispered.

"Yes."

"Lilliane is going to send someone to kill Lola and Jade."

"Whoa," Ryder bolted upright, scanning the vicinity. "Where did that come from?"

"I had a dream, or maybe it was a vision. We can't stay here, and we can't leave Lola and Jade here, alone and undefended."

"Dawn is a few hours away."

Melia knelt beside Lola, hating to wake her. She whispered her name as she rubbed her shoulder.

"What? What?" Lola stammered. "I'm not harming anyone."

"It's me," Melia said.

Lola wiped her mouth with her hand. "Why did you wake me up?"

"We need to leave here as soon as possible."

"Is it the police?"

Melia didn't tell her it was far worse than the police. "We need to travel to the enchanted world."

Lola rubbed her eyes. "This is a good dream."

"This is no dream," Melia said. "Can you call your daughter? Ask her to meet us at the fountain before dawn."

"I don't know that she'll come. She hates to miss her shift at work."

"Please, try to call her now."

Lola dug through the mound of possessions beside her. "She might not answer her phone."

"She needs to meet us here as soon as possible."

The cell phone's small screen ignited with light. Lola punched buttons. "Honey–" Lola glanced at Melia, her eyes glowing. "Yes, they're still here." A smile curved her lips. "Don't wait. Come right now." Lola pulled the phone away from her face. "Should she bring anything?"

"No," Melia said.

Lola nodded a few more times before saying, "I love you." She snapped the phone shut. "She's on her way."

"Good," Melia said. "Let's head over to the fountain."

Lola began to pack her cart.

"You won't need any of those things in the enchanted world."

Lola ran her hand through several scarves. "Everything I own in the world is in here."

"We can't take it with us," Melia said.

"Let me pack it up and push it over there." Lola pointed to the boulders. "For when I come back."

"Yes, fine," Melia said.

Ryder picked up the blanket. Melia helped the woman gather her other things. She wished she could take the book about Melusine back to Aldous, but the chance was less than slim it would make it through. Traveling between the worlds was becoming so difficult.

Lola hid the cart in a shadowed cleft between the largest boulder and grassy wall. Anyone walking by would have to leave the sidewalk to see it. Something Melia noticed most mortals weren't prone to do.

Maybe one day Lola would come back for it, but she doubted it.

They had to get Lola and Jade somewhere safe. And soon.

Melia gripped her elbows. She watched the eastern horizon, willing a streak of sunlight to break the line. "How much longer until Jade gets here?" she asked Lola.

"There shouldn't be any traffic on the freeway, so I'm hoping she'll be here soon."

Ryder draped his arm across Melia's shoulders. "She'll be all right."

"I hope so," Melia said.

"What did you see?" he asked.

Melia shook her head. Lola stood too close. She didn't want the woman overhearing her describe the gruesome images.

Ryder pulled Melia to the fountain's retaining wall. He sat down on the narrow ledge. She moved to stand in front of him. He held her hands.

"I saw two white doves. Blood and death." The revulsion of saying the words aloud caused her stomach to clench. Ryder shifted and she settled on his thighs with her back resting against the brace of his arm. "Blood stained my fingers. It's been so long since I've seen that."

He rubbed her back. The tension in her body didn't abate. He cupped her chin and turned her face to him. "You're doing everything you can to help them."

"Lilliane was there. I couldn't see her face, but I saw her fingers crushing black rose petals. I heard her brittle laughter."

"You mentioned a Huron assassin," Ryder said.

"Yes."

"If Jade doesn't get here by dawn," he said. "I want you to take Lola. We'll catch up with you."

"No."

"We may not have a choice."

"If Jade doesn't get here in time, we'll take Lola to the Veil, and come back for Jade at dusk, together."

"Years could pass in the mortal world while we're gone. Is that a risk you're willing to take?"

A slim figure emerged on the predawn horizon. The tension in Melia's belly eased. "It looks like we won't have to." She took Ryder's hand and led him to Lola.

"I knew she'd make it." Lola whispered to Melia. "She sounded shaken on the phone. Something has spooked her."

Jade had almost reached them. "What's the emergency?" she called out.

Melia, growing up with two sisters, was well versed in subterfuge. Although she did her best to appear calm and casual, Jade was nervous, perhaps even scared. "Ryder and I must return to the enchanted world. We want you and your mother to travel with us." She wasn't going to tell them their lives were in danger. The surest way to enter Faerie was to focus on joy; learning they might be an assassin's target would terrify them, maybe so much they wouldn't be able to cross at all.

Jade evaded Melia's gaze and smiled at Ryder. "Cool." The girl was hiding something, but there wasn't time to press her.

"The doorways between the two worlds are becoming more difficult to pass through," Melia said, "and we don't have time to practice. We have to get it right the first time. We'll need to hold hands and wade into the water."

Jade grabbed Ryder's hand. "Nice."

Melia squelched the urge to rip their hands apart. She took Lola's hand. Mother and daughter entwined fingers and palms. Jade kept a firm grip on Ryder. They approached the retaining wall in a single line. In the cool of predawn, the fountain's spray was icy. Goose bumps sprouted on Melia's legs and arms.

Before she stepped in the water, Melia searched for a natural element to pull strength from. A breeze blew across the courtyard. She angled her shoulders. The wind hit her full in the face. She absorbed its energy as she coaxed her irritation with Jade into a tight coil in her belly and let it light her soul flame. The inner heat—power—extended to her extremities. She leaned into the wind. With each breath, she called the turbulent power of air deeper into herself, and with each breath she became more determined to drag Lola and Jade across the boundaries of time and space, no matter what Lilliane might throw at them.

The four stepped into the water, sloshing to their knees. Water sprayed their arms and faces. "We'll gather as close to the center of the fountain as possible," Melia said. "Lola and Jade, focus on a joyful memory, the most powerful one you can summon. Ryder and I will pull both of you, but you'll need to help us. Once we pass from the mortal plane, we'll hit the threshold between the worlds. It will feel like being in a windstorm. Your bodies will spin. Whatever you do, don't let go of our hands."

She glanced to the east. The first ripple of daylight touched the sky. A sense of dread crawled up Melia's throat and made her mouth dry. She gazed around the fountain's perimeter. A few figures, shaded by the grey light of early morning, meandered the sidewalks that crisscrossed the enormous courtyard, but they were too distant to warrant the dark feeling blossoming within her. Melia could feel Ryder watching her. She pulled more of the wind's energy inside her before leaning past Lola and Jade to lock eyes with him.

He nodded.

Hopefully, Lola and Jade's Albiana blood would help them. "Concentrate on joy—" A sudden gust shoved air in Melia's mouth, knotted her hair, and shoved her shoulders back. She gripped Lola's hand so hard the woman gasped.

"We have to go now!" Ryder shouted.

He was right, and yet—

The fountain floor shifted. The wavelike motion caused all of them to flail. Lola's butt splashed into the water. Melia tugged her back to standing, but on her other side, Jade wobbled.

A black-hooded figure shot from the fountain floor, a silent torpedo.

It was a miracle no one let go. "Now," Melia shouted. She called forth the image of the beach in Tyrannis, shaded by cliffs. The fountain floor swirled beneath her like sand. The doorway opened, a widening funnel. Lola, Jade, and Ryder slid down and across the barrier with her. They bobbed unevenly, but they were together. In her mind's eye, Melia latched onto their destination with ferocity.

When the wind hit, she didn't spin, but Lola did, and the torque felt like it would pull Melia's shoulder from its socket; she refused to let go and willed Lola to hang on.

The heel of a black boot knocked Melia's forehead so hard her neck snapped back with a sharp jerk.

She churned air franticly with her free hand.

39. Flora Gazes into Ormrun

Flora missed her cottage. The isolated yellow A-frame had been her refuge. And oh, how her heart ached for Bella. She pulled her hands from her apron pocket and wrapped her arms around herself as she lurched away from the square wooden table on which Ormrun and the silver pitcher sat side by side.

The spring faerie tottered to the window, gasping for breath. Grief had never been a friend to her. The genocidal burning of her kind had created a tear within her, a rip too great and too formidable to comprehend.

All these years, abandoning Illialei and nurturing her boundless rage for the Albiana queens had been her ballast. Now, with Melia and Ryder away in the mortal world; Ormrun and Koldis secure, here at the Veil; and Sevondi prepared to become regent; the first quiet and uneventful moments since Bella's death crept into Flora's day. And what did the peace bring her? Sorrow reaching its long dark fingers into the empty spaces to strangle the life within her.

She shoved the window open and leaned across the frame to take in fresh air, holding the breaths deep in her lungs. When Melia and her young man returned, all Flora's resources would be needed to see them through Umbra's incarnation and the half-faerie's ascent to the throne; the first true queen of the Realm of Faerie since the Albianas proved themselves despots.

The spring faerie rested her chin in her hands. Hot tears rolled down her face. A loud knock saved her from the oncoming flood she could never seem to dam.

Crossing the room with a clumsy gait, she wiped her eyes and cheeks with her apron. She patted her kerchief, damp beneath her chin, and forced a smile that felt unconvincing even to her. She let it fall after she opened the door.

Gumf pushed past her into the center of the room. "Any news yet?"

The dwarf's question focused her attention on the problem that beset her. Though it wasn't urgent, it troubled her. Whenever she gazed into the silver basin's eye and searched for Lilliane, she found the princess in the same state. Tranquil and reposed, reading in her chamber. Her innocent appearance would deceive anyone unaware of the princess heir's capabilities: a talent for black magic and an aptitude for murder designed to conceal the killer's hand.

"None to speak of," Flora said.

"What do you make of it?"

"The image is so uniform I'm beginning to suspect it's an enchantment itself."

Gumf rubbed his chin. "I've got a thick feeling in the back of my head and an ache in the base of my skull. It claims itself in my mind as a dire foreboding, but of what, I can't discern. These past days, regardless of whatever elixir Nivea brews, it doesn't relent. It grows worse."

As the proprietor and permanent resident of the Veiled Tavern, the mystical layers of reality that ensorcelled the inn affected Gumf's consciousness.

Flora moved to the table and settled her weight into one of the four chairs surrounding it. "I was preparing to look again before you knocked."

He settled in the chair catty-corner to hers. "Don't let me stop you." His left eyelid drooped. The left side of his mouth made a slight dip toward his jowl. The facial tics created an ominous contrast to the sunlight filtering through the open window.

Flora shuddered. "The pitcher."

He slid it toward her.

She filled Ormrun with seawater and gazed into the pool.

Steamy vapors rose from the still surface; the familiar trancelike state possessed her. She welcomed it, allowing Gumf and the room to slip beyond her awareness.

Thick woods surrounded her. The Balyudor.

Sinister laughter rattled her cheekbones. Umbra.

How long since she'd been called to face him? She hardened her mind.

"Old faerie, are we not done with our exchanges?"

"Your preference for youth who have no defense against your enticement to power saddens me."

"About your sadness, you do not lie."

Flora breached dangerous territory. Umbra created a murky bog of truth that sucked the careless to psychic death. She needed to barricade her deep inner wounds far from Umbra's stranglehold. She retreated and regrouped. *"I seek the Albiana heir."*

"What do you want with that dull princess?"

"She throws a veil around her being. I seek her, only to find a false image she projects."

"The princess bores me."

"And yet, the Albiana have drawn from your power. How do they accomplish that when they've never once possessed the basin?"

"The basin was made for Isolt, not the Albiana queens and princesses."

"Yet you have commandeered the bowl."

"Quasimi's death showed me the basin's power. From that moment, I wanted it for myself."

The mage's death showed Flora the basin's power too. *"And Isolt handed claim of Ormrun over to you—at your request?"*

"I loved Isolt of the Waters."

"Did you now?"

"*Her bereavement was dear to me.*"

"*Heartbreak draws you.*"

"*Isolt's infinite lamentations awoke me from my cosmic sleep.*"

Flora pulled at the knot on her kerchief. "*Where is Isolt now?*"

"*She languishes.*"

"*She doesn't care to take vengeance against Vulcan?*"

"*I will avenge Isolt's honor and the death of her son. I have vowed her that. She has no care to return to the mortal world. Such a reunion would only drive home the truth of her betrayer.*"

"*Una, her mother.*" Flora mused aloud, "Earth."

Umbra remained silent.

"*So you intend to assault that planet on Isolt's behalf?*" she asked.

"*I have convinced Isolt she can achieve both vengeance and blamelessness by allowing my hand to wield the sword of justice for her.*"

"*And she's agreed to that?*"

"*In a matter of speaking.*"

"*You profess such noble intentions.*"

"*Old faerie, your attempt to beguile me is transparent. What is the motive of all this gushing flattery?*"

"*The Albiana harness your energy. It fuels their dark magic with power. Even now, Lilliane casts a spell over the basin's eye. I gaze upon her, but it's like a dream that repeats itself. She blocks the eye and hides from its sight. But my greater fear is what she hides, and for what purpose.*"

"*You shoot questions like arrows.*"

"*And how do you answer?*"

"*The Albiana are capable of harnessing whatever energies exist within the Whole. Despite my being vaulted away beyond the Parallel of Shadows, they still drain me. My incarnation will achieve my independence from them.*"

"You fueled the slaughter of my kind," Flora whispered the accusation.

"I have no control over how they direct my power."

"And yet you long to destroy the Whole, and every creature in it. The killing of the spring faeries was just a taste to whet your appetite."

"I will wipe out any who refuse to worship me. Those who acknowledge my sovereignty will live."

"A new god—"

"Will soon be born. My vessel, Jade, is near."

Flora startled.

"You didn't know."

"How close is she?"

"Look out your window and you'll find her. She will not deny me."

Umbra's laugh echoed through the spring faerie's soul. She jerked to full consciousness.

"What is it? What did you see?" Gumf asked.

"The half-mortal Umbra seeks as his vessel approaches."

"Melia?"

"No. He's chosen another."

40. Jade Reaches the Enchanted World

Jade hacked up river water, snorting it through her nose. Beside her, the man in black panted. She rolled over, sprawled in the V of a shadowed gorge, an enormous black bridge overhead. She studied the six towering columns piercing the sky, the thick chains linking each ascending post, the solid black planks creating a walkway wide enough for ten people to walk abreast. Yet no one crossed it.

Eerie. Everything was so still.

He entered the edge of her vision, a coil of rope in his hand. Where did he get that? Before she could slam his face with the heel of her boot, he had her straddled with her legs pinned. She bent her fingers and reached out to claw his eyes, but he caught her wrists with one hand, a grip like steel. Almost twice her size, he bent over her, binding her wrists so tight, she feared he'd cut off the circulation.

"Guess you've done this before!" she shouted, hoping someone would hear her and come to her rescue. Isn't that what happened in the enchanted world? Damsels in distress and all.

No one showed up, and he said nothing. Not a word.

Infuriating. She craned her head. This had to be the enchanted world. It was so different.

But she wasn't about to ask him. He'd already made it clear he was a dangerous asshole. She hoped to God he wasn't Umbra. Oh my god! What if he was the one who'd come to slit her throat! Jade gulped. Where was her mother? Still in Balboa Park, she hoped. That stupid chick and her Max Zander look-alike boyfriend were nowhere in sight, either.

Her mind calculated swiftly as she assessed the lethality of the man eyeing her. She almost giggled out loud. A hysterical reaction? Intellectually, she recognized the precariousness of her situation, but emotionally, all she wanted to do was roll on the ground and laugh out loud. The primal drive to survive slammed through her delirium. She wasn't going to die. She was going to figure out this Umbra-incarnation thing and became all-powerful. Then she'd return to the mortal world and give Ryder another chance to dump his girlfriend.

The plan invigorated her. Jade had always believed she'd never feel sexually attracted to anyone. Ever. Boy or girl. Too risky. Too messy. But her last therapist insisted she'd feel affection and sexual desire when she met the right person. Her sexual anorexia was just a way to protect herself. Jade couldn't put her finger on it, but Ryder was different ...

She searched both sides of the riverbank once more. No one else was in sight. As usual. No one had come to her rescue; she'd need to rely on herself. Okay. She'd need to be hyper-vigilant for any opening to escape. Her insides quaked with fear and a strange exhilaration. Defiant, she bit her tongue to keep from gurgling in terror and readied herself for action.

He stood and yanked on her leash.

Her body, rigid with apprehension loosened. If he was the one the dark voice warned her about in La Jolla, at least he wasn't going to kill her here and now. She had some time.

Jade stumbled behind him, technically beneath him, as he ascended the side of the gorge. His grinding steps showered her with dirt, and the occasional twig, as he dragged her up the steep incline. She tripped over tree roots and slid back down when there were no handholds or toeholds. He grunted and tugged on the rope like a machine.

When they reached level ground, he paused.

Jade had a breath to assess her surroundings. Monstrous trees writhed in every direction. Yep. This had to be the enchanted world. She inched toward the nearest trunk, searching for signs of sentient life, a dryad, something. She reached out with bound hands—her captor didn't stop her—and ran a finger along the bark's deep grooves. Certainly, there was more than wood and leaves here. The tree seemed aware.

She imagined a grand ball with gigantic partners swirling and gyrating beneath clouds and moonlight. But not a leaf stirred, and no limb or trunk moved to embrace her. She sighed. What was the point of coming to the enchanted world if the trees didn't frolic and dance?

But the air was incredible. She gulped breath after breath. No pollution. It was like a feast.

Gabriela should have seen this.

The girl with the blue eyes—Melia—it was her fault. She'd been the one to warn Gabriela away, to make her afraid to come here.

Why? That was what Jade intended to find out.

First, she needed to figure out if this guy was the one who'd come to kill her. But she'd be damned if she was going to ask him in a quaking voice and show her fear.

Her captor pulled the rope, not as hard this time, and disappeared into the woods. She hurried to keep up with him.

How could he tell where he was going? There wasn't a path, or any markers that she could see, but he strode purposefully as she tripped over tree roots and slipped on slick piles of leaves. Where the rope gnawed at her wrists, they burned. Jade wanted to scream at him to slow down. Instead, she pressed her lips together in tight resolution.

They walked on and on at the same relentless pace.

Her sense of time warped.

She'd been in these black woods forever. The world around them grew darker and darker. Her life before was a dream, her future a mirage.

When her stomach growled and her lips cracked with thirst, she wondered if reading about dangerous and fantastical adventures might be preferable to living them.

At the site of a silky lawn and a glimpse of sunset, Jade's heart leapt. She yearned to break free and run for the green, for the swathe of fading light, but her captor held a finger to his lips.

In case she didn't understand, he spun her around, pulled her to his chest, and squeezed one arm across her ribcage. A sharp edge rested against her throat.

A knife; he was holding a knife to her throat. Was he going to kill her now? Was she some sort of sacrifice?

He whistled. It sounded like a bird.

Numerous tweets and coos responded. The woods were thick with his companions. What were they up to?

This might be her last chance to escape. She readied her assault.

One. Two. Three. Jade whipped up her knee and jammed the heel of her boot straight back. It connected with something hard and solid. A tree trunk, not her captor. Damn.

He pulled her back into the woods. Not the direction she wanted to go.

"I prefer girls with some fight," he whispered, all hot air in her ear.

Another man, who almost collided with her head-on, pulled up short. Tall and lean, he wore a brown uniform.

"Gods of Azyllai, who is this, Gavin?"

"A ploy. Stacking the deck in our favor."

His name was Gavin. Not Umbra. Maybe that was a good thing. She wasn't sure. It was almost twilight. Maybe she should try to call the dark voice.

She tuned into Gavin and his friend, exchanging rapid whispers. As best she could tell, they were planning an attack on the nondescript building crouched in the middle of the green lawn. Not her. She observed the brown building with its wraparound porch. It was so plain it looked out of place. Why did they care about it?

"Keep an eye on her," Gavin said.

He was not going to leave her here with a stranger. "No!"

A leather glove slammed over her mouth.

Now the stranger's arm circled Jade's chest, crushing her arms to her side, and Gavin faced her. "Are you going to miss me, love?"

"M. Humph. Hm."

"Don't let her get away," Gavin commanded his friend. "She's valuable to the princess. You understand what I'm saying?"

The princess?

"Yes, sir, Captain, sir."

How had they changed places? Grrr. This wasn't at all like reading about it in books. Sweat trickled into her eyes. Her back hurt like hell. A blister burned on her heel, and everyone shoved her around like a damned suitcase.

"Speaking of the princess," Gavin said, "did she get wind of our plans to seize the sword and basin?"

"We've been sending out knights on a rotating basis like you ordered, sir. A few days ago, we sent out two corps before dawn. The princess took no note when only one came back after sunset. In your absence, she's been less attentive to our presence."

"Good. Good," Gavin muttered. "She wants to make a lap dog of me, but with the sword and basin in our possession, it will be me pulling the strings of our puppet princess."

"Do you know what she wants with this one?"

Gavin returned his hood to his head. "I've got an idea."

"What is it?" Jade blurted out.

"Keep her quiet," Gavin said.

A hand clamped over the top of her head and shoved. "Get down."

339

Wait until she incarnated Umbra and became queen. Then she would show them this was not how you treated someone on their first trip to the enchanted world. Not at all. And who was this princess? And why was Jade valuable to her? Apparently, Melia had withheld some critical intelligence. Boy, Jade's mom was going to be pissed.

If she ever saw her mother again.

No. Stop it. She'd read an article once about surviving a physical assault. You had to believe you were going to escape. Believe. Believe. Believe.

Jade's eyes widened. On the edge of the lawn, ten, twenty, thirty soldiers materialized out of nowhere.

The building remained quiet, the wide wraparound porch empty.

Didn't anyone besides her see them? The soldiers advanced.

Jade screamed and the hand over her mouth muffled it.

"You need to shut up." More hot air in her ear.

41. Bloodshed

The wind between the worlds ate Melia's shouts for Jade. She pushed relentlessly toward the Tyrannis beach in her mind. Her body passed from air into water. Her head broke the surface of the Great White Sea.

Lola spluttered away from her, crawling toward shore.

It was low tide and they'd arrived in the shallows. Melia crouched. A rush of blood pounded in her ears. She turned in circles, crab-like with her hands and feet in the sand.

They were alone. No Ryder. No Jade. And no one else.

An explosion of saltwater erupted from a gentle swell. Dark hair flung water in Melia's face. She gouged the burning wetness from her eyes.

Ryder's emerald gaze, darkened beneath the cloudy sky, returned hers. They waded to each other and pressed their bodies into a reassuring embrace. He picked her up and swung her around as if she were a child of five. She laughed until she saw Lola on the beach, a hand shading her brow.

Melia sighed. "We need to go back to the mortal world for Jade."

"We won't find her there," Ryder said. "She let go of my hand and took his."

"His?"

"The assassin. I dove after her, but couldn't catch hold of her." Ryder touched the tender spot at Melia's hairline. "What happened?"

"He kicked me." Her eyes stung. "I understand Jade not trusting me. But why would she leave her mother to go with a stranger?"

"She didn't know who he was."

"Maybe I should have told them the whole truth. But we were running out of time, and I was worried if they knew their lives were in danger, they'd be too frightened to cross."

Ryder put his arm around her as they sloshed to shore.

"Jade couldn't get away from me fast enough yesterday afternoon," Melia thought out loud, "yet this morning, she didn't argue when we told her we needed to bring her and her mother to Faerie. She didn't ask a single question. Something happened between yesterday afternoon and this morning. Her mother said something shook her up."

They reached land.

Lola wrung her hands. "Where's Jade?"

"We got separated when we were crossing over," Melia said.

"Is she in danger?" Lola asked.

Melia found it harder than she thought it would be to lie.

"We think she's on her way to Illialei," Ryder said. "It's another country in Faerie, but we're near the border—" He scanned the beach and towering cliffs. "Where are we?"

Lola's eyes rounded. "You don't know?"

Melia studied their surroundings. "It's the same beach we left from, just farther north."

"We need to regroup at the Veil," Ryder said.

"You'll be safer there," Melia told Lola, "while we search for Jade."

"Oh, oh, oh," Lola whimpered. "What will happen if you don't find her?"

Melia hugged her. "We will." Until then, Flora would be a calming influence on the woman.

❖ ❖ ❖

They walked along the wet sand in the direction of the Nyssalei River. The wind blew increasingly cold as the cloud-blocked sun dropped from the sky. Icy gusts whipped their hair and poked through their clothes like frozen fingers. Lost in their respective thoughts, no one complained.

Several hours later, Melia spied the dirt trail leading through a cleft in the wall of rock. By the time they entered the Balyudor, the shadows were deep in Faerie's wild woods.

A dark moon night was falling on the enchanted world.

Halfway between the cliffs and the tavern, Melia heard an enormous bang in the gloaming. "What was that?"

"It came from the direction of the tavern," Ryder said.

"Isn't that where you're taking me?" Lola asked.

"It was probably–" Melia tried to imagine something that could make such a loud, sharp noise, something that didn't signal danger. She couldn't.

Ryder took Melia's hand and inched forward.

Melia took Lola's hand.

Shouts rang out. They weren't expressions of joy.

Melia tugged on Ryder's hand to make him stop. When he did, she didn't know what to say. All her thoughts scared her; they would terrify Lola.

"Wait here," he said. "I'll scout ahead."

Melia dropped his hand and chewed on a fingernail.

The shouts, laced with pain and despair, grew more frequent. Something tore past them.

"Hey," Melia called after it.

More shadowy figures raced by.

"Hey!" No one answered her. She tried to grab one of the figures as it darted by, but her hands caught air. A swatch of silky hair brushed her cheek.

"Female trolls," Melia said. "They're some of the fastest creatures in Faerie."

"Trolls. Really?" Lola stretched and twisted, trying to get a better look as they ran by.

Melia wanted to ask one of them why they were fleeing the Veil.

"Do you think Jade is all right?" Lola whispered.

"We're going to do everything we can to protect her." That was the truth.

"If anything happens to her, I'll never forgive myself," Lola's voice quaked. "I've always wanted to come here, even though my mother warned me it was dangerous. From the day Jade was born, I've fed her tales about faeries and whatnot. What if I've misled her and it costs my daughter her life?"

Melia felt her way to put her arm around Lola's shoulder. "For the most part, Tyrannis and Illialei have peaceful histories." She glossed over the chapters about Uriel's burning of the spring faeries and Plantine's murder of the grey faerie. Those were anomalies, weren't they? Melia recalled the vision of the two doves and shuddered. She heard sniffling. "Are you crying?"

"I won't be able to live with myself if anything happens to my daughter."

Melia considered telling her the mortal world was unsafe for them as well. That Lilliane had dispatched an assassin to take their lives, so Melia could never have left them there, defenseless. But if Lola found out Jade was most likely with the assassin right now, what would she do?

The woman was already shaking.

"We'll find her." Melia was no longer sure that they would, but Lola needed to settle down.

A dark figure raced past them, clipping Melia's shoulder.

She whirled around. Her pulse accelerated.

The knight who'd been inside their tree house stood an arm's length from her. The details of his face weren't clear, but her eyes had adjusted to the dark night. His height, his sharp nose, the beard; it was him.

"You!" His hand dropped to his belt.

Melia didn't hesitate. She lowered her torso and charged. Her head slammed into his stomach. He stumbled back, arms flying in the air. They crashed to the ground together, landing belly-to-belly.

His hands gripped the sides of her head. His thumbs searched for her eye sockets. He was wearing his damned gloves! She hugged herself to him, limiting his range of movement as she groped along the leather of his belt for a weapon. Her fingers brushed the hilt of a knife before he bucked her off and flipped. Somehow he landed on his feet while she ended up sprawled on her back, clutching her lower abdomen.

He staggered in her direction.

She rolled onto her stomach and, using her elbows, dragged her body away from him. The sound of his labored breathing gained on her. She wasn't moving fast enough.

His boot smashed down on her lower back.

Lola screamed.

Melia buckled in pain, gasping for air.

He grabbed a handful of her hair and jerked her head up. "I'm going to enjoy slitting your pretty, pale throat." Then he fell on top of her.

"You asshole!" Lola was on his back, pummeling him with her fists.

Their combined weight crushed Melia.

The knight lost hold of his knife when he crashed to the ground. It was so close to her outstretched fingers.

His fingers wrapped around hers and pulled them back.

She screamed.

"Melia!"

"Ryder—"

A leather fist slammed her mouth. Her head lolled to the side then flopped to the ground.

"Melia!"

Her tongue was too heavy. She couldn't make her lips move. The weight on her back lessened, but Melia couldn't think of how to free herself further.

"Do something!" Lola screamed. She was standing somewhere off to the side now. "He's going to kill her!"

A deafening roar filled Melia's ears. Ryder. She closed her eyes. Maybe he'd save her.

Ryder heaved the knight and threw him from her back as if he were weightless.

Melia heard a sickening crack, the knight colliding with a tree trunk. She willed her hand to walk across the dirt and leaves and reach.

Ryder crouched beside her, caressing her hair.

"His knife," she whispered.

Ryder snatched up the blade. "How bad are your injuries?"

"Just bumps and bruises, I think," she said. "Let me lie here for a minute, to gather my strength." She heard more voices. Another knight?

Ryder left her side.

She heard battle cries and the dull thud of body strikes. Then she heard running, crashing through the woods; the chase faded, then silence everywhere. It was a ghastly quiet that prickled her skin.

Lola crept to her. "Oh, oh, oh. Are you all right?"

Melia tried to nod, but she wasn't sure whether or not her head moved.

Lola dabbed the corner of Melia's mouth with a soft cloth.

By the time Ryder returned, Melia was sitting up. Lola had helped her prop her back against a tree.

"They got away," Ryder said.

"How many were there?" Melia asked.

"By the time I stopped giving chase, more than I could count. Can you walk?"

Melia shrugged her shoulders and winced.

"He almost beat her to death!" Lola cried.

Ryder knelt before Melia.

"Why did he attack her?" Lola asked. "Are they coming back?"

"I don't think so. They were heading toward the bridge. They're leaving Tyrannis."

Melia forced herself to sit straighter.

Ryder ran his finger across her cheekbone and kissed her eyelids. "Earlier, I ran into Nivea. She was digging for herbs not far from here. She was distraught and mumbling about a poultice. Gumf was cut open—with Koldis—"

"Where's Flora?" Melia asked.

Ryder's grip on her hand tightened. "I don't know. After Nivea told me the knights attacked the Veil, that it was madness, I came back for you."

"Please, help me stand. We need to find her." She bit her lip hard to keep from crying out as he helped her to her feet.

Lola tripped over tree roots and repeatedly caught herself by grabbing Melia's arm, her shoulder, or colliding against her back. Melia absorbed the impact silently, gritting her teeth.

Ryder slipped through the woods as if he had the eyes of a cat. He stopped often, to wait for Melia to catch up with him. But he was patient and accepted her need to walk on her own.

Ahead of them, someone moaned.

"Wait here," he said.

"No," Melia answered. "We're not going to be separated again."

They almost tripped over a troll, lying on the ground. Ryder held his hands against the creature's stomach to staunch the flow of blood. Melia pulled Lola's scarf from her neck. It was the same cloth Lola tended Melia's wounds with earlier. She pressed it into Ryder's hands. He folded it into a makeshift bandage and pressed it against the ugly gash in the troll's side.

Even without moonlight, Melia could tell the blood seeped fast, soaking through the cloth. She pressed her fist against her mouth, helpless to prevent the troll's impending death.

How many others lay silent and dying, alone and unaided in the woods?

The troll struggled to speak, "They attacked at dusk. There were so many of them."

Melia drew closer to Ryder. She cradled the troll's head and stroked his forehead.

"But Flora, oh, she was magnificent." The sound of his voice was dreamy. "She wielded the blue sword." He choked and coughed. "Until five of them ganged up on her."

Melia trembled at the scene he painted.

The troll continued his story in a raspy, fading voice. "I didn't even try to help her." He grabbed Ryder's arm and pulled himself up. "I ran." His body shuddered. "I've run as far as I'm going to run in this lifetime. One of them caught up with me and pumped my gut with his blade. It serves me right." He dropped back to the ground. "But I saw the spring faerie's glory before I lost my courage. There was a halo around her, a halo of light. I hoped it would save her." He coughed up a spittle of blood. "I hoped it would save us all." His head lolled to one side.

Ryder unwrapped the blood-drenched cloth and covered the troll's face.

Lola batted her hands. "He died. Right here in front of us. He just"—she hiccuped—"died."

"I have to find Flora," Melia whispered. She couldn't think beyond that.

"Who is Flora?" Lola asked.

"The last spring faerie"—Melia wanted to say alive but feared it was no longer true—"to live."

"That sounds lonely," Lola said.

"I think it was." Melia wiped away the silent tears that blinded her. She'd make sure Flora had an honorable burial, that a flaming cross marked her grave. In Faerie, it was the greatest tribute one could bestow.

But she had to find her body first. Numb to her own pain, Melia pushed past Ryder.

❖ ❖ ❖

Ryder overtook her and led them through the woods.

When they reached the back of the inn, Melia saw the building stood as it always had, there had been no burning. At least Flora didn't suffer that indignity.

Melia indicated to Ryder she was anxious to cross the lawn.

His arm shot out to hold her back. "Let's be sure we don't walk into a trap."

"The night has grown eerily still since the troll died," Melia said. "The fighting is over; the knights are gone."

Ryder didn't relent with his arm.

"What if Flora is still alive?" She shoved past him.

Ryder and Lola followed on her heels.

A dark form lay on the lawn. A body. Melia counted four more as she raced to the first, a dwarf still wearing his apron and chef's hat. She dropped to his side, brushing his cheek with the back of her hand. Dead; recently. Ryder and Lola checked the others. By their response, she judged their results were the same. "They're all dead," Melia said. Heat blistered her veins. "If I'd incarnated Umbra, this never would have happened."

Ryder gripped her shoulder. "You weren't ready."

"No. I was afraid and ruled by self-doubt."

"Melia, even Flora agreed you weren't ready."

"I'm ready now."

Ryder pulled her to him.

Although she would have rather flailed at him with her fists, she buried her face in his chest.

"You can't blame yourself for this senseless carnage," he said.

Melia pulled away from him. "This is Lilliane." She spread her arms. "No one believed she'd dare cross the river. Do you see how bold she's become?"

Ryder tried to embrace her.

She blocked his arms. "For the first time in my life, everything is clear. If I find the basin and sword in that building"–she thrust her finger over his shoulder–"I'll incarnate Umbra tonight."

"No!" Ryder said. "That isn't what we agreed to!"

"Can't you see? I was wrong to wait for the Grey Council's approval."

"You're overwrought—"

"What has the council ever done to help Faerie? Did they send aid when Elendah died? What about justice when the spring faeries burned?"

"There are prophecies—"

"Idonnic prophecies? I thought they sickened you. I thought that's why you left Idonne. Now you defend inaction with claims of what? That we must stand by and do nothing while innocents die, because genocide and murder fulfill the lines of a poem? I won't live that way. Not when there's something I can do."

"Melia—" He took hold of her hands.

She pulled away from him. "Let me go inside."

Ryder released a weary sigh and moved aside. He walked behind her with Lola.

Inside, torches burned in their sconces. The well-lit scene and the smell sickened Melia. She lost count of the bodies—some piled one on top of the other—as they fruitlessly checked each one for life. "I'll remember they showed no mercy," she said.

Lola wept over what they saw, but there was no time to comfort her. And Melia had nothing to offer. She'd never witnessed carnage like this. Not the day the Calashai razed itself. Not even in her dark moon visions. She raised her hands in front of her face now. Blood made her palms and fingers black in the moonlight streaming through the kitchen windows. She may not have committed these murders, but she could have prevented them.

She headed toward the inn's large central tavern. When she crossed the threshold, she swayed with nausea. No one had survived.

Lola's sobs grew louder.

Melia sank onto one of the hewn benches and dropped her head onto the table, her body heaving. All hope of finding Flora alive drained away. She sensed the absence of Ormrun and Koldis as well. Temporarily sated, the malignant energy of the dwarf artifacts had moved on.

Melia tried to stand. She clutched her abdomen and caught herself with a hand against the table before she crumpled. Black dots swam across her vision.

Lilliane ordered this; to protect her throne.

Melia would tear the Cathedral Palace apart with her bare hands if that's what it took to keep the princess from becoming queen.

There were over a hundred corpses.

Incapable of remaining in their presence, Lola excused herself. Ryder pointed to the corridor that led to the foyer and out the Veil's front door. She hurried in that direction.

Melia wiped her forehead. Maybe she needed some fresh air too. Maybe they all did. She limped toward Ryder.

"Lights! Lights!" Lola called out, the inn's mahogany walls funneling her shouts from the front porch.

Melia, with Ryder holding her elbow, hobbled to see what excited the woman.

Dots of light, too numerous to count, danced along the edge of the woods.

"Glow sprites," Melia whispered.

Shaded figures emerged from the trees, slinking across the ground. The airborne lights advanced with them.

Lola hid behind Melia and Ryder. "What is it?"

By the time they crossed half the lawn, Melia pressed her hands together. Surrounded by glow sprites, Bertille's face gleamed. She led a band of water nixies.

"Friends." Melia patted Ryder's hand. He released her elbow. She forced herself to stand erect. "Very dear friends."

"Oh, oh, oh." Lola pointed. "They look like giant butterflies."

Melia looked up. An impressive assembly of sylphs fluttered over the treetops to land behind the nixies. As she ran to Bertille, Melia thought she recognized Calista.

"Are you all right?" Bertille asked.

Ignoring the aches of her beating, Melia rushed to meet her

friend on the lawn. "Huron knights attacked the Veil. They've left nothing but death. Oh, Bertille, it's worse than anything I ever saw in my dark moon visions." Melia lowered herself, knees on the ground, hands on her thighs.

The nixie stroked her hair.

"I shouldn't have let this happen," Melia said.

"How can this be your fault?"

Melia reached for Bertille's hand. "If I'd incarnated Umbra, I would have had the power to stop it."

"No." The nixie squeezed Melia's fingers.

"It's true!" Tears rolled down Melia's face. "I could have defended the tavern and everyone in it. I could have saved Flora. I've been so afraid of Umbra's power. But now, I want it! I need it!"

"Shh. Shh." Bertille pushed Melia's hair away from her face. "We have the spring faerie."

"What do you mean?"

"The sylphs saved her."

Melia let out a heaving bellow of relief. "There are so many dead. The back lawn, the kitchen, the hall. How did she survive?"

"When they awoke at dusk, the whippoorwills discovered the knights skulking through the woods. They sent a call for aid along the river. The sylphs arrived first. They traveled the cloud road."

"They saved Flora?"

Bertille took Melia's hand again. "She's alive, but they tortured her for knowledge of the basin."

"Flora survived the genocide of her race, and the deep sorrow of Elendah's death, to be tortured by Lilliane's agents?" Melia doubled over, sobbing with anguish and relief.

"The spring faerie is fierce in battle," Bertille said.

Melia grabbed the nixie's shoulders. "I have to see her. Where is she?"

"She's on her way to the valley, to the marketplace. It's the best we can do on such short notice. Traffic on the Undine is thick. Every vessel in the muannai valley port has been called upon. But the knights' attack was strategic and ruthless. As you've seen, most didn't survive."

"What of the basin and sword?" Melia asked.

"Flora kept the basin safe. Ormrun is with her, but the knights have taken Koldis."

"They also have a prisoner," Melia realized.

"Who?"

"Her name is Jade. She's Queen Luisa's great-granddaughter. They'll kill her."

"Will the queen risk a public execution?" Bertille asked. "Illialei's population is naive, but they won't approve of that."

"Who says it will be public? By annihilating those whose Albiana blood mixes with mortal, Lilliane can prevent Umbra's incarnation. If she does that—"

"There'll be none to stand against her."

"That's my fear," Melia said.

"Then you're in danger here. It's possible they sought you as much as the basin and the sword," Bertille said. "Leave this place. Let us deal with the remains. Go on the next boat to the marketplace. I'll find you there."

"Bertille, I've been so naive about everything, and it's cost so much."

The water nixie shushed her again. "I've heard you've been diving." Bertille indicated Ryder, waiting on the porch with Lola. "And that you saved Sevondi's life at the Muudron Stone."

Melia watched Ryder pace the edge of the wide porch. She was grateful he remained with Lola, allowing her to talk freely with Bertille. "I've decided I will incarnate Umbra."

"And he agrees?" The nixie wound her hand in the air, indicating Ryder.

"Yes," Melia said. "No. I don't know. Witnessing so much bloodshed has changed me."

"It's changed us all," Bertille said. "Who's that on the porch with him?"

"Queen Luisa's granddaughter, Lola."

"The prisoner's mother," Bertille said. "It must be devastating for her to see what the knights who've abducted her child are capable of."

"We haven't told her Jade is with them." Melia tugged on her hair. "It's the first time she's come to Faerie. She showed me books she read in the mortal world. She believed the realm to be some kind of wonderland."

"It is a wonderland," Bertille said. "But even fantastical places have dark shadows. Take her to the valley with you," Bertille said. "For now, it remains peaceful there."

There was no reason except stubbornness to argue. Melia called out to Lola and Ryder.

Bertille signaled to another nixie. "Lead them to the river. Make sure they secure passage on the next boat to the valley."

Ryder took Melia's hand as they entered the woods. "Are you all right?"

"As well as can be expected." She allowed herself to lean on him as she relayed Bertille's mixed news.

"Flora survived, and they don't have the basin," he reiterated.

"I'm deeply grateful for that," Melia said. "But it doesn't lessen the magnitude of the crime committed in Tyrannis tonight."

"No. It doesn't," Ryder said.

Lola chattered about the spectacle of glow sprites, sylphs, and nixies before falling quiet.

The nixie said little.

42. Illiqlei

The chilling screams stopped. Jade shattered the quiet aftermath with her own howls. Her guard slapped her hard with the heel of his hand. Her knees buckled. It felt like he fractured a cheekbone. Jade forced herself to take deeper, slower breaths.

She'd gotten herself into scrapes before and managed to get out unscathed. The Sig Ep party the single semester she attended San Diego State University came to mind.

About 1 a.m., after drinking way too much watermelon punch, going home with the guy who hadn't seemed so hot before he kept her flimsy white plastic cup filled seemed like a good idea.

Until they walked into his apartment and no one else was home.

When he turned on the stereo, Jade rushed to climb up on his sofa, stood on the cushions, and wailed "You Oughta Know" along with Alanis Morissette at the top of her lungs. An excellent anti-aphrodisiac.

By the time she finished—five songs later—he was begging to take her home. His car was rolling when she opened the door, jumped out, and hauled ass inside her tiny Hillcrest bungalow. Despite the stupidity of giving him her phone number earlier in the evening, he never called or texted. She considered that a success and declared Fraternity Row off limits. Forever.

But death hadn't loomed. Only sex.

Not exactly like this.

The storm of shrieks and cries that hailed down on her ears

earlier assured her people had died.

A large number.

The blue shimmer caught her eye before she saw Gavin. Disheveled, worn, and breathless, he gripped a sword. It was magnificent. "Come on," was all he said to the knight restraining her. Another knight followed on his heels.

As they made their way back through the woods, the number of men who gathered around them swelled like yarn twining around a ball of wool.

The light of the blade flickered—disappearing, reappearing—as Gavin threaded through the growing ranks of soldiers.

Jade focused on the ghostly blue light. She longed to possess it.

"It belongs to you," the dark voice said.

Umbra. Finally.

Jade was at the tail end of the soldiers crossing the enormous iron bridge she'd seen that morning; no one heard her when she whispered, "What took you so long?" The rope binding her wrists was uncoiled to its full length, and as long as she kept up with their pace, Gavin and the soldiers ignored her.

"My precious, Jade. I'm never far from your side."

"Then let me be clear on something. Being tied up, pushed around, smashed in the face, and led like a dog on a leash doesn't feel very queen-like to me. So if—"

The soldier holding the far end of the rope cupped his ear. "What's that, love?"

"I'm not your love," she seethed.

"She told you," a voice shouted. More jokes, catcalling, and raucous whistles rippled through the men.

Jade glowered. Apparently, assholes were as ubiquitous in the enchanted world as they were in the mortal one.

The company drew to a halt. The ranks split. Gavin, tall and menacing, marched through the divide. "Are we having a problem with our prisoner?"

"Nothing I can't handle." The thug holding the end of the rope swaggered toward his leader.

"She's going to handle him," a voice called out.

Gavin surveyed his men. "I'll have silence."

They came to attention.

"This is our prisoner." He turned his back on Jade to speak to them. "Princess Lilliane would have me kill her."

Jade would have lost her dinner if she'd eaten any. Rather she experienced wave after wave of nausea with no way to alleviate the discomfort. Melia said nothing about a princess wanting her dead; neither had Umbra.

Gavin stepped close. He traced her cheek with a gloved finger. Jade flinched from the strange caress. He settled a hand on her shoulder. "I prefer to use her as a bargaining chip. Queen Luisa intends us to shield her throne; I intend to take it for the glory of Huros. This slip of a girl is going to ease the negotiations immensely." He stepped away from Jade and addressed his men with increased vehemence. "No one will touch her. For the time being, she remains pure."

Jade cringed at the connotation. Maybe she should have stayed with Melia, and Ryder, and her mother.

"Any questions?" Gavin asked.

"Why does the princess—whoever—want me dead?"

Gavin spun in a tight circle. Jade swore he clicked his heels before advancing toward her. "Has anyone ever told you you're mouthy?"

"No," she lied.

Although she doubted he believed her, he let the point slide with an elegant nod of his head. "She considers you a beast stalking her country's border," he answered her, but spoke to his men.

Another point Melia failed to mention. The beast point. Next time Jade saw her, they were going to have a chat. Until then, she needed to survive.

"But you don't?" Jade asked.

"No. As I've told my men, I consider you an opportunity."

Her feet planted, Jade bobbed up and down from her knees. "Then just tell me what you plan to do with me."

He stood with his chest so close to her forehead, looking at the buttons on his coat made her cross-eyed. The bottom of his beard-covered chin was even with the crown of her head. He glared down his nose. "The more docile and compliant you are, the more you'll appreciate the final outcome."

Jade's gaze traveled down to settle on his hip and the sword shoved in his belt. A large ruby eye on the sword's hilt mesmerized her.

She was going to find a way to steal that sword, and run.

"Understood?" Gavin asked.

"Yes," she mumbled.

"Good." He returned to the front of the group and led them across the bridge.

❖ ❖ ❖

They reached a dirt road. It wound through a different forest. Not so tangled and dark. Tall straight trees with light-colored trunks stood farther apart. Birches. Aspens. Those were the ones Jade could name. It was early in the day and birdsong saturated the air. It sounded like the entire world was wired with speakers.

Sometimes it felt like they were being watched. But whenever Jade thought she caught a glimpse of a face or the shadow of a fleeting figure, by the time she turned her head, it was gone. Her imagination?

Hard to say.

The men continued their relentless marching. The night before, after crossing the bridge, they threw themselves on the ground. Gavin called it sleeping.

Jade begged to differ.

When she put on her combat boots yesterday morning, at home—which now seemed another lifetime ago—she hadn't bothered with socks. The blister forming where the boot slipped on her right heel

358

was only getting worse.

How much farther did they plan to go?

She bobbed and craned her head. In daylight, the sword's illumined glow was hard to keep track of.

The forest came to an abrupt end. To the right, magnolia trees with blossoms the size of her head shaded a large grey boulder and long, high stone wall. Jade stared at the wall as it disappeared behind them, and was rewarded with the glimpse of an ornate gate and lush landscape beyond it.

Another strange longing possessed her. For the hundredth time that morning, she wished they could stop marching and truly rest.

They didn't.

It still felt like eyes were everywhere, watching them. Still she saw no one, except Gavin and his soldiers, who kept moving like they were androids.

A hill grew before them. With each step, it grew wider and higher. When it became clear they intended to climb the hill, Jade balked. She was certain her heel was bleeding. She had a severe case of cotton-mouth. She stopped walking.

The thug tugged on her leash. "Come on."

Jade tripped but didn't fall. She shook her head. "I need water."

"The palace isn't much farther."

The palace? Would that be the home of the princess who wanted her dead?

She no longer cared what Gavin might do to her. She braced herself. When the thug pulled hard on her leash, only her arms jerked forward. "I can't walk anymore," she yelled. "I've got an enormous blister on my heel."

Everyone stopped and turned their head. Gavin approached. "Again, with the mouth."

"My foot is bleeding and I'm dehydrated."

He positioned himself in front of her and squatted down. "Which foot?"

She swung out with her boot and was impressed when he didn't flinch; rather he caught her heel before the reinforced toe nailed his hawk-like nose. She hopped on her other foot to keep her balance.

"Put your hands on my shoulder."

"Fine."

He slipped the boot off and tossed it aside. Her heel was indeed a bloody mess. He released it. "Give me your other foot."

"Why?"

"Everyone goes barefoot here. You don't need shoes."

"You're not barefoot. All your men are wearing boots."

"Faerie is not our home."

"It's not mine either," she said.

"We don't have any bandages." He patted the ground. "The grass is soft the rest of the way. We'll get your heel wrapped and find you some better shoes at the palace."

"There aren't any shoes better than my boots," Jade said. If she managed to escape, how far was she going to get with no shoes?

Gavin stood. He ordered one of the men to pick up her boot. "Let's go."

"You expect me to walk like this?"

"What do you suggest?" Gavin asked. He was weird. Icy and ruthless one minute, pragmatic and patient the next.

"Can he carry my other one too?"

Gavin reached with his large hand. Even in the day's heat, he still wore his gloves. Jade wrestled with her left boot, but it was difficult to work with bound hands.

He raised the blue blade. "Hold out your wrists."

"Are you going to hurt me?"

"Don't run. Stay with us, and I'll free your hands."

Jade considered the offer. She wasn't going anywhere without that sword, but there was no way to take it from Gavin now. If she followed along with him willingly, could she pump him for more information? Could she take the blade when he was off guard? Was he ever off guard? "I won't march willingly toward my death," she said.

"If you'll do as I say, you won't die."

The men watched their exchange with interest. What did that mean?

"What about the princess?"

"I can control her."

"When did you decide not to kill me?"

Gavin folded his arms. "When I realized the greater advantage you offered me alive."

"When was that?"

His hand came toward her. She reared her head back. He ran two fingers down one of her dreads. "There's something worth saving about you."

Jade felt like she stood on a precipice. For all the quiet around them, her heart beat like a drum in her chest. "You and your men killed a lot of people last night."

"The grey faerie died and war has reached Faerie."

"War?"

"The battle between Dark and Light. The fight for Faerie's throne."

Umbra had promised it to her. "You don't want Lilliane to have the throne?"

He dropped the rope of her hair. "You ask too many questions. Hold out your hands."

She did.

He deftly cut the rope binding her wrists. "Give me your other boot."

Jade pulled it off and handed it to him. He gave it to one of his soldiers. "Can I have some water?" she asked.

"The palace is just over the hill. You won't die from thirst in that time."

She glared at him.

He turned around, squatted, and leaned slightly forward. "Climb on my back."

"You've got to be kidding."

He repeated himself.

"If the princess wants to kill me, why are you taking me to her?" Jade asked.

"I'll protect you," he said.

"Befriend him to gain the blade," Umbra said.

This time she didn't answer him aloud, only in her mind. *"Are you sure?"*

"When he lowers his guard, take the blade and cross the river."

He was giving her instructions. This was very cool. *"What about this princess? She wants me dead."*

"As my queen, you will defeat her."

"When do I become your queen?"

"The blade is the key. The basin is the door. When you unlock the door, we will be united, and you will be my queen."

"Some voodoo ritual?"

"My, precious Jade, you'll be more powerful than any mortal voodoo queen."

When Jade had been a teenager, she and Lola spent a transient summer in Louisiana. Jade became obsessed with voodoo and used to leave pound cake at the statue across the street from Mary Laveau's tomb in hopes of cursing her father. As far as she knew, her efforts went unrewarded. Whenever she tried to obtain any information about the suffering she'd hoped to rain down upon her father's anonymous head, Jules erected a steel wall of immutable silence.

It had been one of the rougher patches in Jade's life.

So more powerful than a voodoo queen sounded good right now.

Gavin waited.

She reached out with her hands, leaned forward, felt his scratchy uniform through the thin cloth of her dress, and circled her arms around his neck. Throwing her legs around his waist was more awkward, but she managed.

He stood, and with Jade riding piggyback, assumed his place at the head of his men.

✧ ✧ ✧

An enormous white palace glistened in the afternoon sun. With its steepled turrets and flags waving in the breeze, it looked like it belonged in a storybook. Jade counted six towers of differing heights. Despite its dazzling beauty, her heart fell like a stone. "Please don't take me there."

"I've nowhere else to keep you," Gavin said.

She wanted to scratch and claw her way from his back, but with no idea of the terrain, where would she go? "There's got to be somewhere else. Somewhere the princess can't find me."

"She won't find you in the palace. You'll be tucked away in a tower far from her chamber."

"And she stays in her chamber all day?"

"No, but the places she fancies—the library, the throne room, the rose garden—are in the southeast wing of the palace. You'll be in the northwest tower. Lilliane doesn't wander the halls; her mind is bent on other things. Under my protection, you'll be safe from her."

"What will you tell her when she asks if you've killed me? Will you lie?"

"It won't be difficult to convince her I've accomplished my mission."

"And what is your mission?"

"To kill any half-mortal with Albiana blood."

"See, you've made a mistake and grabbed the wrong girl. I don't have any Albiana blood."

"You're the faerie queen's great-granddaughter."

"No, I'm not."

"Is Gabriela your grandmother?"

"Yes, but there are thousands of—"

"Your grandmother was Luisa's daughter in the mortal world. That I'm sure of."

At this point, Jade didn't find it hard to believe Gabriela's mother had been a faerie. In fact, it explained much of what Jade loved most about her grandmother. But ... "The princess wants me killed because Gabriela was my grandmother?"

"Like I said, all half-mortals with Albiana blood."

"But if what you're saying is true, then I'm related to the princess. We're family."

"Lilliane doesn't dare see Umbra incarnated."

Jade had never questioned why Umbra came to her out of the blue. Maybe she should have. Next time they chatted, she would. "Why not?"

"There you go with your mouth again."

"I'm just trying to understand what's happening to me. If someone wanted you dead, wouldn't you want to know why?"

Gavin's grip tightened around her thighs. "The longer this conversation continues, the more I'm doubting the wisdom of allowing you to live."

A sick feeling crested in Jade's stomach as his words sank in.

When they reached a broad road—it wasn't paved, but the grass was flat and brown from foot and hoof traffic—Gavin ordered his men to continue their march to the drawbridge. When the last man passed, he left the road and entered an orchard.

The thicket of golden apple trees reminded Jade of the first time Umbra contacted her. She couldn't decide if that was a good or a bad thing.

After ducking under and dodging around branches, Gavin reached a plain door in one of the white walls. He knocked a rhythm on the wood. The door cracked open.

Gavin pushed his way through into a shadowy hall.

"Sir, good to have you back at the palace."

"How's everything been since we've been away?"

"Quiet."

"And the princess?"

"Spending more and more time in her chamber, less and less time in her garden."

"Is she well?"

"Yes."

"Good. Don't announce my return. I've some matters to attend to before I greet her in the throne room. She's still making her daily appearances?"

"Only in the morning, sir."

"I'll see her then. First thing." Gavin passed the man, then stopped and turned back to tell him, "Remember, you didn't see me —or this girl on my back."

"Of course, sir."

Gavin kicked open the door. "This will be your room." He walked to a window, scanned the view, and seemed satisfied.

Straining to look past his head—and beyond the thick velvet curtains—Jade managed a glimpse of an endless field. He stepped away from the window and crouched. The blade scratched the floor. Jade released her hold on his neck and slid from his back. The cool floor soothed her aching feet.

It was a luxurious suite with an enormous canopy bed, a marble fireplace with a golden grate, several stuffed chairs, and a lounger. An inlaid trunk stood at the foot of the bed; the design appeared to be lilies in a rich shade of blue. Plush rugs made walkways from the door to the bed and the sitting area.

Jade stepped toward one. Her foot sank into thick fibers. She couldn't decide if the polished stone or deep pile felt better. She stood with a foot on each.

Gavin crossed his arms. "You'll be well fed. I'll send fresh clothes."

"I want my boots."

He canted his head and gave her a hard look. "You're definitely an Albiana."

"What do you mean?"

"Spoiled, demanding queens, all of you."

"I'm not spoiled."

"Humph." He turned to go. "I'll have a tub of hot water sent for you to bathe in. Don't bother trying to escape. I'll have guards at the door."

"You can't just leave me here." She hated the sound of her whining.

"I can, and I will." He left.

Jade walked around the suite, examining everything more closely. Touching things, running her fingers over the rich fabrics and textures. If she was related to the Albiana queens, perhaps that wasn't such a bad thing. They were wealthy and powerful.

43. The Marketplace

Bertille led Melia to the line of lean-to sheds used to stable horses on the west wall of the marketplace. They made their way through a crowd of muannai and trolls.

"Why are they gathered here?" Melia asked.

Bertille greeted many of them. "Flora and Gumf are recovering here and there." She pointed to two sheds directly ahead of them. "News of the attack spread quickly. The response has been swift. Gumf and Flora are beloved throughout the valley. The muannai and trolls are keeping vigil."

Melia nodded at some of them, grateful they cared enough for Flora to watch over her.

Bertille pushed aside a canvas flap that served as a door. A dim lantern burned inside. Flora slept on a pallet, still and pale. Melia rushed to the spring faerie's side, her own bruises forgotten.

"We gave her something to help her sleep. She was distraught. It was a hard thing to see," the nixie whispered.

Melia kneeled beside the spring faerie.

A wide bandage stained with blood ran from Flora's ear to her chin. Deep bruises covered what Melia could see of her arms.

"We can't move her until the internal bleeding stops," Bertille said.

"Internal bleeding?"

"The blows to her stomach were merciless."

Melia closed her eyes. "How could they do this to her? After all she's been through." She pushed a lock of grey hair from Flora's forehead.

"They wanted the basin. Word spread she kept it hidden in her cottage for years. They're outraged at her cunning. The soldiers punished her for that tonight. How dare an old faerie obstruct their ambition to dominate us all?" Bertille maneuvered her torso close to Melia. "The chivalry of the Huron knights goes no deeper than the cloth of their uniforms."

The half-faerie's tears spilled onto Flora's cheek. Bertille wiped them away. "She didn't break," the nixie said. "After everything she's been through, she didn't break."

"Will she be all right?" Melia asked.

"Be here when she wakes. Having you close will revive her spirits."

"I'll stay by her side until she's well."

Bertille squeezed Melia's shoulder. "I'll have a pallet put down for you next to hers. Ryder won't mind if you sleep here tonight, will he?"

"No, he'll understand."

"Come with me." Outside, the nixie glided over the packed dirt, pocked with horse hoofs, that sufficed for a road and into an adjoining pasture.

"We'll prepare a pallet in the shed next to Flora's for Ryder, and one on the other side of him for Lola."

"I promised her we'd search for her daughter in the morning, but —"

"Perhaps Ryder can go? I'll round up some muannai to accompany him. They'll be glad to help."

Although Melia hated to be separated from him, she couldn't leave Flora. She thanked Bertille. "Has anyone found Nivea? She was alone in the woods—"

"She'll be here soon. I put her on the last boat."

"How—"

"I swim very fast." Bertille smiled, her sharp teeth glinting in the light of distant torches.

"How is Gumf?" Melia asked.

"His wound is deep and festers with black magic."

"Will he live?"

"The Veil will never be the same if he doesn't."

"It will never be the same even if he does. It should be burned to the ground, to erase all trace of what was done!"

"Nothing can erase what was done, including burning the Veiled Tavern. But there will be rectification."

Ryder approached with Lola. "How is Flora?" he asked.

"Not good," Melia said.

"But she's alive and she'll survive," Bertille said. "She saved the basin."

"How long until the soldiers come for it?" Ryder asked.

"We probably don't have as much time as we'd like," the nixie said.

"You think they'll attack the marketplace?" Melia asked.

"Although an open attack would be costly to their side, the muannai are preparing to defend themselves," Bertille said. "We'll need to be vigilant."

"What about Jade? I'm so worried about her," Lola said.

"Melia needs to stay with Flora." Bertille turned to Ryder. "Can you lead a search party to find the girl? I can give you the Tasimas diamond and assemble some muannai to go with you."

"Of course," Ryder said.

"I want to go with them," Lola said.

"They'll need to move quickly," Bertille said. "It will be better if you stay here with us."

Lola batted her hands in the air, but otherwise didn't protest.

"Where will you go first?" Melia asked Ryder.

"Southend. It's where we landed when I first arrived in Faerie. It will be easier to blend in at the docks and ask questions. Find out what Lilliane's been up to since the last time you saw her. I've ruled out the palace library because I don't want to step into a trap."

"It's getting late," Bertille said. "Your beds are ready. I'll bring you the Tasimas," she said to Ryder as she took Lola's hand and led her away.

Ryder pulled Melia to him. "How are you?"

"Not good" she whispered. "What we saw tonight, Ryder ..."

He wrapped his arms around her. "War has reached Faerie."

She melted into him and listened to the beat of his heart. After so much death, she needed to hear the sound of life.

"Melia, if I'm going to help you through this, I need to speak honestly with you."

"You're worried I can't handle the incarnation—"

"We need to present our case to the Grey Council and abide by their decision."

"I don't want to wait any longer."

"We don't have the sword," he reminded her.

She turned her face up to his. "When you're in Illialei," she said, "find it and bring it back to me!"

"After Jade is safe, I will."

"But a long sea voyage? Imagine what Lilliane will do while we're gone," she murmured.

"We won't leave Faerie until we've recaptured the sword. We'll take Koldis and Ormrun with us when we sail. We'll make it known they're no longer in the country. If the knights wish to chase us across the Great White Sea, let them. We'll leave Tyrannis in peace."

"But will Lilliane?"

"If both the artifacts and the vessel of incarnation have left Tyrannis, she'll be foolish to squander her resources here."

Melia raised up on her tiptoes. She grimaced at the pain the movement caused her abdomen. "Wake me tomorrow before you leave."

"I'd rather not if you're asleep." He kissed her. "You need your rest to heal."

"Melia? Is that you?" Flora's gravelly voice pulled the half-faerie from her sleep.

"I'm here." Stiff and aching, Melia hobbled to the spring faerie's side. "How are you feeling? Can I get you anything?"

"Water."

Melia pushed some loose hair from Flora's forehead. "Is that all?"

"I don't think I can eat. I can hardly move. When did you return from the mortal world?"

"Yesterday. Just before sunset." Although her abdomen protested, Melia leaned in closer. "I'm sorry—" Tears filled her eyes.

Flora gripped her arm. It was a fragile hold. "Did they hurt you?"

Melia covered the spring faerie's hand with hers. "No. I'm fine."

Flora lay back on her pallet. Her hands fretted with her blanket. "And Ryder?"

Melia told the spring faerie about Jade, Lola, and the assassin.

"You were right to trust your vision, and right to bring them here. Don't doubt that," Flora said.

"But why would Jade willingly go with an assassin sent to kill her?"

"She didn't know who he was."

"Ryder said the same thing."

That seemed to please Flora. She closed her eyes. But Melia was worried. "Flora," she whispered, "What if he's already killed her? What am I going to tell her mother? She'll never believe that I went to the mortal world to help them."

"Wait until Ryder brings back that news before you worry about it."

"I don't like her," Melia whispered.

"Who?"

"Jade. She's infatuated with Ryder." Melia couldn't believe she was confiding this to Flora, but now that she'd started she couldn't stop. "She flirts with him, even when I'm standing right there. She dismisses everything I say." Melia ran her finger along her cheek.

"And she insulted my shield." Spoken aloud, the complaints sounded petty.

"She doesn't respect you," Flora mused.

The answer did little to assuage Melia's discomfort.

Bertille poked her head through the tent flap. She brought a bottle filled with a cloudy mixture. After she handed the bottle to Melia, and determined that Flora was better, she coiled her tail and settled on Melia's pallet. She pointed to the bottle the half-faerie had placed on the ground. "She needs to drink four of those four bottles a day, until she can walk."

"What is it?" Melia asked.

"A mixture of herbs that will stop the internal bleeding and," she addressed Flora directly, "help rebuild your energy. When you finish this bottle, I want you to go back to sleep."

Flora waved her hand. "Help me sit up."

Melia did as she was asked and held the bottle for the spring faerie between sips.

"Have you seen Lola this morning?" Melia asked Bertille.

"I'm not sure she slept. She saw Ryder and the muannai off at dawn."

Melia wished she had too.

Bertille patted Melia's knee. "You'll see him again."

"Your faith is appreciated." Melia wished she shared it. "How is Lola?"

"Worried about her daughter, but–" Bertille paused.

"But what?"

"It's strange. Last night she was so agitated. There was a wild look in her eyes. It wasn't just what she saw at the Veil. A sense of terror seemed to abide deep within her. But this morning, even though I don't think she slept a wink, she's better."

"Better how?"

"She's quite taken with the muannai. After Ryder left, she followed me into the market. At every stop I made, she chatted with the shopkeepers. She can be quite charming."

Flora returned the empty bottle to Bertille. "I'd like to meet this Lola."

"After you take a nap."

"No. Now."

"Your obstinacy is heartening."

"Then please bring her," Flora said.

Bertille excused herself.

"Flora, I've made a decision," Melia said.

"And what is that?"

"I'm going to incarnate Umbra."

Flora absorbed the announcement.

"Someone must subdue Lilliane. It will be me."

The spring faerie scratched the bandage on her face. "This is good news. Determination will serve you much better than vacillation."

"I don't care what the Grey Council says."

"We need their support if we're going to raise an army."

"That's what Ryder said."

"It's wise counsel."

"How will we raise an army?"

Flora's eyes lit up. "With the Grey Council behind us, we can send word to all the countries: Morganna, Typhos. Maybe some of those from Kyrakkos and the Hidden City will join our cause. The Albiana have made a long list of enemies."

"Then you don't believe a long sea voyage is a waste of time?"

Flora paused as if to think the question through. "No, one must always consider the peace before engaging in war. If the Albiana queens are to be evicted from the Cathedral Palace once and for all, the new queen will need allies."

"Will Illialei's population fight against us?"

"That remains to be seen. But the Hurons will. And whoever else Princess Lilliane conjures to her side."

"Do you think it will be awful?"

"What made you determined to go through with the

incarnation?" Flora asked.

"What I saw last night at the Veil. All the senseless death."

"I didn't foresee the knights of Huros taking orders from the princess. Perhaps I should have. You can see where underestimating her has gotten me."

Melia had no response. Silence settled between them. When Bertille returned with Lola, they were still quiet.

"Is everything all right?" Bertille asked. Lola bobbed behind her.

"Resting as ordered," Flora said.

It encouraged Melia to watch the spring faerie's spirit revive.

Bertille made introductions.

"It's such an honor to meet the last spring faerie alive," Lola said.

"Although I would have preferred a different fate, I work with what is mine," Flora said.

Lola nodded. "I'm so sorry for what happened to you."

"It was an ordeal," Flora said.

"I thought the Realm of Faerie would be different. More whimsical, less violent."

"These are dark days on the threshold between the worlds, and the influence is being felt in the mortal world, is it not?"

"They're drugging everyone," Lola said. "Pharmaceuticals. Synthetic chemicals."

"A kind of black magic," Flora said.

"Exactly," Lola beamed.

Melia listened with fascination.

"The war has barely begun here," Flora said. "While it's fought, things will worsen in the mortal world. It always reflects ours to a degree. You should stay here."

"But I'm so worried about my daughter."

"I have a presentiment she's safe," Flora said.

A tear rolled down Lola's cheek. "I want to stay in this world. I have nothing but a shopping cart to go back to."

❖ ❖ ❖

The next two days passed in a blur for Melia. She hardly left Flora's tent. Bertille brought bottle after bottle of the cloudy medicine, and the spring faerie dutifully drank each one. She slept most of the time, but she was gaining vigor.

On the morning of the third day, Flora asked Melia and Lola to accompany her for a walk.

The days were growing colder. Lola produced wool cloaks for the three of them.

"Where did you get these?" Melia asked.

"Telling stories to the muannai. They give me trade credit. Bertille gave me the idea. Telling stories is my talent. When Jade was young—Lord, I hope they bring her here soon, she'll be crazy about this market." Lola wiped the corner of her eye. "Oh, when she was young, she loved to hear a different tale every night. I was her Scheherazade. As she grew older, she lost interest." Lola paused as that far away look returned to her eyes. She shook her head and smiled. "Well, the art of telling a story is valued here, and I was able to trade for these cloaks."

"What kind of stories do you tell?" Melia asked. "Do you make them up?"

"Oh no. I tell magical stories written and collected long ago. *Beauty and the Beast*, *Rapunzel*, *Cinderella*—we call them fairy tales in the mortal world, although they're not necessarily about faeries."

"I'd like to hear one," Melia said.

"Do you know where the food court is?" Lola asked.

"Yes."

"Beyond there is a stage. Come tonight. I'm going to tell the story of 'The Red Shoes'."

"I'll come too," Flora said.

"You don't need your rest?"

"I'll be fine. I can nap this afternoon."

As they walked, Melia watched Lola.

In three days, she'd transformed. She'd bathed and her hair was braided and piled high on her head, held in place with combs in the muannai style. Her eyes were bright, her skin less sallow. She wore a pair of muannai boots, and her brightly colored skirt and brown jacket were replaced with a much prettier flowing skirt—something Sevondi might have worn—and one of the muannai-style ruffled shirts.

When Jade returned with Ryder, Melia didn't think she would recognize her own mother.

Flora led them beyond the pasture to the high grass of the steppes. When she started panting, she stopped. "You're going to need to begin training again," the spring faerie said to Melia.

"I'm ready."

"Lola, I want you to help her."

Melia wondered how the woman could help.

"I'll be glad to assist in any way I can."

"Melia's greatest internal wound—her mother's abandonment—must be healed before she incarnates Umbra. She finds it difficult to express the deep anger and resentment surrounding that pain. It must be drawn out."

"Flora!" Melia said. "I don't want to discuss my mother."

The spring faerie raised her palm. "Lola, you see what I mean."

"She has her own daughter to worry about," Melia said. "Don't burden her with problems I can handle on my own."

"And you've handled all your problems just fine. But you're going to be called upon to shoulder greater burdens. Your heart and your mind must be as clear as possible."

"Bertille has already taught me this," Melia said.

"You've made a first pass, and it was a good one. But the wound is deep. It must heal or Umbra will use it to turn you toward destruction."

"How do you heal the wound of a mother who hates you?" Melia asked. "What is there to do but move on?"

"I want Lola to share her story with you. Gabriela turned on her in a cruel fashion, very similar to the way Pressina turned on you. Both of you were punished for clinging to the truth. Now, when the truth needs defense, Melia, you grow quiet. When you incarnate Umbra, there will be no room for equivocation. The battle will begin within you. It's possible–probable–you won't seek anyone's counsel, or if you do, you won't hear it. Especially, in the initial days. At the same time, your ability to manifest whatever you want will be magnified. You can't risk losing your way because Umbra bores into your shame."

Melia resisted the urge to stomp off. Only because she was curious to hear Lola's story.

44. Lola's Story

"For as long as I can remember," Lola began, "I've seen faeries. Not too many. Maybe one or two a year. Always different ones. Some of them used to slip off their wings when they reached the mortal world—to avoid detection—but now that mortals can't see them, most don't bother. Of course, with their wings, they're easy to identify, but even without them, you can spot them. There's a sheen to their skin, and they seem to glide when they walk, almost as if their feet don't touch the ground.

"Once they get over their surprise I can see them, most faeries are friendly toward me. But the first time I told my mother about my new friend who'd arrived by way of the river, she shushed me. Later that year, I spied one in our garden. After we chatted a bit, I went to get my mother.

"She didn't want to hear about faeries, or creatures who came from other worlds, but I refused to relent. I grabbed her hand and pulled so hard I almost toppled over when she finally rose from her chair. She followed me out to our backyard. The faerie was still there, flitting among her tomato plants.

"Mother was a tremendous gardener. Our flowers and produce were the envy of the neighborhood. But she was generous with her harvest, so no one gave her the stink-eye when their gardens failed.

"When I pointed out the faerie, I saw the flicker of recognition in my mother's eye before she dragged me back inside the house.

"'Lola, if you saw anything,' she said, 'and I doubt you did, but if

379

you did, it was an evil spirit, an agent of Satan, and you must shun it.' She hugged me close and told me about the blue-eyed girl and pixie warning her about Umbra. It was the only time she talked about that experience, even though I could tell it affected her deeply. 'I'm going to teach you how to pray because I don't want anything to happen to you,' she said. 'I don't want them to take you away from me.'"

"I asked her who would take me away from her. She released me and wiped her eyes. 'Edmond and Emma. The government.' She shook me. 'Never tell your cousins about these things you see. Promise me you won't.'

"It was an easy promise to make. Emma was my great-aunt, by way of my grandfather"–Lola's gaze drifted upward–"Ben Silver. Edmond was her husband. My mother called their grandchildren my cousins, although they were actually my second cousins. I didn't really enjoy their company, but they were the only family we had.

"We lived in Austin, Texas at the time. On occasion my mother and I drove the two hours to their farm, but they were different from me and my mother. They were heavier, not physically–Emma was a scrawny old thing–but mentally. Their thoughts were so small and slow, it was hard to carry on a conversation with any of them. All they wanted to do was read their Bibles and gossip about the sinners who attended their church.

"It always made me wonder, if they were the only ones who were perfect in the eyes of God, why bother congregating with the fallen? They seemed to think it was important not to hide their lights under a bushel.

"'Who is the government?' I asked my mother.

"'They make the laws, and they'll take you away from me if you tell them the same stories you've told me. They'll lock you up and perform cruel experiments on you.'

"That sounded unappealing so I promised her I wouldn't talk about the faeries anymore. She squeezed me so tight I could hardly breathe.

"The next Sunday she gave me a new dress and a new pair of shoes. We went to church. After that, she made me pray with her every night. For ten years, we got down on our knees as she made fervent requests I be relieved of the visitations as she had been.

"I was a lonely child. Seeing faeries made me feel special, like a princess. The rare friends I made didn't last. I suppose they got tired of my insistence that they kneel whenever they made a request of me." Lola laughed.

"What can I say? I was young and the feeling that there was something special about me, that I was different, possessed me. It wasn't just seeing faeries. I could see lies and truths that escaped others, big ones and little ones. But I learned to keep those things to myself too.

"My mother's nightly prayer sessions made me angry. I wanted to see the faeries, and no matter how much my mother insisted they were evil, I knew they weren't.

"The Sunday I refused to go to church, I thought she would kill me. I'd never seen such rage in her. I was sixteen, and I'm ashamed to admit the fight came to physical blows. It was a sad turning point for us. Our relationship deteriorated quickly after that. She never asked me to go to church or insisted I pray with her again.

"Boys were always attracted to me, but their attention was confusing. I would catch them staring at me with dreamy eyes in class, then they'd aim a kickball at my stomach or head when we went outside to play.

"I became shy and isolated, spending most of my time in the small woods on the outskirts of our subdivision, dressed in costumes, pretending I was royalty, and reading books. Sometimes I rode my bike down to the river and searched for faeries.

"There was a thrift store on the way, where I could find old gowns, shawls, and things for my hair to make costumes. The owner liked me. In exchange for helping her sort through heaps of donations every week, she let me pick out a few things to keep.

"After the fight with my mother, I spent more time there.

Sometimes, after the shop closed, I headed down to the river. I loved to be there when the sun set and wander along the riverbank in the gloaming. It felt like a magic time of day, and it set my imagination afire. I created incredible stories to keep myself company. Going home became harder and harder. I would sneak in the back door, and the guilt would bear down on me.

"There would always be a dinner plate on the table, covered in foil. I would take it to my room, close the door, and choke down as much of it as I could. Most of the time with tears in my eyes. I knew we were sad people, living sad lives, and that something vital was missing, but I didn't know what it was, or how to find it.

"Mother never had friends over, and she never went out. She was lonely too, but I didn't know how to rebuild the bridge we'd burned. I knew faeries were real, and that they weren't evil. I also knew a lot of the folks who went to church were unkind. I hated that Mother persisted with her prayers and Bible reading.

"The divide between us continued to grow.

"After high school, most of the girls in my class were getting married, or going off to college. I wanted to see the world, but didn't have the means. I began hitchhiking. In the 1950s, things were different. You could get away with taking risks you wouldn't consider today. At first, I only took short trips to San Antonio or Houston. I met all sorts of people and had some interesting experiences. For the first time since I was a young child, I felt free and alive.

"One morning I returned home. The sun was rising, and I was humming and singing. I'd just heard the song *I'm Walking* by Fats Domino and couldn't suppress the urge to dance. I suppose I was making too much noise. I didn't see my mother standing in the kitchen doorway, glaring at me, while I made a pot of coffee.

"You have to understand, Gabriela was a beautiful woman, but she hid it behind thick glasses and plain dresses. She always pulled her hair back into a severe bun and, I swear, she only wore the ugliest shoes she could find. Men didn't exist for her. She never talked about my father, and I'd never known her to go on a date.

"Over the past year, I'd had a few romantic encounters and fancied myself something of an expert on the subject.

"'Where have you been?' my mother asked.

"'Dancing.'

"'Like a heathen!'

"'Like a goddess.'

"She yanked my hair and dragged me into our tiny bathroom. Standing behind me, one hand tight in my hair, nails from her other hand digging into my waist and back, she was a reflection of God's wrath over my shoulder.

"'I won't have a filthy daughter,' she said.

"I couldn't take anymore of her religious insanity. Something inside me snapped. I was young. I wanted to live. I spit in the mirror. 'To hell with your God and your lies. To hell with you,' I said.

"She released my hair with a fist to the back of my head. The blow knocked me forward, and my forehead cracked against the mirror. A thin red line emerged.

"'What is wrong with you?' I screamed.

"She grabbed my shoulders and pushed me out of the bathroom. She shoved me through the hall and into the kitchen. 'Get out of my house. You're not welcome here anymore.'

"'You're crazy, you know that,' I said to her. 'People think I'm crazy, but they're wrong. If they knew you, they'd realize, you're the one–'

"'Get out!' She was screaming. 'Get out! Get out! Get Out! And don't come back home until you're ready to get right with God!'

"'If that's your condition, you'll never see me again. Is that what you want, Mother?' She remained stone-faced.

"I said, 'You're going to die alone with your precious God.'

"I left and never went back. I couldn't. Jade asked me why I wouldn't visit my mother when she was dying. How could I tell her that for me, Gabriela was already dead?"

Melia's breaths were shallow and uneven. A sickening awareness of banished daughters formed a line through time in her mind. Olivia disowning Pressina, Luisa abandoning Gabriela, Gabriela shouting at Lola to get out, and Pressina telling Melia to leave the tree house.

She wasn't sure whether hearing Lola's story made her feel better or worse.

Melia reached out to take Lola's hand. "My mother banished me too. She thought I murdered my father."

"Did you?" Lola asked.

Melia laughed. The question, asked with such sincerity, strengthened the truth within her. "No." She squeezed Lola's hand before releasing it. "He died. My sisters and I were there, but it was an accident."

"Then your mother loved your father very much?"

"I still don't know what she truly felt for him. But, for years, I believed she hated him." Melia shook her head. "I never meant to hurt her."

"She must know that."

"Did your mother know you never meant to hurt her?" Melia asked.

Lola raised her eyebrows. "I see your point."

"What happened when you left your mother's home?"

"I hitchhiked all over the country. It wasn't quite the sixties, but if you knew where to go, things were already changing. I did odd jobs and learned how to volunteer as a research subject at universities. That's how I got turned on to LSD before it became popular. I would trip out and tell everyone about the faeries I saw. Most people didn't care, but I started having breakdowns. I'd have a bad trip with me ending in hysterics.

"I woke up one morning in a room with grey concrete walls, strapped to a bed, in a hospital gown. Things didn't get much better from there. By the time I made it to San Francisco and met Jade's father, I was a mess.

"He was a freshman at Berkeley, and I was his swinging hippie chick. I wore garlands in my hair and called him my king. To him, I was a female creature different from any he'd known. He always said I cast a spell on him. He liked to make sure I ate and he loved to listen to me sing.

"We fell in love, but he didn't like the drugs as much as I did. We were fighting more and more. Even so, when he graduated from Berkeley, he took me with him back to the east coast. But I couldn't stand it there. He changed so fast. I called him Iron Man and told him he was killing the faeries every time he touched me. The first and only winter I was there, I told him I'd reincarnated as the Ice Queen.

"We knew it was over. His family was never going to accept me, and he wasn't the type to marry without their approval. When I hitchhiked south, I didn't know I was pregnant with Jade. I wrote him when I found out. He takes care of her financially, but he washed his hands of me." Lola sniffled.

"I loved him. I hate him. It breaks my heart Jade doesn't know her father, but he wouldn't understand her. She's too much like me. He would break her heart too. Who am I kidding? He already has."

Melia tried to imagine how her life would have been different if she'd never known her father. She might never have had dark moon visions. Nandana probably wouldn't have marked her forehead. She would never have known what it was like to fly.

She would never have met Ryder.

"Jade has never told me about the times she's tried to contact Tom—that's her father—but Jules has. Even after all these years, he refuses to see her."

"Who is Jules?"

"Tom's lawyer. He handles all of Jade's finances."

"Like gold?" Melia asked.

Lola laughed. "Exactly."

Flora had been right to ask Lola to share her story with Melia. It made her realize how much those with a mix of Albiana and mortal blood struggled to find their place in the Whole.

"How did you end up living in the park?" Melia asked.

"I've always felt safer outside. Houses, office buildings, mental institutions feel like traps to me. The air is suffocating. Sometimes, when all the doors and windows are closed, I feel like I can't breathe." Lola inhaled a deep breath now. "The air is amazing in Faerie. I'm getting stronger and more hopeful with every breath I take. If I could see Jade and know she's all right—"

"Ryder will bring her to you."

"The massacre we saw—the ones who did that, are they the ones who have my daughter?"

Melia considered lying if it would help Lola remain calm, but who knew what was ahead of them? As long as Lilliane was in line for the Cathedral Palace throne, Lola would need to stay in Faerie. "We think so."

Lola covered her mouth with her hand. Her entire face quavered.

Melia reached for her other hand. "Jade is going to come back to you." She trusted Flora's presentiment.

As they walked back across the pasture, Melia absorbed more of Lola's story. It saddened her to think of the young Gabriela she met in the cemetery living such a barren life, and Lola living such a lonely one. It made her own life seem easier. A year ago, she might not have thought so, but now she was surrounded by Ryder and friends she cared for deeply.

"I like the marketplace. Will we be able to stay here?" Lola asked.

"The valley is too close to Illialei's border. Until everything is settled, you'll be safer in Aldaine."

"Where's Aldaine?"

"North."

"Is it a long trip?"

"It depends," Melia said. If Flora healed sufficiently, they could use the Tasimas.

"Can Jade come with me?" Lola asked.

"Of course," Melia said. Taking them to the Dragon's Keep made the most sense. While Ryder and Melia went on the long journey to Minnanon, Lola and Jade would be safe under Sevondi's protection.

Later that afternoon, the spring faerie asked to speak with Melia alone. "You did a good thing," she said.

"What good thing was that?" Melia only half-listened to Flora, her gaze scanning the crowds entering and leaving the market, hoping to see Ryder. His absence made her more jumpy than she cared to admit.

"You have a healing presence about you. I've suspected it for some time, but I wasn't sure until this afternoon." The spring faerie pointed across the way. It took a minute for Melia to perceive what Flora wanted her to see—Lola, in the middle of a group of muannai women, laughing with shining eyes. "Do you hear that?" the spring faerie asked.

"Yes."

"She's not the same woman who came to Faerie a few days ago. The air itself always does mortals good."

"But she's only half-mortal."

"Yah. And when you listened to her story, you lightened her burdens."

A glow warmed Melia's heart. "Anyone could have taken the time to do that."

Flora folded her arms across her chest. "When you returned from the edge of death at the Calashai, you brought back a gift."

"I don't understand."

"Forces greater than you came to your aid; they brought you back to life. When their work was done, they left behind a seed. A seed of healing energy. It's growing every day, becoming stronger. I can feel it."

Melia turned her palms up and down. Her own bruises and

soreness from the night of the massacre were long gone. She'd been so concerned about the spring faerie, she hadn't noticed how quickly they healed. "Are you sure?"

"Yes." The spring faerie ambled off. Melia stared after her. Flora called over her shoulder. "Bertille can't believe I'm up and walking around."

45. Wine and Shadows

Although Jade appreciated her luxurious cell, after sleeping most of two days, she wanted out.

From the first night, elves and faeries came and went. Whenever the faeries came, Jade stared at their wings. Some looked more like dragonfly wings; others resembled the intricately patterned wings of a butterfly. The elves were shorter than Jade, and chubby. Friendly and talkative, she enjoyed their company.

The food they brought was delicious—vegan, but the tea was herbal—no caffeine.

No withdrawal headache yet. She feared having a hell of a one tomorrow if she didn't get any caffeine in her system today.

Two faeries brought fresh clothes—sleeveless dresses in tiny floral print with drop waists, the hems right above her knees. Perfect. They also brought a pair of blue slippers—like house shoes—and her boots, which were polished. She asked for some socks, but they had no idea what she was talking about.

Apparently, no one wore socks or drank coffee in Faerie—Illialei.

Jade's head spun with all the information she'd gleaned over the past two days. When anyone brought her food or tea, she asked them questions. Guileless, they answered every one.

Luisa Albiana was Queen of Illialei. Lilliane her daughter. As of now, there was no queen of the Realm of Faerie. The target the knights attacked was in Tyrannis, the country across the bridge. A grey faerie named Elendah used to be the regent of Tyrannis, but she recently died. The muannai—the faeries who lived across the river—didn't have wings; after the grey faerie's death they installed a dragonwitch, who was half-muannai, as their new regent.

Jade wondered if she was a threat.

"What's a dragonwitch?" she asked one of the elves who brought her tea four times a day. Although she never touched it—she poured it out the window, or into the chamber pot—she encouraged them to keep bringing it. The more trips they made, the more information she gathered.

"She calls dragons to her."

"Just calls them. 'Hey, you, dragon, over here,' and they come?"

The elf's eyes popped open. "I never gave it much thought. It's just what we've heard. There was a big carnivale, but that's over. The gossips say she's sailing to northern Tyrannis now. The stronghold of Calashai fell, but they've built a new fortress for her, the Dragon's Keep."

A fortress didn't sound good to Jade. "Are there lots of dragons in Faerie?" She hadn't seen any.

"None that I'm aware of."

If there were no dragons, who cared about a dragonwitch? Jade removed her from the short list of chicks who might threaten her reign. Lilliane and Melia's names remained at the top. Lilliane wanted her dead, and Melia was a liar. A big one.

Jade had another conversation with Umbra. He encouraged her to be bold.

"Seize the sword."

"How?" Alone in her room, she spoke aloud. "Gavin hasn't come back to see me. Even if he did, how would I steal it from him and make it out of the palace without getting caught? Where would I go?"

"Feign pain. Whatever draught they bring you, set it aside. Insist the knight visit you after dark. Lace his tea with the potion they brought you to make him sleep."

"Maybe I could just get him good and drunk," Jade said aloud. She'd become more comfortable with receiving Umbra's telepathic communications.

"Inebriation is an excellent idea."

She grinned. "Do they have whiskey in Faerie?"

"Blueberry wine."

That sounded about as potent as fruit juice. "Will that be strong enough to knock him out?"

"If he drinks enough, yes. You'll need to be convivial."

That might not be a problem. There were questions the elves and faeries couldn't answer. Mostly about the basin. She suspected Gavin could.

While she talked with Umbra, she lay in bed, staring at the bed's canopy. "Can you see me?" Jade asked. "Here, in the palace?"

"What I see is hazy, as through a veil. Looking beyond the Parallel of Shadows requires a reservoir of energy I'm loathe to squander. It's why we cannot converse with more frequency. I must allow my energy to accumulate with periods of silence."

Jade pushed herself up, rose from the bed, and walked over to the table. She fidgeted with the fruit in the bowl at its center. The apples, berries, and melons made a joke of similar fruits in the mortal world. Larger and more beautiful, they exploded with taste a flavor chemist could only dream of. "I still don't get it. When you come into my body, what will it be like?"

"You'll want for nothing and no one else."

Jade thought of all the times she'd longed for her father, or for her mother to be sane and present. Wanting nothing sounded safe. "And I'll really become the queen of the Realm of Faerie?"

"We'll rule as one."

No sex. Not a bad deal.

The morning of the third day, Jade told the elf who brought her tea, "I need to speak to Gavin."

"I'll pass along the message," he said.

"Maybe he could eat dinner with me tonight."

"I'll pass along the message," he repeated.

When her post-lunch tea arrived, the elf told her Gavin agreed to her request. "Could blueberry wine be served with our dinner?" she asked.

The elf didn't bat an eye.

Fresh from a bath, Jade laid her three dresses side by side on the bed. They were similar, but the blue print matched her eyes.

Gavin arrived before dinner with two crystal glasses and a bottle filled with dark liquid.

Relieved he carried the sword in his scabbard, Jade's eyes danced over his face and figure. Something was different. Everything about his nature was rough, but this night, not a hair on his head was out of place. His uniform was creased and his fingernails looked as though they'd been manicured.

That was it.

It was the first time she'd seen him without gloves. He greeted her as if she were a friend before stepping back into the hall and ordering a fire. Although the days were warm in Illialei, the nights were cool. An elf scurried in, pushed aside the golden grate, and built a fire. Gavin motioned for Jade to sit in one of the chairs at the table, filled the two glasses, handed one to her, then settled back into the chair across from her.

She expected the wine to taste like juice, but it tasted like nature itself. Wild and untamed, tart and fermented to perfection. She forced herself to slow down. Gavin was supposed to drink himself into a stupor, not her. "This is wicked good."

"One of the wonders of Faerie." He drank three glasses to her one before dinner arrived.

Jade smiled inside. She whispered to the faerie who delivered honey butter and hot rolls, to bring another bottle of wine. When an elf brought it, Gavin patted him on the back and thanked him. This was going to work.

Jade kept Gavin's glass filled while taking the smallest of sips herself. When he was more than halfway through the second bottle, she ordered a third and steered the conversation to the sword and basin.

"May I see it?" she asked.

To him, she presented no threat. He pulled the blade from his scabbard and held it high. It glimmered in the light of the fire.

"May I hold it?" she asked.

He pushed it into her hand.

"It's so light."

"None can craft metal like dwarves," he said.

She sliced air. "They made it?"

"Along with a bowl."

Jade wanted to laugh as he volunteered the information she needed. "What kind of bowl?"

Gavin glowered. "A fancy one. I don't wish to talk about it."

His sudden change of mood disconcerted her. She couldn't risk angering him. He might storm out. "If it disturbs you to speak of it, let's talk about something else."

"Damned spring faerie," he muttered.

Jade perked up. "Is that a special kind of faerie?"

Gavin filled his glass. Wine spilled, staining the tablecloth. "Flora and her naive allies imagine they'll stand against the entire army of Huros and win."

"Why would she think that?"

Gavin loosened his collar. "Because of Umbra."

Jade's mind went on alert. "What does Umbra have to do with the spring faerie?" Did she need to add the spring faerie to the short list of women who threatened her?

She placed the blade on the table.

Gavin stroked its handle, caressing the ruby. "The bowl and the sword are a pair. They open a portal through which Umbra can incarnate. They're the only means in existence by which he can. The spring faerie is betting the incarnated Umbra will defeat us."

"Is she mistaken?" Jade heard the tremor in her voice.

"What she thinks is irrelevant. Her theory will never be tested because I'm going to rip Tyrannis apart and find that stupid bowl."

The basin was in Tyrannis. A spring faerie had it. Once Jade had the sword, she would need to cross the bridge. "You're going to leave me here, at the palace, alone?"

Gavin waved his hand. "Don't worry. Lilliane won't come looking for you. She believes you're already dead."

The suite shrank around her; her vision telescoped. All she saw was Gavin's face. His heavy eyelids. The pinpoints of rage in his pupils. The thin lips in his planed face that tinged his countenance with danger.

Had he come here tonight to tie up loose ends? To kill her before he left? Jade continued to press. "Why does she think that?"

"Because that's what I told her, and I gave her a dog's heart in the place of yours."

Jade stopped nibbling on her cookie.

He stumbled to his feet and lurched toward the lounger pushed against the wall between her bed and the table. He landed half on and half off it.

Jade tiptoed toward him. She waved a hand in front of his face. He was out cold. She returned to the table and ran her finger over the ruby in the sword's hilt. She picked the blade up, walked to the bed, and slid it between the bed sheets. She went to the door.

Gavin snored.

She opened the door and peeked out. There were two guards. "Could you carry him to his chamber? He's fallen asleep."

They brushed past her. They saw Gavin on the lounger and the empty bottles of wine on the table. They mumbled between each other and agreed to take him from her room.

When they were gone, she returned to the bed. First, she retrieved her boots. She'd already tied the laces together. She slipped them around her neck, so a boot rested against each shoulder. The bundle she made of her dresses was too much to

carry. She pulled the blade from its hiding place and hurried toward the door. The sword's blue light would give her away.

She returned to the bed and wrestled with the bundle of dresses. She wrapped one around the blade, and belted the other one around her waist. When she shoved the wrapped blade into her makeshift belt, she felt rather clever, but it had cost her precious time.

She returned to the door, and hoping the guards were still gone, pushed it open. Small torches lit the empty corridor with a wavering light. Jade raced for the stairs.

She had no idea if she could find her way back over that hill, through the forest, and across the bridge. But she was going to try.

Jade pressed her back against the white palace wall. Overhead, the enchanted world's two moons, one white and one lilac, waxed. She'd watched the sky from her window every night. Tonight, there was enough moonlight for her to find her way.

Shouts cried out in the night.

Jade slid down the wall to listen. They were searching for her.

Footsteps rang in the corridor she just exited. Jade inched away from the door she silently closed, remaining in the deep shadow of the palace walls. When the door cracked open, she bolted. Voices rang around her. Thank God, there were no baying dogs. Gavin probably killed them all! She winced at her own black humor as she continued to scoot along the wall. The sweet fragrance of roses alerted her to a garden.

Could she hide there until the guards passed?

She ran through a swathe of moonlight toward a tall hedge. Confident no one had seen her, she followed along the line of bushes. At their end, she paused. The shouts were fanning out and becoming fainter. No one was looking for her here.

Watching over her shoulder, Jade entered the garden.

She heard the voice before she saw the girl. "Who are you, and what are you doing in my garden?"

Jade rotated her head. A figure, about her height, advanced on her.

"Sorry? I didn't mean to trespass."

"What is your name?"

"Ja—net."

"Jaynit, how did you find your way here? This is my private garden."

All Jade could see of her interlocutor was dark hair, pale cheeks, and lips that appeared deep crimson in the moonlight.

The girl stepped closer. "Where are you from?" She reached for one of Jade's dreads. "I've never seen hair like this before."

Jade took a step back and searched for an exit. She couldn't have this conversation. Especially, if this was the princess, and she feared that it was.

"If you don't answer me, I'll call the guards." The girl pointed in the direction of the retreating shouts. "Perhaps you're who they're searching for?" She grabbed Jade's arm.

Jade jerked away and kicked out. Her foot made contact with the girl's pelvic bone. She doubled over.

"You dare accost me?" the girl hissed.

Fingernails raked Jade's arm. She grabbed for the girl's hair, but got a handful of string. Jade yanked as hard as she could, anyway.

"You're choking me," the girl gasped.

Jade wasn't prepared to commit murder. She panicked. The girl spun and the string in Jade's hand fell limp, it was a shawl.

The girl rushed at her.

Jade pivoted, and the girl careened past her, stumbled, and landed, jamming her elbows into the ground. Jade ran blindly in the opposite direction.

"Stop! Guards!" The girl screamed. "Guards!"

Jade searched for an escape route. The smell of dung wafted in the air. Horses. Jade pushed through a different narrow gap between two large bushes. Thorns scraped her bare arms. She made herself run faster. A wide moonlit field gaped before her. She needed cover.

Although the girl didn't follow her, she continued to scream.

From the sounds of their shouting, it sounded like the guards were circling back.

Jade raced along the edge of the moonlit field toward a dark outline, the shawl still gripped in her hand. The field dead-ended at an outer wall. She considered scaling it, but there were no hand- or toeholds. She slid her palm along it, and let it lead her farther from the girl's shouts. Behind her and across the field, lights flickered.

She moved faster. Finally, the palace gates. Closed. Locked. Two guards slouched against them. She wasn't getting out that way.

Jade slumped in the shadows. What was she going to do?

Then she remembered Gavin didn't carry her through any gate. He crashed through an orchard. The outer wall didn't form a complete circle around the palace. Jade had gone in the wrong direction. Better to backtrack and start over, or to keep moving in the direction she was going? She tried to calculate the distance she'd already covered.

The girl's screams were so faint she could barely hear them, and the two guards didn't seem alarmed. If she could slip past them, and the orchard was close, it was her best chance of escape. She ran her free hand along the ground, but found only soft grass. She needed something to throw at the gate to distract the guards.

Her boots.

She crouched down and wrapped the shawl around her shoulders. Living with her mother, she'd learned to hang on to whatever things came her way. Who knew when something might prove useful? Jade slipped the tied shoestrings over her head and undid the knot. As much as she hated to use it, she got a firm grip on the heel of one of her boots. She picked up the other one and edged toward the soldiers.

When she'd gotten as close as she dared, she hefted and launched the boot by its heel. It crashed into the tall gate and toppled to land between the guards.

"What's this?" One of them bent over to pick it up. "A bloody boot."

Jade was already running.

"Have you ever seen a shoe like that?"

"Don't think so."

"Why did someone throw it at the gate?"

"Maybe they missed. Maybe they threw it at us."

Jade no longer heard them. She ran along the wall until she thought her lungs would burst.

46. A Challenge

Ryder led the muannai through the orchard bordering the palace. There had been no information about Jade at Southend. If she'd been taken to the harbor, or Bryndale, gossip would have reached the port. But there was none. That left the palace as her likely location, but there could be no direct assault. Ryder considered using the Tasimas to reach the stables, he was familiar enough with them. But again, the risk of entering a trap dissuaded him of the idea.

He and the four muannai with him traveled the outskirts of Bryndale for two nights. It was close to dawn. Now they ducked and crouched through the trees.

Two lights—knights carrying torches—came toward them. Earlier, there had been some commotion earlier.

"Gavin will be in a murderous state if she gets away," the shorter knight said.

The other one cast his arm, widening the circle of light. "I knew she was going to be trouble the moment I laid eyes on her and that big mouth."

The two passed within a body's length of Ryder and the muannai, but the deep shadows from the apple trees kept them hidden.

"Where do you think she went?"

"After she kicked the princess?"

Ryder grinned. The girl had spirit.

"I would have liked to see that," the shorter one said.

The knights snickered, but kept advancing. When the torches were only dancing spots of light, Ryder motioned for the muannai to follow him in the opposite direction. "It sounds like she's escaped."

"How are we going to find her?" one of the muannaye asked.

Ryder ran his hand over the bulge of the Tasimas inside the old pillowcase. The slack part of the sack looped over his belt. He'd never used the diamond to take him to a person, only a place, but there was no way to know where Jade had fled.

He considered whether he could hold a clear image of the girl in his mind. He hadn't seen her that many times, but her strange hair, pale skin, and blue eyes were memorable.

"Do you hear that?" another muannaye asked.

It was the soft sound of ragged breathing. Quiet as any creature of the woods, Ryder moved toward it. A lithe, dark figure ran from tree to tree, panting. "Jade," he whispered.

She startled.

He called her name again.

She turned.

He drew closer to her.

Her pale face glowed in the moonlight filtering through the trees. "Ryder?"

"We're here to take you to your mother."

She tiptoed in his direction. "Ryder!" She ran at him and leapt. Her arms circled his shoulders, her legs circled his waist. Something hard poked his gut as she buried her face in his chest.

The greeting shocked him. "What did they do to you?"

"Locked me in a room. Knocked me around a few times before that. The man who grabbed me on the way to Faerie told me the princess hired him to kill me. He didn't, but only because he intended to use me as leverage against her."

"We need to be away from here before the guards double back."

"How? There are so many of them, and they're everywhere."

"We have one of the Rykkiel," Ryder said. "It will take us to the muannai valley in the blink of an eye. I need to set you down."

The girl slid from his arms. "Magic?"

He tugged at the pillowcase. The muannai gathered round them. "We'll be traveling through time and space again. This time, don't let go!"

"Who's there?" a voice called.

Ryder rolled the Tasimas to the ground and stopped it with his foot. He cinched the pillowcase with his belt. The muannai ringed around him, the one next to Jade grabbed her hand. "Put your other hand on my shoulder," he whispered loudly.

"I've found her," the voice shouted. There was more shouting and the sound of boots pounding the ground.

A lone knight burst through the trees waving a torch in one hand and a sword in the other. "Be armed! She's not alone!" He swung the torch at their tight circle.

Ryder bent over to grab the yellow sphere—

One of the muannai screamed. Flames licked the back of his shirt.

"Snuff it out, on the ground!" Ryder shouted.

The knight feinted with his torch, forcing the group against a tree. The Tasimas rolled away, beyond Ryder's grasp. He lunged after it and landed prone on the ground, the Tasimas beneath him. The sharp point of a blade pricked his throat.

The knight and his weapon somersaulted over Ryder's head, crashing at a distance.

Two of the muannai had charged him.

"Grab hold of me and the girl, now!" Ryder shouted. He felt two hands clamp his biceps. "Jade?"

She slammed against him, her belly against his back. She threw her arms around his neck and squeezed. "Get us out of here!"

Ryder concentrated on the green pasture outside the marketplace. He dug his hands beneath him and pressed his fingers around the globe.

When they reached the wall of wind, he pressed harder with his mind. Jade's arms clung tighter, choking him. The wall of wind shoved them into a sticky, impassable membrane.

Blessed Idonne. What was it?

The membrane folded over and around them, wrapping them in a claustrophobic cocoon.

Ryder imagined a wall of heat and fire. Slowly, the membrane melted into a viscous liquid. They rolled onto grass, drenched in oily residue.

"What was that? Where are we?" Jade cried.

Ryder stared at the row of lean-to sheds. "We made it to Tyrannis. We're at the marketplace." He returned the Tasimas to the pillowcase and went to find Melia.

"Hey, wait," Jade shouted. "Don't just leave me here."

"I'm going to find your mother." Melia would know were Lola was. Ryder noticed the long cloth-wrapped thing shoved into Jade's belt. He'd felt it briefly when she landed on his back. "What's that?" he asked.

Slick streaks ran down her face and stained her dress. "A sword."

"Koldis?" Ryder asked.

"How would I know? I took it from Gavin."

Thank the gods of Azyllai, she managed to bring it with her. Now he wouldn't have to return to Illialei to hunt for it. "Give it to me."

She stopped walking toward him. "No."

"You don't want to bear responsibility for that blade." He wiped the goo from his cheeks then rubbed his hands against his breaches. At least it didn't stink.

"And you do?" she asked.

"I made a vow to caretake it."

"I'm sorry, but I can't just give it to you. Umbra wants me to have it."

Ryder's jaw locked. He thrust out his hand. "Give it to me."

Jade darted around him, beyond his reach. Frustrated with her, and the greasy mess coating him, he hurried after her and grabbed her arm.

She whirled around, her blue eyes piercing him. "Let me go!"

"Umbra is dangerous. Far more dangerous than you imagine."

The blue in her eyes darkened into a stormy sea. Like Melia's eyes, when she was upset.

"I don't believe you," she said.

"We went to the mortal world to warn you about him."

"You should have warned me about the princess. I could have been killed!"

"Ryder!"

He dropped Jade's arm and turned.

Melia hurried toward him. She threw her arms around him. "I'm so glad you're safe."

Jade smirked.

"What's all over you?"

"Mucous from a barrier we passed through as we left Illialei," Ryder said.

Melia raised her hand to her nose. "At least it doesn't smell." She acknowledged Jade. "Let me take you to your mother. She's been worried sick about you."

"She has Koldis," Ryder said.

Melia walked toward Jade and held out her hand. "We'll keep it safe while you reunite with your mother."

Jade's eyebrow quirked. "I can keep it safe. Safer than you kept me. Why didn't you tell me you were bringing me to a world where the princess wanted me dead?"

"Fear might have made it impossible for you to travel here."

"How do you think I felt when that knight tied me up and dragged me around like a dog on a leash?" She pointed to her lip. "Another one smashed me in the face and busted my lip."

"But you're safe now," Melia said.

"No thanks to you." Jade pointed to Ryder. "At least he came after me."

"Because I sent him." Taller than Jade, Melia stood with her hands on her hips, cheeks flushed. Dressed in the muannai style, her body was rigid.

"Maybe you could have sent him sooner," Jade said.

403

"He left two days ago."

Jade's blue eyes refocused on Ryder. "You've been trying to rescue me for two days?"

"Yes," he said.

She moved toward him. "Thank you."

Melia folded her arms. "Koldis will call danger to you. If you're afraid of the princess, you should let us relieve you of its burden."

Jade whirled around. "I didn't say I was afraid of her. I said you should have warned me about her."

"You shouldn't have chosen to go with her assassin."

"If you'd told me she wanted to have me killed, maybe I wouldn't have."

"Jade!" Lola ran to her daughter and buried her in a hug.

When she released her, Jade tottered back a few steps. "Mom, what happened to you?" She reached up to touch one of the combs in her mother's hair. "Who fixed your hair?" Jade's voice trembled, her head moved up and down. "You look beautiful." Her eyes watered. "Magical. Like you did when I was a girl."

Her mother beamed. "I was so worried about you, but they promised Ryder would bring you back to me. Are you all right, honey? Aren't you cold? Walking around in that dress, barefoot?"

"It was much warmer where I was."

"What happened to your shoes?" her mother asked.

"I had to use them to escape."

"Let's go find you some warmer clothes." Lola grabbed her daughter's hand. "Thank you," she said to Ryder. "Thank you for bringing her back to me."

He bowed his head.

Lola chattered to her daughter as she swept her away.

Melia shook her head. "If the knights come for Ormrun and Koldis again, their rage will be greater. We need to take them far from here."

"That girl is dead set against handing over the sword."

"Perhaps her mother can persuade her."

Ryder doubted Lola could persuade her daughter of anything. "If we can't change her mind, she'll have to come with us."

"They need to go to Aldaine. Sevondi can keep them safe at the Dragon's Keep. I don't want those two sailing with us to Minnanon. That girl is nothing but trouble."

Ryder didn't say they might not have a choice.

While he and Melia walked to the line of tents, he searched his heart. He would be lying if he didn't admit, at least to himself, that he preferred Jade to take on the burden of Umbra's consciousness.

Later that day, Ryder, Melia, and Flora sat at one of the tables at the back of the marketplace. Flora looked thinner and paler, but her eyes were bright. She refused to remain in the shed that had been converted into a sickroom for her.

The spring faerie pressed Ryder for details about the thick gel that enveloped them as they left Illialei.

"It was like a net, except it wasn't porous," he said. "It was a thin, but strong layer. We didn't hit it going into Illialei, only coming back to Tyrannis."

The spring faerie shook her head. "She's created some sort of bubble around herself, or the palace–a shield."

Melia put one elbow on the table then the other. She searched the crowd.

Ryder settled his hand on her knee. "What's on your mind?"

"Jade isn't going to relinquish the sword."

Flora tapped the table. "Speaking of."

Bertille led Jade and Lola to their table.

"Why is she bringing them here?" Melia whispered.

"They must have something they wish to discuss with us," Flora said.

"I don't want to talk to her," Melia said.

"Good afternoon," Bertille said. "May we join you?"

Flora indicated the benches around them.

"Are you sure you're ready to travel?" Bertille asked Flora.

"Yes. How is Gumf?"

The water nixie stared down at the table top. "He's not doing as well as you are."

"Is it the depth of the cut, or the poison from the blade?"

"I'm afraid it's both," the water nixie said. "Black pus oozes from the cut, and at its depth, the wound exposes bone."

"Do you see the danger?" Melia said to Jade. "If you're careless with the blade and cut yourself—"

"I won't be careless with it."

"We brought you to the enchanted world to keep you safe."

Jade straightened her spine. "I came here to become powerful. When I incarnate Umbra, I'll be a queen, and you'll have to do whatever I tell you to do."

The blood drained from Melia's face. She stood and placed her palms on the table. Leaning over, she said, "You're not going to incarnate Umbra."

The muannai at surrounding tables stopped talking.

Ryder stood and rested his palm on Melia's back. She bucked it off.

"Do you think you're going to do it?" Jade asked. "Has he even asked you to?"

Melia's flattened hands curled into fists.

"Do you even talk to him?" the girl pushed her.

"He'll seduce and corrupt you," Melia said though clenched teeth.

"You're jealous of me," Jade said.

"That's what my sister said before she tried to incarnate Umbra. By the time he was done with her, she wanted to kill herself"—Melia pointed at Koldis, now in a scabbard on Jade's hip—"with that blade. We had to keep it from her, so she couldn't."

Jade's eyes widened.

"So, yes. I know Umbra much better than you."

Lola smoothed one of the girl's snakelike braids. "I want to stay here, honey. Please, listen to her. She wants to protect you."

"From what?" Jade said.

Lola took her daughter's hand. "The first night we were here, we went to an inn. It was a nightmare. Everyone who'd gone there to eat and drink was murdered. There was blood and bodies everywhere—"

"You were there? Inside?" Jade asked.

Confusion flashed over Lola's face.

"That was the first place the assassin took me," Jade said. "To the edge of the woods, outside that building. I listened to the screams all night. It sounded like a slaughter." She faced Melia. "For someone who wants to help us, you're doing a pathetic job. Why would you take my mother there, to a place where everyone was being killed?"

"Jade," Bertille interjected. "Things are happening quickly in Faerie. The attack you heard couldn't have been foreseen. They took your mother to the inn because they knew they could trust the proprietor. As we speak, Gumf hovers near death because of a cut made by the blade you refuse to relinquish. Your mother's life was never at risk. But if she stays here at the marketplace, it will be. As will yours. The princess heir wishes you both dead. You must go north with Melia. There is a fortress there, the Dragon's Keep, where you and your mother will be safe."

"I don't need you to protect me," Jade said, "or dump me and my mother in some fortress where we don't know anyone."

"But you do," Bertille said. "Sevondi can keep you both safe while Melia and Ryder sail to Minnanon."

Jade perked up at the mention of Ryder. "Why are you going there?" she asked him.

"Because I'm going to incarnate Umbra. It's my destiny," Melia answered.

Jade laughed.

Melia straightened her body to its full height, crossed her arms over her chest, and glared. "You think this is a game?"

"You can't incarnate Umbra unless I give you the sword. The

sword is the key to open the portal."

"Which you don't have."

"The basin," Jade said.

Melia arched an eyebrow.

Jade's eyes flickered with thought. "Minnanon; is that where the basin is?"

"No," Melia said.

"Where is it?" Jade asked.

Melia gazed pointedly at Koldis. "It seems we're at impasse."

"If the basin isn't there, why are you going there?"

"To appear before the Grey Council."

"Is that like the U-N?"

"I don't know what the U-N is."

"It's an international governing body in the mortal world; but nothing they do is binding," Jade said.

"The Grey Council is something like that," Melia said.

"Then why go there?"

"With their support for the incarnation, we'll rally an army from across the enchanted world to defeat the Albiana queens once and for all."

Jade's eyes narrowed as she studied Melia. "Why has it come down to you or me?"

"Because of the Albiana blood that runs in our veins. Mixed with mortal, we make the perfect vessels to contain Umbra's consciousness."

"You have mortal blood?" Jade asked.

"My father was a druid," Melia said.

"Honey, do you remember the sad story about those three girls whose mother cursed them for killing their own father?" Lola asked her daughter.

"Are you talking about the French fairy tale? Melusine?" Jade looked at Melia. "That's you?"

"It's her older sister," Lola said. "Melia is the middle child."

"The story barely mentions you," Jade said.

"That's because when the oldest sister escaped to the mortal world, the two younger sisters remained in the enchanted world to fight the battle between Dark and Light. But that part of the story never made it to the mortal world," Lola said. "Surprising when you consider the younger sisters' story is more epic."

"How old are you?" Jade asked Melia.

"Time is fluid between the mortal and enchanted worlds," Ryder said.

"You mean I could leave here and go back to 14th century France?" the girl asked.

"It's not that fluid," he answered. "You can't return to the past in the mortal world. No one can. Once you've moved forward in the line of time, you must stay in the present, or continue moving forward. You can never go back in time."

"But I could go into the future," Jade said.

Ryder nodded. "If and when you return to the mortal world, many years may have passed, but you'll still be the same age you were as when you left."

Jade considered his words. "Then I want to go with you to this island. I want to make a request of this council in your world."

The spring faerie had been observing the exchange with keen interest. "What request would that be?"

Jade flashed hard blue eyes at Melia. "I want to request I be the one to incarnate Umbra."

"A challenge," Flora's words were thoughtful. She tugged at the knot in her kerchief. "Melia?"

Everyone waited.

"When I'm your queen," Melia said to Jade, "you'll do as I tell you to do." She gave Ryder a dark look and stormed off.

The spring faerie held up a hand to him. "Let me go." Flora hurried after Melia.

Jade sat down next to her mother. "I'm going to beat her."

Ryder wished Jade could, but he would never forget the night at the Muudron Stone when Melia saved Sevondi and spewed Umbra back into the Void. If he were forced to bet, he would put his gold on Melia.

"Ryder, if Jade is going to go to this island, I feel like I should accompany her," Lola said.

"I'm sure we'll be able to make arrangements for you to sail with us," he said.

And Sinjiin.

Ryder would beg, plead, and remind the mage of his oath. Whatever it took to convince his friend. He couldn't travel with all these females alone.

Bertille gave him an impish smile, as if she read his mind.

47. Dreaming About Dragons

Melia paced back and forth along the shelf of rock. Ocean spray flicked her face.

"It's freezing down here," Tatou said.

Winter had arrived in Tyrannis, and every day seemed colder than the one before.

Melia pulled up a flap on her long coat. "Come, climb in my pocket."

Tatou pointed her toes and slid into the pixie-sized pouch. "Better."

Melia resumed her pacing. "You've spent time with her. Am I exaggerating?"

"She'd be happier if you didn't exist."

"I'd be happier if she didn't exist. I went to the mortal world to save her and her mother, and this is how she repays me? By attempting to steal Ryder's affection, and refusing to give me the sword. She has no idea what we went through to obtain Ormrun and Koldis in the first place. I almost died in the Calashai's dungeons. Now, I bring her here from the mortal world. I help her cross over! And she thinks the blade is hers, simply because she stole it from a drunken Huron knight? She understands nothing. Nothing!"

"The Jade you know, the Jade we've all met, is influenced by Umbra. Do you remember when Plantine threw a hairbrush at you?"

Melia chewed on a fingernail. "She admits she talks to Umbra. That he came to her in the mortal world."

"So we don't know what Jade was like before Umbra's influence, but we know it altered Plantine."

"Yes, but Plantine only became a worse version of herself, not a different one. Jade treats Flora and Aldous with contempt, dismissing them because they're old. She has no idea of the warrior and scholar she belittles."

"I like her mother," Tatou said.

"Lola is wonderful. It's hard to believe she has such a beast for a daughter. How am I going to survive two, three, four moon cycles on a ship with her? 'Ryder, what do think? Ryder, tell me a story about your days in Idonne. Ryder, when you came to save me that night in Illialei, I thought God had sent an angel'."

"She's very enamored of him."

"Can't she understand he's mine?"

"He doesn't encourage her."

"And yet she doesn't stop, does she?"

"Umbra."

"It would be so easy to blame her ingratitude, arrogance, ignorance, and disrespect on Umbra."

"Would it be so easy?" Tatou asked. "Wouldn't it be easier to believe she's just a nasty person and hate her?"

Melia tossed her head, a wild horse straining at its bit. "She doesn't understand what I gave up to be with him."

Tatou pressed her lips together.

Melia stopped. "Did you say something?"

"I said, when you look at her, see Umbra not Jade. See how the dark force dominates her. Through observing Jade, learn Umbra's tactics and how to defend against them. Use her to augment your training, to help you become more strategic, so that when he's inside you, you control his energy, he doesn't control yours."

"What if the Grey Council chooses her?" Melia asked.

"What did Flora tell you?"

"That I'm responsible for making that outcome impossible."

"And how will you do that?"

"By outperforming her in every challenge set before us."

"And where does victory begin? Tatou asked.

"Within, little professor." Melia had gnawed her fingernail down to the quick. "It's just that I never saw this challenge coming."

"Use it to make you stronger."

"She's such a show-off. Have you seen her? After every training session, she can't resist tossing her knives around. She almost sliced off one of the cook's ears. Everything is a game to her."

"If you can't handle Jade, how will you ever handle Umbra?"

Melia squinted her eyes against a searing cold wind as she grappled with the unsettling question.

"You have to pull your focus away from Jade and strengthen yourself."

"I know you're right," Melia said.

"Can we please return to the keep?" the pixie asked. "I'd like to spend my last days on land toasting by a warm fire, not fending of frostbite. There'll be enough of that on the ship."

"Are you sure you're up to the journey?" Melia dreaded any answer other than yes, but she had to ask.

"I'd never let you face the Grey Council without me."

I'm climbing a stone mountain, but my hands are not my hands. They're covered in aqua-colored scales. I hold one up in front of my face to examine it. Speckled leather ripples in the sunlight. What happened to my skin? I spread my palm. Tiny webs connect the base of each of my fingers. Except they're not fingers, they're blue-black claws. I dig them into the mountain and gouge a mound of dust from the sheer wall as if it was sand.

I turn my head. My eyes must be enormous because the scope of my vision is broader, higher, and deeper than it's ever been. The muscles of my back bunch and release, bunch and release. A shadow flaps against the mountain wall. Enormous wings.

But I'm not an eagle.

I ease the weight of my torso back, letting my monstrous wings carry me. My hands—claws—release the mountain wall as I hover. Below me spans a valley with a river for its spine. I curl my neck. My legs are stout and short. Like my hands and arms, they're covered in aqua-colored scales, and blue-black claws glint where my toenails should be.

The force of my beating wings pulls me farther from the wall.

I need to see what I've become.

I dive.

As I approach my reflection in the river, my eyes widen. Disbelief spews from my mouth in flames, scorching the water. It froths, releasing steam in an agitated boil.

I'm one of Sevondi's beasts, raining fire in the sky.

Melia jerked awake, her heart pounding in her chest. It wasn't the first time she'd dreamed of a dragon, but it was the first time she'd dreamed of becoming one. She stumbled from her bed. Where was the black vial Sinjiin gave her when she began training several moon cycles back? She tore the room apart.

"What are you doing?" Tatou slept in a wooden cradle. Stuffed with cushions and blankets, it was pushed close to the smoldering coals of a fire that had died in the night. The harsh winter invading Tyrannis threatened to turn Tatou into an ice cube on a daily basis.

"I have to find something," Melia whispered.

"What?"

Melia stood in the middle of the room, trying to remember where she put the vial. "Do you remember the oil Sinjiin gave me? The one to help me dream."

Tatou rubbed her eyes. "I saw it somewhere. Do you need it right now?"

Melia crouched next to the cradle. "I dreamt I was a dragon."

Tatou's eyebrows shot up.

"It was incredible. I want to believe that's the creature I'm meant to become."

Tatou flitted to a tall dresser. She tugged on one of the small drawers in a chest that sat on top of it. Melia ran after her.

The drawer wouldn't budge. Tatou stepped aside. "You try."

Melia held the drawer's small handle between her thumb and index finger. It stuck. She pulled it again as hard as she could. The drawer's contents exploded in the air.

Tatou darted back and forth. She caught something heavy and landed with her butt against the dresser. Her arms wrapped around the dark glass, protecting it. "I caught it!"

Melia took the vial from her friend. "Thank you."

Tatou landed on her shoulder, shivering in the cold air. "Now can we go back to sleep?"

"Yes," the half-faerie said, but her heart pumped with questions as she stoked the fire.

Was it possible?

Was she capable of shifting into a dragon?

Afraid to use the oil before she discussed the matter with Sinjiin, she curled beneath her covers, holding the vial against her thumping chest. The mage hinted she might be surprised by her native animal totem. But a dragon? What would Ryder think? A smile broke across her face. If she could shift into a dragon at will, Jade didn't stand a chance on the Isle of Minnanon.

Melia woke before dawn. Although the morning air was frigid, Tatou slept soundly beneath a mountain of blankets. Melia let her be.

Across the hall, she tapped on Ryder's door. He didn't answer. When she pushed on the door, it opened. Melia slipped into the room and advanced to his bed. When her foot crinkled the dry straw spread beside it, she held her breath. The pallet was meant for Sinjiin, but the tiger never slept there. He spent every night with Sevondi.

Ryder didn't move so much as a finger.

Melia tiptoed around the pallet and settled beside him. Not

wishing to jar him awake, she let her hand rest gently on his shoulder. He wrapped his arms around her waist and pulled her to him. Her body fell across his, and he showered her with kisses.

"How long have you been awake?" she asked.

"A while. I saw you open the door."

"I tried to be quiet."

"You might need to work on that."

She grinned. "I forgot about Sinjiin's bed."

"Apparently, so has he."

"Yet, you keep it here for him?"

Ryder shrugged. "Sevondi might tire of him, then he'll need a place to sleep."

"Why do you begrudge their affection for one another?"

"I'm not sure begrudge is the right word."

"It doesn't please you."

"Is that why you came here?" he asked. "To discuss Sinjiin and Sevondi?"

"No. I had a dream."

Ryder pushed himself to sitting. "A vision?"

"Maybe," Melia said. "A few nights ago, I dreamed one of Sevondi's dragons scorched the black roses in Lilliane's garden. Her power to work black magic is linked to those flowers. If we could destroy them–"

"You want Sevondi to go to Illialei?"

"I was thinking about that, yes. Until last night, when I had a different dream."

"And that dream is the reason you're here so early this morning?"

Grey light filtered through the heavy curtains. Day had dawned while they talked.

Melia took Ryder's hand in hers. "I dreamt I became a dragon."

Ryder's green eyes searched hers.

She slipped the black vial from her pocket and gave it to him.

"What's this?" he asked.

"An oil Sinjiin gave me."

416

"You never mentioned it before. When did he give it to you?"

"The day I came back to Tyrannis; the day we fought."

Ryder held up the small jar and studied it.

"Sinjiin told me to dot the oil on my upper lip at night before I go to sleep. It's supposed to help me dream of the creature I can shift into at will. I always thought it would be an eagle. But last night, I didn't even use the oil, and I became a dragon in my dream. It was so real."

"And you think that's the creature you're meant to become?"

"It's more than I ever hoped for."

"A dragon," Ryder mused.

"Do you doubt it?"

He set the vial down and pulled her to him again. "No."

"Then you like the idea?"

"I would like it more if I could become a dragon with you."

"Maybe you can."

"I doubt it. Your Albiana blood is rich with mutable qualities mortals and other creatures in the enchanted world don't possess."

Melia tightened her arms around him. "It was just a dream."

"No. It was more than that, and you're right to be excited. Let's go find Sinjiin. He'll be down at the inlet, chasing his breakfast soon."

She kissed his neck. "I was afraid you wouldn't understand."

He shifted so he could hold her face in his hands. "I've been dreaming too."

"Really? About what?"

He searched her eyes.

"About what?" Melia repeated.

"I walk along a river in a deep gorge with a tiger and a dragon. The dragon is the most beautiful creature I've ever seen. Nothing like the pictures I've seen in books. It's so graceful—"

"Is it blue?"

"The color of the sea reflecting the sky on a cloudless day."

Chills ran up Melia's spine as Ryder picked up the black vial and studied it before giving it back to her.

✧ ✧ ✧

"This is good news," Sinjiin said.

As soon as they found him stalking gulls by the ocean, he shifted into his mage form.

"You're not just becoming stronger." He reached up to tap Melia's forehead. "You're attaining clarity as well."

"Because I had the dream without using the oil?"

"Precisely."

"What will happen now when I use it?"

"You've never used it, not once?"

"No, I didn't even know where it was. Tatou helped me find it in the middle of the night."

"And you"—the mage pointed to Ryder—"dream of walking with a tiger and a dragon?"

Ryder nodded.

Sinjiin rubbed his slim, angular jaw. "The bond between the two of you deepens. That is good news, too."

"Then I should use the oil tonight, before I go to sleep?"

"Yes."

"I want to talk with Sevondi before we sail," Melia said. "Before my dream last night, I dreamt one of her dragons burned Lilliane's black roses. Somehow, her dragons and the one I'm to become are connected within me."

"That's an excellent idea," Sinjiin said.

"I'd like to speak with her alone."

Ryder folded his arms and shook his head. He refused to view the new regent as an ally, and his presence might hinder Sevondi's willingness to help Melia.

"Approach her in the throne hall," Sinjiin advised. "Request a private audience. She'll appreciate the show of respect."

Melia would have to do it soon. They sailed for Minnanon in two days.

48. A Private Audience

Melia squirmed beneath Sevondi's steady gaze. Never had the half-faerie been so aware of her own lack of authority. The muannai, crowded behind her in the large hall, hung on Sevondi's every word and gesture. It seemed they'd be willing to die for her. They had no interest in Melia, though, Or that she was the one who saved their regent's life at the Muudron Stone. The overt disparity in their stations—the dragonwitch calm and dignified upon her onyx throne, Melia sweaty and disheveled from her morning training session—ate at the half-faerie.

It seemed the higher the sun rose in the sky, the more the experience of herself as a dragon thinned. Like some strange illusion, the winds from the Great White Sea blew her dream away.

Melia pushed thoughts of her mother—devoured by envy of Melusine—aside. It disturbed Melia to empathize with Pressina. Yet standing here, groveling before Sevondi, her mistakes became clear. The more Jade embraced her desire to incarnate Umbra with no apology, the more Melia realized the power Nandana's prophecy had bestowed upon her, and how foolish she'd been to reject it. Now, because of modesty, humility, or stupidity—maybe a messy combination of all three—she'd have to stand before the Grey Council opposed.

Jade would press her advantage—that she was the vessel Umbra desired. How much weight would the council give Umbra's preference?

And how much would the scales of destiny shift if Melia could compete as a dragon?

Melia couldn't kneel before the dragonwitch. She tried to bow her neck. It refused to soften. "I request a private audience with you before I sail to Minnanon."

Sevondi's nod heartened Melia. At least she hadn't forgotten the half-faerie saved her from Umbra's rage. "This evening, when the sun meets the horizon, Sinjiin will find you," the muannai's new regent said. "He'll escort you to my chamber. We'll dine there alone, you and I."

The mage, in his tiger form, perched on the dais, close enough for Sevondi to bury her fingers in the scruff of his neck as she greeted the day's petitioners. He acted as though he'd not talked with Melia and Ryder that morning on the beach.

"Thank you." Melia turned to leave.

"I hear the pixie will sail with you to Minnanon."

"Yes, and I'll be glad for her company."

"I've appreciated her progress reports on the sapphire lily. Just the other day, she mentioned the gnomes have created a solarium so they may experiment with its cultivation through the winter months. We'll know whether the lily can grow in Tyrannis by the time you return to Faerie. Ask your friend to choose a representative to keep me apprised of the progress during her absence."

"I'll see that she does."

When Melia turned to leave, the muannai parted, creating an unobstructed path for her exit. Sevondi's deference had raised her value in their eyes.

❖ ❖ ❖

The dinner of roasted fish and vegetables served with a crusty loaf of bread and blackberry wine was delicious. Melia only allowed herself occasional sips from her wine glass. She noticed Sevondi drank little as well. The dragonwitch ate even less. Dark circles beneath her eyes, and a sheen of paleness to her dark skin, undetectable at a distance, or in shadows of the throne hall, were clearly visible now.

Melia tugged on her hair as she wondered what tormented Sevondi.

"You'll win," Sevondi said. "You must win."

"Are you talking about—?"

"Jade."

"She's determined," Melia said.

"Then you must be more determined."

"The misgivings, the fear I have about the incarnation, she has none. Her confidence will give her the upper hand."

"Then you must set aside your misgivings and grow beyond your fear."

"Flora and Tatou offer me the same advice."

Sevondi reached for Melia's hand. "There's no longer a question as to whether the Whole is going to transform. It will. Umbra is going to incarnate. I foresee a golden age if the vessel is you. If the vessel is Jade, I foresee black times ahead."

Melia's hand jerked. Sevondi held it tight. She traced the warding she'd painted on the half-faerie's face with the index finger of her free hand. Melia's skin tingled.

"Set your self-doubt aside. It's a false mask, one that no longer serves you."

"I fear my ambition will consume me."

Sevondi laughed. "Finally, you admit you have desires. Tell me what they are."

Startled, Melia answered. "To end the Albiana reign, and any possibility of another massacre like the one at the Veiled Tavern. To achieve some sort of justice for Flora's race. To unite the inhabitants of Illialei and Tyrannis, as they were in the old days when the Maeldun Bridge was well traveled, and elves and dwarves, faeries and trolls were friends. To show Jade ..." Melia tugged on her hair.

"To show Jade what?"

"That she should be honored to kneel in service to me."

"She'll never grant you that." Sevondi let go of the half-faerie's

421

hand and patted it. "Unless you prove yourself worthy."

"How?"

Sevondi steepled her long, slim fingers, but didn't respond.

"My soul flame," Melia whispered as she relived the flames in her dreams scorching the river's surface.

"It's the first thing Umbra will try to extinguish."

"Is that what he did to you at the Muudron Stone?"

Sevondi closed her eyes, a silent yes.

"How did you resist him?" Melia asked.

"You've forgotten? Your soul flame lent strength to mine. That's what saved me. You'll do well to remember that when you face Jade before the Grey Council."

"I will."

"Now, what did you need to discuss with me in private?"

"The dragons. The way you create them from nothing."

Sevondi's pupils darkened, her eyes hooded.

"I ..." Melia hesitated, uncertain how much to reveal. Should she share the dream about the scorching of Lilliane's black garden, or the one she had last night?

Sevondi pushed her chair away from the table. As she walked to the doors that opened onto her private balcony, Melia noticed a slight limp in her gait. The dragonwitch opened one door in a panel of many. The sound of waves crashing against rocks far below rushed into the room. Sevondi disappeared into the darkness beyond the door.

Melia followed the regent onto her balcony. All day she'd considered her request. If Sinjiin's oil failed to work, if she proved incapable of transforming into a dragon, she needed to learn how to call them. If for no other reason than to destroy the black roses Lilliane cultivated; they gave her too much power. "I want to learn how to call the dragons like you do," Melia shouted to be heard over the surf.

Sevondi's fingers circled the metal railing that enclosed the balcony. "If you return to Tyrannis triumphant, if you vanquish

Jade, I'll teach you my bag of tricks."

Melia exhaled a deep breath. "Then I will win."

Sevondi spun around and glared at her. "You must."

"But there will be many long days on the ship," Melia persisted. "There must be something I can do—to prepare myself for your lessons."

The dragonwitch stared at the half-faerie.

"Flora and Tatou are teaching me to strengthen my mind, and Sinjiin—" Melia fidgeted with the small black vial in her pocket. If Sinjiin hadn't confided to his lover about the oil and its purpose, she wasn't going to.

Sevondi crossed her arms.

"There must be something you can give me before we sail," Melia said. "Some scrap of enlightenment."

"My Aunt Imelda taught me the dragon magic. She knew the way to call them, but was never able to do so herself. Do you understand what that means? It may be that no one else is capable."

"When we return from Minnanon, I fear there'll be no time for lessons."

Sevondi returned to the interior of her chamber with Melia trailing behind her.

"And what would happen, if you incarnated Umbra, and had the power to call dragons to you?"

"I could defeat Lilliane, and win the devotion of the creatures of Illialei, perhaps the devotion of creatures throughout the enchanted world. Flora believes we'll need to raise an army."

Sevondi glared at Melia again.

The half-faerie forged ahead. She'd seen Sevondi's dragons strike awe in the hearts of an audience and inspire their allegiance. She also understood the power of followers who were devoted, as opposed to those who followed because they had no choice. If she was going to incarnate Umbra, if she was going to wear the crown of the Queen of the Realm of Faerie, she would have subjects loyal in their hearts, not because she called the nation of Huros to Faerie

423

and ruled by force.

"You didn't see the bodies piled up at the Veil," Melia said. "It was an abomination. Lilliane must be stopped. We must unite to defeat her."

Sevondi closed her eyes and shook her head.

"Please," Melia said, "there must be some task or ritual I can practice on the long journey ahead of me." She bowed her head and waited.

"True power is balanced," Sevondi said. "It's not light or dark. You must understand that, and that understanding must live deep within you, in your bones and in your blood."

Melia's heart stopped beating. Her thoughts scattered in different directions as she tried to comprehend what the dragonwitch was telling her. She reached for the pearls resting against her heart. A glimpse of understanding flickered by; she grabbed it by the tail. "Elendah said to know light one must travel through the dark. Is that what you mean?"

"The dragons breathe fire. A harsh, burning light. The fuel for that light, what it burns, is the darkness within me."

"The darkness within you?"

Sevondi closed her eyes. "Certainly, you're no stranger to pain and loss, anguish and heartache."

"It's your—" Melia searched for the right word.

"My guilt. My hate. My rage. Everything we prefer to shun within ourselves, that's what fuels the creation of my dragons."

"The truth," Melia whispered.

"The whole truth."

The half-faerie nodded. The vase she used to contain Umbra was fired and shaped by her soul flame; but its substance had come from her inner darkness.

"Then you understand."

Melia didn't understand how to apply it to the creation of dragons. "How—?"

"You want an exercise, something to practice until you return?

Embrace your darkness. Every bit of it. Hold nothing back. The more familiar you become with the black vectors of energy your myriad wounds have given birth to within, the more capable you'll be of harnessing that energy. Most people bury their pain, not realizing it's their greatest source of power."

Melia considered Sevondi's explanation. She wanted to make sure she understood what the dragonwitch was saying. "Do you meditate upon it?"

"With persistence, your ability to acknowledge the truth and contain it will grow. That's the trick. To build an accessible reservoir of black within you, one you can tap into at will. Be measured in the beginning. Only meditate for a minute or two. As you become more adept at containing the dark energy, you can meditate for longer periods. Don't rush the process. It's possible to drown your inner world with black, then the ability to channel it is lost. That's what happened to my aunt. Even though she understood the process and was able to pass it on to me, her darkness spilled out of its container. There's no rebuilding once the inner walls have been breached."

"It's dangerous," Melia said.

"Exceedingly."

"But it will make me strong?"

"It can make you invincible."

"That's what I need to become," Melia said. "Invincible."

Sinjiin raced down the stone stairs with Melia on his back.

A spark sizzled at the base of her spine. She forced her breaths into an even rhythm and focused her inner eye on her soul flame. Certainty engulfed her. She'd become invincible.

When they arrived in the keep's airy kitchen, Yrrick and Ryder bantered at one of the tables, empty plates and bowls stacked between them.

As soon as Melia slid off the tiger's back, Sinjiin morphed into his mage form.

"You're coming with us to Minnanon?" she asked him.

"I don't have a choice, do I?" Sinjiin threw a pointed look in Ryder's direction, as Melia circled the young priest's shoulders with her arms and settled her chin on the top of his head.

Ryder released an exasperated sigh. "I do recall the matter of my saving your life. Twice."

"As long as we're clear." Sinjiin's dark eyes flashed with anger. "The moment we land, I'm free of my debt. What happens with the basin and sword once we set foot on that infernal island is not my concern."

"Always the hero, willing to come to the aid of those in need, with no thought to yourself," Ryder said.

"Don't presume to judge me."

"No judgment, just a simple observation."

"I'll watch over Sevondi while you're away," Yrrick volunteered.

"Thank you," Sinjiin said.

Ryder shrugged. His stubborn dismissal of his friend's devotion to the dragonwitch baffled Melia. The more she observed Sinjiin and Sevondi together, the more she appreciated their union and their ability to communicate without words. She wished Ryder could honor their affection as well.

"If anything happens to her while we're away"—Sinjiin glared at his friend—"I'll hold you responsible."

"If anyone can take care of herself, it's Sevondi," Ryder said.

Melia sighed. He didn't see the exhaustion or limp she'd observed tonight. She suspected Sinjiin was acutely aware of her struggles. Maybe if she told Ryder about them later, in private, he'd be more respectful of the mage's concerns about leaving her for so many moon cycles.

49. Sailing to the Isle of Minnanon

Jade watched Melia, her pearly white teeth exposed as she laughed. A long pale arm, visible beneath her wool cape, draped Ryder's shoulder. The half-faerie exuded a confidence lacking only two days before.

Training among the muannai, Jade's confidence increased. Small and muscular, her body and natural coordination adapted easily to the physical aspects of fighting with fists and her legs, a short knife or a long sword. But what about her mental strength and endurance? It was the first time she questioned herself—and whether she'd become Faerie's queen—since she arrived in the enchanted world.

When Melia smiled, her entire face lit up. Ryder, and everyone else in the vicinity, couldn't take their eyes from her, including Jade, who much preferred her opponent sour-faced and sulky.

How was she going to regain the upper hand?

Jade had eight weeks, maybe less, to find an answer to that question.

Perhaps Umbra could help. But their contact was limited since she'd left Illialei. Their long nights talking in the Cathedral Palace drained his reserves.

Two muannai rowed the dinghy carrying Jade, her mother, Melia, Ryder, the tiger, the old wood elf, the fat old spring faerie, the pixie, and five large trunks to the ship they'd sail to Minnanon. It was a marvel the small boat didn't sink when the trunks were loaded ahead of the passengers. The plainest trunk, bound with steel girders, concealed Ormrun and Koldis.

Jade studied the faces of her fellow passengers.

Melia was surrounded by friends and tutors; no one on the boat was on Jade's side. When it came to incarnating Umbra, not even her mother wanted her to win. Lola hung on every word Flora and Aldous said. She tried to convince Jade to listen to them. But what did they know? They were old. The future didn't belong to them.

When they reached the ship, Jade lurched toward the rope ladder thrown down to greet them. She was eager to move her body after the long moments contorted into an uncomfortable posture so no part of herself made contact with the dinghy's other passengers. She curled her fingers around the ladder's rope. The soles of her feet, in their soft leather boots, gripped one rung after the other as she pulled herself up the side of the enormous ship. The first of their party on deck, she raced to the ship's bow. When she reached the bowsprit, she scrambled up it as best she could, spreading her arms wide like Leonardo DiCaprio and Kate Winslet in the Titanic. It didn't have quite the same effect as when the ship was moving. But at least she could breathe after suffocating in the company of Melia and her cheerleaders.

Someone called her name.

Jade pretended not to hear.

Jade came to hate the ship. As large as it was, it was too small. There weren't many places for combat drills, so no matter where she went —or at what time—she ran into her nemesis. It had been easy to avoid her competition at the Dragon's Keep. The old faerie often dragged Melia away at dawn, leaving the sizable courtyard and the rest of the keep for Jade to claim. As a result, she came to think of the fortress as her domain. The ship never felt that way, and the sense of displacement didn't ease her growing insecurities. Her mother was no help either. Every morning and every night, she begged her daughter to reconsider. The most important opportunity of her life presented itself, and her mother championed the opposing side.

"It's not a question of whether Umbra will incarnate, Mother. They all believe he will. Do you really think she's better than me?"

"Of course that's not what I think. But she's lived here her entire life."

"No. She was born in the mortal world, like me."

"You know what I mean. She grew up in Illialei. They know her. You're a stranger to them."

"I don't care. I don't like her!"

"Honey, you don't like her because you don't want her to incarnate Umbra, but she's a very likable young woman."

"How can you even say that? She's awful. What does Ryder see in her?"

Jade sank onto the bed next to her mother. Rain trapped them in their pittance of a cabin. Jade didn't mind the wet, but the farther north they went, the colder the wind blew. Rainstorms had become sleet storms. After braving the last one, she'd shivered uncontrollably next to the giant fire in the ship's kitchen for hours. She wasn't eager to repeat the experience.

Lola waited until her daughter's shoulder settled against hers. "Have you heard the story about the mark on her forehead?"

"Yes," Jade growled.

"Honey, she saw visions of Ryder before he even arrived in Faerie. They're destined to be together."

"Mom, no! Don't say that!" Jade collapsed in her mother's lap, her shoulders heaving with quiet despair.

Lola rubbed her daughter's back. "There, there. Have you ever considered you might be star-stuck? You weren't there the first night they came to San Diego, but all the women and girls were gaga over Ryder. He's very magnetic."

"It's more than that," Jade sniffled. "I think I love him."

"I thought I loved your father," Lola mused.

Jade's torso whipped up, she clipped Lola's chin with her head. "You didn't?"

Lola rubbed her jaw. "I love you."

"You didn't love my father?"

"I told you, I thought I did."

"What does that even mean? Either you love someone or you don't."

Jade peeked at her mother through half-open eyes. If her father saw her mother now, he'd never be able to walk away from her. With each passing day in the enchanted world, she became more beautiful. Her eyes shined, her skin glowed. As she ate the healthy omnivorous diet of the muannai, her body shrank and tightened. It wasn't just her outsides. Her spirit, which had been sick and tired for so many years, sprang free, vital and alive. Although Lola seemed oblivious, Jade had caught some of the muannai flirting with her mother.

"Lust is always part of the equation," Lola said.

Jade jerked back. "Eww, Mother. I don't want to have this conversation with you."

Lola raised an eyebrow. "Refusing to talk about something doesn't change the facts. Have you ever found yourself attracted to someone you hate?"

Jade bounced up from the bed and crossed her arms. "That's the stupidest question I've ever been asked. If you hate someone, you hate them. You're not attracted to them."

"Jade, I understand I haven't been the best role model when it comes to relationships between men and women—"

Jade slammed her palms against her ears. "We're not having this conversation. Lalalalala."

Lola waited patiently. When Jade quieted down, Lola patted the bed beside her. Her daughter sat next to her. "It's possible the attraction you feel toward Ryder is physical. You don't really know him. I'm just asking you to consider whether the attraction is more lust than love."

"Was your attraction to Dad just physical?"

"Whatever it was, it wasn't enduring."

"Why did he leave you, Mom?"

"I left him."

"But why won't he even talk to us? Why doesn't he want to meet me? I'm his daughter!"

Lola wrapped her arms around Jade's shoulder as she trembled against her. "Your father is dominated by his family. He could never break free."

"That's a lame excuse."

Lola smoothed her daughter's dreadlocks in a comforting rhythm. "I can't defend him. I won't even try. But we're here now, in this new place. We could leave all that behind."

Jade pulled away. "I don't want to leave it behind. I want to make him pay for what he did to us."

"Is that why you want to incarnate Umbra, honey? So you can make him pay?"

"Someone needs to make him understand you can't just have a kid and pretend like she doesn't exist."

"It would be better for you if you could just accept—"

Jade jumped up again. "You don't get it, Mom. I'm not you. I'm not going to accept it, then end up in some psychiatric ward taking meds for the rest of my life." She stormed out of the room, fully aware of how cruel she'd been. In her haste to leave their cabin, she hadn't bothered to grab her coat. One floor beneath the deck, she hesitated in the stairwell. The staccato beat of the rain reminded her of the punishing elements awaiting her if she proceeded. But her insides were on fire. Maybe the ice cold onslaught would calm her down.

Halfway up the steps, Ryder's voice stopped her. "Wait."

She turned to see his outline in the dim shadow beneath her.

"Where are you going?" he asked.

"I need some fresh air."

He handed her his cloak. "Please, take it. I don't want you freeze to death."

She took it from him. Still warm from the heat of his body, she

inhaled the scent of him as she wrapped it around her. "Thank you."
He was alone. "Do you want to come with me?" she asked.

"I'll be back shortly."

She felt his presence dwindle to nothing as she perched on one of
the risers. He wasn't gone long. He'd retrieved a second cloak for
himself. "Let me go up first," he said.

She scooted out of the way as he hurried past her, his boots
cracking against the wood. Jade pulled his cloak tight around
herself and followed him. It was the first chance she'd had to be
alone with him since they boarded the ship.

Above deck, Jade leaned into the icy sheets. Ryder held out his
hand and she grabbed it. He held tight, leading her to the railing.
When they reached the side of the ship, he maneuvered behind her,
standing at her back and blocking the worst of the wind. His hands
gripped the railing on the outside of hers. His breath warmed the
back of her head. Resisting the urge to sink against him, Jade held
her body rigid. She tried to think of something to say, but every
comment that came to mind seemed clumsy.

He remained quiet as well.

What was he thinking? Why had he come up on deck alone?
Where was Melia? Did they have a fight? She turned to face him. He
looked down at her, his green eyes mesmerizing. She reached up to
touch his cheek with her finger. The contact was so light she barely
felt his skin. His eyes filled with questions, but he didn't push her
hand away or pull back. She stood on her tiptoes. His head moved
back in unison with her upward thrust. But his hands still gripped
the railing behind her. She dove into his lips.

The shock registered in his eyes. He released the rail, staggered
backward, and wiped her meager kiss away as he shook his head.

A single hot tear flecked the corner of Jade's eye. She squinted it
away as she ducked around him and raced for the hatch. Her heart
burned as she ran blindly down the ship's corridors.

His rejection, although as wordless as her father's, felt much
worse.

❖ ❖ ❖

One week later, Jade sparred with one of the sailors from Typhos. She was aware of Melia, a few feet away, observing the match. Although the sailor she fought wasn't much taller than Jade, he was more bulky. Jade used her slight frame as an extension of her short blade and danced around him. Until Melia began glaring at her, she'd been confident she could best him. Now, even though the northern air was frigid, sweat coated her body. The sailor feinted with his knife. When she spun out of reach, he twirled with his back to hers to catch her wrist with his free hand. He gouged the tender spot beneath her forearm with his thick thumb.

"Give," Jade whispered.

"Did you say something?" he taunted.

"Give," she said a little louder, but not loud enough for Melia to hear.

"I can't hear you." He grinned, exerting enough pressure with his thumb to make her wince.

"I give!"

He dropped her hand and backed away. "Let me know when you want to drill again."

"Sure." Jade hurried after his retreating figure—away from Melia. "Win one time, and you forget all the times I kicked your ass," she said under her breath.

"Jade," Melia called after her.

Overhead, sails cracked in the wind. Jade pretended she didn't hear her name.

"Jade!"

She moved as fast as she could, dodging coils of rope, a roll of canvas, and sailors washing down the deck. Melia was right behind her. She could hear her running. Jade rolled her eyes and spun around. Melia veered right before she crashed into her.

"What do you want?" Jade asked.

Melia regained her composure in a single breath. "I never intended for us to become enemies."

"You never intended to tell me the truth either."

"If I'd told you the princess sent an assassin to the mortal world to kill you and your mother, would you have believed me?"

"That's not the point."

"Then what is?"

"You want me to just step aside and ignore Umbra so you can get on with becoming queen, with no one to challenge you."

"He's seducing you."

"Oh, that's right. I have no power over my actions."

"Why did you kiss Ryder?" Melia's voice was quiet, her tone more curious than angry.

Jade felt the heat rise in her cheeks. She couldn't believe he told her. Why had he told her? "Who cares?" Jade yelled.

Melia took a step closer. "I do."

"Nothing happened," Jade said.

"Why are you fixated on him?" Melia persisted.

"Do you own him?"

"We're bound to one another," Melia said.

What was Jade supposed to say to that? "Then why don't you just get married? What are you waiting for?"

"Are you telling me if Ryder and I were married, you wouldn't have kissed him? That you respect marriage vows?"

As if Ryder's rejection hadn't been bad enough. Now, everyone on deck was circling around them, watching them. Humiliated, Jade grasped for some defense. "He gave me his cloak. He had his arms around me."

"He's a gentleman. You needed to get some fresh air. He was shielding you from the wind. You misunderstood."

Jade advanced toward Melia, her knife clutched in her hand. "Fine. I misunderstood."

Melia cocked her head. "Don't misunderstand again."

Jade instinctively raised her knife hand. The sharp point angled at Melia. She took a step closer. "Or what? What will you do to me if I misunderstand again?"

Melia's hand circled Jade's wrist before she'd even seen it move. "You don't want to find out."

Jade looked down at the hand locked around her arm. The fingernails dug into Jade's skin. One was deep blue. It looked more like a claw than a fingernail. "You need a manicure." Jade raised her gaze to meet Melia's. "And don't try to glamour me ever again."

Melia dropped Jade's arm. The knife clattered to the deck. "As long as we understand one another. You leave Ryder alone, and I'll leave you alone."

Jade snorted as she squatted to retrieve her blade, but the sickening awareness that she'd lost twice today twisted up her spine.

❖ ❖ ❖

"Umbra, where are you?" Jade pleaded.

Her mother slept next to her.

"My precious, Jade, I'm here."

"I need to know why you chose me. Tell me why you think I'm special."

"The incarnation can only succeed if the desire for union is mutual."

"But you tried to incarnate before, with Melia's sister."

"It was a wasted effort. She was impure."

"But the grey faerie died." Jade tested the truth of what Melia had told her.

"Elendah was very old."

"Then you know Melia?" Beside Jade, Lola shifted in their small bed.

"I am aware of all the half-mortals with Albiana blood."

"Did you ever ask Melia to be your vessel?"

"She rejected me."

Jade got up and paced the cramped cabin. *"Before or after Plantine?"*

"Before and after."

"I can't believe Melia was your first choice! That makes me, what? Number three?"

"A half-mortal with Albiana blood is the most desirable vessel."

He was starting to sound like an Artificial Intelligence program on a loop. Jade rubbed her arms. *"You told me I was special!"*

"You are, my precious Jade. And once you receive me, there will be no one in the Whole more special than you."

"You need to promise me from now on I'll be the only one. You have to promise me you won't make anyone else your vessel!"

"My precious, Jade, my strength is rebuilding. I'm preparing myself with great anticipation for our union. Once that is complete, we will be as one. We will only need each other."

She considered pressing Umbra for help with the upcoming challenge, but that would require enlightening him about Melia's change of heart. If he knew Melia was willing to fight for the right to be the vessel of incarnation, would Umbra abandon Jade? God, that would be so humiliating.

She couldn't let that happen.

The challenge, the Grey Council, Melia, none of it would matter if the incarnation took place before they arrived in Minnanon.

The basin and the sword were on the ship. Jade had to find them.

"Our souls must entwine soon," Jade whispered in her mind. *"I'll make it happen."*

"That would please me," Umbra said.

50. Black Magic Vow

Lilliane sat with her back straight and her chin high in the sitting room of her suite, facing the door.

It opened, and Gavin entered. As usual, his uniform and grooming were meticulous.

"Thank you for coming." She squeezed the chair's armrests. "I wasn't sure you would."

He executed a precise bow. "I'm here to serve you, Princess."

"While the sentiments you express are most agreeable, I must question their sincerity."

He glanced at the door. "You're displeased with me?"

Lilliane rose to cross the room. She picked up an engraved box. When she turned to face him, his face was ashen. "So many knights," her voice lilted as she approached him. "More regiments arrive each day. Illialei is crawling with them, and yet not one of them could tell me who that girl was." She threw the box at him.

He ducked.

"You killed a pack of wild dogs!" She stalked toward him. "How dare you defy me?" She slapped his face.

His eyes snapped. The mask of chivalry cracked. He knotted her hair in his fist. "You're out of control, Princess."

They panted as they glared at one another.

"If you let me go now, I won't order your execution," she hissed.

"Illialei is destined to become quite the bloodbath under your rule."

"No bloodier than Tyrannis! What was your plan? Take possession of the sword and basin behind my back, woo the half-faerie to incarnate Umbra, then steal my throne?"

He thrust his fist at her head. His knuckles thumped her skull as he pushed her away, releasing her in the process.

She smoothed the snarl he'd made of her hair, wincing when she touched the tender spot where he'd struck her.

"You could have stopped her in the rose garden." He marched to her fireplace. There was no fire in it, only cold black coals.

"Perhaps, if I hadn't been told she was dead! It wasn't I who possessed Koldis and lost it," she hissed.

He straightened his sleeves and smoothed the front of his jacket. "Don't presume to lecture me, Princess."

She approached a parchment on the table. "If this message is to be believed, Ormrun and Koldis are no longer in Faerie; Jade and Melia have sailed to the Isle of Minnanon, where they will deliver the basin and sword to the Grey Council for safekeeping."

Gavin jerked his head from side to side to loosen the rictus of his jaw. "I can confirm that intelligence."

"My mother believes this will end the threat against our throne." She locked her eyes with his. "But I don't. My cousin is sly. You must follow them."

"And do what? Storm the Grey Citadel?"

"You must overtake them!"

He snorted. "Unless you possess the means to make a ship fly, that will be impossible. They've been at sea for more than a moon cycle."

"And you didn't bring me this news when you first heard of it?"

"My thoughts align with your mother's."

Lilliane sank in her chair. She poured a cup of tea. After she added a dollop of cream, she took a careful sip. "Pressina and Plantine are already on the island. Melia, along with her mother and sister, have violated the Albiana decrees. Jade assaulted me. I'll craft a missive demanding you be allowed to escort the criminals back to

Illialei. The Grey Council is reasoned, they respect the law. They won't deny an official request from the queen."

The muscles in Gavin's jaw flexed. "Will you forge her seal?"

"It won't be the first time."

He compressed his lips with such force they disappeared in his beard.

"And this time"—she smoothed her skirts—"you'll bring me the hearts of four half-faeries!"

He slouched in the chair opposite her.

She leaned forward. "And before you leave, you'll take a black magic vow."

He raised his head to glare at her.

"Yes"—she stood and looked down her nose at him—"this time you won't lie to me." With a black magic vow she'd own him; his heart would stop beating if he violated the pact.

Gavin ran his fingers though his hair. "And what if the Grey Council is not so accommodating? What if they won't release the prisoners to me?"

"Then you must find some other way to cut out their hearts. My mother and my aunt made a grave mistake, breeding with mortals. My throne won't be secure until the half-faeries with Albiana blood are dead."

He grabbed her wrist. "Your bloodlust exceeds your ambition."

"Hah!" She laughed in his face. "You had no care for life when it was your ambition you sought to further." She waited for him to release her.

He glared at her.

"You so wish for a throne of your own, don't you, Gavin?"

He dropped her hand and turned his reddened face away from her. "Isn't that what we all want, Princess—a throne of our own?"

This time her laughter sounded as pleasant as wind chimes.

His jaw softened.

"I'll need a consort." She leaned forward and touched her lips to his forehead. The impulse surprised her. He grabbed her waist. She

439

trembled in his grip, and knew he felt her excitement.

"I'll not be your consort. I'll rule beside you as a king," Gavin said.

Lilliane stared over his head. In the distance, brownies rolled ball in the Footing Fields.

His soldiers were loyal to him alone. Deprived of his leadership, they were as likely to flee Faerie as they were to settle into lives of debauchery within Illialei's borders. Undisciplined without the command of their superior officer, the average Huron knight was as carnal as any mortal when it came to the faeries of flower and field.

She needed him. "Illialei has never had a king."

Gavin released her, and she staggered away from him, rubbing her wrist. He poured himself a cup of tea. "Together, we could reach farther than Illialei."

Lilliane sat down across from him. "And what about your fiancé?"

Gavin waved his hand. "I've taken no vow." He refilled her cup. "Cream?"

"Please."

"Then we've reached an understanding?" he asked.

"Take the black magic vow. Fulfill it, and our engagement will commence."

The princess examined the latest blooms in her garden. As she harvested the blackest petals for Gavin's vow, her mind wandered to the sapphire lily. For a long time now, she'd considered harvesting the lily and sealing its dead blossoms upon a plaque to display above the queen's throne.

But what if the legend was true? What if the gods of Azyllai gave Gwyneth the seed that secured the right of her lineage to reign over Illialei? What would they do if her descendant destroyed the flower? Would they finally come down from their mountain home and intercede?

The gods never interfered, not even when her great-grandmother committed genocide. But that war ended before it began, and it never extended beyond Illialei's borders.

What would the gods do if the entire enchanted world fought for the right to rule the Realm of Faerie, their precious portal to the mortal world?

Lilliane snipped another ebony bloom from the vine. She counted the petals in her basket. Twenty-three—six more than the potion required. She told the guard she was returning to her suite, that she didn't need an escort.

On the way to the east tower, she stopped by the library. There, in the undisturbed quiet she could think.

Now that Aldous was gone, the place felt abandoned. Lilliane followed a carpeted aisle to a large sitting area. She set her basket on the table before lowering herself into the wing chair. With her feet curled beneath her, she recalled her earlier conversation with Gavin.

A marriage founded upon a black magic vow wasn't exactly the romantic liaison she'd fantasized about when she was younger. She circled her fingers around her waist, reliving the quivering breathlessness she experienced when Gavin seized her. But his boldness tantalized her.

Lilliane threaded her way through the apple orchard. Although her steps were careful, twigs snapped beneath her feet. Her long, dark cloak caught on a leafless branch, and she pulled it closer around her.

Gavin waited for her, at the edge of the trees astride a horse. He jumped down, helped her mount, then returned to the saddle, sitting behind her.

Although the moons were dark, Lilliane had no desire to be identified with Gavin late at night. She arranged her cloak to cover her hair.

They rode to Southend Pier.

At the sound of the sea, Lilliane's anticipation quickened. "Veer south," she whispered.

Gavin stopped the horse before they reached the beach. After they dismounted, he led the horse to a lone tree and tethered its reins.

Lilliane approached the waves. She imagined the entire sea as Umbra. She summoned her memory of the moment she learned the knight lied to her, that Jade still lived. Her nostrils narrowed, her jaw clenched, her shoulders became rigid. She imagined Umbra's black energy filling her, fueling her will.

She felt Gavin's presence beside her. A sachet and dagger hung from her waist. "Kneel before me," she said.

"This is truly not necessary, Princess," he said.

"If you don't do as I say, I'll travel to Huros myself, where I'll seek an audience with my father. I'll detail your gross actions against me, and assure he understands how you've harmed me."

Gavin knelt before her.

"Remove your coat."

He laid it in the sand.

Pleased as much by his silence as his obedience, she smiled. "Give me your wrist." She peeled back the thin cloth of the shirt covering his arm. Keeping hold of his wrist, she slid her hand into the folds of her cloak and slipped her dagger from its sheath. She began just beneath his elbow joint and dug the blade down the length of his forearm.

His body tensed. He let out a long slow whistle.

She dropped his arm and returned the bloody blade to her waist. She threw back her hood, removed the sachet, and tugged at its silken strings. When it was open, she kneeled facing Gavin. She snapped her fingers, and he offered her his bloody forearm. She searched the cut with her fingers. When she found its center, she dug her thumb into the broken flesh.

He winced.

She emptied the sachet's contents—crushed black rose petals, the stingers from two bees ground to dust, and a sprinkling of black pepper infused with a drop of her own blood—into the wound. She pushed the grains deep into the flesh. "Gavin Tovar, bring me the hearts of four half-faeries or your lungs will quit breath."

"Lilliane Albiana, I will do as you command or relinquish my life."

"Go now, and do as I have bid you! Do not seek me again until your vow is fulfilled." A swell of dark energy rose within Lilliane's body. She paused to savor the sensation.

Gavin didn't rise with her.

Lilliane covered her head and walked quickly to the horse. She mounted the beast and galloped to the palace alone.

51. Dragon Claw

Sinjiin examined Melia's hand. The single midnight blue claw remained. She'd taken to hiding it in a loose bandage.

"Tell me about your recent dreams," the mage said.

"Every night I dream I'm a cerulean dragon. I fly throughout the enchanted world to places I've never been to or seen."

"What is your mood?" Sinjiin asked.

"Triumphant, joyous."

"And you fly alone?"

"I do, but I don't feel alone."

"What do you mean?"

"I mean Ryder is always with me."

"Flying with you?"

"No, I always carry him in my heart."

Sinjiin shook his head.

"Please, don't dismiss that," Melia said. "His presence is strong within me, the knowledge that he loves me, that he waits for me somewhere beyond the clouds. That he'll be there when I return."

"Then you're searching for him?" the mage asked.

Melia studied the deck's weathered planks. "No."

"He dreams he flies with you," Sinjiin said.

"I know. He tells me."

"I would feel better if the two of you flew together in your dreams as well," he said.

"Why don't we?"

"You're asking me?"

"I love him. We're bound to one another. What am I missing?"

"Do you feel like you're missing something?"

Melia dug her single claw into the ship's railing, chipping the faded paint before she caught herself. "I'm afraid if we marry, he'll violate his faerie troth. Not on purpose, but in the careless way all mortals do."

"And yet, he isn't a mortal."

"But he has mortal blood."

"We think he does. We know you do. Doesn't that make it likely you'll violate the troth?"

"I'm the one with faerie blood; I won't have to take the troth."

"A half-faerie, half-mortal married to a half-Idonnai, half-mortal would be unique."

"Ryder is half-Idonnai?"

Sinjiin's teeth gleamed. "I've never shared my theory of his lineage with you?"

"No, you haven't. Have you shared it with him?"

"No."

"Why not?"

"If my theory is correct, he doesn't care for his father."

Melia fidgeted. "Your theory might be wrong. From what I've heard, Ryder bears no physical resemblance to the Idonnai."

"Yet his head for details, innate discipline, and talent for research bears a striking resemblance to those who excel in the priesthood."

Melia felt uneasy. Ryder strode across the deck in their direction. "He's coming," she whispered. "You could tell him now."

He stood between them. "Tell who what?"

Melia coughed.

Ryder rubbed her back. "Are you all right?"

Sinjiin shook his head.

Maybe the mage was right. Maybe it would be better if Ryder and Sinjiin were alone when the mage shared his suspicions. Melia raised her hand. "I was just discussing my claw with Sinjiin."

"It's strange, don't you think?" Ryder asked his friend.

"I think we should sit with her tonight, and observe her while she sleeps," Sinjiin said. "We should be able to tell when she begins to dream."

"What will that do?" Melia asked.

"We need to begin somewhere." The mage raised his arm up and down, sweeping the length of Melia from head to foot. "It will get awkward if more of you shifts and won't let go."

"Is that the problem with my hand?" Melia asked. "It won't let go?"

"Let me examine it once more," Sinjiin said.

Melia unraveled the white cloth she'd rewound around her hand. The claw was longer than the rest of her fingernails, its blue-black spike thick and sharp.

"When did it first appear?" Sinjiin asked.

"It wasn't until we boarded the ship," Ryder said.

She nodded.

"Can you remember if there was a particular event that preceded its appearance? Perhaps something made you angry or disturbed?" Sinjiin probed.

Melia scanned her memory. They'd been at sea for almost two moon cycles, and the days were an indistinguishable blur. Although the temperatures dropped the farther north they sailed, there'd been no storms, and the constant south winds aided their speed. If the winds maintained, they'd arrive at their destination soon. It was as if the gods of Azyllai watched over the ship.

Melia's mind clicked. She glanced around, not wanting anyone else to hear her confession. "It was Jade."

"What happened?" Sinjiin asked.

Melia shaded her eyes to see Ryder's face. "It was the day she kissed you."

The mage rounded on his friend. "You didn't tell me the girl kissed you."

Ryder crossed his arms. "There was nothing to tell."

Sinjiin took Melia's hand and waved it in front of Ryder's face. "Someone disagrees with you."

"I told her," Ryder said in a loud whisper.

"You told her what?"

Ryder dropped his arms. "I told her I ran into Jade. It was one of the days when it was raining. It was cold and she forgot her cloak. I gave her mine before joining her on deck. I stood behind her to shield her from the wind. She turned around and brushed her lips against mine. It was brief and meaningless."

"But you told Melia."

"Of course, I told her. Why wouldn't I?"

"Good point," Sinjiin conceded. "And it made you angry?" he asked Melia.

"It made me furious."

"Did you dream that night?"

All her dreams collapsed into a single memory. "I saw them!"

"Who?" Sinjiin asked.

"I saw Ryder and Jade together." She whirled upon him, as if the scene had been real. It had felt real. "I saw them from a distance, two black specks inching along together, but I knew it was them! I flew closer, but they were so focused on each other, they didn't see me."

Sinjiin nodded. "Go on."

"They were walking on a beach and crawling over jagged rocks. Ryder was helping Jade find her way." An inhuman bellow erupted from deep within Melia. Her deep blue eyes rounded with shock. Her mouth shot open as she expelled a stream of dark smoke. "What just happened?" she asked Sinjiin.

Sinjiin raised his eyebrows. "How did it feel to watch Ryder helping Jade?"

"I wanted to claw her eyes out!"

Sinjiin reached for Melia's hand and flicked the hard blue-black claw that extended from her finger. "This would do the job."

Melia pulled her hand from his and studied the blue-black spike.

She opened her other palm and dragged the claw across it. A thin line of blood emerged.

"What are you doing?" Ryder asked.

"Sinjiin's right. I could do a lot of damage with this."

"Precisely," the mage said. "Now that you understand your power, you must stop pretending it doesn't exist and learn to wield it with more precision."

"I don't understand," Melia said.

Sinjiin squatted and motioned for her and Ryder to do the same. He traced a circle on the deck. "This is the core of you, the deepest truth of your experience. It never lies." He drew four concentric rings around the central circle. "These layers of consciousness both protect and obstruct your central core. Your history of dark moon visions has left you wary of your darker emotions, but you mustn't repress them. Especially if your animal totem is a dragon."

"I can't give them free reign. I'd—"

Sinjiin tapped Melia's forehead. "To mediate your desires you must acknowledge them. You wish to harm Jade. She's challenged your right to incarnate Umbra and become queen. She tries to steal Ryder's heart from you."

"You see it too!"

"I do. I also see his unwavering devotion to you. Do you see that as well?"

Melia flinched.

"No, you close your inner eye to that," Sinjiin said.

He was right; she was quick to follow any path her worst fears laid down, and just as nimble to avoid any road that required her to have faith in someone other than herself.

"Melia, if you incarnate Umbra—"

"If. If. If. If I can acknowledge my darkness. If I can channel it. If I can balance it with my light. If I can have faith in Ryder's love."

Sinjiin rocked back on his heels. "Was that so difficult?"

Confused, Melia looked to Ryder for help. Judging by the crease between his eyebrows, Sinjiin's lesson wasn't any clearer to him.

She returned her gaze to the mage.

"You're afraid you can't do what needs to be done," Sinjiin said. "Instead of burying that fear and pretending it doesn't exist, face it." He stabbed the central circle drawn in the residue of salt and dirt. "Your love, your hate. Your fear, your anger. Your joy, your hope. It's all energy. It's all you. Embrace all of it. Harness all of it."

Melia shook her head. "You make it sound so easy."

"You can't see how far you've come, but I can," the mage said. "Do you remember the first time you saw me in the palace library? When you turned to run, you tripped and lost your balance."

A small laugh escaped her as she felt the blush rise in her cheeks.

"The girl I met that day could never have forgiven her sister's crimes, or saved Sevondi at the Muudron Stone. She could never have sacrificed the freedom of flight for the possibility of love. Have faith in yourself. Have faith in who you are. Every single bit of it."

Melia squirmed. Could she do that? Could she stop fighting herself? A strange milky fog descended as her thoughts spiraled in on themselves. The white mist swirled and thickened. The world around her receded.

I hop from boulder to boulder. My claws gripping and releasing rock. Ryder winds his way between the large stones. He's laughing, and the sound of it fills my heart with joy. We approach a riverbed.

There's someone on the other side, a woman. She's watching us. Her long dark hair is familiar. Her nose ring glints in the sunlight. It's Nandana.

I flap my wings and rise into the sky. Excitement propels me in her direction, before I remember Ryder. I circle back and land beside him. Like Sinjiin, I press my belly to the earth.

"Fly with me," I say.

He swings his leg across my back. I feel his hands on the twin ridges that run the length of my spine.

I return to the sky. We soar as one. It's the most magnificent thing I've ever felt, a physical expression of the union of our hearts.

On the other side of the river, Nandana layers twigs, kindling, and logs with great care. She slips a box of flint from a fold in her tunic. With a single strike, a flame dances. She places it against the smallest twig. Its tip reddens, and the flame jumps from the flint to a slender stalk of wood. The flame multiplies. The fire grows.

When it burns as tall as Nandana, she pulls one of the burning sticks from it.

"Eat this," she tells me. "To extinguish the doubt that thrives in your belly."

I open my rectangle of a mouth.

She shoves the scorching heat down my throat. I swallow it whole. To me, in my dragon form, it's smooth like golden honey.

Nandana shows me the palms of her hand. They're covered with blue ink. The same ink she used to mark my forehead many moons ago. Instinctively, I fall before her, dropping my belly to the ground.

She presses one palm against my forehead, the other she presses flat against the crown of my head.

Blue lightning flashes before my eyes. Thunder echoes through the skies.

"Your destiny is near," she says. "Ryder came to you. He's never doubted you. He'll be by your side forever. When you comprehend that, comprehending right and wrong will be easy."

I look down at my hands. My fingers are pale and long. The skin of my face is soft to touch. I run along the edge of the river. I've returned to my faerie form.

Her eyes fluttered open.

Ryder held her in his arms, bracing her back with his hands.

Sinjiin watched her carefully.

"I ..."

The mage pointed to her hand. The claw was gone.

❖ ❖ ❖

"Where has Flora been hiding?" Melia asked Tatou.

"She's guarding the trunk."

"From whom?"

"Who do you think?"

"Jade?"

"Yes, she's become Aldous' best friend, following him everywhere, and asking him a lot of questions about the incarnation. About how it's supposed to work."

"Does she think she's going to incarnate Umbra here on the ship?"

"Flora is suspicious."

"Why didn't anyone tell me?"

"Your hand and all." The pixie landed on her shoulder. "Don't be upset we kept it from you. We all came on this trip to help you, and that's what we've been doing. Keeping an eye on Jade."

"Where is the trunk?"

"Locked up in Flora's room, but Jade must think it's down in the hold with the rest of the cargo. She's been caught snooping around down there several times. She always has a different excuse for why she's wandering around."

Melia pointed to the fog-covered grey mound in the distance. "If that's what Jade's up to, she doesn't have much time. There's the Isle of Minnanon."

Tatou walked down Melia's arm. The half-faerie flipped her hand over so the pixie could sit shielded in the cup of her palm. "Are you ready to see your mother and Plantine?"

"So much has happened since the last time I saw them. I'm not sure what to expect." Melia wanted to feel invulnerable the next time she saw Pressina, yet she still couldn't do the one thing she really wanted to do. "I'm still unable to transform into a dragon at will. I'm afraid I won't ever be able to do it."

"But you're making progress. Are you meditating?"

Melia turned around and leaned against the railing. "On my darkness?"

"The way Sevondi told you to."

Melia slouched. "Have you ever tried to meditate on the darkness within yourself? It's unpleasant."

"I'm not sure it's supposed to be pleasant."

"Yes, I've been practicing."

"And?"

Melia gave her head a slight shake. "If it's truly a source of energy, I don't think I'll ever run out. There seems to be an endless pool inside me. I'm still angry with my mother, and hurt she left me to die in the Calashai's dungeon. Olivia's treatment of her, along with me and my sisters, is another sore point. And don't get me started on Lilliane or Jade." She stiffened.

"What?" Tatou asked.

The half-faerie pointed.

On the opposite side of the deck, Jade's slim frame trailed behind Aldous. She juggled what looked like several large manuscripts as Aldous' loud tenor boomed over the sounds of the sea and the crew.

"I wonder what they're up to," Melia remarked.

"Aldous is polishing his presentation for the council. He wants his conclusion to be unimpeachable."

"Jade's helping him build the case for my incarnating Umbra?"

"I suspect she doesn't know that's what she's doing, exactly."

"She should never have underestimated Aldous or Flora. Let's go say hello to them," Melia said.

"I thought your strategy was a wall of silence."

"Maybe it's time to change it."

Tatou flitted to her friend's shoulder as Melia dodged ropes and ducked beneath booms.

"Good afternoon," Aldous called out.

52. Peppermint Tea

Two more days. The reality played over and over in Jade's mind. Two more days.

She crept down the rickety steps to the bilge. She'd searched for the plain trunk with steel girders in every area cargo was stored except this one. The smell in the lowest level of the ship had kept her away. It was hard to imagine something as glorious as the blue shimmering blade with its ruby-embedded hilt among this filth.

She pinched her nose as she sloshed through ankle-deep water. Ahead, two sailors worked with pails beneath a swinging lantern. Moving through shadow, and between towers of crates, she was invisible to them. Jade paused as her eyes, squinting in the glare of winter sunlight moments before, grew accustomed to the gloom. She felt in her pocket for the stub of wax and matches leftover from her previous searches.

If she could just find Ormrun and Koldis, it would be easy enough to fill the basin with seawater. There was an incantation, but Aldous hinted it was more of a ritual than a necessity. If she made contact with Umbra prior to plunging the sword through the basin's center, it might be enough. She had to try.

The smell of brackish water mixed with waste forced her to take shallow breaths as she headed toward the other end of the ship. The machinery, supplies, broken equipment, torn sails, rope, and chain she passed by didn't lift her hopes.

Jade slammed her foot into the hull of the ship. She'd reached the farthest point, and the trunk wasn't down here. She'd waded through all this shitty water for nothing.

Jade joined the others for dinner. It was the first time she ate with them since they left Tyrannis. Other than a brief greeting, she didn't say anything to anyone; no one spoke to her, either. But she watched their faces. One of them knew where the basin and sword was.

It wasn't the captain.

Jade studied Aldous next. He was incapable of subterfuge. Besides, she'd been in and out of his cabin many times. There was no place large enough to hide the trunk in there. Her eyes landed on Melia. The first time she saw her in Balboa Park, Jade dismissed her as insignificant. Now she seemed to glow with some inner strength Jade was denied.

It wasn't fair—but Melia didn't have access to Ormrun and Koldis. She would have already incarnated Umbra if she did. Scratch her and the pixie off the list; they shared a cabin.

Ryder, Sinjiin, and the spring faerie remained as the most likely suspects.

They each had their own cabin.

If Ryder caught her searching his cabin after their ill-fated kiss on deck, it would be mortifying—or worse. Ryder didn't keep secrets from his girlfriend. If he had the trunk, Melia would know, and Umbra would already be incarnated. Scratch him off the list.

That left Sinjiin and Flora.

The spring faerie bored into her with those cold, dark eyes.

Jade averted her gaze to the untouched food on her plate.

She knew where the trunk was.

Jade lay awake, her eyes open in the dark. *"Umbra!"*

Deafening silence met her plea.

Umbra came to her because Melia rejected him and Plantine

failed him. She needed to make the incarnation happen before he discovered Melia wouldn't reject him again.

How to get inside Flora's cabin? She wasn't like Aldous, easily flattered with an onslaught of questions. Jade would have to find another way to search the fat old faerie's things. Tomorrow.

After tonight, she had one more day.

One more day.

A lightbulb went off in Jade's mind. It was an awful, terrible idea. She hated it immediately.

But she only had …

One more day.

The next morning, Jade took a metal cup down to the bilge. She filled it with the disgusting backwater and snuck through the ship's galleries.

Outside the kitchen, she looked for a crevice to hide the cup.

"My mother's not feeling well," she told the cook. "I'd like to take her a pot of peppermint tea." It would cover the bad taste and potent smell.

"Poor dear," the cook said, as she boiled a kettle over the fire.

Outside the kitchen, Jade retrieved the cup of brown liquid she'd set aside. It looked like something from a spittoon and smelled worse. Apologizing to some unnamed benevolent spirit, she poured as much of it into the brewing tea as she dared.

When she reached the cabin she shared with her mother, Jade pushed the door open with her foot. "Morning," she chirped. "I brought you some tea."

"You're up early." Her mother, still in bed, pushed herself to sitting. "Aren't you a sweetheart?"

All those years of pharmaceuticals had made Lola's stomach sensitive. The slightest thing could set off a bout of nausea. Despite the health she'd regained since she arrived in the enchanted world, Jade counted on her stomach remaining sensitive. Because when her mother became ill, Jade would run to Flora for help. The spring faerie was a healer, and she adored Lola. She wouldn't be able to say no. While she tended her patient, Jade could search her cabin.

Jade tensed as her mother took a sip of tea. She tried to appear cheerful when Lola patted her hand.

Her mother's nose wrinkled. "Do you know if the tea is leftover from yesterday? It has an unpleasant aftertaste."

Jade gazed at her fingers clenched in her lap. The tea wouldn't kill her mother. "No. I watched the cook make it before I brought it to you. Maybe it's too strong."

Lola took a few more sips, her face contorting after each one.

If she would just finish the cup. "Do you want me to try it?"

"Why don't you?"

Jade plastered a patient smile on her face as she took the cup from her mother. It was already half empty. Her mother wiped her forehead and gazed out the CD-sized porthole. Jade held the cup to her lips and pretended to take a sip. "Oh, I think it's just extra strong." She gave it back to her mother. "I'll tell the cook she used too much peppermint. Would you like me to bring you another pot?"

Lola waved her hand. "Heavens, no." She gulped the remaining liquid before setting the cup down on a short barrel that served as a precarious table. She wrinkled her nose again and wiped her mouth with the back of her hand. "I'm not sure it was too much peppermint. Maybe the water was polluted or something. Which is strange, since everything in the enchanted world is so fresh. It almost tasted like there was salt in it." Lola doubled over, clutching her abdomen.

"Mom, what's wrong?" Jade tried to sound sincere.

"The tea isn't settling well."

Jade reached for a bucket and held it as her mother heaved into it. Lola fell back on the bed, her face white and forehead clammy.

"I'll get Flora," Jade said.

Lola's face spasmed. "Please, tell her to come quickly."

Jade raced through the corridors. Her heart pounding in her

chest was louder than her feet banging against the plank walkways. She hammered on the spring faerie's door. "My mother is sick!" She heard movement on the other side of the door and banged harder.

When the door swung open, she almost hit Flora. The spring faerie's eyes were black slits, but she held a basket. Jade gazed beyond her, searching the cabin. It was much larger than the one she shared with her mother.

"What are you looking for?" Flora snapped.

Jade refocused on the spring faerie. "Nothing."

Flora whistled a shrill, piercing sound. The walls shuddered around them as the tiger bounded into view.

"This one came to get me." Flora pointed at Jade. "Her mother has taken ill. I'm going to tend to her. Stay here, would you, while I'm gone?"

Sinjiin roared.

Jade saw sharp teeth and a huge tongue. Crap.

"Lead the way," Flora said to Jade.

Two hours later, Lola slept soundly in her bed.

Jade glared out the porthole. The grey mound that was the Isle of Minnanon grew larger with each passing second.

The spring faerie packed up her basket. She began sniffing around Lola's bed. Her brow crinkled.

Jade lunged for the tea pot, but Flora's reflexes were quicker than hers. The spring faerie jerked the pot from her grasp. "You did this to your mother."

It wasn't a question.

"Mixed bilge water with her tea, did you?"

Jade squirmed.

"And you fancy yourself fit to be queen of the enchanted world? There's no question the Albiana blood runs thick in you. If it were up to me, I'd send you to Lilliane wrapped in a big bow."

"She wants to kill me!" Jade shouted.

"And who do you want to kill, missy? I don't see a saint standing before me."

Jade opened and closed her mouth.

Flora tossed her head in Lola's direction. "You're a shame on her."

Jade struggled for a retort, but Flora's uncanny grasp of her crime rendered her incapable of speech. "Are you going to tell her what I did?"

Flora snorted. "Don't think she doesn't already know."

Jade's stomach felt like it was spewing its contents into her throat. "No."

"You should have thought of that when you set your mind on cheating. I supported your challenge when you made it, you remember that. But what you did this morning; you've disgraced yourself. Shown your weakness for all to see. Even your poor mother, who's done nothing but love you with all her heart."

"Don't judge me!"

Flora huffed again. "When we land on the Isle of Minnanon, you're going to meet Melia's mother. Those two have their quarrels with one another, but Pressina's fire runs in her daughter's veins. Don't say I didn't warn you." The spring faerie turned and left.

Jade smashed the teapot against the wall.

Lola didn't move. Flora's sleeping draught had knocked her out.

Jade collapsed on the floor.

53. The Isle of Minnqnon

Melia walked down the gangplank, holding Ryder's hand. "Where are the grey faeries?" she asked.

The docks appeared to be deserted. Beyond the stone walkway and a row of flat rectangular warehouses, all she saw were deep green trees, casting dark purple shadows beneath a cold, grey sky. The smallest snowflakes swirled around them, the dots melting as soon as they touched the ground.

Ryder indicated the tall mast in the deck's center. "Once the ship's cargo has been unloaded, they'll raise a flag. A greeting contingent will arrive to welcome us. They'll carry us to the populated part of the island. As soon as I get you settled onshore, I'll help the crew finish unloading."

Tatou poked her head from Melia's pocket. "Tell Petey to raise the flag now! I'm dying of cold." She wrapped her new fur coat tighter.

During the sea journey, whenever it became too cold for the pixie to leave her room, Petey sorely missed her presence on deck. Handy with a needle and thread, the crewman labored over a miniature coat. Delighted with the gift, Tatou perched on his shoulder every day the icy gusts didn't threaten to carry her away. Petey credited Tatou's presence for the *Silver Dolphin's* uneventful trip from Tyrannis. Undeterred by the discrepancy in their sizes, he proposed marriage to her. Tatou politely declined his offer.

Melia and Tatou waited with Flora and Aldous, while Ryder and

Sinjiin helped the sailors unload their baggage, along with most of the ship's cargo.

Sevondi had shipped the grey faeries several trunks of Tyrannis exports, a gift from the country's new regent. They weren't the only gifts she sent on the ship. In the hold, there were trunks from the dragonwitch for all the major countries in the enchanted world: the Black Magic Islands, Idonne, Kyrakkos, Morganna, and Typhos, even Huros and Misgradde.

Despite Huros' current alliance with the Albiana, Sevondi thought it wise to make a friendly gesture. As far as the dwarves of Misgradde, they were isolationists, but Sevondi believed sending them a few chests of raw metal extracted from the Ruadain Mountains might tempt them.

"I'm frozen solid," Tatou squeaked.

"They've raised the flag." Melia searched the trees for movement. At first glance, the woods reminded her of the Balyudor, but the trees here were quite different. Tall and straight columns, they towered to the sky. "I don't see or hear anyone coming."

"If I was warm and comfortable inside, I wouldn't be in a rush to greet us either," Tatou said. "Maybe you should start walking."

"Which direction do you suggest?" Melia asked.

"Away from the ocean."

A sailor in the crow's nest shouted and waved his arm.

"He's spotted something," Melia said.

Several carriages rolled into view. Their grey enamel exteriors, shiny black wheels, and the glossy horses pulling them, suggested unlimited wealth. Their drivers remained impassive as Melia and Aldous waved.

Flora kept her hands jammed in her apron pocket, which was tied over a bulky coat. The deep frown on the spring faerie's face betrayed no emotion. The grimace was her typical expression when she observed her surroundings.

At the sound of the many wheels grinding against the rock and shell road, Tatou peered out again. "Why are they passing us by?

Hey!" she yelled.

None of the drivers heard the pixie.

A ways behind them, Lola and Jade also watched the carriages roll by.

Melia counted seven in all.

"I thought they were supposed to greet us," Tatou said.

"There," Flora grunted.

A white carriage, shinier than the others, rolled into view. Six white horses with plumed headdresses pulled it. Their high steps made them look like they were dancing. The driver wore a great white cloak with epaulettes and puffed sleeves embroidered with silver thread. His white hair coiled over his shoulder in a single long braid. The carriage rolled to a stop, its door even with Melia.

The door opened. A white gloved hand beckoned as a deep, melodious voice spoke. "My name is Threldor. As a member of the Grey Council, I welcome Melia Albiana, second daughter of Pressina Albiana and the Great Mortal Druid Elynus, to the Isle of Minnanon."

"Here we go," Flora grunted. "I suppose if she weren't with us, we'd have been left to turn into ice blocks, our thawed bodies discovered in the spring."

Threldor leaned forward to show his face. It was a face that made Melia take a sharp inhale. He could have been Elendah's brother. "The last spring faerie will always hold a place of honor among our kind," he said. "We would never forget you, Flora Della Snapdragon."

"Wouldn't your words melt a frozen brick of butter?" Flora huffed.

Although the rest of his face remained unreadable, Threldor's eyes twinkled. "I am likewise charmed."

Melia crawled into the carriage behind the spring faerie. As they jostled on the velvety seat across from their host, Aldous filed into the carriage. After Threldor acknowledged him with a lengthy title, the old elf settled next to the grey faerie. Threldor closed the door, but didn't secure the latch. Shortly, the carriage rolled to another slow stop. When Threldor leaned past the old wood elf to open the door again, Lola and Jade waited outside, their mouths gaping.

"Welcome to the Isle of Minnanon, Lola Blue Silver and Jade Rae Silver."

Lola blushed and Jade fidgeted under Threldor's gaze.

"And where is the tiger and the brave priest from Idonne?" he asked, after Lola and Jade squeezed in next to Aldous.

"They're helping the sailors unload the ship," Melia said.

"We'll wait for them," Threldor said.

Tatou fluttered from Melia's pocket. The grey faerie held out a palm. She landed in it.

"I've never had the honor of meeting a pixie," he said.

Tatou executed the most gracious curtsy she could muster, swamped as she was in her fur coat.

Threldor's face lit up.

Melia heard Ryder's voice.

Threldor opened the door. "Welcome to the Isle of Minnanon, Ryder, son of Anton, head of the Order of the Idonnai."

Melia's mouth dropped open as a dozen emotions thundered across Ryder's face.

Outside the carriage, Sinjiin's roar was deafening.

The heritage of the grey faeries lay in the depths of the Great White Sea. They revered and worshiped the water that birthed their kind. Indoor pools and aquariums were interspersed throughout the gleaming grey and white walls of their great city. Melia and Ryder walked along the edge of an indoor pool.

"Did you know?" Melia asked Ryder.

"No."

"How do they know?"

"I don't know. Perhaps Anton trades information with the council or has an ally among them."

"Do you doubt it?"

"Grey faeries don't deal in half-truths and rumor."

"But he's a priest—"

"And I'm surprised he remains at the head of the order if his paternity has become common knowledge."

"It must come as a shock to you."

Ryder laughed. "A greater shock to him when I stole Koldis."

"Do you think he'll forgive you?"

"I don't intend to seek his forgiveness."

"Then you'll never return to Idonne?"

"The only reason I'd return to that sandbox is to see Garrick and Shilda. Garrick was more of a father to me than Anton ever was."

Melia recognized the controlled anger in his voice. It dominated any other emotion the unexpected news and its method of delivery stirred in him. She understood the complicated feelings secrets regarding lineage engendered. "It seems we have more in common than we realized."

"The truth of our blood being kept from us," he agreed.

"You didn't ask Threldor about your mother."

"If he knew who she was, he would have announced it. It's unsettling," Ryder said. "To realize I've known my father my entire life and have always hated him."

Melia recalled the conflicted feelings she had for her father. He'd been absent and troublesome to her throughout his life. But in death, his soul, spirit, or whatever it was, came to her aid in a moment of dire need, and that's the way she chose to remember him.

Observing Ryder's struggle, she wondered if her father's death, by freeing her to remember their relationship as she chose, made her dishonest. Perhaps it was a gift she should simply accept. In a few hours, she'd face her very alive mother. She had no doubt she would wrestle with that relationship as much as Ryder did with the revelation of his father's identity.

"What about you?" he asked. "Are you ready to reunite with your sweet sister and her devoted mother?"

Melia laughed. His teasing eased her tension. "If I can't face my mother, how will I ever be able to handle Umbra?"

Ryder's eyes sparkled. "Pressina is more formidable than Umbra. And Plantine ..."

"She survived the incarnation. I must ask her about the experience. Do you think my mother will oppose me?"

"I doubt it. You're the last hope to dethrone her sister."

"Threldor said nothing about Plantine's judgment, only that they would be at dinner. It must not be too bad—"

"If they allow her to eat," Ryder completed her thought.

Melia released another soft laugh. "Yes."

Ryder took her hands in his. "I know you didn't want to come here. I know, after what you saw at the Veiled Tavern, you believed this journey would be a waste of precious time. But I'm relieved we're here."

Melia gazed at the gleaming stone walls. "Being here brings home the weight of our hopes."

"There's a court in Idonne. On occasion, I sat in on the proceedings. Their methods could be tedious, but there was a purpose to the detail, and great wisdom in attending to it when much was at stake."

"Then you're still committed to the Grey Council's decision, whatever the outcome?"

"Yes. You're not?"

"Since we've landed, my emotions swing from extreme to extreme—fear that Jade will win the challenge, terror that I'll destroy her with my newfound dragon strength. But I'm prepared to defer to the council. I confess, meeting Threldor has increased my confidence in its merit. If each grey faerie that sits upon it possesses a tenth of Elendah's wisdom, then we're in good hands."

"They won't approve of the incarnation if they think it will fail."

"I suppose I can take some comfort in that," Melia said.

"It may be the only comfort we'll have," Ryder said.

"Are you still dreaming about flying with me?"

"Every night."

"It's strange. Every day I feel a quiet strength and determination grow inside me. Yet it doesn't seem to reach my skin. I don't understand why it won't radiate fully outward. I'm sure that's why I've been unable to shift. In my dreams, when I become a dragon, I feel that strength and determination burn from my fingertips to the end of my toes. The feelings and sensations are so strong, and yet, when I'm awake a cool bubble encapsulates it. I wanted to master the shifting, to have confidence in it, before I faced the challenge. I've been counting on it to help me win."

"I've given it some thought," Ryder said.

"And?"

"I think it will be an issue of necessity."

"What do you mean?"

"I think as long as you keep dreaming, as along as you remain prepared, then the moment you need to become a dragon, the need will propel you across the invisible boundary that's impossible for you to cross before that time."

"Is that what Sinjiin told you?"

"Not in so many words. But I've quizzed him about the first time he shifted. There was an inciting incident. One day, his younger sister needed his protection. Two children, they'd wandered into forbidden territory and found themselves isolated and vulnerable. When he became aware of that need, in that moment, he became a tiger. It was effortless."

"And he led me to believe it was because he'd eaten tiger meat."

"I'm not saying that didn't play a part—"

"I'll not eat any dragon flesh," Melia said. "I don't even know where to find any. Where do dragons live these days?"

"The largest of the small surviving population lives around the volcanoes in Kyrakkos. They feel an affinity to that fiery land. Although there have been sightings of a lone dragon here and there in the Black Magic Islands, the Nameless Islands, and the mountains between Huros and Idonne."

"Have you ever seen a real one?" Melia asked.

"No."

"I've been thinking," Melia said. "The Ruadain Mountains would make such a lovely place for a dragon to live."

"Better than the Rolling Mountains that circle Lake Vivientiana?"

"You prefer Illialei to Tyrannis?" she asked.

"In my dreams, we fly over that lake and live peacefully among the stone faeries."

"Those ancient people?"

Ryder nodded.

"I've never met one. They never come down from the mountains."

"Perhaps when peace reigns once again in the enchanted world, they will."

"Do you think they shun the Albiana queens, and that's why they never venture into the valley?"

"From what I've read about them, stone faeries aren't fooled by appearances."

"You think they see through the Albiana beauty?"

"I do."

"Then they could also see through a half-faerie, half-mortal queen, who's incarnated Umbra and shifts into a dragon at will."

"They would see through to her sincerity, her generosity of spirit, her need for justice, and her determination to hope. In fact, that might be the kind of queen they could believe in."

A line of heat traveled from Melia's heart, through her arm, and flowed into her hand. Melia dipped her fingers into the pool's cool water. As soon as she touched the water's surface, it sizzled.

"What just happened?" Ryder asked.

"Your faith in me set my heart ablaze."

His green eyes sparked.

Melia traced a wet line across his cheek. "Is love dangerous, then?"

Ryder opened the brushed silver door. "Tuck."

Melia ran to greet the tree elf. She threw her arms around him and searched the empty hall behind him for her sister. "Where's Plantine?"

The elf stepped inside the room. "She'll meet us in the gallery. It's quite a maze, the inner labyrinth of the citadel."

"We went for a walk earlier and were barely able to find our way back to our rooms." Melia indicated her cobalt blue gown. Swathes of violet gauze floated in a train behind her. "Are they always so formal here?" She took a step back to admire Tuck's long, brown velvet jacket and high boots. The style matched the clothes Ryder wore, a deep black jacket and equally dark shirt, pants, and boots. "You both look dashing."

"The grey faeries are particular. Nothing about the citadel, the island, or their approach to life is careless. They cultivate discernment and objectivity in their every endeavor."

"Do you like it here?" Melia asked him.

"I do," Tuck said.

"Will you be staying much longer on the island?"

"It's likely that Plantine and I will make our home here."

"They embrace her, even after ..." Melia found it difficult to speak of Elendah's death as her fingers reached for the remaining pearls hanging from the chord around her neck.

"Plantine doesn't remain here by choice. Her detention is a condition of her judgment. That, and she wears a lead bracelet—to prevent her from performing unsupervised spells. She was found responsible for Elendah's death."

Melia sank into a pewter chair. "And my mother?"

"The council recognizes your mother's part in encouraging your sister's reckless behavior. She received the same sentence: detainment and she must also wear a lead bracelet."

"And you?"

"I remain with Plantine by choice. I love her, and I'll not abandon her. I'm fortunate the work I do here is useful as well as satisfying."

"What work is that?" Ryder asked.

"The grey faeries are reserved by nature. Naturally attuned to the passage of time, they're loathe to judge events which haven't fully played themselves out. But they recognize they've remained too aloof with regard to certain events. They've come to regret their lack of involvement in Illialei's affairs, especially the genocide of the spring faeries. They've initiated an investigation into the aptitude for magic by those with Albiana blood. Plantine and Pressina are of great interest to them. Their agreement to be studied allowed for leniency in their sentencing. I'm assigned to research related subjects by the grey faeries as they arise."

While she listened to the elf, Melia traced the intricate pattern of metalwork on the side of her chair.

"The skills I gained while serving as Aldous' apprentice are helpful to my work here." The tree elf paused. "Do you think he'll be upset that I'll be unable to help him establish the new library in the Dragon's Keep?"

Tuck's concern was so earnest Melia couldn't bring herself to mention the gnomes.

"I'm sure he'll understand your need to remain with Plantine," Ryder said.

"Yes, I'm sure he will." Melia embraced the meaning of her mother and sister's punishments: Pressina and Plantine wouldn't be sailing from Minnanon; they couldn't interfere with Melia's incarnation of Umbra; and the alliances Melia would build throughout the enchanted world under the guidance of Flora and Aldous would be safe from her mother's mercurial demands.

Her neck and shoulders softened. Perhaps, it would be nice to visit her mother and sister—for a short time.

Melia's pulse quickened as they climbed the steps leading to the gallery. Her eyes traveled the long room, searching among the crowd of silver and white-haired grey faeries for her mother's dark blond hair and her sister's pale golden halo.

There, at the far end of the hall, she caught a glimpse of her mother's ivory wings.

Ryder squeezed her hand. He must have spotted Pressina, too. Melia turned to face him. She needed a moment to collect herself. There was no way to predict what her mother's mood or frame of mind might be. She was a fool if she hoped for Pressina's support. Yet, the sight of her mother awakened some dormant desire for reconciliation Melia tried to cage.

Tuck, a few steps ahead of them, didn't stop moving.

Melia's gaze flitted left to right. "Where are Flora and Tatou? What about Aldous?" She emitted a burst of surprise.

"What?" Ryder followed her line of sight.

Jade climbed the galley steps wearing a blood-red gown. Every head turned to watch her ascent. Lola followed behind her, demure in caramel velvet. The girl's wild hair and tiny frame radiated pride and defiance. The crowd lavished her with curiosity.

Melia's stomach pitched. In spite of Jade's brash arrogance, Lola loved her daughter; Pressina banished Melia from their tree house– and abandoned her to death on the day of Plantine's misguided wedding.

The difference in their states was stark: one beloved by her mother, the other abhorred by her mother. The awareness hit Melia hard.

Ryder must have sensed her downward spiral. "The Grey Council found your mother and your sister guilty with good reason. Don't allow them, or their cool feelings toward you, to define your future. Yes, Jade has her mother by her side. But you have me. Here come Flora and Aldous. And there's Tatou, with Threldor and Sinjiin."

Melia had to admit Jade's striking appearance paled next to Tatou, astride the majestic cat advancing at the side of the regal grey faerie. Every head in the gallery watched as the newcomers entered the throng.

"Have you spoken to your mother?" Flora asked, when she

reached them. Melia shook her head as the spring faerie took her hand. "Be generous with her. To be detained against her will is worse than chains for her."

"Your sympathy is unexpected," Melia said.

"Pressina has many shortcomings, but at heart, she's a free spirit. Let's see how she's faring. I'm curious, aren't you?"

"Curious isn't the word I'd use," Melia said.

"You're not the same young girl she raised. Or should I say neglected?"

Melia hurried to keep up with Flora. Ryder and Aldous flanked them. Melia lost sight of Tatou, Sinjiin and Threldor. Her eyes remained focused on Pressina's wings as Flora threaded through the crowd.

"Pressina, dearie," the spring faerie called out when she was within earshot. "Look who's come to visit you in your fancy jail."

Melia's mother turned. Her violet eyes widened, her pale cheeks flushed. "Flora. Melia. Aldous and Ryder." Pressina held her long slim hand out to the young priest.

Melia flinched. "Mother."

Pressina paused, scanning Melia from head to toe before leaning in to hug her in a stiff embrace.

"Sister!" Plantine cried out. She shoved past their mother and suffocated Melia in a tight hug. "I've missed you," Plantine whispered. "Ryder, Flora, Aldous," Plantine acknowledged them all.

Bells chimed.

"Dinner." Plantine grabbed Melia's hand. "Give Mother a chance," she whispered as they headed to a row of open doors. "The time here has changed her." Plantine led them to a large round table. When Jade approached them, Melia stiffened. "Mother is going to take care of her," Plantine whispered.

At surrounding tables, the grey faeries found their places and sat down.

With fluid movements, Pressina moved through the crowd,

waving a diamond-studded fan. A slim, black bracelet circled her wrist. "Allow me to introduce myself, Jade." Her words dripped with condescension. "I'm your great-aunt, Pressina, Queen Luisa's sister, and Melia's mother."

Jade stared at Pressina's proffered hand as if it were a snake. Lola attempted to insert herself into the conversation.

"And you must be my sister's granddaughter, Lola?" Pressina ignored her extended hand.

"We've not had a chance to meet Luisa or Lilliane," Lola said.

"A pity. The grey faeries are so interested in learning more about our mutual relatives," Pressina said. "Perhaps they could arrange an introduction. A game of time and chance. They're so obsessed with time here. I wonder how many moon cycles it would take before Queen Luisa issued some new decree denying your bloodlines, as she has mine. Or perhaps her sweet daughter might slit your throats." Pressina trailed a fingernail down the skin of Jade's neck. "I've heard blood red is the princess heir's favorite color. Do you wear the gown in her honor?"

Melia watched her mother's cruel display.

Two red spots inflamed Jade's white cheeks. Lola floundered beside her.

Pressina leaned toward them. "It might be cold here, but I've heard things have gotten hot in Illialei. Our young Lilliane has a temper. I'd watch my back—and my neck—if I were you." Pressina slapped her fan closed, turned in a graceful swirl, and came to sit on Melia's right side. "How was the trip?" she asked her daughter.

"Slow but uneventful," Melia spoke carefully, so she wouldn't stutter.

"Slow and uneventful describes this godforsaken island." Her mother tapped the table with her fan. "Now, this challenge between the two of you—what a treat that will be." She waved her fan at the surrounding tables. "Don't let their even-tempered facades fool you. The grey faeries are as ecstatic as I am about your upcoming competition. We were on the verge of dying from boredom before you arrived."

54. The Grey Council

Awakened at dawn, Ryder and Melia were instructed to bathe and eat breakfast–a spicy fish soup in a clear broth with hot tea. The clothes laid out for them were more comfortable than the formal things they'd worn the night before. Warm shirts, slacks, and capes. Melia's grey shirt and slacks hugged her slim body. Ryder's clothes were equally fitted. When they entered the cold tunnels that burrowed through the citadel, they were grateful for the sumptuous capes that reached almost to their ankles.

"The day's proceedings will be lengthy, and there's no fire in the council chamber," their guide said. He was a small, dark-skinned man who reminded Ryder of Sinjiin. Although it seemed unlikely a mage from the Hidden City would serve as a guide anywhere. "Where are you from?" Ryder asked.

"The Black Magic Islands."

"Then you're far from home."

"I have no complaints."

"You don't miss your life there, your family and friends?"

"I don't miss going hungry."

Ryder fell quiet.

"I like the peace of the citadel," the guide said. "Everyone who serves here is taken care of. Food, clothes." He indicated his cape, as thick and beautiful as the ones Melia and Ryder wore. "As long as I'm here, I'm required to study a profession. I've chosen to study the law. I prefer it to black magic."

Ryder sensed more than saw Melia wince. "What branch of law?"

"Comparative analysis. The social consequences of breaking a vow are quite different in the mortal and enchanted worlds, as I'm sure you're aware. If the rumors swirling around you are true, then you were once a priest of Idonne—before you violated your Oath of Non-Interference. My current project concerns external punishment. Does it remain effective when no internal guilt is present? Is internal guilt effective without external punishment? How to achieve a social milieu that allows for optimal individual growth?"

Now Ryder winced.

"I communicate regularly on this topic with your father," the guide continued.

Ryder's throat tightened. Melia squeezed his hand. "I have no father," he choked out the words.

"You're aware he no longer denies you as his son."

"Then the benefit of announcing his paternity must now exceed the benefit of denying it."

"Perhaps," the guide said. "He'd like to hear news of you."

Ryder wanted no reconciliation with Anton. "Pose this question to him: When you realized the woman you'd coupled with was with child—and chose to abandon her—did the lack of external punishment stunt your spiritual growth?"

He felt Melia watching him as his boots rang out against the marble halls. He couldn't afford to become distracted. She needed him by her side during the ordeal ahead. He smiled at her and pointedly ignored the guide.

As they continued toward the heart of the citadel, he observed the high ceilings and ornate walls they walked through. It seemed as though the city was carved from a single monstrous block of grey marble, and the smooth coolness it radiated calmed everything in its vicinity—including him. By the time they arrived in the enormous chamber that housed the council, his pulse had returned to normal.

The council chamber was no less awe-inspiring than the rest of the citadel.

An abundance of sea life swam behind a thick pane of glass in the rear wall. Ryder and Melia stared at the large and small finned creatures swimming among the waving plants. Tatou, Flora, Aldous, Plantine, and Pressina sat in the observation balcony overhead. Tuck was conspicuously absent.

The guide led Melia and Ryder up a side staircase to join their friends and Melia's family. When Jade and Lola arrived, they were seated in the balcony with everyone else.

Soon after, the council officially convened.

"We are here today to address a momentous matter." Threldor sat in one of thirty grey marble chairs. Four were to his right and four to his left. Ten were carved into the row behind him, eleven in the final row. Each row behind Threldor was slightly elevated, so each member of the council had a clear view of the central dais. All the seats in the tribunal were filled.

"There have been prophecies, both hopeful and dire, concerning the incarnation of Umbra. Of all the creatures in the Whole, we, the grey faeries, have a vested interest in this controversy. It was only after the last grey faerie was born"—Threldor's arm swept to the side. On the outermost seat of the final row, a tall, slim male with a nose as thin as parchment stood, bobbed his head, and sat down —"that Umbra was born. We think of Umbra as a parent might think of a wayward child. Like Umbra, we're born from the ash of mortal failure. Unlike Umbra, we are balanced by mortal success, our passions cooled in the waters of the Great White Sea. Since Elendah's death, only thirty of our kind remain. We welcome Flora Della Snapdragon, the sole surviving spring faerie in the Whole to our island. We offer you sanctuary in our citadel."

Flora's chin raised as her back straightened. She adjusted her kerchief. "Would have been thoughtful to offer sanctuary to my kin before Uriel Albiana killed them all."

"Could you please speak up so we might hear you?" Threldor asked.

The spring faerie huffed. "Great words amount to little when real action was never taken."

The grey faerie swept his hand toward the dais. "Flora, please, we would like to hear your words. The acoustics in the chamber are designed so the tribunal may hear all speech from the central stage."

Ryder sensed Flora's hesitation. He wanted to urge her to take her place on the dais. Many believed speeches in chambers like these amounted to little more than useless banter. But the power of words, honestly and simply spoken, could awaken hearts long asleep.

Threldor continued. "You were a dear friend to our beloved sister, Elendah, and we understand you were there when she crossed the threshold to the Unknown Beyond. We thank you for your loving watchfulness. The spirit transcends these planes with greater peace when a loved one attends to the body's death."

Flora stared at the back of her hand, specifically at the ring with the blue stone Elendah gave her. Ryder couldn't remember the last time he saw it on the spring faerie's finger.

"I don't like to wear it," she whispered. "It calms me down. But I knew today was going to be long. No sense in letting myself become all worked up when they expect me to sit motionless like a lizard in the sun."

Ryder smiled proudly at her when she stood up. Aldous rose with her. Flora steadied herself with a grip on the rail in front of them. The old elf took her hand and led her to the dais. Ryder relaxed against the back of the padded bench with his shoulder and thigh pressed against Melia.

"I was in the mortal world when Uriel Albiana cast her dark spell." Flora's gravelly voice imparted the sorrow she'd carried alone for years. "The spring faeries were great warriors, the only ones with the strength and will to oppose the Albiana queens. They understood the purpose of the sapphire lily, a purpose which Uriel denied. She refused to accept her role as nurturer of the flower; rather, she turned the formidable talent the Albiana possess for magic to death and destruction."

Flora hung her head. Her hands dug deep in her apron pocket. "On that cursed day, I was in the mortal world. The cries of my kind echoed across time and space. By the time I returned to Illialei, it was too late. From the smallest bairn to the longest lived, I saved no one. It's the burden I live with." Her voice cracked. "I still hear their cries."

Melia sat on the edge of her seat.

Threldor stood. The rest of the grey faeries rose with him, but Threldor alone ascended from the tribunal gallery. He crossed the central stage to kneel before the spring faerie. He held out his hand and waited for her to pull hers from her apron and place it in his. He bowed his head. "We acknowledge the unpardonable crime committed against your race. We seek your forgiveness." He raised his head and gazed into Flora's eyes. "I, Threldor, custodian of the Grey Council, ally with you in your quest for justice. I commit the power of the council to end the Albiana reign."

Aldous thanked him.

Flora extended her hand.

Threldor kissed Elendah's ring.

Flora lifted her gaze to the grey faeries standing in the tribunal. They bowed their heads one by one. She tugged on the knot in her kerchief.

After a brief recess, the tribunal reconvened.

"The matter of Umbra's incarnation is before us." Threldor spoke from his marble chair. "We wish to thank Aldous Elosius of the White Oak wood elves for the treatise he presented to the council. We also wish to acknowledge the help Tatou Camellia Insons contributed in its preparation. It details the extent of the Albiana crimes through the current day.

"The tribunal has dispatched a missive notifying Queen Luisa Albiana of the crimes her ancestors and descendants stand accused of. However, we will not delay our course as we await a response.

We have waited far too long to take action as it is.

"It is our collective understanding that the Albiana amplify their power through a kind of telepathic connection with Umbra. They are able to reach through the Parallel of Shadows and drain the dark pool of energy to fuel their black magic spells. It seems Uriel Albiana was the first to comprehend the power of this connection and use it to devastating effect.

"While black magic is practiced routinely throughout Kyrakkos and the Black Magic Islands—and the muannai of Tyrannis are obsessed with its nature—no crimes of genocide or comparable atrocity has ever been committed by those populations. Nor does the ability to draw directly upon Umbra's energy seem to be available to any other bloodline or creature in the Whole.

"Therefore, regardless of Queen Luisa's response, we believe the psychic relationship between Umbra and the Albiana must be severed. This brings us to the point of incarnation.

"Will incarnation within a single vessel contain Umbra's power, so that those with Albiana blood may never draw from that reservoir again? We believe it will.

"There is also conjecture that Umbra's incarnation will cause a greater rebalancing of the Whole. We suspect the incarnation—and death of Umbra as a discrete entity—will end the birth of the muannai, in the same way the birth of Umbra ended the birth of grey faeries.

"Is this an acceptable outcome? Are we objective enough to make a determination?

"We believe the end of a species or race through lack of birth differs from genocide. We also believe a new iteration of mortal ember and ash will evolve, the third since the beginning of time. The time it took to birth a grey faerie became unsustainable as the mortal population exploded; as a result, the muannai/Umbra split emerged.

"We have hoped a similar organic evolution would correct the grave power imbalance accumulating in the Void as a result of the

Umbra/muannai split. However, that has not come to pass. It has been proposed to the council that the challenge required by the Whole at the present time is for sentient beings to act upon their own behalf. The incarnation of Umbra would qualify as such an action.

"Having arrived at this point, another question arises. Who would be the appropriate vessel of incarnation? There is consensus that a creature with mortal and Albiana blood would be the most viable candidate for incarnation. The mortal blood will satisfy Umbra—who cannot be forced from the Void, but must be enticed—while the Albiana blood will bestow the vessel with the ability to harness Umbra's will to their own."

Ryder squeezed Melia's hand.

"Two candidates with the desired mixed blood are present in the council chamber today. How to choose between them? Once infused with Umbra's power, the vessel will become the most powerful entity in the Whole." Threldor raised his right fist—"The power to create"—he raised his left fist—"and the power to destroy will be theirs. How they choose to wield that power will belong to them alone. As both candidates are willing to shoulder this grave responsibility, we have designed a series of tests to aid our decision. The candidate who we believe exhibits the greatest capacity to steer Umbra's energy toward creation will win.

"Melia Albiana, do you agree to accept our ruling in this matter?"

She stood. "I do."

Ryder's heart pounded. There could be no turning back now.

"Jade Rae Silver, do you agree to accept our ruling in this matter?"

"Umbra has chosen me to be the vessel, not her." Jade's expression and tone conveyed her distrust. "Other than my mother, I don't really know any of these people. When they realized I possessed Koldis, they persuaded me to come here. Then they took the sword from me, along with my choice in the matter."

"You did not issue a challenge to Melia Albiana in the muannai

481

valley marketplace?"

"Not exactly," Jade replied.

"Then you are here under protest?" Threldor asked.

"I'm here because I want to incarnate Umbra."

"Will you agree to accept the Grey Council's ruling?

"Do I have a choice?"

"Is that a yes?"

Jade shook her head and crossed her arms. "Yes."

Threldor continued. "With the power vested in the Grey Council by the enchanted world, we agree to administer and arbitrate this competition. We will set before the candidates three challenges. Jade and Melia, please come down to the dais."

Ryder knew this moment would come, and yet, as it arrived, uncertainty engulfed him. The thing he most feared since Nandana had uttered her prophecy closed in on him. He wanted to grab Melia in his arms and carry her away from all this madness. Because it was madness.

The volatile psychic residue that was Umbra—the infinite bitterness, rage, and sorrow—would become a part of her.

Who could withstand such an inner assault?

And yet he'd vowed to stand by her side no matter what. It was a vow he would never break again.

55. The Choice

Melia stood even with Jade on the dais. Wary of her opponent, she faced the council, awaiting instruction.

The grey faerie to Threldor's right descended to the stage. She faced Jade and Melia. "My name is Jelina. I hold two pairs of dice, one for each of you. You will cast them at the same time. The one who casts the highest roll will make the choice Threldor sets before you first. That choice will impact the three challenges. Do you understand?"

Melia's mouth dried as she held out her hand.

Jelina dropped two hard, cold silver cubes in her palm.

They reminded Melia of the rocks used in the game of stones, except these cubes were polished and smooth with numerals—10, 20, 30, 40, 50, and 60—engraved on each side. Melia crouched opposite Jade on the grey marble floor. She wished Ryder was beside her. The balcony seemed miles away as she waited for Jelina's command. With the dice in one hand, Melia pressed her other palm flat against the stone floor of the dais. Her mind fell silent as she drew energy from the marble.

"I will count now," Jelina said. "Cast the dice when I say four."

Melia tucked her hair behind her ears. She didn't spare a glance for Jade.

"One. Two. Three. Four."

Melia tossed the dice—a 20 and 50. She looked at Jade's pair—a 40 and 50 taunted her.

Jelina faced the council. "Jade will choose first."

Threldor's face remained impassive as he addressed the contestants. "When we are finished here, you will be escorted to your living quarters for the duration of the challenge. During this time, your contacts will be restricted. Your ability to manage this isolation will be part of the competition. However, the isolation will not be complete. You'll each choose a companion to remain at your side during this time of testing. The choice of your partner is the task before you. Jade you may choose now."

Melia's pulse quickened. She stared at the floor.

Jade didn't hesitate. "Ryder."

A feeling of fire erupted in Melia's chest. It radiated against her ribs as it climbed in her throat. Energy scorched her limbs. She threw back her head and roared. Flame shot from her mouth.

Melia flapped her arms, her feet lost contact with the stone floor. Her vision widened. With a twist of her body, she saw the balcony and the tribunal gallery in a single glance. Threldor and the grey faeries stared, as did her mother and sister, Lola and Aldous. But Flora nodded, and Ryder's eyes sparked. Tatou pulled her hands from the pockets of her fur coat and beat them against one another as Sinjiin met Melia's roar with one of his own.

Other than in her dreams, she'd not flown since the first time she kissed Ryder. The exhilaration of flight collided with her rage at Jade's choice. She'd have to face the ordeal before her without him.

Melia circled the chamber's high ceiling, lashing her tail. She used it to pivot and tighten her movements with quick flicks and hard swipes in the air. She settled her feet, hooked with claws, upon a ledge near the height of the chamber.

Dull purple leather and blue scales as shiny as gemstones covered her body. She didn't require a mirror or pool of water to see she was magnificent, though not enormous. As an eagle, she'd been four times the size of a normal bird, but as far as she could tell, she was a petite dragon. Her gaze scanned the gathering below her. She searched for Jade.

The half-mortal's eyes were dark and wide, perfect targets in her pale face.

Melia launched from her perch to perform a graceful dive onto the marble platform between the balcony and tribunal gallery.

Ryder had yet to join the girl, who trembled before her.

The smell of fear wafted from the girl. To a dragon, the smell was sweet and inviting. A morsel she'd like to taste. Melia craned her long neck and pushed her rough snout as close to Jade's face as she could without touching the girl's white skin.

Jade jerked back, stumbling and tripping on the hem of her wool cape.

Melia's deep throaty laugh came out as a roar.

Jade cowered.

Every ounce of anger that had simmered over Jade's attraction to Ryder became available to Melia. She wagged her dragon snout and showed Jade her rows of piercing teeth.

The girl's hand rested on the hilt of a stone knife.

Melia arched her back and lifted her wings to their full extension. Her dragon shadow stretched across Jade, who took another step back. Tempted by the increasingly sick-sweet aroma of the girl's terror, Melia searched for her beloved. For as much as the emotion of hate became more available to her in her dragon form, so did the emotion of love. Content with the results of menacing Jade, she craved the one whose very breath seemed to fill her lungs. There he was, in the balcony, green eyes shining. She lifted a clawed hoof to hail him.

"Melia." She turned her head to Threldor's voice. Although the rest of the grey faeries stood, he remained seated with quill in hand. "I don't find anything in Aldous' treatise about your ability to shift into a dragon. Have I overlooked something?"

Melia stepped away from Jade. She would rip the girl's body to shreds and gorge upon the bones right t here in front of everyone if she inhaled the perfume of the girl's fear much longer. Her claws clicked against the cool marble. Instinctively, she crouched low, bowed her head, and covered her body with her enormous wings. Focusing her determination, she pressed her claws against the cool stone of the stage. She imagined slim, pale fingers, and legs of muscle and skin. She imagined arms without scales.

An orgasmic force exploded in her belly. Coolness like a welcome pool in the heat of summer coursed through her. A black cloud descended, then receded. She shook her head. Tousled hair fell across her face and shoulders.

She'd shifted at will.

She loved Ryder, and Jade had taken a terrible risk by putting herself between them.

The grey faeries took their seats.

Threldor tapped his quill against the parchment before him. His grey eyes assessed Melia. "Unexpected and impressive," he mused. "How long have you possessed this talent?"

Melia tugged a strand of hair. "Today is the first time I've ever achieved it."

He pushed himself back from his desk and crossed his arms. "You've never shifted into the shape of a dragon before?"

"I used to become an eagle at sunset—"

"Yes, your mother's curse." Threldor shuffled the stack of parchment to his right. "I read about that. But this is something altogether different." His eyes raised to the balcony. "Pressina, have you violated the terms of your sentence by practicing black magic here, on the Isle of Minnanon?"

As Melia faced the balcony, her eyes searched for Ryder. Their eyes met. She pressed her hand against her heart. He did the same. She curled her fingers into a fist. *I'll never let go.* When he mirrored her gesture, she knew he grasped the full meaning of what had just occurred. By claiming Ryder, Jade awakened Melia's dragon heart. The ability to shift at will was a full flowering of who she was. In her reptilian form, genuine emotion trampled every simpering fear of vows that might be broken. Her dragon heart burned away doubt like dry moss.

"I would love to claim responsibility for my daughter's impressive transformation," Pressina said, "but I can't."

Despite their troubled history, Melia's heart glowed.

Threldor called upon Sinjiin next. "I would have you address the council on this matter."

The tiger shifted into his mage form.

"Beyond the walls of the Hidden City," Threldor said, "there are few who have the capacity to shift their form at will. Did you teach Melia this trick?"

Sinjiin bowed to the council before speaking. "It's no trick. The Albiana blood possesses a mutability that extends to their form."

"Then each of them—Pressina, Plantine, Jade, and Lola—have the ability to shift into a dragon form?"

"I can't say which animal would be true to their individual natures, but yes, it's possible that, with proper training, they each might develop their capacity to shift at will."

"Without the use of black magic?"

Melia slipped her hand into her pocket. She'd taken to carrying the small black vial of oil wherever she went. Once she began to meditate upon the dark within her, as Sevondi instructed, her obsession with shifting at will deepened. The more she hoped to call forth dragons in the sky, the more the dragon within her yearned for release.

Sinjiin's weight shifted. "There's an intersection where the line between black and white magic blurs."

"And what does this blurring entail?"

"There's an oil that activates the deepest layer of the mind at the base of the neck. The vehicle for penetration is smell."

"You procured this oil?"

Sinjiin's hands disappeared in the pockets of his red silk pants. "I don't know anyone who sells it, not in the Hidden City or here in the enchanted world."

"Then how did you come by it?" Threldor asked.

"I distilled it."

The grey faerie nodded. "Do you have any of this oil with you?"

"I don't."

"Melia?"

She looked to Sinjiin for guidance. The mage tipped his head. Melia pulled the small black vial from her pocket and held it up so Threldor could see it.

"Jelina," he said.

The grey faerie again descended.

Melia relinquished the empty bottle.

Jelina carried it to Threldor.

"The council will schedule a thorough discussion of this revelation for a future session. My concern today was whether black magic was employed in this chamber. I am satisfied that it was not. Now, Melia, you have a choice to make."

Melia considered her remaining options.

Tatou was the most familiar to her. Besides her mother and sister, she'd known the pixie the longest. But Tatou suffered in the north's icy temperatures. Who knew what challenges would be set before them, or where they would take place? The tiny faerie would freeze outside. Endangering her friend wasn't acceptable. She wouldn't consider her mother or sister, either. She needed someone she could trust. Melia lingered over Flora. The spring faerie's wisdom and faith in her had already seen her through so much. Yet Flora didn't feel like the right choice either. Leaving her in peace to spend time with Aldous resonated more with Melia's heart.

"Sinjiin."

Her gaze returned to Ryder. He approved her choice with a tilt of his head. They would be apart in body, but never in spirit. In a flash, her dragon heart burned away a wall she erected long ago. For the second time, Melia recognized the folly of Jade's mistake.

"Ryder, Sinjiin, join Jade and Melia on the dais. The rest of you are free to go," Threldor commanded.

Three guides appeared. One led Flora and Aldous away. The second escorted Pressina and Plantine from the council chamber. The third offered Lola his elbow. Tatou perched on her shoulder. As much as she disliked Jade, Melia cared for Lola. It relieved her to see that she wouldn't be spending the days of her daughter's confinement alone.

When the others were gone, Threldor addressed the four who remained.

"The deep cold of winter approaches. Soon, ice floes will make it impossible to sail from our island. The freeze endures three moon cycles. Each challenge will last approximately a full moon cycle. Once the third challenge has been completed, we will choose a victor." Threldor called for two more guides.

Melia recognized the guide from that morning. He led Ryder and Jade from the council chamber.

Sinjiin returned to his tiger form. Melia climbed upon his back. The great cat padded behind their guide through the marble halls.

56. The First Challenge

Jade ruminated as they walked down the hallway.

Ryder hadn't said a word since Threldor ordered him to join her on the dais. It made it harder to stop thinking about what she saw in the council chamber today: Everyone riveted with awe while Melia transformed into a dragon.

Then she threatened to roast Jade alive with those enormous, glowing blue eyes, and no one did or said anything to stop her. Not even Lola.

Jade had almost gotten used to watching the tiger change. Now this. It hardly seemed fair, she and Ryder competing with a tiger and a dragon. Maybe she'd lodge a formal complaint.

It didn't help Jade's mood that Melia didn't become just any ordinary dragon. Oh no. She became a sparkly, spangly, sleek Victoria's Secret dragon, and Ryder was impressed.

Jade wondered what her own animal totem might be. It was hard to imagine something more exotic than a shiny lavender-sapphire dragon.

A few steps ahead, Ryder and the guide were talking.

"He expects some report. What would you have me tell him?"

Jade wondered who "he" was.

"I'm alive," Ryder said.

Pithy. Jade could appreciate that in a guy. Although it was going to make living together for the next three moon cycles a challenge.

"I keep him updated on events. Anything of note that happens on the island."

"Anton always appreciated a well-placed spy."

"The letters I send your father aren't secret."

His father?

"We'll sail when the ice melts, I'll be gone before your letters reach him."

"Snowy owls carry my correspondence through the winter moons."

"Then report what you will."

If Ryder and his father were at odds, they had something in common.

The guide stopped beneath an arch. "Your suite."

Jade's heart did a little flip. She looked at Ryder to gauge his reaction. His face remained a hardened mask.

"There are separate sleeping chambers," the guide added.

Ryder stepped aside to let Jade enter.

The suite was much larger than the room she'd shared with her mother the night before. There were two doors on either side of the main room and one on the far wall opened onto a patio.

"Three months—moon cycles, I mean—is a long time," she said when Ryder closed the door.

He grunted.

It was going to be a really long time if he didn't talk.

For the first time since she left Illialei, Jade missed Gavin. Give him a little blueberry wine and the knight was downright chatty. Jade wondered if Ryder drank inebriating liquids.

"Did the guide mention anything about dinner?" she asked him.

"It will be delivered."

"So, we're like prisoners?"

"The less distractions, the more you'll be able to focus on what lies before you."

"It lies before you too," she said.

"Because you chose me."

"If I hadn't, she would have."

"That's true."

"What do you think about her choosing the tiger?"

"He was the next best choice for her."

"They're spending three moon cycles in a suite like this, just the two of them. Doesn't that concern you?"

He stood like a statue. "They'll unite for the purpose of winning this competition, that's all."

"You mean they'll focus on beating me," Jade said.

"Yes. You're going to lose. Have you considered conceding?"

"No, I haven't!"

He crossed the room and exited through the door that led to the patio.

Jade tagged along after him. A stunning view of the Great White Sea made her catch her breath before a gust of wind almost blew her back inside. "You don't get it!" she yelled. "You have to help me!"

"I'll do everything in my power to ensure your success."

Wasn't he freezing? She was turning into a human Popsicle. "You better!" She slammed the door as she headed back inside.

The suite's other rooms, two bedrooms, were as spacious as the main room but indistinguishable. She picked one, threw herself on the bed, and pounded it with her fists. After she wore out her arms, she flipped over and smashed her heels against the mattress.

How was she going to beat a chick who could morph into a dragon? This was so much worse than any video game she'd ever played. And if Ryder remained Mr. Sheer Steel Wall for the next three months, it was going to wear down her determination.

Gavin would help her win if he was here.

Who was she kidding? He was an assassin. If their paths crossed again, he'd probably kill her.

The guide returned with the rising sun. "The council requests your presence."

Jade hung on the door. "What do they want?"

"To instruct you regarding the first challenge."

Ryder remained MIA in his bedroom. As much as Jade wanted to destroy his relationship with Melia, she needed to win the competition. Maybe the council would let her pick again. After a night of no sleep, Lola looked like a much better choice.

Jade led the guide back into the hall and whispered that Ryder was ill. "I'll go before the council without him." The guide's forehead raised in question, but he didn't press for further explanation.

A few moments later, shock and curiosity flitted across Melia's face when Jade entered the council chamber alone. Of course, the tiger stood beside the half-faerie, his golden eyes probing. She hated they would witness what she was about to do.

At least, she'd prevented Melia and Ryder from being together for three moon cycles. Maybe during that time they'd grow apart. She'd seen it before, friends distracted by a summer romance, falling out of love.

"Where is Ryder?" Threldor asked.

Jade felt less comfortable lying to him. "I'd like to request a different companion for the challenge." After their initial conversation on the patio, Ryder ignored her the rest of the night. When no one said anything, Jade continued, "I need a partner who will help me win." She couldn't say, I need a partner who will at least talk to me with Melia standing right beside her.

Jelina stood. "You chose first. It came with the responsibility of choosing wisely. Whatever trials arise in the partnership are part of the challenge."

"Are you kidding?"

"We do not take this matter lightly," Threldor said with an air of finality. "Are there any other concerns before we proceed with instructions for the first challenge?"

If she didn't get another partner, she was going to lose. Her mother understood her. Her mother believed in her. In Lola's eyes, she could do no wrong. "I want to choose my mother."

The grey faerie to Threldor's left leaned toward the council's custodian. Jade watched his lips move. She didn't dare turn her head. The last thing she needed was an eyeful of Melia's smug face.

Threldor finally spoke. "If you choose a second time, your challenger will also choose a second time."

Jade gripped the hilt of her knife. These grey faeries—everyone in the enchanted world—were on Melia's side. Umbra had probably abandoned her too. It was all so familiar.

She would lose with Ryder before she let Melia win with him.

"Will you choose a second time?" Threldor asked.

"No."

Threldor stood. "We'll reconvene when all parties are present."

Jade's guide popped in front of her like a jack-in-the-box. "What do you want?"

"It's my responsibility to assure you don't violate the rules regarding contact with anyone other than your partner."

She held out her wrists. "Why don't you just drag me around in chains?"

The guide's forehead puckered. "I don't understand."

Jade dropped her arms. "Never mind." She followed him off the dais. When she was sure they were well out of Melia and Sinjiin's earshot, she added, "Don't tell Ryder I asked to choose someone else."

"As you wish."

"Did you see the way Jade gripped her knife?" Melia chewed on a fingernail. "Do you think she would hurt him?"

"She might want to hurt him. He can be stubborn," Sinjiin said. "But I doubt she will."

"This is going to be more difficult than I imagined. Yesterday, when I shifted into a dragon, my love for him was right here." Melia placed her hand over her heart. "It roared through me like a gorged river. I was furious when Jade chose him, even though I knew she would."

"A dragon's heart is passionate and loyal."

Melia smiled. "It felt wonderful."

"The council might prohibit you from shifting into a dragon during the challenge proper. But I want you to do as I do. I want you to stay in your dragon form as much as possible. Your greatest vulnerability is your doubt. If the love you feel for Ryder drowns that out when you're in your dragon form, then you must live there as much as you can."

Melia settled on one of the sofas in their shared front room. She crossed her legs, with her elbows on her knees and her chin in her hands. "Would that be considered cheating?"

Sinjiin settled opposite her. "Is being who you are cheating?"

Ryder paced.

When Jade entered the suite alone, he asked her where she'd gone. It was a chore to make himself speak to her.

"The council summoned me."

"Alone?"

"Why do you care?"

"I don't. However, I was under the impression they wish us to be partners."

"How can we be partners if you won't even talk to me?"

Ryder exhaled roughly. "My situation is difficult."

"Your situation is difficult? Every single person in the enchanted world hates me. Umbra—"

Ryder walked toward her. "What about Umbra?"

"Nothing. The council wants to know when you can appear before them."

It was an odd request. "I have nowhere else to go," he said.

She left the suite briefly. When she returned, she said, "They'll send for us."

"Why did you choose me?" Ryder asked.

"I want you to help me win."

Jade didn't understand how she tempted him.

If she won, Melia would never incarnate Umbra.

✧ ✧ ✧

The next morning, when Ryder saw Melia standing on the dais with Sinjiin, everyone else faded away. Her proximity tormented him as much as it aggravated his dilemma. If he helped Jade win, would Melia ever forgive him? Yet, if he didn't do his best to help his partner, wasn't that another way of betraying Melia?

He liked that line of thought. By helping Jade become the best she could be, Melia would have to become the best she could be to win. And that would increase her chances of subduing Umbra's will to her own—if she won.

"The first challenge will be hand-to-hand combat in an arena." Threldor drew Ryder's attention back to the council chamber. "It will be a test of physical strength and agility, as well as mettle. Are there any questions?" Threldor asked.

Ryder had none. Nor did anyone else. Their respective guides escorted them from the council chamber. By the time they arrived at their suite, Ryder had made up his mind. "We must begin your training. There's no time to waste."

Jade's sulky face lit up. "You're actually going to help me?"

"Yes, I am."

57. One Hundred

The citadel was an elaborate marble hive.

Every day, thousands of inhabitants from all over the enchanted world swarmed through the cold grey tunnels. Other than her mother, none of them were full-blood faeries; they had no wings. Melia never detected the distinctive musky scent of full-blood mortals wafting in the halls, either. Though everyone she saw was dressed in a similar manner, wearing capes and boots, their physical features and skin tones varied. Until now, they'd been out of sight. Sections of the marble city were off-limits to the island's general population. The council chamber and dining gallery where they ate their first meal, the living quarters where they spent their first night —those areas were exclusive to the grey faeries.

Elendah's chamber had been secluded on the Calashai's highest floor. Had it served as her refuge? As the regent of the stronghold, she'd been famous for nurturing passionate engagement in a daily salon, but perhaps as a grey faerie, she required a balancing quiet as well. Older than any other creatures in the enchanted world, grey faeries were deep thinkers. Perhaps the energies of normal daily life disturbed them.

Melia often wondered whether their cool charm was a mask which hid deeper emotions. Or had their long lives really imbued them with wisdom so profound little could jar or upset them? She admired them if that was the case, but she had little desire to emulate them. Experiencing her dragon self Melia understood, her

499

heart was the root of her strength and clarity not her head.

Twice a day, their guide led Melia and Sinjiin on a lengthy hike to a large room designed for physical exercise. Despite the traffic in the halls, whenever they arrived at their destination, it was empty. The walls were lined with shelves of metal balls and bars of all sizes. Ropes and chains hung from hooks in the ceiling. The drills Sinjiin forced her to endure were as rigorous as any Flora had devised. No one ever interrupted their work. Most days she wished someone would. Sinjiin was brutal. After each session, she practically crawled back to their suite.

Her low energy made it hard for her to shift into a dragon, but in that too, her companion was relentless. Sinjiin seemed aware that, day by day, her distance from Ryder made it harder for her to remember how whole she felt in his presence. How necessary he was to her life.

Yet once she shifted into her dragon form, her heart was aflame. She wanted to tear down the marble walls to find him.

Ryder had trained with the Idonnai Guard. He drew on everything he remembered from those days to develop drills designed to increase Jade's physical stamina and dexterity. She was smaller than Melia, shorter and lighter, but that didn't mean she had to lose. Used to proper advantage, speed could demolish size. So Ryder focused on training Jade to react and think fast. She was naturally quick with her movements and impulsive with her thoughts.

He spoon-fed her discipline. Bite by bite. He never chastised her carelessness, only forced her to repeat a task until her execution matched her speed. There wasn't enough time to integrate as much structure into her processes as he would have liked, but excessive demands risked swamping her confidence. If she moved too slowly, she'd lose her single advantage.

❖ ❖ ❖

Jade touched the pants laid out on the bed. They felt like microfiber, but they weren't. The shirt was made from the same pliable fabric as the pants. When she held the shirt to her nose, it was odorless. She tugged on the fitted pants, then struggled to get her arms and head inside the tiny shirt. Once she was dressed, the clothes felt good. She performed a roundhouse kick, jabbing her heel in the air. The tight outfit didn't restrain her movement. In fact, it felt like she wasn't wearing anything at all. If she could figure out how to manufacture this fabric in the mortal world, she'd make a fortune.

Backup plans surfaced more than she cared to acknowledge. If she lost this stupid challenge, she wasn't going to hang around in the enchanted world to become Queen Melia's slave–that was for sure. Nope. She was going to cross the borders of time and space as soon as she could. Surely, Gavin–and the faerie princess–would lose interest in eliminating her and her mother if Melia incarnated Umbra.

Knock. Tap. Knock. Tap.

Jade smiled when she recognized Ryder's code. She didn't know what changed his mind, but ever since they received the council's instructions for the first challenge, he was a changed man. Not exactly chatty, but clearly committed to helping her beat Melia. And he did talk to her, as long as she didn't steer the conversation toward subjects which were too personal. Like his father.

Jade opened the door.

"Are you ready?" he asked.

She shrugged. She was never going to be ready to get her ass kicked by Melia. "You're sure she won't be allowed to shift into a dragon?"

"It would defeat the entire purpose of hand-to-hand combat."

"And remind me of the purpose again."

"It's a raw contest, the most equal pairing possible."

"Right. Like she's not four inches taller than me and twenty pounds heavier."

Ryder frowned. He wasn't good with jokes, especially when it came to his precious Melia. "Without weapons or other parties, and no animals or magic to assist them, the combatants are forced to rely on their own resources—body and mind. What did I tell you about size?"

"Speed is a greater advantage than size. You really want me to win?" In less than an hour, she would face Melia, and his answer to that question was critical.

"Yes."

She believed him. She didn't know why. But she did. Jade's heart thumped. Ryder wanted her to win. For the first time since Melia morphed into a dragon, Jade's confidence returned.

Someone rapped on the door.

Ryder opened it.

They followed their guide on a new route through the endless marble halls and indoor pools.

"Where are we going?" Jade asked the guide. His name was Raffi.

"To the arena, Miss Jade." That's what Raffi called her—Miss Jade.

Sometimes Ryder did too. It was the closest thing he came to cracking a joke. She snuck a sideways glance at him.

He seemed far away.

The arena wasn't much larger than the training room or the Grey Council's chamber. There was a square mat in the middle. It looked like a boxing ring, except it wasn't elevated, and there weren't any ropes or other barriers around it. About five feet from the edge of the mat, on all four sides, there were two rows of five seats, carved from marble stone—like almost everything else in the citadel.

Melia and Sinjiin were already there. Not a dragon or a tiger. Jade's body pumped adrenaline.

Ryder walked to the pair. He shook their hands. When he held Melia's hand longer than Sinjiin's, Jade wanted to kick something. She decided to save it for Melia.

Grey faeries filed in around them, filling the seats.

Then she saw her mother.

If Jade thought her mother had been returned to her former beauty in Tyrannis, her transformation since she'd been on the Isle of Minnanon was nothing short of miraculous. She looked twenty years younger. If Ryder could shake Melia's hand, she could hug her mother. Jade ran to her. When Raffi thrust out his arm to stop her, she wanted to spit in his face. But Threldor was watching, he'd probably give her demerits. She acquiesced. Her mother waved.

Jade turned back to the arena with more righteous anger revving her up.

Melia approached her, head high, hand out.

Jade clenched her opponent's fingers as hard as she could. "Don't expect any mercy from me."

Melia didn't flinch.

That made Jade even angrier.

A grey faerie stood in the center of the ring. He motioned for Melia and Jade to join him.

Her mother wasn't the only non-grey faerie there. Melia's entire cheerleading squad was in attendance. Along with Pressina and Plantine were the fat old faerie, the gaunt white-haired elf, and that shrimp, Tatou.

The referee's name was Enidor. He explained the rules: Any move with their fingers, hands, toes, feet, elbows, knees, or head was allowable. There would only be one round; the goal was to immobilize the opponent for a count of one hundred.

Great. All Melia had to do was sit on her.

Enidor sent them to opposite sides of the mat.

Jade couldn't believe they weren't using gloves, tape, or face masks. Punching Melia's beautiful face was going to hurt.

The referee raised his arms. When he dropped them, the challenge would begin.

Jade focused like Ryder taught her to do.

Enidor's arms fell.

Jade zigged and zagged toward Melia, whose first line of offense was her long legs. Other than a clip on the chin, Jade bobbed in and out of her range, giving her opponent little to show for all the energy she expended. If she kept this up, Jade might just wear her out and pounce on her when she was exhausted.

No sooner had Jade enjoyed the pleasure of that inner laugh than Melia came at her with a head butt. She connected with Jade's abdomen. Jade made claws of her fingers and dug into Melia's head. She tried like hell to slide her fingers in the direction of Melia's eyes.

Melia jerked away. Jade got a handful of hair and yanked hard. She shot up with her knee and slammed Melia's nose. The impact shot a spike of pain down the back of Jade's calf. What did it feel like to Melia? Jade cocked her knee for another slam, but Melia slipped out of her grasp. Jade cracked a smile at the sight of her opponent's blood-smeared face.

Ryder was right. Speed could demolish size. She just needed to pay attention and think and move fast.

She danced around Melia, taunting her and forcing her to spin in tight circles.

"Ring around the rosy, a pocket full of posies, ashes, ashes, we all fall down," Jade singsonged.

Melia wiped away the blood dripping from her nose and into her mouth. Those blue eyes glared. A thread of smoke curled from her left nostril, but she didn't shift into a dragon.

Emboldened, Jade wanted to jam her heel into that long pale throat, but if Melia got hold of her foot or ankle, she'd be dead meat. As she watched for an opening, Jade realized she was getting impatient. Ryder had warned her to take her time. The right moment will present itself: Wait for it.

What if it didn't?

Jade considered a head butt. Bent in half, she'd reduce the size of herself as a target. If she could get a grip on Melia's pants ... That would be tricky. Maybe too tricky. The fabric didn't have a lot of give. What if she aimed lower? Smashed her head against Melia's knee and grabbed for her ankle? It would hurt Jade's head, but she'd be standing. If Melia landed on her tailbone, that would hurt like hell. Jade knew from experience. It had happened to her once when she was a kid. She'd been jumping on a trampoline, lost her footing, and smashed her tailbone against the metal frame. It had taken years for that little injury to fully heal.

Melia started kicking again.

Jade kept her distance, noting the height of Melia's range. If she gauged it right, she could aim low, rush in, and head butt her one standing leg. She liked that strategy.

One. Kick. Two. Kick. Three. Jade doubled in half and tore across the mat. Her head connected with Melia's knee as Melia's other leg came down on Jade's back. Jade thought cannonball and pushed forward. Melia was falling and Jade was crashing down on top of her. Something cracked. Or popped. The sound made Jade gag. She mowed forward. Melia pummeled her back. Was she aiming for her kidneys? Jade cocked her elbow and slammed it down. Melia heaved.

No one broke them up. For all their put-on civility, these grey faeries were a bloodthirsty lot.

Jade cocked her elbow again and again.

Melia strained beneath her.

Jade pounded blindly. Tears salted her eyes. Why didn't someone stop her?

Melia made one final buck.

Jade slammed her shoulders against Melia's torso. Finally, she stilled.

Jade heard Enidor counting. When he reached one hundred, Ryder pulled Jade off Melia.

Sinjiin hovered over the loser, wiping her down with towels that became blood-soaked as soon as they touched her.

Ryder pulled Jade away.

No one clapped or cheered.

Back in their suite, Jade hid in the shower. The citadel was the only place in the enchanted world with overhead faucets. She stayed under the steaming water for hours. Not even Ryder's knock-tap-knock-tap drew her out.

When she couldn't stand the water anymore, she turned the shower off and sat for a long time, alone in the steam. She couldn't believe she'd won. She couldn't believe how violent she'd become.

When she finally wandered into the shared room for something to drink, Ryder was there. Like he'd been waiting for her. It was late. She'd hoped he was already in bed. "You must hate me."

"You did what you had to do to win. You did what I trained you to do."

"But I hurt her," Jade said. "I think I hurt her really badly."

"She'll heal."

"You seem awfully unconcerned for someone who's in love with her," Jade observed.

Ryder stared at her without speaking, like he was rolling something around in his mind. Finally, he shook his head. "Umbra doesn't like to share."

Sinjiin crouched over Melia, who was lying flat on her back. The mage had pushed all the furniture from the center of the room and spread a pile of thick blankets on the floor. She didn't want him to touch any part of her, especially not her nose.

Sinjiin gave her a pillow.

"Please, wait," she said.

"If we don't do it now, and your perfect nose heals crooked, we'll have to re-break it later. It will hurt more the second time."

"I don't care if it's crooked."

"You will. Take a deep breath and squeeze the pillow with both hands." He showed her his fingers and thumb shaped into an arch. "I'm going to get as close to the injury as I can without touching it. The swelling is too great for me to assess the extent of the damage by sight. But if I hold my thumb and fingers right here, I can sense the bone, and whether it's fractured."

"What are you trying to feel?"

"Heat," he said. "Here it is. Are you squeezing the pillow as tightly as you can?"

She wasn't– "Ouch!" When she dug into the pillow, her fingers ached too.

"Hold still," Sinjiin said.

With his first slight touch, pain shattered her face. Her stomach erupted with nausea. "I can't hold still." Melia struggled to sit up. More crushing pain radiated from her tailbone, forcing her back to the floor. "Everything hurts!"

Sinjiin rocked back on his heels. "I know it hurts, but this will be quick."

"My nose is fine. I can breathe."

Sinjiin reached for the pillow she'd discarded, and handed it back to her. "Let me finish."

She held up a hand. "Wait. Have you ever done this before?"

"The bar fight at The Crossroads wasn't my first."

"You've had your nose broken?"

"More than once."

Knowing he really understood the throbbing pain shooting through her cheekbones and eye sockets made her more trusting. "Who fixed your nose?"

"I did it myself. When you have no choice, you do what you have to do. But you already know that."

He always called her attention to "lessons". Most of the time she appreciated his nudges toward wisdom, but this afternoon, his effort only made her head ache more.

"Can I finish what I started?" he asked.

She couldn't bring herself say yes.

"It's the last time I'll hurt you today. I have a salve that will reduce the swelling throughout your body. It will help the bruises heal too."

"What about my ankle?"

"It's not broken."

"It feels like it is."

"My salve will help with that too. First, let me fix your nose."

Clutching the pillow, Melia slipped back into the pile of blankets. "I feel like I should be more demoralized than I am."

"Why?"

"I lost. She broke my nose." Melia reached for one of the bloody cloths Sinjiin piled on the edge of the blanket, evidence of her defeat. But it hurt too much to roll over. She couldn't grab the proof. "She made me bleed, and I didn't spill a single drop of her blood."

"Tell me what else you didn't do," Sinjiin used his teaching voice again.

"I didn't shift into a dragon."

"Was that hard?"

Melia closed her eyes, recalling the inner war that waged within her while Jade circled her on the mat. "The moment I saw her, my dragon-self wanted to manifest." When Jade drew first blood, it took every fiber of Melia's being to quell the cataclysmic ripples within that, left unchecked, would have erupted in her exterior metamorphosis into a dragon. The effort severely hobbled her performance.

"But you didn't lose yourself," Sinjiin said.

"Threldor isn't going to give me any points for that."

"As far as I'm concerned, you won today," Sinjiin said.

"You're the only one."

"I was afraid you wouldn't be able to control your emotions."

"You never told me that!" Over the past fortnight, Sinjiin coached her to identify the emotions that triggered her change. Those were the keys for controlling the shift. She needed to master accessing them when she wanted to shift and controlling them when she didn't. Emotions linked to truth and loyalty seemed to be the surest triggers. The truth was: She wanted to destroy Jade.

The mage shrugged. "Yes, Jade beat you in today's match. But you won against yourself. That was more important."

"You keep saying that, but that won't matter if she wins this competition."

"You haven't lost your destiny yet. Two challenges remain. Now, lie still, and let me fix your nose."

Melia inhaled a deep breath, squeezed the pillow tightly, and gritted her teeth to keep herself from screaming. She couldn't see Sinjiin's hand, but she could see his arm. He didn't warn her when he gripped the bone to pull and push. The room wavered around her. Sinjiin rocked back. She put her hands over her face with her fingers spread. "I'm not going to let you touch it again."

He showed her his mouthful of gleaming white teeth. "I don't need to."

Melia gingerly let her hands drop from her face.

The next morning, Sinjiin woke her before the sun rose. "I want to rub some more salve on your wounds and bruises before the guide arrives."

Melia's body still ached, but in comparison to the night before, the pain had dulled. Although she still didn't want anyone to touch or poke or prod her, Sinjiin's salve had made a difference. "Did you make that, or bring it with you?" she asked.

He was massaging her ankle. When he didn't answer, she knew he didn't want to confess to anything that might get them both in trouble. For all she knew, Flora sent a snowy owl to their porch with the jar of ointment tied around its leg.

"Ryder trained Jade well," Melia murmured.

"You hoped he wouldn't?"

She shrugged. A stinging spike ran across her shoulders. It reminded her she would have to face her small but fierce opponent— and her trainer—again soon. "If he hadn't done such a good job, I wouldn't have gotten such a sound beating yesterday."

"It's going to make her overconfident," Sinjiin said. "Challenges, wagers—competition is common in the Hidden City. It's always a mistake to believe you're invulnerable. I've seen it repeatedly. A single win, and they think no one can beat them. "

"Maybe," Melia said.

Sinjiin stopped massaging her swollen elbow. "You're upset with Ryder."

"I have to face them today, bruised and crippled. He helped her do this to me."

"Did you dream last night?" he asked.

"No."

"As soon as you heal, you'll need to shift into your dragon state."

"Sure."

"You don't expect him to sacrifice his honor, do you?" Sinjiin asked.

"His honor? He's never wanted me to incarnate Umbra. If Jade wins, he'll get his way. This isn't about honor."

This time, rather than stopping the application of the salve, Sinjiin pushed deeper into her muscles.

"Ouch!"

"When you incarnate Umbra, it will be the pettiest emotions that put not just you, but the entire enchanted world at risk. That is what you have to understand, Melia. It doesn't matter what Ryder's motive is. You have to become stronger. You're not fighting to beat Jade. You're fighting to beat Umbra."

58. A Whole Sand Dollar

Melia forced herself to stand as straight as she could in front of the tribunal. She couldn't bear for Jade to know how much damage she'd inflicted. Sinjiin, in his tiger form, stood by Melia's side. She let the weight of her right leg and hip press against him.

"The second challenge shall be a contest of time and ingenuity. It will begin when you leave the council chamber today with your instructions." Threldor held up two pieces of parchment before he handed them to Jelina.

He continued to speak as she brought the parchments down to the dais, giving one to Melia and one to Jade. Melia avoided eye contact with everyone. Regardless of Sinjiin's insistence she won the greater victory by not allowing her dragon self to emerge, she burned with humiliation.

"The challenger who collects the most items from the list you're being given," Threldor continued, "and delivers them to the tribunal on the morning of the next full moon, will be the winner of the second challenge. If all ten items are delivered by both contestants, the quality of the items will be evaluated to determine the winner." Jelina carried a second set of parchments down to Melia and Jade. "These maps of the island will aid you. Are there any questions?"

None.

Threldor dismissed them. "May the gods of Azyllai watch over you all." The grey faeries turned from the contestants to talk among themselves.

Melia hesitated. As much as she longed to brush her hand against Ryder's, or gaze into his eyes, she couldn't separate him from Jade's victory; he helped Jade hurt her. When he and Jade exited the dais, Melia hung back.

Sinjiin waited with her.

She strained to hear the echo of Ryder's footsteps over the tribunal's conversations. When she was certain they were long gone, Melia knelt next to the tiger, gasping when her tailbone reminded her it was still tender. She moved more slowly as she spread the first parchment across the cool stone.

They gazed at it together.

Down the left side were five pictures: a gold coin, a silver ring, a clump of purple berries, a sand dollar, and a plant from the ocean with long green fingers that looked like seaweed. On the right side, there was a list of five more items: a book from the mortal world, words of cherished wisdom, the definition of a true friend, a recipe for love, and a self-portrait.

A moon cycle seemed like a long time to collect the ten items. Puzzled by the challenge, she gazed into the tiger's eyes. "It looks too simple."

Sinjiin wagged his head in the direction of their guide, who waited on the edge of the dais to escort them from the chamber.

Melia's lower back pitched as she returned to standing. She had several questions for Threldor. Did she dare ask them?

She held one finger up to the guide as she waited to see if the grey faerie would notice her standing below. He never acknowledged her. Melia considered climbing the stone stairs which led to his seat. Sinjiin nudged her. He wanted to go. Maybe their guide could answer her questions. She let the tiger lead her from the chamber.

"Will we be able to roam freely over the island?" she asked the guide.

"I must accompany you wherever you go," he said.

"Are we limited to whom we can speak with?"

"As with the rest of the challenge, you may not speak with your family or friends."

"Then we are free to speak with anyone else?"

"You may not speak to the other team."

What would she say to Ryder? *Are you enjoying your time with Jade?* Her mind seized on images of them together: running across a beach, laughing over the sand dollar they found; Ryder beaming as Jade painted a perfect self-portrait; both of them smiling as they concocted a special recipe for love.

Her fantasies made her heart hurt as much as her cheekbones.

It was going to be a long moon cycle.

Jade watched Ryder from the corner of her eye.

This morning, Melia entered the council chamber, limping. Her face, more purple, yellow, and green than black and blue, looked nasty.

To keep from smirking, Jade bit her tongue. The tip still smarted.

Now, Ryder was on the patio because he needed fresh air. She didn't point out they would be spending plenty of time outside over the next moon cycle. Several of the things on their scavenger hunt could only be found outdoors. Because that's what this was: A scavenger hunt. Jade loved them as a kid. She studied the parchment again. When her gaze settled on *a recipe for love*, she felt giddy. She'd make sure to have him help her with that one.

Later, when Ryder came inside, they went over the list together, but he took charge.

He divided the list of ten items into groups. Things they would find outside: the purple berries, the green-fingered seaweed, and the sand dollar. Things they'd need to borrow: the gold coin and silver ring. And the things they could research in the citadel library and/or create themselves: the book from the mortal world, the words of wisdom, the definition of a friend, and a recipe for love. The self-portrait was the only thing he hesitated over. "This will require parchment and charcoal or ink, perhaps some paints and a looking glass." He stared at the map.

"Are you looking for an art studio?" Jade leaned closer to him. When her elbow slid against his, he jerked his arm away.

The reaction was as bracing as a glass of cold water splashed in her face. She forced herself to remain calm. If she yelled at him, he'd withdraw. "You're upset about what I did to Melia yesterday."

He covered his mouth with his hand.

Jade's impulse to touch him was strong. Instead, she pushed her chair away from the table, stood, and crossed her arms. "I did what you trained me to do. It probably looks worse than it is. If she were seriously injured, she wouldn't have been able to stand in the council chamber for so long. They would have canceled the next challenge." Wouldn't they?

Ryder lifted his head. "I miss her."

Jade threw up her hands. "And I need to know that because?"

He rubbed one eye and then the other. Oh my god. Was he crying? No. No. No! She needed the stoic Ryder. When he focused on a challenge, he didn't talk about Melia. Jade pulled the map out from under his fist. "The beaches are the obvious places to look for the seaweed and the sand dollar. They all look like long walks." Although she wanted to bolt from their suite right now, it would be more efficient if they could find the berries on the way to the coastline. "I'm going to go ask Raffi some questions."

Ryder didn't stop her. His face was blank, his eyes dull. He looked like a zombie.

It creeped her out.

She shook her head in disgust as she stalked across the suite.

Several weeks later, Ryder rifled through a collection of love poems. With eleven days left, six items were checked off their challenge list: the berries, a gold coin, a handful of dried seaweed, and a silver ring; Jade had been uncharacteristically ecstatic when she'd discovered the book, *To Kill a Mockingbird*, in the citadel library, murmuring Atticus Finch was the best father ever; and inspired by memories of her grandmother, she settled on a short quote from the Christian bible, *The truth will set you free*, as her words of wisdom.

Now Jade struggled with her self-portrait. Ryder suspected it was more an exercise in seeing oneself than a drawing contest.

While she worked on her portrait, it gave him time to consider Melia. His recent revelation unnerved him. From the day they met, Melia distrusted his ability to keep a vow. Most times, he understood her fear as a product of her parents' failed marriage, but sometimes he became angry when she insisted it would be impossible for him to honor a faerie troth, whatever that might be.

However, since they'd left Tyrannis, Melia's faith in him had shifted. She no longer doubted him. Now, it seemed, he doubted her.

He was helping Jade win because he didn't trust Melia's love for him could withstand Umbra's seduction. Facing Melia's doubt, he often felt superior. Now, he faced his own, and it looked ugly. He wanted Jade to win. Not for the good of the Whole, but to make his own life easier.

He should be helping Jade win because he had faith in Melia, not because he doubted her.

Ryder puzzled over the council's list. The only item left in question was the whole sand dollar.

Jade had found pieces of sand dollars, halves of sand dollars, and even one sand dollar that looked like something had taken a bite from it; but she had yet to find a whole, unblemished one.

When the dark moon phase reminded them they were halfway through the challenge and still minus a single whole sand dollar, they decided to scavenge the beaches twice a day—once at low tide in the morning, a second time at low tide in the evening.

Every day it grew colder, and the winds blew harder, slicing their cheeks with icy air. But the single whole sand dollar eluded them.

Ryder closed the book of love poems and reached for the map of the island. Maybe there was a better beach.

✧ ✧ ✧

Ryder reached down with his hand to pull Jade up onto the large rock. Despite the increasingly stormy weather, he preferred traveling to beaches farther and farther from the citadel to being trapped in their suite discussing a recipe for love.

Jade had prepared a satisfactory response for the council in that regard, but it had become her favorite topic.

Heavy grey fog enveloped them. Ryder could barely see two arm lengths in front of him. He didn't know where Raffi was, or if he was even still with them.

"How are we going to find a sand dollar in this bowl of clam chowder?" Jade asked.

"I have no idea what that is."

"A thick, creamy soup perfect to eat in weather like this, but it's opaque."

Ryder nodded. "Not a broth."

Jade punched him in the arm. "Exactly."

"All right, Miss Jade. Take it is easy with the right hook."

She giggled.

"Do you see Raffi down below?" he asked.

"Nope. We're alone. Unchaperoned. Do you remember that ledge before we dropped onto the first line of sand? He's back there, resting. He said he'll wait for us there."

Raffi had divulged the existence of the pristine beach they were seeking this morning. He'd described the wall of volcanic rock as an impassable barrier, and advised them the tides along this side of the island were unpredictable.

Ryder had dismissed the guide's warnings. They had four days to find a whole sand dollar. "Good. I won't have to worry about him drowning." He turned to the sound of the sea, searching for his next landing spot.

One minute Ryder was standing with Jade, deciding which

direction to leap, the next minute he was slammed by a huge wave and submerged, being dragged out to sea by the undertow. He flailed and kicked, fighting to reach the surface. The seawater was numbing. He bounced against hard, smooth blocks that burned his hands when he grasped for purchase. Ice.

Groping for air, his head butted against the moving blocks. His body begged for breath. An intense pressure squeezed his empty lungs. They were going to explode. What would happen to Melia when he was gone?

His body drifted down.

Melia couldn't believe what she saw.

Ryder and Jade standing on the rocks. Ryder and Jade wiped away by the tide.

She swooped down, barking for Sinjiin. Surefooted, the tiger bounded across the volcanic rock. This beach, the farthest one from the citadel, was their playground, where they came to let off steam far from the grey faeries' watchful eyes.

Blocks of ice extended beyond the shoreline. She searched the enormous puzzle with her penetrating gaze. A dark shadow drifted beneath the floes.

She barked again for Sinjiin. She called it barking, although it sounded like a cross between a goose's honk and a tiger's roar. Sinjiin sniffed and tread the mounds of rock. Melia arced and swooped, nose-diving for the shadow. The dark form plummeted deeper into the sea's abyss.

She smashed the water's surface, sensing the cold more than feeling it. She was cold-blooded, but the air was cold too. Guided by unwavering instinct, she pushed deeper into the freezing water. She would dive to the bottom of the ocean if she had too. Her snout knocked into an object too soft to be rock or ice. Ryder's body spun away from her. The sight of his stiff arms and legs flung wide as if he were paralyzed stoked an inferno in her heart. She sliced through the water and clamped her boxy mouth around a lifeless limb and pulled up. Jettisoning from the water's surface, she dragged Ryder, slamming his limp body first against an unforgiving block of ice, then against several of the volcanic rocks. He was heavy, and she was panicking. He showed no signs of life.

She flew inland with him, leaving Sinjiin to find Jade.

At the edge of the fog, she saw Raffi, Jade and Ryder's guide. She aimed to land a short distance from him. Raffi's eyes widened when he saw her; when he recognized Ryder, he screamed. Melia dropped Ryder gently onto a narrow strip of flat land. Raffi attacked his charge's chest, pumping it to resuscitate him.

Melia shifted and raced to Ryder's side.

By the time she dropped to her knees, he was coughing, choking, and gurgling up seawater. Raffi dragged his arm across his face in relief. Melia threw herself across Ryder.

At dawn, she awakened with images of this beach seared in her mind. It hadn't been a vision, but the feeling to fly here had been so strong, she'd been unable to shake it. If she'd ignored that inner insistence, the tide would have swept Ryder away. He would have died. Her entire body trembled with the shock of the realization.

A little while later, Sinjiin caught up with them, a bedraggled Jade draped across his back. Although Melia was glad to see her alive, her dislike of the girl had only deepened throughout the challenge.

When everyone had achieved a calmer state, and Jade and Ryder were able to walk, the four challengers looked to Raffi.

"I must tell the council about today's events," he said.

Melia was willing to bear whatever punishment their transgression brought down upon them.

"Where is your guide?" Jade asked Sinjiin, who remained in his tiger form.

Melia tugged on a strand of hair. Sometimes, Sinjiin slipped their guide a sleeping aid so they could run and fly unfettered in their dragon and tiger forms. They always made sure to be back on their patio before he woke, but it would be better if Raffi didn't report that to the council.

Melia pointed in the direction of the citadel. "He's over there. If you're both all right, we'll go now and catch up with him."

Raffi nodded. As they walked away, she overheard him commiserating with Ryder. "All that, and still no sand dollar?"

"No," was all Ryder said, but his frustration was evident in the single word.

She and Sinjiin found a whole sand dollar the first day they came to the beach. Or maybe it found them.

That night Melia dreamed for the first time since the hand-to-hand combat. She was her dragon-self and flew with Ryder on her back, far away from the Isle of Minnanon.

When they stood before the tribunal on the morning of the next full moon, Melia wasn't surprised that Jade and Ryder still hadn't found a whole sand dollar. And yet, she was curious about the deceptively simple challenge. When Threldor solicited their questions, Melia asked, "What did this challenge test?"

Threldor bestowed her with a rare smile. "You are familiar with how grey faeries were born?"

"The soul ember and ash from certain mortals settled on the floor of the Great White Sea. Over time, the accumulated ember and ash cooled to form grey faeries."

Threldor nodded. "While we came into being on the bottom of the sea floor, sand dollars watched over us. Ours was a symbiotic relationship with our protectors, an oxygen exchange which allowed us to breathe before our lungs developed."

"I had no idea," she said.

"Few do. When our time to surface came, an army of our protectors escorted us from the depths. However, in the final stage of our transformation, the oxygen exchange between ourselves and the sand dollars who sustained us was severed. Having become dependent on that exchange, they could no longer survive on their own. In essence, they sacrificed their lives so that we might become land creatures who breathe air. To us they are sacred, a symbol of the circle of life that is the essence of the Whole. The nine other items in this challenge were somewhat meaningless. The council wanted to learn whether a whole sand dollar would offer itself to either or both of the challengers."

A strange sensation stirred in Melia's belly. As it grew and moved through her body, she was able to name it: intense joy.

59. The Grey Citadel

Gavin cursed the cold. "When will we be able to land?" he shouted over the wind.

"The floes are breaking up!" The ship's captain blew into his hands. "In a few more days, we'll be able to dock in the harbor."

"I need to send out a scout."

The captain squinted. "There's a beach a few miles west of the port where a small boat can land."

"Have one ready within the hour."

Gavin traveled with a single regiment, thirty armed men. He carried Lilliane's letter to the Grey Council, sealed with Queen Luisa's sigil, in the breast of his jacket. If the council refused to relinquish the half-faeries to his custody, he would drag them from the island by their hair.

He whistled as he walked by a cluster of knights huddled against the fierce wind. One of the knights dropped away and followed Gavin to his cabin.

"Lock the door." Gavin shuffled through the sheaf of diagrams that papered the table in the room's center. He found the most current schematic of the Grey Citadel and placed it on top of the stack. "You see how the city is laid out like a large horseshoe with these chambers at its center?"

The officer nodded.

Gavin dragged a finger along an entire outer wing. "This part of the citadel is off-limits to all but the grey faeries. We needn't concern ourselves with it." He circled the area in the center along with the horseshoe's central wing—more than half the map. "It's likely these corridors are also of no concern." He pressed his gloved palm flat on the tip of the remaining leg of the horseshoe. "The island's most prestigious guests have always been quartered in these suites, and I suspect this is where you'll find the half-faeries. However, I must be certain before we land. If the council denies the queen's request, we cannot linger. We'll have to move quickly to seize the targets. Confirm the precise location of their rooms and all access routes." He stroked his chin. "Ascertain the shortest routes from the council chamber to this beach, as well as to the port." He spun the map. "Before you leave, I'll ask the captain if he can anchor the ship in that cove. The elevation of the ridge should keep the ship hidden from any observation point in the citadel. If that's the case, you'll need to document these routes as well." Gavin dragged his fingers from the tip of the horseshoe to the cove, and from the council chamber to the cove. He straightened. "The grey faeries are pacifists. They don't believe in war or weapons or violence. Confirm that's still the case. We need to know if any of the foreigners are armed, and if they are, we need to ascertain their numbers. We need to know if there are any weapon caches on the island."

The officer continued to nod.

"There's one more thing." Gavin shifted the parchments, searching for the sketch of Ormrun and Koldis. "An ancient basin and sword are on the island." When he found the parchment, he spread it before the officer. "If you're able to gather information about the whereabouts of these artifacts, you'll be generously rewarded. I'd like to carry them back to Illialei with us."

The officer studied the images.

Gavin clasped his shoulder. "Be quick and unobtrusive. We'll not go ashore until we receive your report."

❖ ❖ ❖

Gavin rolled up his shirtsleeve. He unwound the blood-soaked bandage and grimaced. The cut festered, and the skin didn't close.

Two moon cycles later, the wound bled as freely as the night the princess carved it in his arm. He submerged his forearm in the copper bowl and sucked in his breath. The hot saltwater stung.

A knock came at the door. He pulled his arm from the bath and wrapped a strip of fresh cloth around it. The knock came again. He tossed the old bandage in a bucket and rolled down the sleeve of his shirt as he crossed the cabin.

The scout stood at the door.

Gavin ushered him into the room. "Tell me all you've learned."

When the scout left, Gavin considered his strategy.

Plantine and Lola slept at a distance from Melia and Jade. If the council refused to release the targets, abducting the four half-faeries from their rooms would require the knights split into two groups. Performing the operation as a single unit reduced the risk of failure.

Gavin studied the map. The council chamber was nearer to the cove than the private quarters. It was also a restricted area. The daily activities of the foreigners, many of whom carried weapons—bows and arrows, daggers, knives, and swords—were carried out at some distance from the council chamber.

A dragon had been sighted flying over the island. An exotic pet?

Gavin's wound throbbed.

The scout also learned Pressina and Plantine wore lead bracelets by order of the council; the lead inhibited their ability to perform magic. But no one spoke of the dwarf artifacts.

Information about the sword and basin was non-existent.

Gavin swept the stack of parchments to the floor. He pounded his fist against the table and winced.

60. The Mother Tree

The next morning, when Ryder knock-tap-knock-tapped on the door, Jade pulled the covers over her head. The exhilarating confidence surge from the hand-to-hand combat had been vacuum-sucked out of her when Threldor divulged the truth about sand dollars.

She didn't even try to connect with Umbra last night. What was the point? Ever since they landed on the island, she couldn't get through to him.

Ryder knock-tap-knock-tapped again.

Jade threw off her covers. "Go away!"

"Raffi is here."

"Already? What time was it?" She jumped out of bed and scrambled to get dressed. When she opened the bedroom door, Ryder and Raffi were in deep discussion. As soon as she appeared, they fell quiet.

"What were you two talking about?"

Neither answered her question. Jade studied both their stone faces and sighed.

"We're keeping the tribunal waiting," Raffi said.

As they followed him through the citadel's busy corridors, Jade's feet dragged. If she lost the final challenge, she was toast. Her dream of becoming the most powerful creature in the Whole, and the Queen of the Realm of Faerie, was slipping away.

When she saw Melia standing on the dais with Sinjiin, a cold rush of anger surged through her. She'd underestimated Ryder's girlfriend from the start. She wasn't going to make that mistake again. Sports clichés rattled through her brain. *This could get ugly. It ain't over til it's over. Never say die.*

"Before we proceed to the final challenge, there is a matter before us." Threldor's voice ended Jade's cheerleading session. "The council has received information that the competitors, along with both their companions, had contact during the past moon cycle. Do any dispute this report?"

No one did.

"The report also states that Jade and Ryder's lives were saved as a result of this violation of challenge rules. Do any dispute this fact?"

Jade wished she could deny it, but Raffi had witnessed everything.

"Then our facts seem to be in order," Threldor said. "We will proceed with the remedy the council has recommended. Melia and Jade, as it stands, one of you will incarnate Umbra. For this reason, your personal histories, and the events that have brought each of you to this moment, are of great interest to us. We have assigned a scholar to prepare a detailed account of each of your lives to-date. To assist in this endeavor, you will both make yourselves available between the hours of sunset and dusk to answer questions about your history, for the remaining days of the competition. This means there will be no traipsing around the island."

Melia's cheeks flushed red.

"Do each of you understand this restriction?" Threldor asked.

"Yes," Melia said.

Ryder nodded, Sinjiin roared, and Jade rolled her eyes.

Whatever.

Threldor steepled his long fingers. "There is a grassy field on the north side of the island. In the center of the field is a tree. It is known as the Mother Tree."

Jade fidgeted. More metaphysical B.S. What had she expected from a council of grey faeries, after all? Another round of mixed martial arts fighting? Damn, she just wanted to kick Melia's ass again.

"For the final challenge, each of you will spend a dawn-to-dawn cycle beneath the tree."

The mere thought of sitting outside for twenty-four hours made Jade shiver. "Doing exactly what?" she blurted out.

All thirty grey faeries gaped at her. She'd interrupted their precious leader. Jade couldn't care less. The entire challenge was stacked in Melia's favor.

"Time spent in the company of the Mother Tree has proven to be enlightening. You will report whatever insights you gain during your time there to the council."

Jade's fear of Threldor evaporated. The entire challenge was a farce. "Like, you want a book report?"

"No. You will take no books or other distractions with you." He didn't understand she was being a smart ass. "Some things must be experienced to be known," Threldor said.

Or maybe he did.

"Time spent beneath the tree during the moons' dark phase has provided the most insight to the seeker. Since there are three dark moon nights each moon cycle, the challengers will roll for the first two nights. On the morning of the third night, the challengers will face the council for the final time."

Jade didn't want to roll. "I'll take whichever night she doesn't want."

"You're foregoing the opportunity to choose first?" Jelina asked.

"Yes."

Jelina scribbled something down. "Is that acceptable to the other challenger?" she asked Melia.

Much more of this ridiculous ceremony and Jade was going to puke.

"Yes," Melia replied.

"Which night will you choose?" Jelina asked Melia.

"The first night."

Jelina made another note. "The second night goes to Jade."

"Is that acceptable?" Threldor asked.

"Yes," Melia and Jade replied in unison.

"What is this garbage?" Jade asked Ryder, as soon as they were alone in their suite.

"Are you referring to the interviews, or the challenge?"

"Both."

He shrugged. "Be flattered they wish to make a record of your life."

"It's not flattering, it's creepy."

"It's a gentle reprimand for violating the competition rules."

"It means we can't leave our rooms." She shoved the empty chair next to the one she sat in with her heel. "And do they really expect me to sit under a tree all night and freeze to death?"

"You won't die."

"How do you know? Have you ever sat under the Mother Tree?" She couldn't believe she was having this conversation.

"The council would never send you to your death," he said.

She didn't bring up their near drowning. To know she lost a round of the challenge because a whole sand dollar hadn't deemed her worthy was one thing; to say it out loud, she just couldn't. The grey faerie tribunal was worse than all her mother's government helpers, new age believers, and aging hippies rolled into one. "But sitting under a tree doesn't even make any sense!"

Ryder dragged his chair closer to hers. Wary of this out-of-character gesture, she scooted back in her seat. He rested a hand on her shoulder. It felt good. She wanted to fall forward and bury herself in his arms, but if he pushed her away, she would probably shatter into a thousand pieces on the spot. She sat still.

"It sounds like this is going to be difficult for you," he said.

She shook her head. She was not going to cry, but something hard and solid cracked inside her. He pulled her to him and wrapped his arms around her. She heaved and sobbed and snotted all over his shirt. When she was finished, he gently released her.

Jade had never hated Melia more. Because in that moment, Jade didn't just want to incarnate Umbra, she wanted Ryder to be in love with her.

After Jade went to bed, Ryder sat alone in the front room of their suite. Melia and Jade's mild punishment had gotten him to thinking, as well. Scenes from his entire life, the journey that brought him to this moment, paraded through his mind. No simple coincidence had brought him here.

Over the past two moon cycles, he'd grown fond of Jade. She was different from Melia or Shilda, but he couldn't deny his feelings for her anymore. Jade had become like a sister to him, and he was going to help her do her best in this final round.

The next day, Ryder waited for Jade to come out of her room. He wasn't surprised that half the day was gone before she finally showed herself, grumpy and hungry.

When she finished eating, he asked if she was ready to train.

She laughed. "You want to train me to sit under a tree?"

"I want to teach you how to listen."

Jade's smile reshaped into a grimace. "Meditation is so not my thing."

Ryder pushed back his chair. He leaned forward, elbows on his thighs.

When he was younger—and as angry as she was now—Garrick had been the one to help him see beyond the walls of the priesthood. Imagining a world beyond them had allowed him to breathe and survive. What walls were closing in on Jade now? What bigger picture did she need to grasp?

"Why is incarnating Umbra so important to you?" he asked her.

She struggled to answer. He waited. When she finally met his gaze, he smiled.

"I've never met my father," she said. "I want to meet him, but he doesn't want to meet me," she whispered.

He reached for her hand. It was so small in his. Her eyes widened at the contact. "I've met my father," he said, "but I don't ever want to see him again."

"Why not?" Jade asked.

"He's a liar."

"What did he lie about?"

"I grew up in his world, but the entire time I lived there, he never claimed me as his son. I was raised, eating as an orphan at his table."

Jade frowned. "That's so weird."

Ryder nodded. "Tell me something about your father."

"There's not a lot to tell. He's from a very wealthy family in the mortal world. When he learned my mother was pregnant with me, he agreed to take care of me financially. He sends money every month, but he refuses to have a relationship with me. Every time I've ever asked to meet him, I've been rejected or ignored. Or he threatens to stop sending money through his lawyer. It's humiliating."

"That's why you want to incarnate Umbra?" Ryder asked.

"It would be nice to show up and make him feel humiliated for a change."

"Revenge."

"I think about it more like making him take responsibility for his actions."

"Responsibility is a strange thing," Ryder said.

"What do you mean?"

"Do you like it when anyone forces you to take responsibility?"

"No."

"Most of us don't."

"What's your point?"

"If we don't choose to take responsibility, if our heart isn't in it, it's somewhat meaningless."

"Then what am I supposed to do? Just move on?"

"Your mother loves you very much," Ryder said.

"I know that, but sometimes it's just not enough. I want my father to love me too."

Ryder didn't think it would be wise to use Melia's difficult relationship with her father as an example. "Have you ever dreamed about your father?" he asked.

"Yes."

"When you woke up, did it feel real? Like you really saw him or spent time with him?"

Jade's eyes lit up. "Yes. That's why I want to meet him in real life. If he only knew how happy we could both be if we were in each other's lives."

"Umbra exists in the Void," he explained. "Between the Void and our plane is the Parallel of Shadows. The purest forms of energy exist in the Void as incorporeal entities in a mass of nothingness. Once something reaches the Parallel of Shadows, it has enough form to be like a shadow, a wisp of smoke, a layer of fog. By the time something manifests in our plane, its form is dense enough to be seen and touched. The idea of each of us is born in the Void. However, that idea, of who we are, will never manifest unless it accumulates enough focused energy to move all the way from the Void, through the Shadows, to activate Primal Essence on our plane. You exist in our plane, as did the circumstances that birthed you. However, your father is unable to express his love for you in this plane. It's trapped in the Shadows. The dreams you have about him connect you with those ephemeral fragments that can't be touched or experienced on this plane, and yet, they're very real."

"Like Umbra is real?" Jade asked.

"Like that."

"So there are different layers of reality, and my father's love exists in some of them, but not in all of them?"

"Yes."

"Is it the same with your father?" she asked.

"I never dream about him."

"That's sad," she said.

"It is what it is."

"You're very Spartan," she said.

"I try to listen."

"To your dreams?"

"To my dreams, to my heart, to however the Whole is communicating. It's one of those things that gets easier with practice."

"Have you ever thought you heard the Whole and gotten it wrong?"

"Yes. That's why practicing is helpful. Are you going to let me help you prepare for this last challenge?"

"Do I have a choice?"

Melia entered the carriage behind Threldor. Sinjiin leapt in behind her. After Melia settled across from the grey faerie, Sinjiin stretched out on the floor between them. The heat from his body warmed her legs and feet. Although her clothes—a cloak twice as thick as the one she wore inside the citadel, thick socks, gloves, and a hat—kept out the cold, the proximity of Sinjiin's body was a great comfort to her. Threldor rapped the carriage wall behind him. The cabin jostled as it began to move.

Outside, a sprinkling of stars and two thin slivers of the moons reminded Melia that, in the coming night, the sky would be black. It had been a long time since she'd spent a dark moon night alone.

"We'll arrive at the Mother Tree just before sunrise," Threldor said. "You might want to nap."

Melia closed her eyes and allowed the carriage's steady rhythm to lull her into a doze.

When Threldor woke her, she startled. The grey light of predawn spilled into the carriage when the coachman opened the door. Sinjiin exited first. Melia followed.

The first thing she noticed was the air. She took in deep gulps of it. Threldor pointed. Melia turned.

She'd expected something magnificent, but the tree looked plain, and there was nothing special about the field's appearance.

Disappointed, she returned her gaze to Threldor. "That's the Mother Tree?"

"Yes. We'll leave you shortly. I'll return at the same time tomorrow morning."

"Sinjiin won't come with you?"

"I'll want to hear the account of your experience. It's best for it to remain private."

"I have no secrets to keep from him."

"Then you may share your experience with him when you return to the citadel." Threldor took her gloved hand in his, led her to the tree, and then past it. Sinjiin padded after them. The grey faerie escorted Melia to the far edge of the field. Beyond a steep embankment, there was a small river.

"If you find you're thirsty, you may come here for a drink. However, it's common to forego all forms of physical sustenance while in this field, and in the tree's presence."

"And there's nothing I need to do to have this experience?"

"There is something unique about this location," Threldor said. "Fanidor, a grey faerie who is scientifically inclined, has been performing studies of the area. It's possible the effects experienced by those who visit here might one day be explained by the presence of a magnetic field, or perhaps an odorless gas released from a deep fissure in the ground not too far from here. At present, they remain a mysterious but reliable reality."

Mysterious was the word that kept coming up whenever the Mother Tree was discussed.

Threldor led Melia back to the tree.

Sunlight edged the eastern horizon.

Threldor bowed and gestured for Sinjiin to accompany him. Melia watched as the spirited white horses and gleaming carriage retreated into a line of brush, and then disappeared altogether.

She gazed up at the tree. Its limbs and leaves emanated a pleasant odor. The lowest branch was well within reach. Impulsively, she raised her hands. The gloved tips of her fingers trailed the bark. She followed the length of it to the tree's trunk where she pressed her palms flat against the rough wood.

The tree hummed. It was a slight but steady vibration. Melia turned around and pressed her back against the trunk. She slid down until she crouched with her butt and feet wedged between two of its sizable roots. She realized she was enjoying herself. Her sense of time blurred.

How long had it been since she ran through the Footing Fields, laughing and wild, with Tatou flitting beside her?

A euphoria gripped her. The desire to return to Illialei consumed her. Why did she ever leave? She closed her eyes and found herself sitting at the table in the kitchen of her mother's tree house. She was alone, but she heard the clack of boots against the hardwood floor in the hall behind her.

"Melia," her mother said. "I never expected to find you here."

"I've missed Illialei so much, and I've missed you, too. I've even missed the tree house." She laughed. "That's why I decided to come home."

Pressina sat in the chair across from her middle daughter.

Melia studied her mother's face. It was the face of a great beauty. "Do you like being beautiful?"

"I think it suits me."

"It does," Melia agreed. She couldn't imagine her mother otherwise.

"Where are Plantine and Melusine?" Melia asked. "I've missed them too."

"Have you forgotten everything that's happened?"

Melia's breathing became labored.

"Your father is dead," Pressina said.

"I-I know."

Her mother shook her head. "Melusine and Plantine are never coming home."

"Do you miss my sisters?" Melia asked.

"I do."

"Do you miss my father? Did you love him?"

"What is love?" Pressina asked.

"I'm in love," Melia said.

Her mother's eyes sparked. "Tell me about it."

"All my life I've been yearning for something I couldn't put a name to. I believed it was some place far away, but I didn't know where. Now I know it's not a place, it's a person. When I'm with him, I feel like I'm exactly where I'm supposed to be. And even though we don't always see things the same way, we're learning to talk to one another. To trust one another. But it's more than that, his presence fills something inside me. Something that's always been empty."

"Where is he now?" Pressina asked.

Melia looked around the kitchen. "I don't know."

They fell quiet.

Melia had the feeling there was something important she needed to ask her mother, but she couldn't think of what it was. She toyed with the pearls on the cord around her neck.

"Where did you get those?" her mother asked.

"They were a gift from Elendah before she died." A torrent of images roiled in Melia's mind. "Mother, why did you leave me to die on the floor of the stronghold?"

Pressina closed her eyes. "You were determined to stop Umbra's incarnation."

"But you never came to visit me in the dungeon. Why not?"

"Your sister needed me, and there was nothing I could do for you."

"You could have held my hand—"

"What would that have done? You were unconscious!"

Melia reached for her mother's hand now.

Pressina pulled away. Her hand disappeared beneath the table.

A bruising ache filled Melia's chest. "I hate you," she whispered.

Her mother offered an icy smile. "That hate will be the door Umbra enters to destroy you."

Melia's eyes flew open. It was so cold. She rubbed her arms and tried to stand. Her foot was asleep. She kept testing it until the tingling ended and she could walk. She hurried away from the tree. When she no longer stood beneath its long arms, she studied it.

Residual energy from the fight she hallucinated having with her mother reverberated in her body. It had felt so real. Yet, here she was, standing alone in this field in winter.

Melia experimented with the tree the rest of the day. Dozing with her back against its trunk produced the most powerful hallucinations. The emotional truths that erupted from deep within troubled her, until she realized how cathartic it was to release them. More and more, as the day went on, it felt like the tree was pulling her darkest energies and emotions from her. The result after each encounter: she felt purer, lighter, cleansed.

She began to crave the intensity of revealing and reveling in truths she'd shunned her entire life. It became addictive, a game she never wanted to end.

After the sun set, the hallucinations changed. Rather than scenes from her past, visions of her future came.

I walk through crumbling stone. The hem of my long gown trails in the vines and twining ivy that choke the walls, and every chair, table, surface, object within them. I stop before a long window.

Low grey clouds flood the sky. Winter has reached Illialei. The endless summer is gone.

Carriage wheels woke her.

"Open yourself to whatever happens," Ryder told Jade before he left her beneath the tree.

Sure thing. She stretched out beneath the canopy of limbs and leaves and fell asleep.

"Jade."

She opened her eyes. From the height of the sun, it was midday.

She'd slept for several hours. She looked around, but no one was there. "Umbra?"

Nothing. She rolled on her side and repositioned her long, thick cloak to make both a pillow and a blanket. She curled her knees into her stomach and went back to sleep.

"Do you love him?"

This time Jade didn't open her eyes. "It doesn't matter."

The ground quaked.

Jade smacked her hand against the dry grass. "Stop it."

"My queen cannot love another."

Jade sat up. She hugged her knees to her chest. "Your queen." She snorted. "You'll take anyone who'll have you as your queen."

A wind that made it hard to breathe blasted across the field.

"Why do you toy with me, precious Jade?"

"Why have you avoided me for the last three moon cycles when I needed your help to win this stupid challenge?" Jade hissed. "It's too late now. I'm going to lose. So go away."

"He doesn't love you."

"Don't you think I know that?"

"I am here now."

"Great. I don't have the basin or the sword."

A sour smell, like rotten eggs, washed over her.

God, this tree stinks. She pushed herself up and headed toward the embankment and the river. The nauseating odor lessened. She couldn't take a breath without feeling as if she was going to gag. Another sharp gust of wind sliced through her. This was the most miserable and stupid challenge yet. The tree was the only form of shelter, but she couldn't stand its awful smell.

If she pressed herself flat against the ground, there would be less surface for the wind to attack. Lying spread-eagle on her back, she stared at the sky. It was one enormous grey cloud.

She came to the enchanted world to incarnate Umbra and become queen. What happened?

Melia happened. And this stupid challenge.

Now she was lying in some field next to a tree that smelled like a dumpster. Or sulfur. Pollution. For the first time since she crossed the borders of time and space, Jade wanted to go home. She missed her cottage in Hillcrest, her job at Starbucks, and Jules. Maybe if she went back now, things could be different. She wouldn't have to worry about her mother. She wasn't sick anymore.

A soft wind blew across Jade's face. It brought a pleasant scent. She sat up. Maybe it wasn't the tree that stunk. She walked back to it and went right up to the trunk and sniffed. The tree smelled good.

She settled with her back against the trunk and her legs straight out, mingled with the roots. Jade drifted off.

"Honey."

"What, Mom?"

"I brought someone to see you."

A man Jade had never seen before stood beside Lola, yet there was something familiar about him. Like Jade had known him all her life.

"This is your father, Tom Conroy," her mother said.

Jade felt her body light up, like she was a football field and someone popped on the stadium lights. "You're my dad?"

"Your mother wanted me to meet you."

"That's the only reason you came, because my mother wanted you to?"

"I'll always love her. I knew it would make her happy."

"What about me? I'm your daughter. Don't you want to make me happy?"

"You may be my blood, but you're a stranger to me."

"You're an asshole," Jade said.

"Then I guess you'll have to live with the fact that your father is an asshole."

"Mom! How could you have slept with this prick?"

"Hormones?"

"You two deserve each other," Jade yelled at them. God. After all the fantasies she'd had about him, she couldn't believe her father was such an idiot. If she ever made it back to the mortal world, she was going to make things official and adopt Jules as her father. Ever since she could remember, he was the one who looked out for her. His face was the one that lit up when he saw her. Why hadn't she ever paid attention?

Jade jerked awake.

Her pulse raced. The hallucination had been so real.

Ryder had told her to open herself up to anything.

She tried to catalogue all the visions, illusions, and hallucinations she'd had since the carriage had left.

She surveyed the field. It was as if a veil had lifted, and she'd been gifted with stark-raving truth.

She didn't care about Umbra. She didn't want to be the Queen of the Realm of Faerie. She'd wasted her life yearning for a father who was incapable of caring for her, while she ignored the man who loved her like a parent.

She wondered if her mom had ever slept with Jules.

No. Too disgusting to consider.

Her thoughts moved on to Ryder, who didn't belong to her.

Yet, because of him, for the first time in her life, she'd embraced the possibility of falling in love, being in love. That had to be a good thing, didn't it?

Jade wrapped her arms around herself and smiled. It felt like some cosmic force had wiped her slate clean.

She loved new beginnings.

Two days later, Jade stood with Ryder, Sinjiin, and Melia on the marble dais facing the tribunal for the last time.

Lola, the fat old spring faerie, the old elf, the pixie, and Melia's mother and sister watched from the balcony.

Umbra hadn't tried to contact her since their pathetic exchange beneath the Mother Tree. The more she thought about it, the more she decided it was Umbra who brought the smell of sulfur to the fields.

Jade wasn't about to dwell on the parallels between sulfur and brimstone, Umbra and the devil. Her grandmother had warned her, maybe she should have listened. She was ready to go home. It was time.

"Jade and Ryder, we acknowledge and thank you for your participation in the competition," Threldor said.

Everyone except the contestants clapped.

"Melia and Sinjiin, we also acknowledge and thank you for your participation in the competition."

More polite clapping.

"Melia and Jade, we acknowledge your compliance with the documentation of your stories, and thank you. If you desire a copy of these accounts, one will be provided to you.

"The third challenge pitted each contestant against herself, and herself alone," Threldor continued. "The insights and awareness you each gained beneath the Mother Tree will serve you for the rest of your lives. Both contestants have been challenged emotionally throughout their lives. However, only Melia shared her full experience beneath the Mother Tree, withholding nothing."

Jade squinted at the council. How did they know she withheld her encounter with Umbra?

Threldor held Jade's gaze. "Our darkest sides are revealed to all who spend time beneath the tree."

Jade snorted. She should have known the final challenge was just another trick.

The grey faerie shifted his gaze to Melia. "After a thorough evaluation of the results of each challenge, the Grey Council declares Melia Albiana as the chosen vessel for Umbra's incarnation. We shall reconvene in a fortnight to determine the optimal time and location for the incarnation."

A deathly silence consumed the tribunal, the chamber, and everyone present.

The first sound Jade registered was the thump of her heart. It was over.

Ryder turned away from her, to embrace Melia.

Jade's eyes watered. She lowered her head and rubbed her eyes with her fists, hoping to look tired, not teary. Losing the first guy she ever had romantic feelings for–and the competition–to Melia needled her pride, but the sharp edge that had possessed her since … since Gabriela died was fading. She just couldn't workup a huge case of ill-will for Melia or the stupid council. Ever since her night under the Mother Tree, Jade felt as though all her desires and emotions were being flung around the cage of an amusement park ride. And there was this idea growing in the back of her mind. She'd never wanted to write a book, but what if she returned to the mortal world and wrote all this crazy stuff down? No one would believe it was true, but she could call it fiction. Plus … she really missed Jules.

"Jade!" Lola threw her arms around her daughter's neck. "I know how important this competition was for you, but I'm so glad you didn't win."

Jade half-laughed. Her mother might have spent years as a bag lady and pharmaceutical experiment, but she'd always been honest with her daughter. For the first time in ages, Jade responded to her mother's affection with a heartfelt hug.

As they held each other, Jade scanned the council chamber. The audience was filled with men. Her heart skipped a beat. Every single one of them wore the same brown uniform Gavin had worn. She patted her mother's back and released her.

Jade studied the men's faces and quavered.

"What is it?" her mother asked.

Jade shook her head as her gaze locked with his. What was he doing here?

61. The First Battle

"There is one more matter before the council adjourns," Threldor announced. He waved his hand, motioning someone to come forward. Everyone turned to see who it was.

Melia's blood raced. The row of seats behind her friends were filled with Huron knights. She'd been so focused on Ryder and Threldor when she entered the council chamber she hadn't noticed them.

One of the knights rose.

Melia gasped and squeezed Ryder's hand.

He gave her a questioning look.

She shook her head. In her peripheral vision, Jade trembled.

Lola covered her mouth with her hand.

Melia located Tatou in the front row of the balcony. The pixie's wings blurred in a panicky rhythm. Melia wasn't imagining it: The knight who'd chased them to the enchanted gardens, the same one who'd tried to kill her the night of the massacre at the Veiled Tavern, was descending the marble steps, whistling, as if he didn't have a care in the world.

Melia swung her head to observe Threldor's reaction.

It was rare to observe emotion in the grey faerie's demeanor, but on the day he addressed Flora concerning the genocide of the spring faeries, his eyes had darkened and his brows had furrowed. Now, his expression was mild. He didn't know.

The knight reached the dais. He smiled at her!

Melia's heart roared.

Ryder shifted to stand behind her, his hands circling her biceps.

Sinjiin, in his tiger form, rose. He stood, his haunches taut, his ears perked. After three moon cycles together, he could read Melia's emotions.

Jade and Lola shuffled closer to one another.

"Your name?" Threldor asked.

"Gavin Tovar." The knight bowed with a graceful flourish that made Melia's teeth grind. "I come before you"—he fanned his arm indicating the council—"as an emissary of Queen Luisa Albiana." He pulled a folded parchment from his jacket and waved it in the air.

Threldor motioned to Jelina. She descended the stairs. Gavin gave her the parchment. She delivered it to Threldor. The seconds dragged on as he read the document.

Knights coughed and shifted in their seats.

Melia studied Gavin. Despite his carefree demeanor, she noticed he was careful with his arm.

When Threldor finished reading, he gazed down at his folded hands before raising his eyes. "Queen Luisa has accused Pressina Albiana and her daughters, Melia and Plantine, of violating the decrees set forth as law in Illialei by Uriel and Olivia Albiana. The queen accuses Jade Rae Silver of physically assaulting her daughter, Princess Lilliane." The grey faeries shook their heads and murmured to one another. Threldor held up a hand. "While we appreciate the queen's attention to protocol, she offers no reply to the council's accusations against her—"

Gavin stepped forward and raised his chin. "On the day I sailed, no document setting forth any accusations against the queen had reached Illialei." He stepped back.

Threldor canted his head. "Be that as it may. We cannot comply with the queen's request until the matter of her own crimes have been resolved."

Gavin stepped forward again. "I feel confident Queen Luisa Albiana has committed no crimes."

The grey faerie to Threldor's right leaned over and whispered in Threldor's ear. Threldor nodded. He motioned for Gavin to take a step back. "Be that as it may, crimes have been committed in Faerie —"

Melia stepped forward. "This knight participated in the massacre at the Veiled Tavern." She could feel Gavin's cold stare. "If he didn't beat Flora himself for knowledge of Ormrun and Koldis, then it was done at his command. He would have murdered me that night, but Jade's mother and Ryder interceded. It's an outrage he stands before this council issuing demands."

"Are Melia's accusations true?" Threldor addressed the knight.

"She's mistaken me for another. I—"

"I've mistaking you for no one!" Melia shouted.

Jade stood even beside her. "He ... Gavin ... that princess sent him to the mortal world to kill me and my mother. Ryder ... and Melia ... saved us."

Gavin strode in front of Melia and grabbed Jade's wrist with his good arm. He began to twist—

Jade struggled as her body crumpled.

Lola screamed.

Ryder rounded Melia and slammed the side of Gavin's jaw with the heel of his hand.

The knight stumbled. He didn't fall, but he lost his grip on Jade's wrist.

Jade found her feet and raced to shield her mother.

"Seize them!" Gavin shouted.

Shouts and screams broke out from the balcony.

Melia whirled around to face chaos.

A knight dragged her mother—rendered powerless by the slim lead bracelet circling her wrist—by the hair. Pressina's pale face reddened as she swatted air in an attempt to strike her assailant. Two more knights wrestled with Plantine. Wearing a bracelet identical to her mother's, she fought to free herself. Although she was too short and slight to throw off her attackers, she bought herself some time. Flora stood back-to-back with Aldous, covering him, as the old elf eased toward the head of the stairs that exited the balcony. The spring faerie gripped a knife in each fist. Tatou darted above the melee tossing pixie dust like confetti. Four knights sprawled upon the two highest rows of bench-like seats, loopy grins on their faces.

Sinjiin roared.

Melia crouched and let the fire in her heart consume her. Her arms stretched long and wide. She curled her fists, now studded with deadly claws. Her legs shortened and thickened into stumps of solid muscle. She curved her neck, her long snout thrusting toward the ceiling, and bellowed.

A sharp pinch stung her underbelly. Melia looked down. The long shaft of an arrow protruded from her scaly skin. Three more glanced off the tough hide of her wings. Melia scanned the chamber for the archer. Three knights stood equidistant across the lower rows of the balcony wielding bows. They all aimed at her.

Melia flapped her wings. Slowly, she rose from the marble floor. Four more arrows flew at her. Two hit their target. Their sharp stings annoyed her but didn't disable her. She ripped them from her hide as se climbed higher to the chamber's domed ceiling. There, she coiled, arched, and sent a sheet of flame across the knights who shot at her.

Two of the bows ignited, scorching the bowmen's hands and faces. They threw their weapons down. The giant wood frames clattered against the stone floor to burn and smolder. Melia shot another tide of flame, and the pair tore down the aisle.

Flora and Aldous had almost reached the bottom of the stairs.

Jade's arms circled Lola. They were trapped together in the center of the dais. Ryder shielded them, wielding a dagger he'd wrested from a knight. Sinjiin tread a menacing perimeter. Three knights taunted the tiger from a safe distance.

Gavin urged them on.

Threldor intermittently banged his gavel against his podium and called for order. The rest of the grey faeries crowded around him, their alarm and helplessness etched on their faces. Although they were unarmed, no knights attacked them. Jelina hurried down the steps leading from the tribunal gallery to the dais. She skirted the platform and ran into the hall. One of the guides followed her.

A shrill scream pulled Melia's gaze back to the balcony.

A knight carried Plantine, her hands knotted with rope, over his shoulder. He bolted down the stairs.

The unending wail came from Pressina. Her assailant held a knife against her throat and murmured in her ear.

As a dragon Melia's hearing was as sharp as her vision, she heard every sickening word.

"Hush, hush, now," the knight said. "Don't fight, my beauty."

Pressina's gown was torn, her cheek bruised, her eyes pools of dismay. "Please, let my daughter go."

"You have to believe I'd do it, just to see you smile, but those aren't my orders, love."

Pressina collapsed, as if all the fight left her body in a single exhale. She'd lost consciousness.

With one arm cinched around her waist, the knight returned his dagger to his belt. He leered as he slid his arms beneath Pressina armpits and dragged her toward the end of the aisle.

Melia's vision tunneled. She erupted from the ground with a thundering growl and landed, gripping the balcony railing with her hind claws, her tail whipping behind her. Her burning eyes glared into those of her mother's captor.

"Now, now," he cooed.

Melia wagged her head and roared.

The knight took an awkward step back, but didn't release Pressina. "Your mother wants to go home. I'm only helping her."

Melia lunged at him, aiming for his head.

The knight ducked.

The benches she landed on shuddered. Melia whipped around. The knight had almost reached the stairs. Melia bellowed and launched herself again. He raised his hands to protect his face. Her claws lacerated his forearms. The sweet smell of terror filled the air. He turned and ran, leaving Pressina crumpled on the ground.

Pressina's chest rose and fell. She was alive.

The only knights remaining in the balcony were in a pixie haze.

Melia rose into the air and circled the chamber.

Volcanic heat rose like bile in her throat. Sinjiin's mighty bulk stretched across the dais. Blood stained his fur. Three separate blades pierced his throat, flank, and hindquarters. Their hilts quivered as the tiger gasped for air.

Jade and Aldous knelt beside the large cat. Jade eased the blade from the wound in the tiger's throat as the elf stemmed the flow of blood with a strip of cloth. Lola hovered over them, batting her hands. Ryder and Flora parried with two knights.

Four bodies in brown uniforms lay lifeless on the chamber's marble floor.

Plantine, Gavin, and the rest of the knights were gone.

Threldor descended the tribunal gallery stairs.

Melia swooped, aiming for the two knights battling with Flora and Ryder. They heard the thunder of her wings and fled. Melia released her anguish in a guttural blast that shook the entire chamber.

Flora joined Aldous and Jade.

Threldor hailed Melia. "Go and save your sister. We will save your friend."

Melia caught Ryder's eye. He lowered his gaze to the ground. Melia circled the chamber and landed beside him. She flattened her belly against the floor. Ryder settled astride her. Once she felt his fingers clutching the spiny ridges that ran down her back, Melia flew from the chamber.

More than a hundred foreigners clogged the grey-marble corridor, easily blockading a handful of knights. At the far end of the hall, seven more knights, their wrists and ankles bound by cuffs and chains, lined up behind Jelina and the guide.

Melia and Ryder weren't needed here. She soared beneath the citadel's high ceilings, carrying Ryder as she had so many times in her dreams. Her heart expanded in her chest—until the delectable scent of terror flooded her nostrils.

Her dragon-self followed it to the sea.

The ship was anchored in a cove.

From a distance, the knights looked like rats as they scampered on board.

Melia circled overhead. Gavin commanded his reduced number of troops from the deck. Melia counted eleven knights pulling canvas covers from four brass cannons. Crewman passed along bags of gunpowder to gunners who rammed the packs into cylindrical muzzles. They wheeled the guns into position.

"It's a trap," Ryder said.

A few of the knights waved their arms and shouted.

"How about a bellyful of iron?"

"That hide will make a nice blue jacket for my lady."

"I've always wanted a dragon claw to wear around my neck."

Melia swooped, and they scattered. She circled the vessel, searching for her sister.

Gavin marched to the front of the ship where two knights jerked on the ends of the rope that bound Plantine. She was on her knees, blindfolded and gagged.

"Come and get her!" Gavin shouted.

Melia exhaled a stream of fire.

Gavin and the knights shrank from the deadly heat. A sail behind them burst into flames. Plantine and everyone else on deck choked on black smoke.

"We need a plan," Ryder shouted over the roar of the sea.

Melia wheeled to the shoreline. As soon as she touched ground, Ryder leapt from her back. She lumbered across the sand. Hidden behind a bluff, she transformed into her half-faerie self.

There was no time to marvel over the fluidity of her form, a fluidity that had once been impossible. Over the past three moon cycles, Sinjiin had pushed her to master the shift until it required the same effort as taking a deep breath. "I can breach the ship's hull," Melia said to Ryder. "The ship will take in water and go down. They won't drown, but their cannons will."

The wind whipped their hair and stole their voices. "It's too dangerous," he yelled.

Melia curled her toes in the sand. "If I come in from a low enough angle, I'll be out of firing range. But you'll have to swim out to rescue Plantine."

Ryder ran his fingers through his hair. Melia could almost hear what he was thinking, *You're damned reckless*. But he didn't say it. He rested his hands on her shoulders. "Are you sure you want to do this?"

"We need to get Plantine off the ship, and I don't intend to let Gavin escape."

Ryder squeezed her in a tight hug. "All right."

She soaked in his strength.

He let her go.

Melia touched her lips to his and met his gaze before she crouched with her palm flat against the sand. Like the flicker of a match, her love for Ryder combusted with an image of Sinjiin lying half-dead on the chamber dais. Melia exploded into her dragon-self and launched into the air. She flapped her powerful wings, drawing energy from the dark grey clouds, the frigid wind, and the Great White Sea. Her breath was like a bellows, fanning the furnace of rage in her belly.

She flew farther and farther out to sea. When the ship was nothing but a dot bobbing among the waves, she rounded back and aligned herself with her target. Gradually, the beat of her mighty wings increased. Her body cleaved air.

The ship gained in size.

A cannon exploded. A ball of iron shot across the sea in her direction. Another one came. And then another. The distance and height of the eruptions guided Melia's path. Her experience as an eagle served her well. She manipulated the angle of her body, her tail, and her wings with nuanced skill. She shot through the air lower and faster. She tipped toward the sea. A cannon ball whizzed overhead. Heat grazed her tail.

Melia bowed her head. She slammed into the ocean. And plowed into the ship's hull with the spiny ridge of her back. Wood splintered. Her body shook with the impact. She reeled beneath the waves. Water rushed into the ship's hold.

She swam as far away from the wreckage as her breath would allow. When she surfaced, the ship careened among the waves. Melia rose from the sea, and slowly approached the deck. The cannons had rolled from their positions to collide at one end of the vessel. They were useless now, deadweight sinking one end of the ship more quickly than the other.

Several knights and the ship's crew already slogged to shore, navigating the ice floes which had begun to melt and shrink. A band of armed foreigners awaited them with cuffs and chains. Melia scanned the crowd for Gavin. He wasn't among the deserters. She returned to the sinking ship. A strange scent attracted her attention. It wafted from the nearest hatchway. She inhaled a big whiff. It was the scent of terror, but there was something else. Blood and roses. She waited for Gavin to show himself.

When he finally appeared, clawing for air, she glided to him. He screamed and thrashed when he saw her. She spiraled behind him and gripped his shoulders with her claws. He grabbed debris and kicked, but she lifted him into the air. She searched the shore for Ryder. At the far end of the beach, he waited with Plantine. Both were drenched and shivering, but they were safe.

Melia dropped Gavin a short distance from them.

The knight somersaulted to land in a collapsed heap. He protected his wounded arm. A grimace contorted his face when Ryder pinned him to the ground. Debris from the ship washed ashore, and Ryder had salvaged some rope. When he jerked Gavin's wrists behind his back, the knight screamed.

Melia landed and transformed into her half-faerie self. "Something is wrong with his arm," she said to Ryder.

"I'm going to die!" Gavin shouted. "I'm going to die!"

Ryder yanked him to his feet.

Gavin uttered another shrill cry.

"We're not going to kill you!" Ryder shouted.

Melia approached the knight and rubbed her nose. The sick-sweet smell of blood and roses lingered. She tugged on his sleeve. A bloody wrap circled his forearm. "What's this?"

He spit at her.

Melia returned to the waterline. Rather than a fiery dragon, she imagined her rage in the form of ice, and retained her half-faerie form. She drew power from the frigid water splashing against her shins and knees. When she was filled, and brimming with power, she stalked back to Gavin.

The knight sagged in Ryder's arms.

Despite the cold temperature, beads of sweat ringed the knight's forehead, the musky, metallic odor rolling off him thickened.

"You smell of black roses," Melia said.

"Your cousin demands four bloody hearts."

"Whose?"

Gavin glared. "Those whose Albiana lineage is tainted with mortal blood."

"And if she doesn't receive those hearts?"

"Then I'll die."

Melia crouched before him. She needed to gaze into his eyes, to see what kind of evil lurked there. "Then my decision is easy. Because I won't allow you to take another life."

He turned away from her.

Melia took hold of his chin and forced him to face her. "I know that Huron knights follow orders. Did Lilliane also order you to attack the Veiled Tavern? Did you beat Flora at her command?"

Gavin laughed. It was a strange, maniacal braying that awakened a memory in Melia.

She quivered. "Umbra," she whispered.

The knight's face jerked up. A dark cloud passed overhead. Gavin's blue eyes sank beneath his brow bones until they appeared dark and menacing. "I won't suffer another Daughter of Light to rule the Realm of Faerie."

Ryder's hands gripped the knight by his armpits. He sagged on his knees.

"What you would or would not suffer means little," Melia observed.

"So does your victory!" Gavin seethed. "The Grey Council may have crowned you as Umbra's vessel but he won't have you!"

A flame licked at the ice in Melia's belly. She jerked to her feet, her jaw tight. She wanted to take the knife in Ryder's belt and slit the knight's throat. Instead, she turned away from him.

Her gaze settled on Plantine sitting in the sand, shivering. Her sister's arms were curled around her knees. Her wet clothes offered no protection against the cold air.

"We need to return to the citadel," Melia said.

"Besting Jade proved nothing!" The knight yelled.

Melia glared at him. She remembered the Veiled Tavern. "Although you don't deserve it, you'll receive mercy at the hands of the grey faeries." The knight lunged at her, baring his teeth. Ryder held him back. Melia recalled Flora, pale and near death in the muannai valley. "But you don't want mercy, do you?"

"He's goading you," Ryder said.

Melia's mind returned to Sinjiin, clinging to life on a stone cold floor. An icy desire formed in her veins. It was as sharp and brittle as the crazed gleam in Gavin's eye.

"Fight me," he challenged her.

Ryder shook his head.

She could end this now.

Gavin sensed her willingness to do battle. "The princess heir would have me bring her your heart."

Melia saw Aldous withering under a black magic spell. "But you won't." Her response was soft but clear. Adrenaline surged through her. She spoke to Ryder, "Gavin is Lilliane's fist, and I will pulverize it."

He canted his head.

Melia raised her closed hand to her heart.

Ryder held her gaze.

She closed her eyes in a slow blink.

He shook his head.

She pleaded with her eyes.

He gave her an imperceptible nod. He wasn't pleased, but he understood what she needed to do, and wouldn't stop her from doing it.

The next time Melia spoke, her voice was much louder, "The knight and I will duel."

Even though Ryder's body hardened against her announcement, he supported her. "It will be an honorable fight," he said.

Gavin didn't respond.

Ryder shook him. "Agree you will fight with honor."

"I'm a Huron knight. We only fight with honor. She must swear not to turn into a dragon."

Melia shifted her weight. "I swear."

How many times had Flora told her: When it's not training, when it's a real battle, your mind will distort everything. Drill until your body executes each move without thought—and then keep repeating the routine. Melia sparred most frequently with a dagger. It was a weapon she favored and the one she'd mastered to the greatest degree.

"Release him, and give him your blade," Melia said to Ryder. "And someone," she yelled to the crowd of foreigners gathering around them, "bring me a dagger."

A dark-skinned, dark-haired mercenary hurried to offer her a shiny knife.

Melia hefted it, familiarizing herself with the grip and the balance of its blade.

Another foreigner drew a large square around them, dragging the heel of his boot in the sand. Plantine stumbled beyond its perimeter.

Ryder met Melia's gaze. He slammed his fist against his heart. She saw his confidence in her. And his respect for her decision. Slowly, he untied Gavin's hands. The knight staggered to his feet. Ryder handed him the knife and backed away.

Melia assessed their arena, a sloping square of sand. It was mid afternoon, and churning clouds blocked the sun's rays. The tide was rising. Her attention shifted to her opponent. A dagger was an extension of the hand, and Gavin's lethality had been cut in half. He already angled his body to protect his wounded arm.

Similar in height, each paced an invisible line along opposing sides of the square. Melia was light on her feet. Gavin's heavy boots made him less nimble. Melia lunged first. She aimed for the inside of his good elbow and missed. He raised his arm, and her blade tore the cloth of his pants. She threw herself forward, and his blade came down on air. Melia stayed on her feet as she ducked beneath him. She straightened and pivoted.

The small cut on Gavin's thigh seeped blood. He registered the wound. When he raised his head, his eyes bulged. He cocked his elbow, blade high, and charged. Melia's mind cleared. She balanced on the balls of her feet and focused all her attention on his leading arm. At the last second, she whirled to the side and smashed her fists, holding her blade in a single grip, down on his good arm.

He grunted but managed to keep hold of his blade. He staggered uphill, forcing Melia to retreat to the waterline. The rising tide turned their square into a rectangle. Melia allowed the sea water to lap around her feet, her ankles, and her calves. She pulled energy from the waves as she regrouped. She was failing at her primary goal of disarming him.

She edged out of the water.

Overhead, the grey clouds rumbled. Their movement across the sky picked up speed. A gap opened, a ray of light pierced Melia's eyes, blinding her. The gap closed.

Gavin was already on her. He'd charged again, leaping on her, and throwing her back into the sea. He was on top of her, choking her, holding her underwater. She squirmed beneath him flailing with her dagger. Saltwater stung her eyes. His grip tightened around her throat. She tried to buck him with her hips. He mounted higher, squeezing his legs around her ribcage.

Through the water she saw his face contorted into a mask of glee.

She would be just another kill for him. Her death would have no meaning. Lilliane would win. Blackness erupted within her. Everything slowed down. Before, Melia stabbed blindly, hitting nothing. Now she angled the dagger's hilt and aimed. She slashed his wounded arm. He screamed. It was a far away sound, but his stranglehold on her throat loosened. She slashed his arm again. He released one hand, to ward off her next blow. It was enough.

Melia's torso exploded up. She gasped for air. He still straddled her. She twisted and slammed her blade into his throat. Blood spurted from the wound. He collapsed across her, dead weight. Blood turned the sea water around her a deep shade of red. She pushed him from her, found her hands and knees, and crawled to shore, gasping for air.

Ryder pulled her up and into his arms. "You're damned reckless," he whispered as he stroked her wet hair and held her close.

"Just never let me slip over the edge," she whispered into his chest.

Around them, the crowd of foreigners cheered.

Melia craned her head. Gavin's lifeless body rocked in a gentle swell of bloody waves. Her teeth chattered, and she was exhausted, but she still held the dagger. The weapon had saved her life, and she couldn't let it go. Someone offered her a blanket. Ryder wrapped it around her.

She'd survived her first battle.

Ryder led Melia and Plantine along the trail that led to the citadel.

"Where's Tuck?" Melia asked, when she could finally speak. "I haven't seen him since the first night we arrived on the island."

"He sailed to Kyrakkos."

"What is he doing there?"

"Researching a potential location for the incarnation."

The answer shocked Melia into silence.

Raffi met them at the citadel entrance. "Take us to Sinjiin," Melia said.

The tiger slept on an enormous cushioned pallet in a room of cool grey light. His wounds were bandaged, and he would live.

Melia asked to be left alone with him.

When Ryder closed the door, she knelt beside the big cat and dug her fingers into his fur. She kneaded his skin, then collapsed against his body and sobbed. Her entire body shook.

If it weren't for Sinjiin she would never have discovered her dragon-self, if it weren't for Sinjiin she wouldn't have won the challenge, if it weren't for Sinjiin her nose would be crooked! She laughed into his fur.

He draped a heavy paw across her back and shoulders.

She rolled to her side.

His golden eyes held hers.

"As soon as you can sail, we're going to send you back to Sevondi," she whispered.

He closed his eyes.

When his breathing was even, she tiptoed from the room.

Although they were minor and mending quickly, Flora tended Melia's wounds.

"I don't feel guilty," Melia said.

Flora's deep brown eyes studied hers.

"For killing Gavin. I don't feel guilty. I feel—"

"Like you set something right?"

Melia searched herself. "I feel like I stopped something that needed to end. He was under Umbra's influence, and he wasn't going to stop killing. If I hadn't killed him ... he would have killed me ... and many others."

The spring faerie fiddled with the lid on a jar of ointment.

"Shouldn't I feel something else?" Melia whispered.

"If you had killed him for your own purposes, if you had killed him for greed or pleasure, if you took joy in the bloodshed, I imagine you might feel something else."

Melia reached for Flora's hand. The roughness of the spring faerie's gnarled fingers felt gentle against hers. Melia held on to them.

A current deeper than words ran between them.

After they'd been quiet awhile, Melia asked, "When will we begin training again?"

Flora patted her knee. "Tomorrow will be soon enough. Despite all the commotion, Threldor has refused to cancel your celebration."

❖ ❖ ❖

Melia felt like royalty when she entered the gallery in her burgundy gown with Ryder at her side.

The grey faeries parted as the couple passed by, clapping softly.

Right before they entered the dining area, Pressina approached the pair. Her gown matched her ivory wings, and she glimmered from head to foot. "Melia."

"Mother."

Pressina took her daughter's hand. Melia held her breath as her mother studied her fingers. "You've always underestimated yourself"—Pressina paused—"as have I." She shifted her gaze to Ryder. "But not you. You've believed in my daughter since you first laid eyes on her, haven't you?"

"Yes."

"Elynus believed in me." Pressina shook her head. "But I lost faith in him." She gripped Melia's hand. "You won't do that. You won't make the same mistake I did."

Melia leaned forward to kiss Pressina's cheek so her mother couldn't see the tears glistening in her eyes.

Ryder's hand rested on Melia's back. She closed her eyes to absorb the sensation of his touch.

Inside the dining hall, Tatou greeted them. "You make the most beautiful dragon!"

Melia's cheeks flushed.

"Can I fly with you someday?"

"Of course!"

The pixie landed on Ryder's shoulder.

Melia couldn't remember her ever riding there before.

He turned his head to gaze down at the small faerie.

"Everyone is waiting for you two." Tatou pointed to a table where Plantine sat with Aldous, Flora, Jade, and Lola.

Melia sat in the empty seat next to Flora. Ryder sat on Melia's other side.

Plantine raised her glass of wine. "To Melia. And Ryder."

Melia raised her glass. "To Sinjiin." Over the rim of crystal, she lost herself in Ryder's green eyes.

He raised his glass to hers.

Everyone else at the table raised their glasses, even Jade. Later, when she laughed at something Ryder said, the exchange was warm, not threatening.

"Will you stay and fight with us?" Melia asked her.

"My mother will remain in the enchanted world," Jade said. "She belongs here, but I've come to understand that my home is in the mortal world."

Tatou landed on Melia's shoulder. She whispered in her ear. "I told you it was Umbra."

Melia wrung her napkin.

Across the table, Plantine laughed. It sounded like the peal of bells.

Melia watched her sister. Her gaze shifted to Jade, then back and forth between them. Under Umbra's influence, they'd both become

559

the worst possible versions of themselves.

Plantine looked up. "Are you all right?" she asked.

"I'm fine." Melia wanted to ask her sister about her experience incarnating Umbra. But not tonight. She glanced around the table at her friends and loved ones.

Ryder caressed Melia's shoulder.

She sipped from her glass of wine. Tonight, she would cherish her victory.

Epilogue

"Do you see how the entire enchanted world plots against us?" Lilliane asked her mother.

Luisa sifted through the parchments her daughter had brought her. "The list of charges is thorough."

"Is that all you have to say?"

"I can't think of a single thing they missed."

Lilliane leaned over her mother's writing table and picked up one of the quills. She tried to put it in Luisa's hand. "Then write a reply that says, We're guilty."

"Darling, you're overreacting."

"You expect me to remain calm when the Grey Council enumerates my family's crimes, and publishes them for the entire enchanted world to see?"

"Perhaps when they realize our power, they will be less quick to strike."

The princess crossed her arms. "By all means, that's good news. They'll take their time. Perhaps they'll be more strategic, or strike with greater force."

"Or perhaps they'll do nothing," her mother said. "As they always have." She sighed.

"Or perhaps my cousin will incarnate Umbra and tear down the walls of this palace with her bare hands!"

Luisa rubbed her temples. "You're making my head ache with your hysteria."

Lilliane gave a short, angry laugh. "Then perhaps I should leave you to your draughts, and your palliatives, and your mysterious ailments."

"Where is Gavin?" Luisa asked. "It's been ages since I've received a report from him."

Lilliane crossed her arms and stalked to the window. "My father ordered him to return to Huros." The lie came easily to her lips.

"Then he's been replaced? I understand more knights arrive on our shores each day."

"It's true."

"Yet, you fear words on a parchment."

"I'm surprised you don't."

"What do you suggest we do?" her mother asked.

Lilliane stared into the distance, at the fountain shooting from Lake Vivientiana. "I want to destroy the sapphire lily once and for all."

Luisa stood abruptly. "No!"

"Mother, please! Let me do it!"

Luisa crossed her arms. "You'll bring the wrath of the gods down upon us."

"What gods, Mother? Have you ever seen one, with your own eyes?"

"The gods sent Gwyneth here, with the lily's seed."

"And what if the gods are just some fairy tale meant to frighten us?"

"If you destroy the sapphire lily, and they're more than a fairy tale, you'll never inherit the throne."

Lilliane glared at her mother. "Then we must find out if the gods are real."

Thank You

I appreciate you spending your valuable time reading *Half Mortal*. If you'd like to share the story with other readers, please tell a friend, or post a review on any book-ish site.

I'd also like to invite you to sign up for my newsletter: http://eepurl.com/wWKUj. It's quirky–like me:D–and I confess, it comes out sporadically, but I send a variety of things, including some (hopefully) pleasant surprises along with updates on all my new releases.

Sincerely,

Acknowledgments

So many people and readers have helped this book come into being. My first editor H. Danielle Crabtree played a huge part in the creation of Half Mortal, when we discussed the story concept in December 2012. Vince Dickinson, the book's second editor, pounded structure and pacing. I also want to thank the trilogy's early readers on Goodreads—Brenda Ayala, Kasey, Meghan, Maria Bonano, Monica, Pamela, Stacy, Susan, Tiffany, and Toni—you all provided rich feedback, and sharing what you loved about the story encouraged me to keep going. Sheila of Frostbite Publishing read the earliest completed manuscripts and patiently answered all my questions. Rachmi Febrianty continues to provide invaluable feedback as the trilogy develops. (Thank her for the maps!) She offered her usual insightful critique of this installment pre-publication. Finally, I must thank my husband, he not only designed the gorgeous cover; but this book could not exist without his faith and support. He is my heart.

The Daughter of Light trilogy is inspired by my beloved grandmother and the transformative effect she had on my life.

I hope you continue to delight in Melia's journey.

Sincerely,

Heidi Garrett

About the Author

Heidi Garrett is the author of the *Daughter of Light* fantasy trilogy about a young half-faerie, half-mortal searching for her place in the Whole.

She's also the author of *Once Upon a Time Today*, a collection of modern fairy tale retellings for adults who have already left home. *The Magic Cupcake* series is paranormal romance trilogy she writes with Billie Limpin.

Heidi was born in Texas, and attempted to reside in as many cities in that state as possible. She made it to Houston, Lubbock, Austin, and El Paso. After spending a decade in southern California, she now lives in Eastern Washington state with her husband, their two cats, her laptop, and her Kindle. Being from the South, she often contemplates the magic of snow.

You can find Heidi on her <u>blog</u>.

Glossary of Characters and Creatures

The Albiana: Although they are of unknown origin, the Albianas are considered flower faeries. However, they are taller than most flower faeries, and their alabaster skin remains pale even when exposed to sunlight. They are the most beautiful of all the faeries.

Basil: The Grand Library's ginger tabby cat.

Brownies: Ruddy-faced, dark-haired, playful creatures, they usually stand about three feet high. Some choose to serve in the Cathedral Palace Guard.

Aldous: A wood elf, he is the head librarian of the Cathedral Palace Grand Library.

Anton: An Idonnai, Ryder's mentor, and the head of the Order of the Idonnai.

Ava Albiana: The second queen of Illialei, she was Gwyneth Albiana's daughter.

Captain Tom: Captain of the Lucky Seahorse.

Cult of Umbra: An army of muannai who will serve the incarnated Umbra.

Dwarves: Dwarves originally populated the planet Una in the mortal world. However, when Isolt of the Waters, an ancient water elemental, was banished from Una by her husband, the god Vulcan, the dwarves abandoned Una with her. Una became known as Earth, and the dwarves migrated from Earth to Misgradde by way of the Realm of Faerie. A sizable population of dwarves never made it to Misgradde. They remained in Tyrannis as chefs when it was discovered their talent for cooking was as great as their talent for metalwork.

Elendah, the Grey Faerie of Aldaine: The only grey faerie who does not dwell on the Isle of Minnanon, Elendah sits on the throne of the Stronghold of Calashai in Tyrannis. She is known as the regent of the stronghold.

Elynus: The Great Mortal Druid. Estranged husband to Pressina. Father to Melia, Melusine, and Plantine. Exiled to the mortal world.

Evangeline: A mermaid Melia meets in the mortal world.

Field Faeries: The faeries related to non-blooming plants. Typically, their physical appearance is plainer than that of the flower faeries. They have wings and are capable of short flights at low altitude. Average height is five feet.

Flora: The sole surviving spring faerie in the Whole.

Flower Faeries: The faeries related to blooming plants. Typically, the females are of great beauty. They have wings and are capable of short flight at low altitudes. Average height is five feet. Verbena, Clementine, Brigitta, Giselle, and Marguerite are flower faeries.

Garrick: An Idonnai and baker, husband to Shilda. He is like a father to Ryder.

Glow Sprites, Nixies, and Undines: The water creatures native to Tyrannis. They live in the Undine River.

Gnomes: Stand about two feet high and wear red hats. Native to the Ruadain in northern Tyrannis, they are taciturn creatures and not friendly.

The Grey Council: Composed of grey faeries and located on the Isle of Minnanon, it is the supreme ruling body in the enchanted world.

Grey Faeries: Wise and ageless, a small population dwell on the

Isle of Minnanon in the enchanted world.

Gumf: A dwarf, the proprietor of the Veiled Tavern in the Balyudor in Tyrannis.

Gweff: The dwarf who forged the magical basin, Ormrun.

Gwyneth Albiana: From unknown origins, she was Illialei's first queen.

Haff: The dwarf who forged the magical sword, Koldis.

Huron Knights: The fair-haired natives of Huros. Considered to be the most chivalrous inhabitants in the enchanted world.

Isolt of the Waters: An ancient water elemental banished to the Void by her husband, the god Vulcan.

Lilliane Albiana: Illialei's faerie princess and daughter of Queen Luisa Albiana.

Luisa Albiana: The reigning queen of Illialei.

Malachi: A cat-like creature. The result of one of Pressina's botched spells.

Melia: A half-faerie. The middle daughter of the mortal druid Elynus and the full-blooded faerie Pressina. She has no wings.

Melusine: A half-faerie. The oldest daughter of the mortal druid Elynus and the full-blooded faerie Pressina. She has no wings. Melusine's story was legend in 15th century France.

Mermaids: The water creatures native to Illialei. They enjoy traveling to the mortal world.

Moog: A troll, he serves Lord Zachariah Goring. He transports communications between the mortal and enchanted worlds for the mortal druid Elynus.

Morgannai: A warrior race, they are the dark-haired natives of Morganna.

The Muannai (singular muannaye): Tall (over five feet) and lean, they are the wingless dark faeries native to Tyrannis. They are the only creatures in the enchanted world who cannot travel to the mortal world.

Nandana: A mortal, also known as the Illustrator, she lives in

Illialei. Her body art is popular among the faeries and elves.

Ogres: Huge creatures from Kyrakkos. They are strong, but simple-minded and slow. Often described as smelling of mold.

Olivia Albiana: The fourth queen of Illialei, she was Uriel's daughter. She is Queen Luisa's mother.

The Order of the Idonnai: An order of priests in Idonne. They chronicle and observe events in the Whole. However, they do not intervene.

Pixies: The most petite faeries. They are approximately four to six inches tall and dwell in the enchanted gardens. Known to be mischievous.

Plantine: A half-faerie. The youngest daughter of the mortal druid Elynus and the full-blooded faerie Pressina. She has no wings.

Pogo: A troll and Moog's twin brother. He has served Sevondi's lineage for centuries.

Pressina: A full-blooded faerie. Estranged wife to Elynus. Maintains a private life in Illialei with her three daughters: Melia, Melusine, and Plantine. She studies and practices black magic.

Ryder: A young priest fleeing his duties as a member of the Order of the Idonnai. An orphan, he was abandoned at the priesthood's gates as an infant.

Sevondi: A dragonwitch. She is a muannaye. Her great-great-grandfather was a sorcerer from Kyrakkos.

Shilda: An Idonnai and skilled herbalist, wife to Garrick. She is like a mother to Ryder.

Sinjiin: A mage from the Hidden City.

Spring Faeries: A race of warrior faeries native to Illialei.

Tatou: A pixie. She is Melia's best friend.

Tree Elves: Thinner and taller than wood elves, they are native to eastern Illialei.

Trolls: Both the males and females of the species stand about three feet tall. However, the males tend to be balding, with swarthy skin and large noses, while the females—though often stout—have thick, luxurious hair, bewitching eyes, and cherubic faces.

Tuck: A tree elf, he is Aldous' apprentice at the Cathedral Palace Grand Library.

Typhons: Natives of Typhos, considered to be the enchanted world's best sailors.

Umbra: A non-corporeal entity dwelling in the Void. He is a growing mass of mortal psychic ash, a result of rapid population growth in the mortal world. Umbra has developed a discrete identity and seeks to incarnate in the material plane. He requires a living material person/creature as a vessel for his consciousness. He seeks to ruin and rule the Whole.

Uriel Albiana: The third queen of Illialei, she was Ava Albiana's daughter.

Wood Elves: Mostly rather round, they stand about four feet tall and are native to western Illialei.

Zachariah Goring, Lord: A muannaye, he collaborated with the mortal druid Elynus to incarnate Umbra.

Glossary of Places and Things

Achill Island: An island in the country of Ireland in the mortal world. Birthplace of Elynus and Pressina's daughters: Melia, Melusine, and Plantine.

Achill Head: The most westerly point of Achill Island.

Aldaine: A city in Tyrannis located on the highest, north most peak of the Ruadain Mountains in the enchanted world.

Ashleam Bay: The western coast of Achill Island.

Azyllai: A country in the enchanted world. Home to the gods.

The Balyudor: The wild woods in Tyrannis.

Bryndale: The largest city in Illialei.

The Cathedral Palace: The primary palace in Illialei. Gwyneth Albiana's husband, a lesser god, built the palace for her. She ascended the Cathedral Palace throne as the first queen of Illialei.

The Cimmerian Inlet: An inlet to the Great White Sea, located in northern Tyrannis, in proximity to the Stronghold of Calashai.

The Crossroads: A popular tavern in the seaport of Typhos.

The Danu Meadows: A large meadow in central Illialei.

The Enchanted Gardens: Home of the pixies. The gardens border the Sylvan Forest in western Illialei.

The Enchanted World: Known territories include: The Realm of Faerie, the Great White Sea, Idonne, Morganna, Typhos, Huros, Kyrakkos, Azyllai, the Isle of Minnanon, and Misgradde.

The Flower of Isbelline: A striking flower with creamy white petals that blooms on the northern most sea cliffs of the Ruadain

Mountains.

The Footing Fields: The fields of Illialei where brownies roll ball and play other games.

The Glen: A wooded valley that lies between the Rolling Mountains and the Nyssalei in western Illialei. Home to the largest population of wood elves in Illialei.

The Grand Library: The library in the Cathedral Palace.

The Great White Sea: The largest body of water in the enchanted world. Reputed to have mystical and healing properties.

The Hidden City: Home to the most powerful mages in the enchanted world. Its location is hidden from all who do not dwell there.

High Hill: A large hill in Illialei.

The Hive: A cafe in Bryndale that caters to wood elves. Honey is an ingredient in all the items on the menu.

Huros: Home of the fair-haired Hurons. Huron Knights are considered to be the most chivalrous in the enchanted world.

Illialei: One of two countries comprising the Realm of Faerie. In older days, it was known as the Territory of Light. It is considered the heart of the enchanted world.

Idonne: Home to the priesthood of the Idonnai. Idonnai, who are not members of the priesthood, are considered to be the finest artisans in the enchanted world.

The Idonnic Library: The priesthood of the Idonnai's work and purpose for existence. Its pristine architecture is the seat of Idonnic power and influence in the enchanted world.

The Isle of Minnanon: An isolated island in the northern waters of the Great White Sea. The Grey Council and the largest surviving population of grey faeries reside on the Isle.

Koldis: The dwarf, Haff, forged the magical sword in the bowels of the Ruadain Mountains.

Kyrakkos: Considered the font of black magic, it is home to the most powerful sorcerers and witches in the enchanted world.

Lake Vivientiana: A lake in eastern Illialei.

The Maeldun Bridge: The iron bridge that crosses the Nyssalei River between Illialei and Tyrannis. It is an in-between place.

Mare Cliffs: (pronounced mah-**ray**) The high cliffs that follow the Nyssalei River as it runs through eastern Illialei. Sylphs from Tyrannis have been known to cross into Illialei to dive from the cliffs into the river.

Misgradde: The country with the largest population of dwarves in the enchanted world.

Morganna: Home to the dark-haired Morgannai. The Morgannai are the enchanted world's warrior race.

The Mortal World: Home to mortals. Although it is not part of the enchanted world, the mortal world and the enchanted world must sustain a dynamic equilibrium of metaphysical energies for the Whole to function optimally.

The Muannai Valley: Borders the Undine River in southeast Tyrannis. Home to the largest population of muannai. Where the Muannai Valley Marketplace is located.

The Muannai Valley Marketplace: A large market in the muannai valley.

The Nuada: The plains of central Tyrannis.

The Nyssalei River: The river that borders and runs through Illialei. It runs from Lake Vivientiana into the Great White Sea.

Ormrun: The dwarf, Gweff, forged the bejeweled basin in the bowels of the Ruadain Mountains to be used as a portal by Isolt of the Waters.

The Parallel of Shadows: The shadowy realm between the Void and the enchanted world.

Pebble Rock: A large boulder with a natural cleft comfortable for sitting. It marks the head of the most popular trail through the Sylvan Forest.

The Primal Essence: Where all life—mortal and enchanted— begins.

The Realm of Faerie: A single land mass in the enchanted world comprised of two countries, Illialei and Tyrannis. The Realm of

Faerie is the only country in the enchanted world that shares contiguous borders of time and space with the mortal world.

The Rolling Mountains: A hilly mountain range spanning eastern and western Illialei.

The Ruadain Mountains: A seven peak mountain range in northern Tyrannis.

The Sapphire Lily: The flower that grew from the seed Gwyneth Albiana planted on the shores of Lake Vivientiana when she first arrived in Illialei.

Southend: Illialei's port.

The Stronghold of Calashai: The four-towered stronghold in the center of Aldaine. Elendah, the Grey Faerie of Aldaine, sits on the stronghold's throne as regent.

The Summer Palace: A smaller palace in Illialei, located on the shores of Lake Vivientiana.

The Sylvan Forest: A light-filled forest located in northwest Illialei.

Typhos: Home to the Typhons and the enchanted world's largest and busiest seaport, Maris. Typhons are considered to be the best sailors in the enchanted world.

Tyrannis: One of the two countries comprising the Realm of Faerie. In older days, it was known as the Dark Lands.

The Undine River: Branches from a fork in the Nyssalei River and flows through Tyrannis.

The Unknown Beyond: A place beyond the Whole, about which little is known.

The Veiled Tavern: A mystical inn located in the heart of the Balyudor. Gumf, a dwarf and devout epicurean, is the inn's proprietor. He employs a large number of dwarves at the tavern as they are reputed to be the best chefs in the Whole.

The Void: The realm of incorporeal existence.

The Whole: Includes: The mortal world, the enchanted world, the Void, the Parallel of Shadows, and the Primal Essence. (The Unknown Beyond is not part of the Whole.)